BLACK AMBER

BLACK AMBER

Book One of The Elrolian Hunter

ELI MEADOW RAMRAJ

Wing and Wheel Press

ISBN 978-1-312-04222-3

Wing and Wheel Press

The text of this book is set in 11 point Gill Sans
Titles are set in 36 point Boycott
Design by Sandra L. Meadow

PART I

THE DEFENDER

THE BOMB

Seldom do we ever get any large animals near our camp, but of course, we live in the wild. Animals may go wherever they wish. They have as much freedom as any human does, if not more.

You see, I was in the survival-training arena, heading to our meeting room for our morning conference, where we pretty much just discuss the events from the previous day, and what we need to do. Important things, but still, no less boring than it sounds.

I was only a few metres away from the entrance to the meeting room. Over all the years I've been here, it's definitely become a habit – my routine, coming over here every morning to see what new things were going on – but routines can be interrupted.

That was when I heard deep, loud, ragged breaths. These breaths came from no human. I turned around very slowly. I saw its shiny golden-orange fur, glinting in the sunlight that was passing through the few cracks between the branches that gave us cover from rain, and its jet-black stripes. It was a tiger, very young by the look of it. Probably about three to four years old. It had large, round ears that were pointing straight up, and its eyes were open wide, observing its surroundings. I would have guessed that tigers would be at the Tigers River at this time of day, having a nice bath in the early morning sun.

I had no idea how I hadn't noticed it earlier. You would think I would be able to hear it coming, but it was early in the morning and I was drowsy, having just gotten up from a lovely long sleep.

It was looking right at me now, scared or disturbed by something. I hoped there was no hunter out there. I would go check it out. I could already hear myself saying the words.

'*Excuse me, I am Wolf, from the Animal Defence Organisation, and you are not permitted to hunt here, or, as a matter of fact, really be here at all. This is a protected area, so please leave this range at once.*' If they refused, I would get mad. *Very* mad. And if they'd already done some hunting, I would get more than very mad. Slowly I walked away, quite calmly, to the archway to the meeting room. I had been doing this all my life, since I was only a toddler. I had grown up here.

The tiger growled. I stopped moving. It could kill me at will. I had only my knife, and under no circumstance would I kill any animal, no matter what would happen to me. Our lives are worth no more than theirs – probably less.

Then, even more slowly, I entered the meeting room, like I was in a room with a sleeping snake, taking care not to frighten the tiger.

Now, before you meet the team, let me tell you a little bit about myself. I am twenty-eight years old, for a start. My name is Wolf. Just Wolf. Nothing else. I, unlike most people, remember how I got this unique name. Our leader, Lance Ocrinus, had found me when I was two, abandoned somewhere in the city of Spheria, south of here, and he had brought me here, to the forest in Wouldlock. Four years later, he said to me, 'I will name you Wolf, because your eyes look like theirs. Observing everything. Nothing escapes your sight.' He would tell me this over and over again, until I knew, without even thinking, why I had this name. He'd been working on something for a few months now – he said it was a lock, but would not tell us what for. It didn't interest me at the time though.

Of course, having this name got me interested in wolves, and they very soon became my favourite animal. Unfortunately for me, not much of our job includes wolves. We do of course have them, yes, but they take care of themselves well, and very rarely need our assistance in anything.

People call me 'the hunter' sometimes, or more commonly, 'the defender,' because I make sure I hunt all things that threaten my home. Not animals. No, as I've already stated, I protect them. I do not kill anyone, or anything. There are other ways of defending the things you care for.

Now, back to wolves. I have seen a few of them in Wouldlock, and I know where most of them live. They like the shade by the trees, where they also have a fair amount of cover from other animals, and have their territories marked near to their natural prey. Intelligent creatures, they are. Of course, not all of Wouldlock is forest. Wouldlock is especially known for its wide variety of habitats, so here live almost every single animal species you can think of. And even the ones you don't know exist. Now, I know that if you didn't know about any of these fantastic creatures, you would strongly believe that I am making them up, but let me just straighten that up. If you think it isn't real, that's your choice, and you're fully entitled to it, but the thing is, you're wrong. You don't think so? Show me your evidence. It is good to be imaginative.

In Wouldlock we have mountains, swamps, rivers, the beach, and even the ice. To the north it can be up to minus ten degrees, but to the south, about twenty degrees, near Elrolia, a castle and smallish region ruled by Elrolians, south west from here, near the Black Trees. I don't know anything else about Elrolia, and have never actually been there. I also know there is another Elrolian castle to the north where only the very best Elrolians stay. When I say 'best,' I mean the most highly trained, the ones that cannot be beaten in battle. Elrolians take combat very seriously, and if you are above their expectations, there are awards. Anyway, to the east lies the Alrian Sea, and to the northeast, Alria itself. Wouldlock is very big; about two thousand square kilometres, leaving lots of space for animals, though about a fifth of Wouldlock, the Elrolians call Elrolia, and see it as their land.

We don't have a house, but a camp made from natural resources, that more or less formed on its own. We didn't fix it up that much besides adding some furniture and stuff, but from the outside it looks pretty normal, especially to animals. I had brought some supplies from Spheria. Seeing as it is so cold, all eight members of the team wear warm, fluffy winter coats. Our purpose here, as I told you before, is to secure the safety of the animals. We are the Animal Defence Organisation.

'Good morning, Wolf.'

'Hey, Lance.'

Lance Orcrinus was our leader. He's forty-nine, and he doesn't look old at all, but still has silvery hair. His face is a little bit wrinkled from smiling a lot. His right leg was bloody, as the day before, on the twelfth of November, a protective mother crocodile had bitten him. He organizes us, giving us jobs, and dealing with anyone who questions our authority over preventing hunting in Wouldlock.

There is also Stream, the technology expert. He fixes our computers, our heat tracker maps, and anything else that needs repairing. We don't have many electronic devices though, because we like to live as much as we can without technology, but he is in charge of all of those kinds of things that we do use. These days there is more of a need for technology, for the world is changing, and we need to change along with it.

The two brothers, Blade and Raider, specialise in more specific things. Blade does habitats, while Raider does endangered animals, so I would ask him to help with the tiger.

The sisters Rovia and Sora also have distinct areas. Rovia does animal healing, for the animals that are hurt either by nature – falling trees or things like that – or if a predator hurts them, but doesn't kill them. Sora tries to discover new species. Even though we all scout around Wouldlock, when she does, she's trying to find something new, while we protect the other animals we already know of. She happened to be the one to discover the liasers, an incredible species that has been of use to us in the past by providing us transport, for they are known for carrying great loads on their strong backs. This will come up again later, I am sure. Then finally, Shade, who does various jobs around the camp with Lance. Come to think of it, I can't really describe what he does exactly. He is very secretive with his work. I think he tries to keep hunters away from here, and to protect the area of Wouldlock, not the animals in it. It's a pretty important job, but he doesn't discuss it much, if ever, for he isn't the friendliest of people.

Blade was attempting to read his brother's future in a snow globe. Or so it seemed.

He waved his hand mystically over the sphere, his slightly open eyelids quivering. 'I see… I see an old man…'

'Where, in your reflection?' he said, snickering. 'You know, you don't need that orb, 'cause if you look in a mirror, you see the same thing.'

'Morning.' I said, patting their heads to get their attention. 'Hey Raider, I need your help.'

He was lying back casually in his seat, with his legs propped up on Sora's lap, who was trying (with no luck) to push them off. Obviously he was enjoying watching her struggle. The brothers entertained themselves by doing things like that.

'Yeah, man, what's up?'

'There's a tiger in the training arena.' I said hurriedly.

He stopped smiling. 'I'm on it,' he said, taking his feet off Sora, and set off to the arena.

Sora breathed a sigh of relief.

'Something scared it, I know,' I said to the rest of the team. 'It seems uneasy about something. I think it might be a hunter. Nothing natural does that to a tiger.'

Lance nodded, looking at me carefully. 'You may go investigate if you wish. We can't have animals dying by the hands of a hunter. If they refuse to come, you can use some force. Not too hard, mind you.'

I liked this about Lance. He was always offering opportunities. He trusted us with everything. If there was a problem, he believed that anyone could help, no matter how small, or young. He was always like this. He was like a father to me.

'Alright. Thank you.' I pulled the lever that pushed aside the boulders to give me access outside. It was a clever contraption that Stream had worked out, and I still don't completely understand it – not that I usually spend my time examining boulders. I went out of the camp and put up my hood. The tiger followed, accompanied by Raider.

'Wolf, it looks well, so I'll just send it out back to the river. I think you're right. It wasn't hurt, just frightened,' said Raider calmly. Normally Raider is not serious, and is always playing pranks, but not when it comes to animals, thank god.

'Okay, thanks.'

'No problem. It knows its way through. You don't have to go with it.'

'Oh, it's okay. I'm heading in that general direction anyway.'

He nodded and went back inside, pushing away the boulder doors.

I looked at the tiger strangely, but it didn't go to the river. It followed me, so the both of us set out for the Black Rocks. They absorb the heat from the sun and make it *very* hot there. It was fairly easy to get there from our place, you just cross the field and you're there.

So that's how I came to be running out in the bright sun by the side of the tiger. This was not an unusual experience, however. When animals get used to you, it's incredible how close they dare to come. I don't think there was an animal in Wouldlock that thought we meant harm. I think the tiger wanted to see to it that the case was resolved.

It took me about fifteen minutes to get to the Black Rocks, walking through the tall grass. I decided not to ride on the tiger, because I didn't think it really knew where it was going, and was just following me. It was, like I said, going to make sure the problem was sorted out. I had started to sweat. I liked the cold more. It's easier to get warmer in a cold environment than cooler in a hot place.

Something was wrong. I couldn't see a single animal anywhere, except for the tiger. I took off my hood and listened. I heard a kind of beeping noise. I went further. Then I saw it, lying on one of the hot and flat rocks. A bomb. It was a flat panel, just a few centimetres thick. I ran over to it. I saw it had the time until it blew. Two minutes.

I snatched it up, and saw hinges. I opened it. It gave no creaking sound, and looked very new, like it hadn't been here roasting in the Black Rocks for long. There were just lots of wires and buttons. That was no help to me. Even though they didn't look that complex, I had only been to a city once and had no real experience with these things since we don't use them often, even when they are brought in – and even when they are, I don't like them. They're so complicated. There are other ways to live life. But if Stream had been here he probably could have done this in seconds. And now, seconds were what I had until every living thing in Wouldlock was destroyed. I could just take out every wire, but that might set it off sooner. I didn't have enough time to get Stream.

Hopeless, I tried punching it.

Nothing.

One minute left. I clenched my fist again and gave it a powerful blow. The numbers disappeared. I had destroyed it! It was easier than I thought.

Then I saw words on the back: *Spheria, Inphonate.* It was just what some rich country like that would do. The other countries would not have done anything like this. They would not have the technology to produce something like this – that much I knew. With the disabled bomb in hand, I ran back to the base, the tiger following carefully in my footsteps. When I finally reached camp, the tiger left, galloping back to its river, and splashing in the cold, shallow waters nearby.

'It was a bomb.' I panted.

I showed the team the device. 'It says Spheria on it.'

'We have to go there and demand to know why the President dared to plant a bomb here!' shouted Stream, enraged. 'Or even dared to *allow* it!'

'I do agree, I would go myself, but I have my leg injury from the crocodile. You and Wolf may go, if you want,' said Lance calmly.

Lance's injury had had a very big effect on him. He hadn't been able to walk for a week.

'How do we get there? I asked. 'Do we walk?'

'Oh no. That would take more than an hour. We want to get there as soon as we can,' said Stream.

'How do you usually get there?' I asked.

'The liasers take me,'

'Ah, I see. Well, let's go.'

You see, Spheria is a big place, though the smallest of the Eromies, and there are lots of cities, but people just refer to the place as *Spheria*. It's a huge country, but people refer to the part where the President lives as central Spheria – the place with the president's office. I know, not in the exact centre, but still.

Half an hour later we were at the Beach Tree. It was a huge, solitary tree by the Alrian Sea, and one of the only ones without leaves. The liasers normally rest there. I saw them under the tree, resting comfortably. I don't think you would have ever seen one, as they are very rare and only live in Wouldlock, so I will describe what they look like. They're about the size of a very small bear, smaller than a human, and they look like deer, with antlers, and wings. They really are beautiful creatures. Normally their fluffy fur is a deep brown. Stream can kind of communicate simple phrases across to them, like you could use sign language to a trained gorilla, but for this you're using their language and *you're* the one who needs to be trained.

Anyway, Stream told them of our needs, and in no more than ten minutes we were soaring in the skies of Wouldlock. We saw some amazing birds on the way: eagles and hawks that were very common here, and then we were there.

Spheria is a tropical country, like Alria, where Lance was born. Most of the buildings are white, or some a light grey. Spheria is a very rich country. Most doorknobs are real gold, and almost every person here owns a three-hundred-dollar watch. It's a very sci-fi looking place. A big change from Wouldlock. We flagged a taxi.

'The President's building please,' said Stream.

Stream is nice, but kind of secretive. He's thirty, and has a beard and jet-black hair. His hair is always combed and tidy, whereas mine is always messy. We paid the driver and entered the building.

Being the President's place, this was even more fancy than the rest of Spheria. Right now we were in central Spheria, where the President normally lived. On the front door there was a golden ocelot, the symbol of Spheria. The building had white marble floors and spiral staircases, and every hallway held a fake bear-skin rug. How do I know they were fakes? I've lived in Wouldlock for twenty-six years. I just know. Also, there were lots of statues of more ocelots, a particular type of rather rare cat. But the Spherians don't worship them. They hunt them. According to the government, they were a danger to citizens. Nonsense, that was.

I went up to the front desk. A very long-haired woman sat at the desk in (of course) a very expensive uniform.

'Good afternoon. I need to see the President. It's urgent.'

'I'm afraid he's busy,' said the woman at the desk without looking up.

I stared at her in disgust. 'It's urgent.'

She turned her black eyes to me. 'His meeting is urgent. It'll be finished in thirty minutes, but he doesn't have a lot of time before the next appointment.'

'We're take it,' I said walking away, only remembering to give a thank-you when I was at the couch.

'Thank you.' I heard Stream say.

He came back to the seat, and I spoke to him. 'I can't believe the lack of security here. They just let us go in without ID or anything.'

'Oh, they have a lot of security, we just can't always see it,.'

We made our way up the marble spiral staircase and strode down the long clean red carpet to the President's large fancy office. On either side of the door was the head of an ocelot. It was staring down at me with its large, sad-looking dead eyes.

I pointed it out to Stream and he nodded sadly. He banged his fist powerfully and loudly on the polished oak door.

'Come in,' said a gruff voice.

We stepped through and I looked around nervously. I knew I had nothing to fear, but I was in a room with one of the most powerful people in Spheria. The President was at a fancy wooden desk, with his glasses on, reading a file. He looked about sixty, with combed grey hair, and wrinkles on his face.

'Good afternoon. My name is Wolf, just Wolf, and this is Stream Runflome. We come here from Wouldlock. We're from the Animal Defence Organisation,' I said, attempting to be as formal as possible. It was not often that I went to these fancy places like Spheria, so I sucked at it.

'I am Dormanant Scale, the Spherian President. And the Animal Defence thing, I have never heard of. Let me just find your files, so I can have a better understanding of who you are.' He called someone in, and briefly whispered to him. The man nodded and left.

We had files? Whatever. I doubted it.

'Well what is it that you have come to tell me?'

Stream spoke. 'Well, Mr. Scale, Wolf here found a Spherian bomb in the forest. Only you could have authorised it to be placed there. We want to know why.'

'Why, yes, I authorised it. Well actually, I was paid a very large amount of money to authorise it. We want the space for building. There are too many obstacles there at the moment – the plants, caves, and *especially* the trees. The bomb would have instantly wiped out all of this and we could make a huge improvement to the country. Money would come rushing to our doors, and the population would grow greatly. We will be in even more control of Wouldlock than we are now. Wouldlock is uninhabited. This is about the demand of the citizens. More and more people are moving to Spheria from Alria *and* Raverand, and we need to expand our share of the land to be able to meet these immigrants' needs!'

'But yes it *is* inhabited, by our organisation, by the Elrolians, and not to mention all of the billions of animals there. You could wipe out entire species! Also, if you blow up their home, the Elrolians will get angry. Like, kill-you angry. And you don't want them as your enemy, or us, as a matter of fact. You would be responsible for the extinction of over five hundred species after you *met the needs of the immigrants*. We would never leave you alone after that' said Stream.

'*Mr. Scale*,' he added.

The president looked like he was about to angrily retort, but the man he had called to fetch the files had returned.

'They don't seem to have any files sir.'

'Whatever. Look more,' said Scale distractedly.

'Yes, sir, but they're from Wouldlock, so I'm not sure...'

'*Go!*' snarled the president.

The man nodded, shaking, pushed the door, and went out, quietly closing it behind him, leaving us alone with Scale again. The president regained his anger.

'Did you just threaten me? I could have you killed in an hour if I wish.'

'No, you couldn't, actually,' I said coldly. 'I am also known as the Hunter, not of animals, but of those who dare to threaten them. If you touched Wouldlock, I would not kill you, but would teach you a lesson that would make sure that if you ever saw my face again you would evacuate the city. Believe me. The lives of animals are not something you should trade for building space. If I were in a battle, I would take five smart foxes over an army from your city.'

Stream had been smiling through this. He knew I could, and would, do what was necessary to protect Wouldlock.

The president looked uneasy, but was attempting to hide it. 'Well, as a matter of fact I am creating a vicious army of highly trained hunters. Maybe in a year's time, no living ocelots will exist.'

I just stared at him in his fancy suit, with his stupid little fancy glasses on, enraged. How dare he threaten animals in front of me? He didn't care about their lives, like a lot of stupid people don't.

'Very well. You have made your point. Get out now,' he spat.

We went back out into the long hall. I didn't like this place anymore. Not that I ever really had. They used animals as decoration. How would they like it if it were *their* heads on the walls?

They're very stupid I thought. No, more than stupid. *Cruel.* I hate Spherians. Or at least the ones I've met so far.

'That idiot,' I growled aloud. 'He only cares about money. I mean, wiping out a whole Eromie just because someone pays you to? We should find out exactly whom he's doing this for. And I bet he was lying about that army. Just trying to scare us ... right?'

Stream smiled, but didn't look too sure. 'Maybe ... hey, you want to go get a snack? There's a café on Oak Street, about two blocks away from here. Want to have a bite?'

'Yeah, sure, why not?'

We stepped down the marble steps, out onto the clean sidewalk. It was so different from Wouldlock. Instead of trees, there were buildings. Instead of animals, there were people. We watched the people walking past us, going about their usual business, and we discussed our meeting with the president.

The café Stream had suggested was a quiet little place called The Three Leaves. It wasn't very fancy or anything, but the food looked good. There were old paintings of trees and beaches on the walls, and the fake moss and seashells that were placed around the room made it look very tropical. We sat down at a smooth wooden table and took a glance at the menu displayed on a chalkboard. A woman with long brown hair came over to us.

'Good afternoon, my name is Slare, and I will be your waitress for today. Are you ready to order? Any drinks?' she asked in a cheerful voice.

We gave our orders and within ten minutes they had it set out on our table. Slare was very friendly, and after we finished eating, she was telling us about all the attractions you could find near here, and about her life. She said she was looking for a new job, and thought the one here – waiting tables – was boring.

'There's the gemstone museum not too far from here, as well as the library.'

She gave us a map of the city, and invited us to come back anytime.

'Well, thank you very much Slare,' said Stream. 'And you were talking about a new job. We're always happy to accept a new member at the Animal Defence Organisation, so stop by soon.'

'Thank you, I most surely will!' she said brightly. The liasers had been waiting in a deserted carpark. We found them again and flew back to Wouldlock, the wind blowing in our hair, soaring over Spheria's magnificent towers.

RAVENWOOD

You might think I was crazy, but after all that had happened I wanted to go explore for the last few hours of daylight. I would go to the Ice, also known as the Iceberg. It would, of course, be very cold. Maybe even snowing. I got a warm black scarf and a knife. I have never seen blood on this knife. I use it for climbing, and it has a compass on its hilt, so that's useful too. It is a product from Raverand, and although we got most of our supplies from Spheria, after my meeting with the president I was starting to like Spheria less, and Raverand and Alria more. The last of the five countries is Lorothia. I'll tell you more about that later! It's a beautiful place, Lorothia- rather like Wouldlock, with hardly any humans living there, but not as many animals either.

They are called the five Eromies. Eromies are pretty much countries, and they're all in Ortus, which is the name for the whole piece of land – like a continent. We're also called simply the Risen Island. So in each Eromie, or country, if you like, there are about three to six states, in which there are then villages. Wouldlock doesn't have any villages actually. Just Elrolia and the Seven Gates, and then, well, Wouldlock. Not too complicated.

Anyway, Wouldlock is one of the five Eromies. It is in the centre of all the Eromies, actually. Eromie means *powerful country*. The Eromies had been under water for 2004 years, since the beginning of time, and eighty years ago, on December 8, they had risen. We have been called Atlantis, even though that is actually another place entirely, although it still exists. It all happened because of what is called global warming. Ten percent of the world's water evaporated when some nuclear experiment elevated the world's temperature and increased the level of heat in the atmosphere. So then, the Eromies lifted. In the same way as water evaporates, they lifted. And they have stayed lifted, one thousand metres above the rest of the world, for ten entire years. And now it was 2084. Now, there are people older than eighty on this ... small world. Yeah, there are. Although I really have no idea how they got up here. It sounds kind of unrealistic, but it happened.

There are other places inside the Eromies, such as Elrolia. Eromies are our way of splitting this large piece of land into smaller areas, like countries, as I have said before. I believe that only sixty percent of the land here on Ortus is actually populated by humans, and the rest is completely untouched, which is pretty incredible, but the population is growing.

Anyway, I went out of the camp again and walked towards the Ice. I would have to pass near the Silent Mountains to get there. I'll explain about them when we get there. The best and shortest way to get to the Ice was to go to the edge of the Silent Mountains, where it meets with the Alrian Sea. So it was this route I followed.

And I was safe until I got to the edge of the sea. I tried to jump over a large boulder, but it caught my left shoe, and I slipped into the freezing cold Alrian water, struggling to keep myself above the surface while my heavy clothes threatened to drag me down.

'Help!' I shouted, splashing around wildly.

It was not very deep here, but the cold sea made my legs numb and weak. The sea grew deep only metres in, and the current wasn't on my side. It was a sense of survival that saved me. I had to live. There was so much more I could do with the time I was given in my life. That's what life is all about. Making a change. But let's not get too sentimental here. I'm freezing.

I pulled myself back onto the shore, my arms giving a big push out of the water, arms that had grown used to dealing with trees, rocks, and animals. I felt very tired. I had heard this sea could do this to you, but had never been eager to try it out. I waited a few minutes to regain my strength, and then got up.

I almost had a heart attack when I saw what was lying next to me: a bloody skeleton, with flippers and a crushed beak, like a broken seashell. It was a dead penguin, which had probably been killed by a leopard seal, or some such creature. The way leopard seals kill is to grab their prey in their two-centimetre sharp teeth and smash the animal against the surface of the water, ripping it apart until it's dead, and the seal has a nice big meal. The seal then drops the rest of the bones and what's left of the carcass somewhere in the water, but sometimes, if it kills near the shore, it can find its way onto land.

I kicked the skeleton back into the water, and looked out at the sea, trying to forget that terrible image.

I saw a movement in the water. A killer whale! And it was hunting. That's even more rare. Killer whales are amazing hunters. They surround their prey, leaving no escape for them, or they tip over icebergs and kill the penguins on them. And they are smart. They have good camouflage. When you look at them from above, they blend in with the ocean, and from below are as blindingly white as the sun. They are just incredible. This one grabbed a fleeing seal in its huge jaw and bit down.

When Lance started this organisation, we decided we would not interfere with animals hunting each other. They need food. If we prevented it, it would be like keeping them as pets, not able to do what they usually do. I had mixed thoughts about keeping pets. I hated how they had no freedom. On a leash, stuck in a boring house. On the other hand, it may be hard to live by itself. I don't know.

Now, the reason why it's called the Silent Mountains is because you can't hear anything further than twenty metres away when you are there. The high mountains tower above you, and block out all sound. The way they are shaped makes it so that sound waves bounce off and into the sky, and don't return. No animals live there for some reason.

I ran by the seaside for a while, but then I abruptly stopped. Just like when I had heard the bomb, it was very sudden. It was coming from the sea. A sound like the beginning of a huge wave gathering its energy. It sounded like waves, but last I had looked it had been perfectly still after the killer whale had gone back down. Then I saw a moving dark shape heading towards me under the water very quickly. It rose up and burst out of the water. It rolled onto the ground and stood up. It was a man, Dressed in jeans, a t-shirt, a cloak, and silver armour guarding his legs, chest, and arms. He had a gleaming silver helmet that looked Lorothian over his short black and white beard (the few Lorothians out there normally have silver battle helmets, and short beards). In fact, once I took a better look at it, I realised that it *was* made in Lorothia – another of the five Eromies. He was also holding a staff in his hand, and engraved on the side of it was the word *terra*, meaning earth in Latin. Then I realised he had a scar over his right eye, but it didn't seem to be bothering him. After I took in his appearance, I realised he had probably been swimming in the water for hours without breath. Unless he was an Elemental Lord, that wouldn't be possible. He looked at me like he was analysing me.

'This is Wouldlock, yes?' he demanded, in a deep, growly voice.

'Um ... yeah.'

'You know Lance Ocrinus?'

'Yes. He's my friend. Who are you?'

He paused before answering.

'Ravenwood Sphalerite Spears.' He growled.

'Wolf,' I said, holding out my hand. He looked at it disapprovingly, and didn't shake it.

'Um, nice to meet you Mr. Spears.'

'Not Spears!' He barked. 'Call me Ravenwood.'

'Right, sorry,' I said quickly.

'You know where Lance is?

'Yeah, that way.'

'Thanks.' He walked off.

I started walking again through the sandy beach, stepping on shells and stones, my feet sinking into the sand until it changed to grass, and finally found myself at the Ice. I lay down. It was cold, but comfortable. Then, very suddenly I stood up and squinted at the huge iceberg across the water. There was a black object lying there. I was very curious, and waded a bit into the icy water to get a better view, without almost drowning this time. It was an axe. That was strange. I had never noticed it before. I turned around and ran back, very carefully, to our camp.

'Hey, Wolf!' said Sora. 'I saw some strange animal by the Silent Mountains, black, big, and winged. I didn't see it clearly though, it was really fast. Any idea what it might have been?'

'No! That's really strange. Try to see if you can find it again, maybe you can borrow Stream's camera.'

Inside the cool wooden camp, Ravenwood was in the meeting room talking very seriously to Lance.

'Are you sure it was the Ice Axe?' Lance asked.

'Yeah, believe me, when that Liaser scratched my eye the only thing it did was make my sight even sharper. It's there,' He growled.

'Well, as you are one of the Elemental Lords you may claim it. When did you see it?'

'As I was crossing from Alria. And I'm only the son of an Elemental Lord,' he added.

So Ravenwood had seen the axe before me. And he *was* an Elemental Lord, or at least a descendant of one. That explained how he had got here. And if it really were the Ice Axe, then it would have extraordinary power. I had never been tempted by power before, but this time I felt a strange urge, like I *had* to have it. Why should some random stranger claim it? Should it be his because he had spotted it first? Did it matter if he was some Elemental Lord? Surely he would already have great weapons. But the thing is, I almost felt scared of him, despite only knowing him for half an hour. And that was saying a lot, because I wasn't scared of any animals at all, and there are quite a lot of dangerous animals that I'd encountered.

I shook my head. I didn't *really* want this axe. Did I? I wouldn't need it. I wondered why Ravenwood would though.

'Wolf? Do you have something to say?'

I looked around surprised. Apparently I had been included in the conversation.

'Oh, um, I also saw the axe,' I said stupidly.

'Do you have any objection to Ravenwood receiving it?' said Lance.

'What? No! No, not at all.'

'All right then, Ravenwood. I don't see why you shouldn't get it. Although I suggest you check in with the Elrolians first.'

Ravenwood stayed at the camp, and over the next few days I grew to like him. He was fierce, but kind.

I wondered why the axe had just been lying around on an iceberg that just happened to be found by an Elemental Lord.

'Hey! Wolf!' a voice said, and strong arms pulled me into an area covered by the shadow of a large lemon tree. 'Go make me a spear for tomorrow's training session. And make it *well*. Last time it was dreadful. Well, what are you waiting for? Now!'

It was Shade. He was always ordering me around, making me make weapons for him. I hated him. But I knew if I didn't do it, he would get back at me some way. He always does.

'Out of what?' I asked glumly.

'Platinum.'

'We still haven't received our order from the Crystal Miners. I'll have to wait until tomorrow.'

The Crystal Miners gave us all the metal we needed for free, because we had helped them out of a tight spot once, and also saved Elfax Reltake's life. He's their leader. It's a long story.

Then Ravenwood came in, limping, holding himself up on his staff, because a lion had scratched him the day before, and he had a big scratch on his left leg, which was concealed at the moment by his long, dirty jeans.

'Shade!' He barked. 'What do you think you're doing, ordering Wolf around like that? It isn't your place to get him to make weapons for you!'

Apparently his eye scratch really *had* improved his sight, because no normal human eye could have seen us in the shadows from where Ravenwood had been.

'I – I can do what I –'

'No, you will not! If you want a spear, you make it yourself!' Ravenwood growled.

Shade backed away and almost tripped, his eyes glinting with fear.

'He bother you a lot, son?' Ravenwood asked once Shade had left.

'Yeah. Thanks,' I said gratefully.

I went outside and lay down on the field, watching the birds soaring gracefully. I loved the way they flew. It was amazing. It was so ... *normal* for them. I wished I could fly. It would make life so much easier. But no living thing as big as a person could fly like that. But then that made me wonder. *Was* there an animal, maybe tiger-sized, that could fly? I would never assume that I had discovered all of the species that Wouldlock held. Wait! There was a way to find out if a human could fly! I could ask an Elemental Lord, and we had one, right here at camp.

'Ravenwood! Hey! I had a question.'

'Yeah,' he said, nodding. 'Go on.'

'Well, I was wondering if there was any way that a human could fly.'

His scarred eye glistened as his face twisted into a friendly smile.

'Trust me Wolf, you aren't the first to want the ability of flying. To answer your question, there are three Air Riders still alive. Used to be ten 'til the days of Hunter. One of them is just plain evil, another one only ever listens to you when you give him something valuable, and he has to be convinced you are the right side to join, and the last one ... well, she's an Elrolian, so that makes it hard for any human to join with her. But I have to say, if somehow you got her – well, any Elrolian, really – on your side, you would probably win every battle you ever fought.'

'Who is she? I mean, what's her name?'

'Her name's Eleria,' he said, with some admiration in his voice, 'the queen of the Elrolians. She's the most powerful one that's ever existed. The second Air Rider I mentioned is Atlantian, called Androma Faithly and she's just as powerful as an Elrolian. Well, maybe not, but you get the idea. Hold on, you know what an Elrolian is, right?'.

'Um, no. I think they are like, really powerful and stuff, but that's all I know,' I said, rather embarrassed, as he spoke of them as if everyone should know about them.

'Well, it could be a short story, but to get the idea, you need the long version.'

'So could you tell me?'

'All right,' he grunted, 'But first let's sit down somewhere. Yeah, there.'

We sat down on an old wooden log, and Ravenwood took a deep breath, gazed up at the celling, and then started his tale.

STORY OF THE ELROLIANS

'Elrolians are the best warriors that have ever existed. Ever. In the whole universe. One Elrolian would easily beat me in any one on one battle. It would take them at the most, one minute to kill me.'

This was saying something. I had heard that no one in the camp had beat Ravenwood in training of any sort. I couldn't wait to actually see him train later today.

He smiled, seeing the look of awe on my face. 'And the ones to the north are even better, nothing against the southern ones. I'm actually part Elrolian. I don't have any Elrolian powers though; because only one of my parents was Elrolian. Anyway, one could beat a whole Spherian army. They could destroy a Lorothian fortress, which is saying something, and they're extremely hard to kill. You're in luck if you have even one Elrolian on your side. They make great allies, but deadly enemies. Now, they only ever trust animals. Maybe occasionally Arigor – you know, the little elemental people in the Seven Gates – and maybe the Orians, the fully grown ones, but *never* humans.'

'Why not?'

'Because once, almost exactly thirty years ago, when they were more flexible, and didn't have anything against us, they teamed up with a human. Or at least he said he was human. I'm pretty sure he was at least half Elrolian, with the skill he had. His name was Hunter. He was only about twenty then. You probably know, the whole other side of Wouldlock is theirs. They call it Elrolia. I'll bet there are about one hundred animals there you haven't seen before. Anyway, when war threatened them, thirty years ago, Hunter betrayed the Elrolians. While they fought their enemy – creatures called Lanxians – Hunter killed twenty of them, before he disappeared. He was an amazing strategist. No one could outsmart him. After the Elrolians won the battle, they searched for Hunter. Many of them wanted revenge. But they never found him. And that's why they don't work with us anymore. They don't trust us.'

I decided to drop my nickname, the Hunter, from then on. He had killed *twenty* Elrolians. Ravenwood spoke of Hunter as if he'd had personal experience with him.

'Wait, you said Elrolians are hard to kill, right?' I asked.

Ravenwood nodded.

'Then how did Hunter kill so many of them, and why?'

'Ah. You see the reason they are hard to kill is because the only way is to use one of their own weapons against them, because their hearts are coated in a thin layer of Elrolian Onyxus, the same stuff their weapons are made of, and only their weapons can destroy it. The Onyxus coats all of the parts of their body that are essential to living. And you can only get their weapons if they let you. The weapons are made by Eridruluths, the blacksmiths of the Elemental Lords, and no one besides them has the skill to craft an Elrolian weapon. That's why sometimes you can find Elemental Elrolian weapons.

'They trusted him, but when Hunter decides to kill someone, he never stops hunting, but even he could only kill an Elrolian if he had an Elrolian weapon, and he did. He killed all twenty of the mountain explorers before he disappeared. One of the explorers he killed was Elrace Orthoclase, my good friend. He and his wife were the friendliest Elrolians I ever met. I think Aria, his wife, is still alive. She said that their children, Storm and Swayvera, were about twenty when it happened, so they were old enough to fight. You see, you need more than just a weapon to kill an Elrolian. You need skill. And Hunter is by far the most skilled human ever to live, if he *is* human. Why he killed all of them, I have no idea.

'As a matter of fact, this Ice Axe is Elrolian. But don't worry, I told the king and queen I knew where it was, and they gave me permission to keep it. I don't have the skill to kill one of them.'

I took a closer look at the axe. It was extremely well-crafted. The most beautiful weapon I'd ever seen. It had an octagonal grey and black half-metre-long handle, and its blade was dark silver, with no curves, but straight, sharp edges. One side of the blade was a normal axe, but the other side was like a flat, rectangular blade. On the top and bottom of the handle, there were skeleton heads, their eyes glowing icy blue. On the left side of the blade was an embossed tilted square, and on the right side what looked like a helmet, also in silver.

Ravenwood had been watching me closely, and, pointing, started to tell me about the axe.

'This square is the symbol that is almost always found on an Elrolian weapon. This is the helmet of the king and queen. The skull at the top is the queen, and the bottom, the king. This helmet is also symbol on the door of the Elrolian mines, where this axe was created. By the way, you should know, most Elrolians have crowns on, small spiked ones, and so whenever you see one, my advice is to bow. It's polite. So anyway, what was I saying – oh, right, Elrolian weapons. Well, they're known for not being curved, but they're always straight, and razor sharp.'

I frowned. 'Ravenwood, if you're human, how come they let you take the axe?'

'Because I once helped them out in a hard case, even for one of them. They had to find the trident of Atlantis for some unknown reason, and only I could hold my breath under water long enough to find it. So they can trust me. And even if I tried to betray them, they would have me dead long before I could even reach for a shield. As a matter of fact, they also gave me this silver ring.'

He showed me a dark silver ring, showing a tilted square, and inside the square a black 'E,' that probably stood for Elrolia.

'It doesn't have any powers I know of yet, but it's a gift that means they can trust me. You can see the same square that was on my axe here. I heard they only made ten of these things.'

'Oh. Why is it that they're so good at fighting?' I wondered if I could be like one.

'Well, I never asked. I would guess that they just train from an early age, probably know a lot of complex battle techniques. People say that the Elrolian Onyxus in their blood makes them skilled,' Ravenwood said.

'Is that why people always bow to them and everything? Because they're so powerful?' I asked.

'Yeah. But they also bow because they're scared of them. The Elrolians are, as you said before, extremely powerful.

'Does Hunter still have an Elrolian weapon?' I asked.

'I would think so,' he said bitterly. 'But even he would not try to kill them again. Even with one of their weapons, they are nearly impossible to kill.'

'But he killed twenty already! He could do it again.'

'I have no doubt he could, but he hasn't been seen for a long time. I think he's working on something. He wouldn't normally rest for this long. One of these days, he's going to strike hard, and we won't realise what he's planning until it's just too late. He still has those weapons.'

'What happens if you stab an Elrolian with a normal weapon?'

'They will feel extreme pain, but will not die. As I said before, their hearts cannot be touched by any normal blade.'

I heard loud footsteps, and then Raider, Blade, and Stream came in, arguing loudly.

'Come on, man! *You* made us wear a tie and suit when we went to Spheria for your conference!' said Raider.

'Yeah, well, Spheria is a formal place, where you wear formal clothes,' said Stream.

'Yeah, but who says you can't wear formal clothes when you go swimming!' said Blade.

'You just *don't* wear things like that to go swimming. Besides you aren't going to wear suits are you?'

'No, because we are the hosts,' said Raider, with a smile and a deep bow. 'We'll wear *swim* suits.'

Stream rolled his eyes.

'You guys are going swimming? Where?' I asked.

'In the Tigers River,' said Blade, smiling mischievously.

'Listen, it's a special occasion,' said Raider to Stream.

'What makes it special?'

'This will be the first time you go swimming in a suit,' said Blade simply. 'An historic moment.'

'You'll never forget it,' said Raider, tapping his head.

I always thought it was amazing how they always knew what the other would say. Like it was from a script.

'Listen, you wouldn't want to go there with your hair dyed blonde, would you?' Raider asked.

'No way!' Stream said.

'Why?' Asked Blade.

'I hate that colour!'

'Yeah, exactly. *You* don't like it on yourself, when others might. Yet, we didn't like the suits, but since *others* liked it, you made us go in it with no choice.'

'Yeah,' Agreed Raider, 'so we're not giving you a choice either.'

'Yes,' said Raider firmly. 'You will go swimming in a suit.'

'You think Stream should go in a suit right?' said Blade.

I opened my mouth to reply.

'Of course he thinks he should!' said Blade, as if me opening my mouth meant yes.

'Well –' I tried to say.

'It's alright, you don't need to come if you don't want to.'

'But *I* do?' asked Stream indignantly.

'Yes,' they said in unison.

'Would you stop making a racket?' shouted Shade who had stormed up angrily from the meeting room. 'Just go in *swim* suits and be done with it!' He glared at them as if daring them to argue. When they didn't, he went off again.

'You know, I've always hated him.' said Raider, shooting Shade a dirty look.

'Ah, my brother, we shall have our revenge,' Blade said.

They too went out of the arena, plotting what they could do to get back at him.

Ravenwood had been very quiet. He had watched over the whole discussion emotionlessly.

'This isn't going to be good,' I said. 'Last time Shade annoyed them, he ended up in his room for four days. Something about vinegar and melted tree bark stuffed in his pancake. You would think he had learnt his lesson.'

'Have you ever thought that you haven't seen all the life in Wouldlock? Like there might be something else out there?' asked Ravenwood suddenly, turning to look at me.

'Well, I don't know. I don't know where else an animal could hide. I mean, besides the Black Trees and the Silent Mountains, but I doubt any animals could live there. I definitely haven't seen all the animals in the sea though ... like the ones down deep.'

'Strange,' he growled. 'I swear there was something I saw in the tree by the beach yesterday. Some black, flying shape.'

'Well, it was probably a liaser. They live by that tree.'

'No,' he said, 'it wasn't. See, I went to investigate, it soared away, all black, like a shadow, and it was definitely bigger than a liaser. And all of the liasers were on the ground, dead. They had been ripped apart. You wouldn't believe it. There was blood everywhere.'

I was astonished. Those poor animals! I felt hatred for whatever had done this, human or animal.

'Well, we won't be going far without any transportation for a while. What could have killed it?'

'Don't know. Very fast beast, I couldn't make it out.' He growled in approval. 'I love animals with such agility. Always liked animals. You've got a good job, son, working here. You know I have an Elrolian Wolf? Well, I don't really *own* it, but it follows me around, like it's mine. But of course it could go anywhere it wants. I don't control it. It really is an amazing creature, the Elrolian Snow Wolf. It's the fastest animal in the world. Five hundred kilometres per hour, and can hold the speed for about twenty minutes, and it's big enough to ride on. It didn't want to come through the water with me, so it went around. Came in yesterday. Have you seen her yet?'

'No! Where is she?' I asked excitedly.

'Follow me,' he said.

'Hey, can't they, like, smash through walls?' I asked.

'No, that's the Stone Wolf. This one is a Snow Wolf, and is much faster, and it can stand any freezing temperature,' he said proudly.

It turned out she was out in the field, running around wildly. She looked beautiful. She had shiny pure-white fur, silver teeth, and looked very healthy. She had long, powerful legs, which was probably the reason she was so fast. When she saw Ravenwood, she leapt to him and sat obediently at his side, rubbing her head against his leg. He stroked her head. I patted her back, and her fur was the softest thing I'd ever felt.

'Name's Spirix. She's very smart. She is so used to hearing English, it seems like she can understand it by now. She chose to follow me the day I left Elrolia, after I had brought them the Trident of Atlantis from, well, Atlantis.'

'Hey!' said Blade peering at us from the camp. 'Lance says it's training time.'

'Alright. Let's go, Ravenwood,' I said, and we walked over to the huge training arena.

Why do we need to train in an arena? Well, most of it is survival, and of course we need that if we're to live in the wild, with millions of untrained animals around us. But a small part of it is combat, to protect us from the humans. There have been times when we have had to defend ourselves from hunters, and, as you could tell from the meeting with the President, there was a chance they would send someone to kill us, even for a little thing like money. If we didn't train, we would probably be dead. But we never attack animals.

After all of the talk about Elrolians and how they were such good fighters, I was rather inspired, and was determined to train very hard. Especially with Ravenwood watching me. I wanted him to see what I was capable of.

There are six stations at the arena: Fencing and swords, archery, the Forge, survival, climbing, and water training. My favourite was archery, so I went there first.

I took my personal black bow and my silver arrows. There was a board that you normally shot at, but it was too easy for me. Now I aimed for falling leaves.

Out of the twenty shots I took, I only missed six of them, which was a considerable improvement from my last score of ten out of twenty.

'That last one was quite a shot,' said Ravenwood.

'Thanks,' I said, feeling quite proud of myself. I imagined myself shooting with ease in a battle, with an Elrolian crown on, very skilled, and respected by friends, and feared by my enemies.

I watched Ravenwood sword-fight with Raider for a while, and he was *very* good. If that was how a human was, I wondered what an Elrolian would be like. And he wasn't all that young either.

Then I moved on to the Forge. If it hadn't been for Ravenwood, I would be making Shade a spear now, but I decided I would sharpen my knife. I got it out and pulled out the diamond wheel. Then I slowly spun it, which turned smaller gears, making it go very fast, with sparks flying everywhere.

I finished up at the forge station, and went to the water training one. It was set up at the sea, with Stream supervising.

'Hey Wolf! Having fun?' Stream said.

'Yeah, just came from the forge,' I replied.

'Cool,' he said, grinning. 'So, how about snorkeling today? You'll enjoy it.'

It was my very first time snorkeling, and, as Stream had predicted, I loved it. So many creatures and colours, and with the sun shining through, it looked stunning. A few times I accidently swallowed some water, but other than that it went fine. I saw several schools of fish, a stingray, and two huge hammerhead sharks.

'That was great!' I said once I had pulled myself out of the water.

'Hey, I forgot, could you deliver these files to Lance? He wants to get them up to date,' said Stream.

'Sure.'

He handed me the files. When I entered the camp I tripped and fell to the rocky floor, bruising my right knee. The files spilled out everywhere. I got to my feet and collected them.

'You all right? Here you go.' Ravenwood got down to his knees and snatched up the files, placing them delicately in my hands.

'Yeah, thanks,' I said gratefully.

He nodded, and then limped away. I looked at the file he had given me. My own face peered up at me: long rusty hair, rough beard. It had been taken very recently. I opened it as I walked. What had Lance said my skills were? I stopped and read it to myself. At the top right corner was a key for the levels you could achieve for each skill.

Platinum (P)

Diamond (D)

Silver (S)

Gold (G)

Bronze (B)

I had heard that Stream had got five Ps and one S, and I was curious to see what I had got.

Climbing: P

Water: G

Fencing: D

Archery: P

Forge: G

Survival: S

I was exceptionally happy with my results. Below each of them were small comments from Lance. I decided that for my next training session I would focus even more on my Water skills. I reached Lance's office and knocked. There were no doors, but boulders we could shift for privacy.

'Come in,' Lance said.

I entered.

'Ah, Wolf, are those the files?

'Yes, Lance,' I said, handing them to him.

'Thank you very much. Have a good day.'

I made to leave, but when I reached the boulders, Lance said, watching me carefully, 'I hope you're proud of your marks.'

VIPER

I had heard we were getting two more people for the team who would be arriving very soon to join us. I only learnt that two major Elemental Lords were coming, two minutes and thirty-two seconds (or so Raider tells me) before they arrived, and I was quite unprepared. But they were only staying for a few minutes. It was the day after the bomb incident, and I had just had breakfast. The sun sparkled and reflected off the Tigers River. I could feel the cool breeze against my face. I heard Ravenwood talking outside of the camp. The people had arrived.

Of the four, I only recognised one. It was Slare. She had, as promised, stopped by to join with us. She was dressed casually, and she seemed much less formal than she'd been when she had been serving our food. She waved and smiled when she saw me.

Another one of the group was dressed in black, with a beard and sunglasses. The other two I guessed were the Elemental Lords. One was a woman, dressed in a stunning bright green, with long black hair, and lots of jewelry. It was seriously all over her. She had rings, bracelets, necklaces, everything. Each item had some sort of gemstone in it. The other wore black and orange shining metal armour, with a black helmet. He took the helmet off and smiled at me. He had a small beard, and looked about sixty. He looked like the woman, and I bet you they were related. They had the same smile, and the same warm eyes.

'Hey man,' he said. His metal glove retracted into his chest armour revealing his bare hand. 'My name's Stringer, Lord of Metal, and the unofficial lord of parties and destruction, and anything that goes boom.' He gestured carelessly to the jewelry woman. 'And this is Cryslia, my caring sister.'

Cryslia rolled her eyes. They were a deep purple colour, like amethyst. 'Hello. I'm Cryslia, Lord of Crystals. We just came by to visit. We're good friends of Lance Ocrinus'

'I'm Wolf. Great pleasure to meet you.'

'Wolf, this is Earthum, he will be staying with us, as well as Slare. I believe you have met her before?' said Ravenwood.

'Yeah,' I said, 'it's good to see you could make it.'

'Yeah, Stringer gave me a ride.'

'Great. So you're staying here?'

'Definitely. It will be so much cooler than the Three Leaves.'

'Well, you guys can come in!' Ravenwood said.

He limped in, gesturing for the others to do the same. Not gesturing for them to limp, but to come in, I mean. We all pulled back one of the tree stumps we used for chairs and sat down around the circular wooden table. As Stringer came in the rest of his armour retracted so only his gleaming black chest plate showed. I guessed he could just control the armour with his mind. After all, he was an Elemental Lord. It looked pretty awesome when he did it.

'So, sis, should I ask them?' said Stringer.

'Do not call me "*sis*"!'

'Sorry… bro.'

'Not bro! I'm not your brother!'

'You're right … bro-sis.'

'Just shut up, Stringer.'

'Okay. Well anyway, I was wondering if you guys want to come to my place. It's pretty sweet.'

'Sure! Now?' I asked. I imagined the home of an Elemental Lord would be awesome. It was pretty nice of them to offer, since they'd just got here.

'Yeah, maybe about … ten minutes? That'll give you time to get ready, and that'll give me and Cryslia enough time to go say hello to Lance. It's kind of cold where I live, so get on something warm.'

'Wait, isn't the Elemental Lords' palace on Eridrulus?'

'Yeah, but my *other* place is at Lorothia. You see, they didn't appreciate the parties I would throw, so they moved me down to my own separate place. I can still go up to Eridrulus though. Just, no parties.'

'Oh. Alright.'

'I know. They don't like parties! What idiots.' He said with a wink.

I went into my room to get everything I would need together. I took Stringer's advice and put on my furry winter coat. I packed my knife just in case I needed it. I never liked to be off guard. Especially that now the Spherians would be after me after that argument with the President. Also, it wasn't good I had no file. And they knew where I lived, more or less. Sooner or later, they would probably come for me.

I met Stringer and Cryslia at the beach, where he had told me to meet them. In front of them was a black turtle, with silver and fiery-orange armour. It was huge, about the size of a truck. It looked amazing.

'Hey man. Are you ready?'

'Yeah. What *is* that?'

'Ah, that's a Lorothian Turtle. I guess you don't have them here in Wouldlock. They're extremely strong. I gave it the armour. Do you have everything?'

'Yeah, I won't need much.'

'Okay then. Let's move.'

I could see his place from about five kilometres away. It was huge, and built on the side of a rocky cliff, overlooking the sea. Two metal doors slid into the sides of the rocks and we went through. It was even grander than the President's place. It had all of his different sets of armour displayed, and a large black and orange metal lion standing motionless in the centre of the room.

The place was five-star fancy. The doors and cabinets were made of polished wood, all of them with gleaming wavy silver handles. The couches looked more comfortable than beds – or at least more comfortable than any I'd slept in before. The legs of the chairs and tables were wavy as well, and he had his own bar and hot tub right there on the first level.

Stringer helped us off the turtle and spread out his arms, bowing deeply. 'Welcome, to my luxurious home! Make yourselves comfortable.'

He showed me to a nice white, fluffy sofa and sat down.

'Want any drinks? Pizza?'

'Sure, I'll have some sparkling water. And pizza sounds great.'

'You got it, man. How about you, sis – I mean *Cryslia*?'

'Same please, Stringer.'

'Okay, coming right up.' He went up a marble staircase to get everything, leaving me with Cryslia.

'Do you know if there's anyone else here?' I asked her.

'Yeah, Stringer said the son of the Elemental Lord of Energy is here working with Stringer on something.'

'Really? Who's the Lord of Energy?'

'Her name's Industria, she's really nice, and extremely powerful. Being the Lord of Energy means you can control movement and electricity, and I've heard she can make anything out of pure energy just by thinking about it. I imagine her children would have relatively the same powers.'

At that moment, Stringer came back in with our food and drinks, accompanied by a young boy – a teenager, by the looks of him, maybe near his twenties.

'Hey guys,' said Stringer, laying down our drinks and pizza, 'this is my friend Viper. He is the son of Industria, Lord of Energy.'

Viper had a short-sleeved shirt, black jeans, and was growing a small beard, that he obviously didn't shave much. He was very muscular, and looked sweaty, as if he had been sprinting or working very hard. His hair was messy, and stood up with some sort of gel, making him look taller than he really was.

'Hello, I'm Viper,' he said, extending his hand.

I took it. 'I'm Wolf. Pleasure to meet you.'

We took our seats, and ate our food.

'Wolf, how would you like to come to my room and see what I'm working on?'

'I'd love to!'

He led me to his place. It was like a whole workshop, with metal parts everywhere, along with a laptop that looked as if he had made it himself, as it was bronze, and extremely thin, with the symbol of energy on it: a circle with lots of wavy lines on it, all joining up to make another small circle in the very centre. It glowed every colour you can think of, slowly changing. He had a cover on it too – random cards scattered over, with the energy symbol where the ace of spades logo should have been.

On one of the desks was a black folder labeled 'Black Aqua' in lake blue, and below it was 'TOP SECRET' printed in red.

That's the type of thing that gets you to want to open something. When it says secret, you want to know what it means. But I was not the type of person who interfered with other people's business. I left it alone. Viper saw what I was looking at.

'Yeah, that's a little project that Stringer and I have been working on. Well, I guess not exactly little. It's the reason I'm here – to help Stringer with it. I'll be happy to show you the final product, but it'll take a long while to complete.'

There was a crash, and a shout of laughter outside. I jumped, but Viper merely chuckled.

'Oh, those will be my brothers. Mac and Icon.' He said Icon pronouncing the 'I' like in the word 'is.' 'They're three and four years old. You should probably meet them now, so they know that you're not an intruder. They like jumping on people they don't know.'

We went out into the hall and into the room where the noise had come from. Viper opened the door. Something smashed me to the ground.

'Whoa!' I shouted in surprise.

Viper walked to me and pulled off a small child. I stood up and saw there was another kid staring at me.

The one that had jumped onto me spoke, in a soft voice that you would expect someone that age to have. 'Who is – ?' he said, pointing vigorously at me.

'That's Wolf, he's my friend, Mac,' said Viper, and the boy calmed down. 'I was showing him my room.' Viper said, patting his head gently.

'Hello!' said the other one, cautiously stepping forwards towards me. 'I'm Icon!' He said loudly, pointing at himself with one of his tiny little fingers.

'Hello, Icon.' I said, smiling warmly.

Mac was on the ground now, holding some cards in his toes, in a perfect fan. He started doing faro shuffles with his feet

'This is Mac,' said Viper apologetically. 'He's kind of nervous around strangers, but when he gets to know you, he's very talkative. He's amazing with his feet. He can eat with them, throw a Frisbee with them, he can even type with them.'

Mac smiled, throwing one of his cards at a dartboard, hitting it right in the middle, I noticed, before it fell like a leaf to the polished marble floor.

'You should see him on the monkey bars,' Viper added.

Icon rushed to a drawer and pulled out something. He ran back to me and showed it to me. 'Widget!' he said proudly.

The thing was a gleaming black robotic animal. I recognised it as a misticon. We have them at Wouldlock. They are sky-dwelling monsters, also known as Sky Biters, snapping at anything from birds to fully grown liasers. It's a mystery to me how they stay aloft though. They have six long tails, and they're sphere-shaped, with six rings around them, like on Saturn. It had large, sharp teeth, and two perfectly round eyes. They have smooth skin, which turns transparent around the time they turn three years old. You can find them in colours of green, blue, violet, and sometimes orange. This robotic replica was extremely accurate.

'Wow,' I said, truly impressed. 'Did you make that by yourself?'

He nodded happily, and turned something on its back. It started flying around the room, looking very alive.

'Yay! Look, tails make it fly,' he explained, catching the model and showing me the six tails on its back. 'They push Widget through air.'

'He has been working on it for half a year. It's amazing. Maybe he can go help out the elemental weapon-creators soon. Anyway, want to go back to my room?' Viper asked.

'No, wait!' Mac said, pulling me back. 'I want to show you.' He went into the back of the room and picked something up from the desk, which was littered with random pieces of metal, rock, and wood. Engineering certainly seemed to run in the family.

'Look-it! Look-it!' He said, holding up a little sledgehammer. And not just any hammer. The most well-crafted hammer I'd seen in my life. The head of it was black rock, not all even, but it looked better unpolished. On either side of the hammer was a small silver elk head in a circle. The handle was made of wood, a light brown type, with silver wire wrapping around it like a snake. I wasn't sure what tree it came from though. I know, living in a forest for almost all my life, but not being able to identify the tree? Still, this *was* polished! How was I supposed to know what tree it came from? Anyway, he told me right after I saw it.

'It's made of Elkwood,' he said. 'It's the Elkwood hammer.'

Ah, Elkwood. Elkwood trees were all over Wouldlock. Beautiful things they are. Let me tell you about them – don't worry, it won't be boring.

Elkwood comes from an Elkwood tree, obviously. It's a humungous tree that grows individually. What I mean is they don't grow in groups. You can see lots of them in one area, but they usually grow spread out from each other, for they are all connected to a master tree, from which the roots, when they grow out enough, grow even more full trees that carry on the system. Therefore came the name known as the family tree – the oldest at the centre, or top, and then roots to other people, or in the case of Elkwood, trees. The trunks are dark brown, but they grow lighter as the branches grow. They are the strongest, hardest living thing on the Earth. *Almost* as hard as diamond. Diamond is the only thing that can penetrate them. If you cut off a branch, it grows right back, very quickly, for the tree knows the length of its branches, and those that are cut off will grow faster, so they can catch up with the rest of the tree. Even if the branch is cut off, if you leave it in water, it grows like normal. Amazing, eh? That would make that hammer incredibly strong. You see? That was a long explanation, but not *that* boring, was it? I hope not … it probably was … sorry. I sometimes get a bit carried away with these things.

'Wow, that's amazing!' I said, very truthfully.

'Thanks!' he said.

'Sure. I'm going to go with Viper now, okay? Bye!' They waved back at me, Mac with his foot. Viper led me into his room again, and I followed him to a desk, which, like the others, was cluttered with random bits of metal.

He looked around for something for a minute, and then showed me a pair of black and silver gloves. 'You see I haven't yet learnt to control my powers to their best effect, so these gloves kind of help me harness the power. I've used a special magnetic force, and voice-controlled devices, so I can control these knives,' he said, showing me. 'If I say 'knives' when I am wearing them, they will come directly to these gloves, if I say 'hunt,' then *I* go to them. Like flying, but I fly directly to them. It only works for me and Mac and Icon though, 'cause we're the only children of Industria. Want to see?'

'Sure!' I said excitedly. This was amazing. If he found a way to make this work for anyone, and he sold it, he would be rich. It was a surprise to me that he wasn't already … or perhaps he was. I didn't know. But he probably liked that he was the only one to have it. It was unique.

We went to Stringer's arena, on the top of the place. Viper put on the gloves, and threw the knives, and they landed point -in on one of the boulders.

'Watch carefully now. *Knives!*'

Both of them soared right into Viper's hands.

'Whoa,' I said in amazement.

'Now look at this.'

He hurled them back at the rocks, higher up this time. They stuck into the rocks, the handles trembling slightly.

'*Hunt!*' he murmured.

This time his whole body flew to the knives, and he grabbed them, and dropped back to the ground.

I gaped at him. 'That's so cool.'

He showed me the rest of his stuff, which included what he said was an elemental disk. It was wafer-thin, made of metal, and extremely light. It was about the size of a playing card. He said you could change them from fire to light, if you had the right disks. He spread out the red fire disks on the cover of his laptop, and then flipped them over, and the disks that had been red and orange were now a blinding silvery white.

'Wow,' I said, turning the disks over to see that they were all white, not with two different sides. 'That's so cool.'

'I practice with playing cards.'

He showed me how he could throw them by using a certain technique, and how they could cut through Lorothian rope (Lorothian rope is made of lots of small strings of iron, and is therefore very strong). He also said that when you threw them, they could activate their element, the air disks making a small tornado, and the fire disks erupting in flames. Each disk had some cool ability. He gave me an air disk to keep, which I thanked him for a million times.

Then he showed me a shiny black and silver sword, the blade of which could retract into the handle, just like a measuring tape, and then come back out again the same way.

All of it was just incredible. And made only by him, with no other help.

'In case you ever need me,' he said, handing me the number to his phone, which he had also made himself. I did not have a phone, which I didn't admit to, but I took it anyway. Viper was a cool guy.

An hour later, Stringer and I got the turtles, and we travelled back to Wouldlock.

It was lunchtime by the time we got there. I said farewell to Stringer, and went to camp. After lunch, I went out to give

Earthum a tour of the place. On the way to the Silent Mountains, I told him about the bomb the day before.

Then as we walked through the woods, we saw the snake. It was a five-metre-long boa constrictor. Earthum gulped.

'What should we do?' he asked nervously, staying very still.

'I don't know. Our rule is, no killing animals,' I said, keeping my eyes on the snake.

It stared back at me, and then blinked. I took out my knife and without hesitation, threw it at the snake. It hit the snake's eye and it didn't move.

'You said you couldn't kill animals!' exclaimed Earthum.

'That isn't real. Snakes can't blink.'

'Oh. Right.'

I took the snake's body up and ripped it open. It was robotic. It was very convincing though. Inside was a bomb, identical to the one that I had found yesterday.

Spheria.

The stupid President had tried to kill us again, with a better weapon. What was wrong with this guy? There were five minutes left until it went off. I tried punching it as I had done before, but this one seemed to be made of a tougher material.

'I'd better get this to Stream. He'll know how to destroy it.'

'Alright. Do you mind if I stay here? You know, to look around? Please?'

I was apprehensive, but I didn't want to say no. After all, he was an adult. He'd be fine. 'Um, alright. Are you sure? I mean, you're new and everything. Are you going to be alright?'

'Yeah, I can take care of myself. See you.'

'Don't go too far.'

I rushed back to camp. By the time I got there, there was only a minute left. I gave it to Stream, explaining to him what had happened, and he had it sorted out in a few seconds, shaking his head and mumbling things about the president that I didn't quite catch.

'So where's Earthum?' He asked me.

'He said he wanted to look around by himself. He's at the Silent Mountains. I should go get him,' I said, making for the door.

'Oh, that's alright, Wolf, I will. I need to get some exercise, and make sure that there aren't any more bombs. Besides, I haven't spent that much time with him. I should get to know him better.'

'Thanks. See you for dinner.'

I sat outside the camp, the wind whipping my hair, playing fetch with Ravenwood's wolf, Spirix. I did some archery too, hitting leaves like in training. I kept imagining being an Elrolian, with extreme power and skill.

I felt rather guilty about leaving Earthum alone out there, by himself in a forest inhabited with dangerous creatures that would love a nice fresh dinner.

No. I couldn't think like that. He would be fine. He would come home, having a nice talk with Stream, and we would carry on with our life, talking about the bomb like it had been a fun adventure.

As it steadily grew darker and colder, I saw Stream coming back, a shadow in the night. I heard no voices. As they came closer, and into better focus, I saw why. Next to him, being dragged and hanging limply, was Earthum. He was bloody, and extremely pale. His clothes were ripped, and it seemed as if something had bitten off his right hand, because all that was left of it was a bloody stump. Just looking at him made me shaky. His grey shirt was stained with dark blood, leaving almost none of its original colour. I could see the deep scratches all over him; so deep I had no doubt they would have gone as deep as the bone. His eyes were opened wide, with no life in them, staring beyond space.

Earthum was dead.

DEATH ASSEMBLY

I couldn't believe what I was seeing. My whole body went numb. Undoubtedly some animal had done it. No human killed like that, and nothing natural could have done it either. Lance called a Death Assembly. We had one whenever someone died, to discuss the cause of death. The last time we had had one had been for someone named William Rollers. He had fallen from the Silent Mountains and broken pretty much every bone in his body. He had been with us for five months. Earthum had only been here for about five hours. The person who had known him best had been Shade, as they had been friends before this, and he had been the one to invite him. But as I found out at the meeting, Shade blamed *me* for Earthum's death.

I could not help but feel extremely guilty. Shade made it much worse.

'Wolf, how could you let a new team member out of your sight!' Shade shouted in rage. 'You find a bomb, and then leave

Earthum on his own, in the middle of a forest inhabited with *thousands* of predators. If you had just insisted he come with you, he would still be alive now! Or you could have just given him a knife to defend himself!'

'*Defend himself!* You mean kill the animal that did this! I feel just as bad as you do, Shade, but killing an animal? We have rules against that! They don't deserve to die! It was probably scared!'

Shade glared at me menacingly. 'Stupid *rules.* Are you saying that some animal's life was so important that he should have just let himself die? If you had been there, would you have killed the thing to save him?'

I had no answer. I honestly didn't know. Ask yourself, would you kill an animal to save your best friend, or a friendly stranger? Of course, I would not have killed it if *my* life were in danger, but with another's? I would hate myself forever, no matter what way I went.

'Now, now, settle down,' said Lance. 'The purpose of this meeting is to discuss *how* this happened, not how it could have been prevented. There is nothing we can do now. What I would like to know is what animal did this. None live close to the Silent Mountains.'

'I have no idea. Maybe it was a hyena. The ones by the Hyena Territory are usually very aggressive,' said Sora.

'No,' said Blade, expert on habitats, 'the Silent Mountains are too cold. They wouldn't go wandering off like that.'

'What about the liasers? They live near the Silent Mountains,' said Raider.

'No, they are all dead. You know, maybe the thing that killed them is also responsible for the death of Earthum!' said Ravenwood.

'Maybe. But that brings us no closer to finding out *what* exactly did it. We should all keep an eye out from now on,' said Lance.

'Maybe it was a new species. Sora, do you know of any other predators around here? Any that wouldn't mind the cold? Maybe it was from the sea, and Earthum slipped in,' suggested Raider.

'I haven't seen any new species, but I wouldn't know what else lives down in the sea. And I don't think that any predators would come too close to the shore.'

Rovia and Slare entered the room.

'I buried the body by the Tigers River. That's where you wanted him, right?' Rovia asked Lance.

'Yes, thank you. You didn't see anything unusual, did you?'

'Well actually, I saw a flying black shape by the Silent Mountains,' said Slare.

'It was probably nothing more than a bird,' snapped Shade. 'Now, this is not the point of this meeting. Let's get on with it. Wolf, this is all your fault.' He muttered, 'he died because of *you!*'

'*Shut up!*' roared Ravenwood, and everyone fell silent. 'It was *not* his fault, and you will stop saying so. Wolf could not have known!'

Shade nodded quickly, gulping. 'Yes, back to the topic now. I believe that these sightings have nothing to do with it. The thing you saw, Slare, was nothing more than a vulture.'

'No, Shade, this was about the size of a truck. I couldn't see it clearly though, 'cause it was very fast. It headed for the Black Trees,' said Rovia, agreeing with Slare.

'Well, this could be the creature. We have never ventured into the Black Trees, so we know nothing of what lies in there. Has anyone else seen something similar to this?' Lance asked.

Both Sora and Ravenwood nodded. They had both told me what they had seen.

'I saw one by the Beach Tree. I'm pretty sure it was responsible for killing the liasers.'

'Yeah, I saw one too, but it was by the Black Trees.'

'Well,' said Stream, 'we can't just go wandering into the Black Trees, it's extremely dangerous. And if what you have seen really is the killer ... you saw what it did to Earthum. It would be very strong.'

'He didn't use any defence. He probably just let himself die. *We* would be prepared' Shade said angrily.

'I'm not saying it's a good thing that Earthum died,' I said, 'but he wasn't stupid enough to kill it, even for his own life. It sounds to me that what you're suggesting is we try to hunt it down, and kill it! Earthum had honour, and saved an animal life with his own.'

'Wolf is right,' Lance said. 'We can't kill it, no matter what it did to Earthum. That is our rule.'

'Are you saying we should just forget about it? We must avenge our fallen friend!' exclaimed Shade.

'Spoken like a true hero,' said Raider, trying to keep a straight face while sniggering along with his brother. 'Since when have you started using huge words for simple sentences?'

'Are you saying that *avenge* is a big word?' Shade sneered.

'Never would I suggest such a thing!' said Raider. 'I was unassumingly stating that the usage of immense words in unimportant statements could give the impression to any spectators that you are a scientific, large-mouthed, extremely talkative *idiot*.'

Shade snarled, looking murderous. 'I'm tired of this.'

'You're always tired for some reason,' said Blade.

'No! Not always.'

'You're sometimes always tired,' said Raider.

Stream sighed and shifted uncomfortably. It was always bad news when Shade and the brothers started arguing.

'It still sounds to me that you are suggesting we attack the creature,' I said to Shade.

'Alright, that's enough,' snarled Ravenwood. 'We will not

kill it. If anyone kills an animal and I know about it, they'll be worse than dead.'

That silenced everyone.

Ravenwood continued.

'No one can go out alone. We have to be on full alert. Prepare to *escape* anything. Under no circumstances will we kill an animal, no matter what it may have done to us.'

It felt natural to take advice from Ravenwood. Perhaps it was because he was an Elemental Lord, and was extremely powerful, and skilled.

'Of course, only if that's okay with you, Lance. I'm not in charge here.'

'Oh, yes, it's a fantastic idea,' agreed Lance. 'Definitely. I wonder how many of them there are? Three? Or is there just one of them, which keeps showing up? Or possibly, there could be a pack of them? In any case, how is it we have never seen them before? Or perhaps, have we seen them before, and just do not recognise them?'

'Maybe it's a cross-breed?' I suggested. 'Maybe someone experimented with the blood of two or three animals. Sora was telling me that if you mix the blood of animals, and then inject the blood into the animal, it could start to grow similar parts to the other animal. Maybe someone recently did some experimental breeding, then let the result go free in Wouldlock.'

'True, I did say that. I think that's a very reasonable explanation,' said Sora. 'It would create a creature that we would not have any idea or record of. Why anyone would do such a thing, I don't know.'

'Perhaps someone from Spheria created a new monster to kill us!' said Stream. 'If they got rid of us, they would have a clear road to gaining control of Wouldlock. We wouldn't kill it, so they wouldn't have to worry we'd stop them, like we did with the snake.'

'Whoa, wait just one second here,' said Raider. 'We are still going off topic. We are saying that we should think that *Spheria* has done all of this. What proof do we have? Sure, there are the others. It doesn't mean that Spheria also created this monster. What you have seen may just be a Lorothian Shadow Eagle.'

Only Slare looked like she hadn't heard of it.

'A what?'

'They're these massive black eagles from Lorothia,' said Blade. 'They're called Shadow Eagles 'cause they're mostly seen under cover of shadows, like the shadows of the Silent Mountains, or the Beach Tree. They can be very aggressive. The Black Trees would be perfect for their habitat. And this animal might be out of the question. What if something else did it?'

'I still do not care. If it hadn't been for Wolf, he would not have died, the *end.* Who cares how he died, that information will not help him, if he is dead already,' said Shade irritably.

'Neither will the information that *I'm* responsible help him,' I muttered.

'I told you before, Wolf could not have foreseen this. From what I understand, Earthum was the one who wanted to stay. Wolf let him, and did not imagine he would come to any harm, am I right?' asked Ravenwood.

I nodded. After everything I had heard Shade say, I felt even guiltier. I could have saved him, just by insisting he come with me. He probably would have agreed. And if, just *if*, I had left him a knife, would he have used it? I would not have, but I may have understood animals better. Would he have been so scared that he would have attacked? He had probably come too close to it, or maybe frightened one of its children. He had looked extremely bad, with his hand nowhere to be seen. I couldn't even come close to imagining the pain he must have gone through.

'For how the information of the killer would help, it would help *us,*' Lance said. 'We will be able to prepare ourselves in case the animal tries to attack us. Prepare not weapons, but *ourselves*. We would be able to know how it moves, and where we would most likely encounter it.'

'Well I think we're done here,' said Ravenwood. 'We just need to be alert and look for all the hints and details of any new creature. I don't think we will be able to actually decide which animal did this, just from discussing it among ourselves, so just be meticulous. And don't get started with me and *big words*. Meticulous means "careful,"' he said, silencing Raider, who was opening his mouth.

'Wait a second,' said Stream, biting his lip in thought. 'There's a terrorist organisation called the Silver Claw. Anyone heard of it?'

Rovia sat up a little straighter, and Shade looked up.

'Yeah,' muttered Shade. 'In the newspapers.'

'I think I've heard of them,' said Rovia. 'They unleash animals into cities, with a metal claw on their foot, to cause a distraction. Usually they use animals with enhanced abilities which they have created by taking genes from other animals, and let them cause destruction until someone kills them. Then they show someone really important whom they've captured – they hack into all electronic devices and show this to and make the people watching give whatever they want. That's how they got their hands on the Sapphire Staff back in April last year. They first sent a tiger into Spheria, and it got killed. They broke into the President's room and captured him, then demanded the staff from the artifacts museum. I think he lived. But no one's seen the staff since.'

'Of course the President lived – he runs Spheria right now! The one Stream talked to, when the bomb was found,' said Shade, acting like I hadn't been involved. 'And who cares about the Silver Claw – they probably aren't connected. Why bring that up?' He glared at Rovia as if she had personally insulted him.

'Well, it was just an idea,' said Stream. 'You know, we've been talking here long enough, I think we should go. But, you know, I found that meeting with the President in Spheria incredibly strange. He used to care for all animals, including ocelots,' Stream said, looking at me. 'But when we went there, he was cold, selfish, and power-hungry. He's changed. Whatever. I guess people just … change like that sometimes. You know, I never got to get the equipment for the phones. Wolf, want to come back to Spheria and get it with me?'

'You're making us phones?' I asked.

'Yeah. Lance thought we'd better find a form of communication because of what happened to Earthum. We want to be able to make sure we can find each other without scouting around for an hour. Slare, you want to come? We could try to drop by the Three Leaves.'

'Sure! It'll be fun. Let's go.'

'I shall accompany you two on this treacherous expedition!' said Raider. 'With what method do we travel if the liasers are deceased?'

'Shut up,' muttered Shade.

'I offer my complete apology, my cherished acquaintance.' Raider smiled.

Shade snarled.

'Well, I'm actually not sure how we *will* get there,' said Stream thoughtfully, as if there had been no interruption.

'We could walk,' I said. 'It takes only about an hour, if we're quick, as you said before.'

'Well, I think that's the only option,' said Slare. 'Getting a vehicle to take us there would take too long.'

Blade started arguing loudly with Shade.

'What are we trying to do, you ask? We are trying to teach you a lesson!'

'Well, you are telling me not to use "big words" when you use them yourself, to try and *teach* me.'

They glared at each other, like two animals crossing territories.

'I think it's time for some music,' said Blade, smiling. He took out a little circular metal object, and fidgeted around with it. Then without warning, extremely loud music filled the room. It seemed to come from all around us, not from the device. Shade yelped and then growled.

'Wow,' said Slare, impressed, though covering her ears along with the rest of us.

'Made it myself. The music, I mean,' yelled Blade over the music. 'Stringer gave me the disc.' He raised the device that was creating the sound.

Shade banged the table with his fist, and then stormed out of the room.

Blade stopped the music, and the smile slid off his face.

'Sorry,' he said sheepishly. 'I didn't mean for anything like that to happen.'

'Never mind that. Let's go.' Stream said. 'We should start now. Do you two have everything you need?'

I patted my pockets to make sure I had everything. 'Yeah,' I said.

'You bet,' said Raider nodding. 'I'm ready for anything.'

'Let's go!' Slare said brightly.

We went outside the camp, pushing the boulders away, breathing in the fresh air. A leaf swayed and fell onto Raiders head.

'Ah!' he shrieked, brushing off the leaf, which fell to the ground.

'Oh. It's just a leaf,' he said, getting to his feet. 'I knew that.' He frowned, and then slapped his face. 'I'm stupid. But I'm ready now.'

Slare laughed. 'We know you're stupid.'

Raider laughed sarcastically. 'Yeah, right.'

I smiled. 'Don't worry Raider, lots of people in the world are mortally terrified of falling leaves. They stay indoors all autumn.'

We all laughed and talked a lot during our hike, telling stories, and I told them about what Stringer's place had been like, and about Viper, and all of his new technology. Stream was very interested.

'He must have been using the gloves to help control his energy power, and use magnetic force to bring it back to him, along with his original power. He might even use negative magnetic force to push the knives away when he was throwing them. I would really love to see that! Theoretically, anyone could do that, but only using magnetic force, but it wouldn't be as powerful as it is when he uses it with his energy. It would only about half as powerful. In fact, it might not even have enough power to pull *you* to them.'

He seemed to be talking to himself, like he was planning a lesson. I hoped he wouldn't teach us. Stream's ideas were usually cool, but he could get kind of carried away.

'Stream? You should really shut up,' said Raider irritably.

'That's not a very nice way of asking,' he said crossly.

'You're right. *Please* shut up.'

We got there at eight o'clock, and decided to get some dinner before we got the equipment for the phones.

'So, want to go to The Three Leaves?' I asked.

'No, we can't!' Slare said. 'I just remembered it was closing for renovation. There's another good place about a block away on Brick Street called The Lemon. It's a nice place there by the ocean, we could get some pizza or pasta or tofu or something.'

'That sounds good,' said Raider.

'Yeah, sure,' I said.

We walked on, and then Raider went crazy. He always does this, and here's a good example. He likes awkward situations.

He'd done this once when Lance's friend from Raverand had come to the camp. He'd asked her if she had ever seen the President of Spheria sing, and showed her a video of himself dressed as the President, with glasses and everything, singing a song in a super high-pitched voice. It got worse when in the middle of the video he ripped off his expensive suit and waved it around like a lasso.

Now, he went up to a thin guy who was sitting on a bench, reading a newspaper. 'Um, excuse me.'

The guy looked up.

'My name's Raider. I was just wondering do you do drugs?'

The guy stared. 'No.'

'Thank you for your kind feedback.'

He walked back to us, and then went across to two teenage girls walking along the street. I opened my mouth to protest, but it was too late.

'Hey girls, listen up. I'm not attractive,' he said seriously, not cracking a smile. Then after a few seconds he said, 'And neither is the chipmunk on your shoulder, okay? Don't let anyone tell you anything else.'

He walked away, leaving the girls speechless, awkwardly searching their shoulders.

My eyebrows rose. 'Why did you do that?'

He shrugged. 'How would I know? I'm just bored I guess.'

I shook my head, muttering an apology to Slare, and we continued walking.

Slare led the way, and by quarter past eight we had arrived. It was a fancy place, and had a view of the ocean from the tables outdoors. The 'O' in the word 'Lemon' on the sign was the form of a lemon.

'Hey, Stream! Slare!' said the man at the counter. 'Here for dinner?'

'Eltz! Yeah, we're staying. How are you? It's been a while,' said Slare.

'Oh, I'm fine. So, inside, or out?'

'Um, we will all stay out. We'll enjoy the view, you know? This is Wolf, and Raider, they're friends from the Animal Defence Organisation. Also, this is Stream.'

'Oh, yes, I know Stream. He's been coming here for five years, after he stopped working here with me.'

'Oh, really! He never told me. Well, we're getting some supplies for phones, so I thought we could stop by and eat here.'

'Well, it's great you're here. Come and sit!' Eltz said, gesturing for us to sit at a nearby table. 'When you're ready to order, call me.'

'Wait, you know him 'cause you worked here with him, Stream?' ssked Raider.

'Yeah, I used to work here part-time. We became good friends.'

'You too, Slare?' I asked.

'Yeah, I came here a lot too, 'cause my mother worked here. You know, Eltz puts lemon on *everything*. Like, you have to ask for no lemon if you don't want it. See, look on the menu.'

Sure enough, it said 'Lemon is squeezed on every dish. If you would not like lemon with your meal, please inform us when ordering.'

'Whoa, this looks nice,' said Raider pointing out the picture of the salami-lemon pizza. 'It says it's an Italian-salami pizza, soaked in lemon, then baked again to make it dry. I am so getting that.'

After a few minutes we decided what we wanted, then called Eltz over to order.

'I'll have the salami-lemon pizza, please,' said Raider.

'And Stream, Slare, and I will have the fizzy lemon pizza, please,' I said.

'All right, any drinks?'

'I'll have the lemon-lime fizzy, please,' said Raider.

'Sure. Hey, Stream and Slare, I got these for your birthdays last month, but I never had any chance to give you them.' He held out two pieces of paper, one for each. 'They're tickets to The Lemon Kingdom. You can see the giant lemon tree, how the lemons get packaged, everything. It really is a great experience.'

'Thanks! Man, thank you so much!' said Stream.

'Yeah, thank you!'

He smiled and went off to get our food ready.

In less than ten minutes our meals had arrived, and we talked about the phones Stream was planning to make.

'I just want a small one. Maybe blue and green,' I said.

'Sounds good,' said Stream. 'I think I'll be able to make it project the screen onto a wall, the use a sensor so you can touch the projection and operate the real screen.'

'Cool,' said Raider. 'Can I have a blue and orange one?'

'Yeah, sure, but for both of you the blue will have to be really dark, that way I might be able to make the screen dark blue when it's turned off.'

We finished our dinner, thanked Eltz, then set off for the supply store. Stream directed us there. We walked down the quiet streets of Spheria, all of the lights from the lampposts shining around us, like stars.

'It's next to The Three Leaves,' he said. 'Ah, here we are. It's a hardware and software store. Has everything.'

It wasn't exactly fancy, but not beat up either; it was in good condition and was very crowded, and very big. There were lots of lights everywhere. Millions of different metal parts lined the walls and shelves around us. There were boxes on the floor, undoubtedly containing more parts. They had tools like drills, screwdrivers, hammers, nails, everything. They also sold flooring, like marble tiles, and doors and windows. You could get all the stuff you would need for a house here.

There were also lots of wooden poles, stairs, and a whole lumberyard outside. The place was called Aroma.

Stream gathered everything we needed and while he did told us what the things were for, and even about some other products that had nothing to do with phones.

'You see, this is the sensor, for when it's projected onto the wall, and this is the actual projector. Then this disk is the battery, but I'm going to make some changes to it later.'

He would explain things like that. They were extremely boring. But it only took about half an hour.

The woman at the counter was rather surprised. Perhaps she never saw that many things bought by a single group of customers.

'Um ... are you buying all of this?'

'Yes. We're planning a little project. We need a lot of supplies,' said Stream.

'Well, that adds up to be... um, two thousand three hundred twenty four dollars, please,' she said, adding up the prices on the computer in front of her, looking as though she was scared he would get mad about the price, but Stream seemed to be happy with it.

'Whoa, these things are expensive,' said Raider, checking the receipt. 'I mean, look at this, the touch sensor alone is ninety dollars. *One* touch sensor!'

'Well, it will be worth it once the phones are made. These things will be better than anything you can find in the store,' said Stream happily. 'I mean, I'm basically paying this much money for ten custom phones. It's a good deal.'

You might be wondering how we can afford to live, if an official company does not sponsor us. All of those organisations and charities that help donate to protect animals give us the money to help, and we use ten percent of that to live. Also, some of us work other part-time jobs to get money.

We stepped back out of the automatic sliding doors into

the cool fresh Spherian air. My eyes were slowly adjusting to the sudden darkness. There were a lot of lights on around the place, but none on in Wouldlock. It's amazing that we live so close to Spheria. Almost right on the border between the two Eromies.

'Man, we have to walk all the way back in the dark,' Stream said, following us outside and peering into the dark trees of Wouldlock.

I could hear all the insects, and the rustle of the leaves. It gave me an eerie feeling.

'Well, let's get this over with,' said Raider, and he plunged into the darkness of Wouldlock, stepping carefully over fallen branches and streams.

'Let's go then,' I said, and we followed him in.

When we finally got back to camp after a long, tiring walk, we could see no sign of light in the camp. The only source of light I could see was very small, and far away, by the Bear Cave. The crysillium crystals were glowing brightly as usual. It seemed that the team had decided to get a good night's sleep. I thought about Earthum. If I hadn't left him, it could have been both of us coming back tonight. Or would I have made any difference at all? Maybe I would have been killed as well. Maybe I wouldn't have been fast enough to escape either.

'Well, see you guys in the morning,' said Stream with a yawn, walking off to his room.

'Later,' said Raider with a sleepy wave.

I was not tired. I walked down to the beach, staring up at the stars. I walked to the Beach Tree, a huge tree that looked like a hand sticking up out of the ground, and jumped in fright. Lying in front of me was a dead liaser. Its body was bloody, and I could see the rib cage. Ravenwood had told us they were all dead, but I hadn't been imagining it would be this bad. I looked around and saw there were about a dozen bodies. I ran back to camp. I wouldn't wake anyone. They already knew.

But it had left me shaken. What had done this? Maybe it was the thing that the other members claimed they had seen.

As I entered the camp, I heard loud breathing. I turned around, and breathed a sigh of relief. It was Spirix, the Elrolian Snow Wolf. I didn't feel comfortable leaving it out by itself. I knew it would probably be able to hold its ground, being Elrolian, but I led it to my room anyway, where it kept me company, resting its head on its paws. If I was here, nothing would kill her tonight.

BARELY A CHASE

Spirix was still sleeping soundly when I woke up, her body moving up and down as she breathed. The gentle breeze blowing through my room was nice and cool, and the sun shone brightly above the trees of Wouldlock.

I got myself out of my sleeping bag, and put on a winter coat, for it was growing colder as winter crept towards us. I walked out into the training arena, where I found Ravenwood sitting on the same log we had sat on when he had told me the story of the Elrolians. He was treating his scraped leg.

'Morning, Wolf,' he said.

'Morning. How's that scrape?'

'Oh, it's fine, just stings occasionally. It's a nice day. You planning on going out?'

'Yeah, I think I'll just go for a little walk before breakfast. I'll be back around eight or so.'

'Alright, I'll tell the others, if you're sure. Listen up though:

I'm not sure it's wise to be going out there after what happened to Earthum.'

'That's the reason I'm going; to try and find out what did it. I'll be all right. I've lived here practically all my life. And I'm still alive,' I said.

'Okay, if you're sure. Good luck.'

'See you.'

I stepped down the stone stairs, and left the camp, and realised just how cold it was getting. Maybe I would go down to the Bear Cave. That way I would pass through the Black Rocks, and I would have a chance to get warmed up a little.

I started walking, observing watchfully for anything unusual. It seemed normal. The birds were singing, I could hear the waves crashing down on the beach, and the leaves were rustling in the breeze.

I thought back to when I had seen Earthum's mangled body. I remembered all of the blood, and how his hand was even missing. I felt a shiver down my spine.

'What could have done that?' I wondered aloud.

I continued walking, wading through the tall grass of the Field. *This would be a good place for a predator to hide,* I thought. Then I saw a large black shape jump in the grass. Perhaps it was my imagination, but I started to jog through the plants. I could imagine some huge animal, leaping at me before I could react, tearing me to pieces.

I finally reached the end of the Field, and took a moment to catch my breath. I looked back, but saw nothing. Could that have been the thing that everyone else had seen? The others had seen something flying. No bird I knew of was that big, or quick on the ground. I was very cold. Luckily, the Black Rocks were just up ahead. I raced to them, and rolled up my long sleeves, letting the heat flow over my skin. I waited until I almost started to sweat before going again.

The cave I was going to was called the Bear Cave, since it

was the place bears usually slept and lived in. It was also know for all the crysillium in it. Crysillium is a type of gemstone that glows, usually found in the same colours you find misticons in. The ones in the cave were a sea-blue. People say that it grows in the water. Aquarius Seabell, leader of the underwater discovery group called the Ocean Divers discovered the biggest one ever found. Apparently he had recently sold it to the Spherian Museum of Nature, and was now a millionaire.

Anyway, it's everywhere in there. We suspect it's the light it emits that attracts the bears. After what happened to the liasers, I wanted to check on the other animals too.

The wind was growing stronger, and the sky was now cloudy and dark, the clouds looked like huge shadows in the sky, as dark as a raven's feather. It was such a sudden change from the beautiful day it had started off as. It felt as if there was a storm coming on – and a very big one.

I was at the cave now, and it was radiating an eerie glow, from all of the crysillium inside. I stepped in, and could tell immediately there was no creature inside. It was quiet, and the crysillium illuminated the walls, showing no animal there. I looked around the floor, hoping to find some loose crysillium to take back to the camp. The cave was big, and it took a while to search properly. I managed to take out a small chunk from one of the walls. Crysillium is very light. I stuffed it in my pocket and turned around.

It was storming furiously. I had been too distracted with finding the gemstone to take in the sounds, but it was pouring now. I heard loud claps of thunder and saw flashes of lightning. It would be too risky to go back to camp, for the lightning could easily strike in the large open field. I sat down and leant against one of the walls of the cave and waited for the storm to stop. After forty minutes, nothing had changed. I was starving, and cold. There were some apple trees by the Tigers River. I decided to go fetch one of those. There were small caves in the Black Rocks, so I could again pass through there, and hide from the lighting, then quickly go to the river.

'Let's do this,' I breathed to myself, and I got up and dashed through the rain. Water lashed at me, droplets hitting me like bullets from a gun, wind blowing rapidly around me.

In five minutes I was under the shelter of the hot Black Rocks, heating my clothes up. I took off my wet coat and spread it out on the hot floor to let it dry for a few minutes. Then I put it back on, and raced to the trees. The tigers where still there, awake (no living thing could have slept through the sound of the storm), but they didn't try to stop me as I climbed a tree and grabbed an apple. I waited under cover of the trees, watching the rain, ravenously eating the apple.

Maybe I would be able to make it back to camp safely after all. No sooner had I thought that than a huge bolt of lightning hit the ground not twenty metres from me.

'Whoa!' I yelled. I scrambled backwards.

It would probably be safer to go back to the Bear Cave. I ran as if my life depended on it – with all the lightning, it probably did – and finally reached the cave.

I sighed in relief and lay down, exhausted, breathing heavily. Weather changed quickly in Wouldlock, as you've probably noticed by now. That wasn't always a good thing.

'I always get bad luck,' I muttered. By now it would be much later than eight o'clock. I hoped the others weren't worried. Would they think the same creature that had killed Earthum had come for me, and that I was dead? If so, what would they do? I hoped they wouldn't try to look for me. They had sense. They would hopefully assume I was stuck in the storm. After what I saw in the grass earlier, I wasn't sure it was safe out here anymore. But if we couldn't go outside, we couldn't protect the animals – we couldn't do our jobs.

I tried not to think of that. I needed to get back to camp. I couldn't stay here forever. Who knew when the storm would stop? And where were the bears? If one came, I would be pretty hopeless, cramped in this cave. My only option would be to outrun it, and what chance did I have of that? Or maybe something even worse would come. I certainly hoped not.

I picked up a sharp rock from the ground and scraped it against the wall of the cave. It gave a screech that sent a shiver down my spine, but it made a mark on the wall. I did it some more and drew a picture of a howling wolf.

I waited for another twenty minutes and by then the storm had settled down, and though it was still raining, the lightning had stopped. I was very tired still, but I slowly got to my feet.

'Finally,' I said, rubbing my eyes.

Then I heard a growl. At first I wasn't sure, because with the rain pounding on the ground it was hard to hear, but then I heard it again, more loudly this time. I took my hands away from my face.

There was an enormous grizzly bear pawing the ground not five metres in front of me. I hadn't even heard it come. It was big, brown and very wet. Its sharp teeth and claws were clearly visible. I tried to think about what I knew about them. Around ninety five percent of the food it eats includes grass, berries, and nuts, but it occasionally eats deer and fish. I knew how it found me. A grizzly bear's scent-detecting part of its nose is a hundred times larger than a human's. It has one of the most powerful senses of smell of any animal in the world. They say it can smell trash, other bears, and carcasses from more than a mile away.

None of this, however, would help me escape from it. I didn't want to startle it, but I knew it would not leave me alone for long. It was blocking the exit to the cave. I leaped up and grabbed a stalactite of crysillium from the roof, and swung off it as it snapped, my feet nearly hitting the bear's head.

I didn't dare look behind, so I kept running. I could hear the bear's paws hammering the ground as it chased after me. I dodged through the pillars of stone in the Black Rocks, and jumped over the tall clumps of grass at the Field. I was slower, after so much running, and at times I didn't feel that I could run much more, but I continued to push myself. Then I made the mistake of turning to catch a glimpse of the bear, and tripped on a stone that was jutting out of the earth like a hand.

My back screamed with pain as it hit a sharp rock. I saw the bear running towards me, and in seconds in was upon me. I kicked away one of its clawed arms, but the other hit my cheek, sending another wave of pain through me. I rolled to the side and stood up. It stared at me. Then it charged towards me as fast as it could. I waited until the last moment before jumping over it. It turned around again. I remembered the crysillium in my pocket. I waved it in front of the bear.

'Want this? Yeah? Well go and get it!' I said, hurling the crystal in the direction of the cave. It ran after it, leaving me alone.

I was breathing heavily, my legs aching. I put my hands on my knees and rested there for a bit. Then I walked back into the camp.

The team was sitting down at the table, looking as if they had just been having a serious discussion. Stream was looking at me as if I was a ghost, and Lance looked extremely relieved.

'Wolf! We were just wondering where you were. What happened to your cheek? Ravenwood told us how you went off to find the creature that killed Earthum. He also told us you said you would be back by eight o'clock. It's nine-fifty now. What happened?' He didn't sound mad, just curious.

'I got held up by the storm. Then I encountered an angry bear that tried to attack me, so I had to run for it. That's where I got the scrape. I'm really sorry. I hope you weren't worried.' But from the expression on their faces, I could tell they had been worried.

'Wait a sec,' said Raider. 'You got chased by a bear?'

'Well, it was barely a chase. Just a little … well, yeah, I guess you could call it a chase.'

A smile spread across Raider's face. '*Barely* a chase?'

Stream smiled, and even Lance laughed. A grin came across my face as well. Then everyone was laughing. It wasn't all *that* funny, but considering all of the horrible events that had occurred in last few days, it felt good to laugh again.

I looked around again, noticing that something was missing. *Someone,* actually. The whole team was there sitting at the table except for one person.

'Where's Shade?'

Everyone else stopped laughing too.

'He's … gone,' said Lance grimly. 'Left the camp.'

I gaped at him.

'It appears he left somewhere after that incident yesterday. Nobody has heard from him since. I believe he has had enough of protecting animals.'

'But how could he just *leave?* He promised to protect animals for all his life!' I exclaimed.

The rest of the team looked interested. Perhaps they hadn't heard much of what happened to Shade either.

'He lied to us,' said Sora sadly. 'I thought he was truthful. Well, at least most of the time. He said he would devote his life to this'

'I don't know why he left. I think that Earthum's death upset him, and you know how he is … he doesn't forgive easily,' said Lance. 'You saw how upset he was about you leaving Earthum.'

I was about to protest, but I knew Lance wasn't really accusing me.

'Where could he have gone?' asked Rovia. 'Shouldn't we try to look for him? He could be hurt!'

'I think he is better left to his own decisions. I'm sure he's fine,' said Lance. 'Besides, we can always hope he will come back.'

'How do we know that he didn't get killed like Earthum? What if he met the same creature?' asked Slare anxiously.

'He lied to us,' said Blade in disbelief, ignoring the others.

'Yeah, well we lied to him as well sometimes.'

'When did we ever lie to him? If we ever did, we didn't mean it to harm him,' frowned Blade. 'It was just a joke.'

'Sometimes we did lie, though. Remember on his birthday card, we said we were glad he was on our team and part of the living world?' said Raider.

'Oh, yeah. A lie,' said Blade vaguely.

'Let's get back to our discussion here,' said Lance. 'I don't know what he could have done if he met the same creature, but for his sake, I hope he didn't.'

I didn't want to say so in front of the others, but I was pretty sure that if he had encountered the creature, he wouldn't have hesitated to kill it. Maybe that was the reason he had left: to hunt down the killer. It was the type of thing he might have done.

'I certainly hope he's alright. But Wolf, did you see anything unusual?'

I thought about the shape I had seen in the Field, but decided it probably wasn't any threat, and also, I didn't want to worry anyone.

'No. Nothing,' I said. A lie.

'Well. We'll just have to keep on looking. I need to go now, I'm afraid. I have something to discuss with Stringer on my computer. Technology these days,' he sighed

He stood up and quietly left the room.

Everyone else left too for something they had to do, leaving me completely alone. I stared outside. The rain had stopped, and it was back to the fabulous day it had started out to be.

Then I saw a small orange shape across the Tigers River. I squinted. Next to it was what looked like a sand-coloured person. They were getting nearer. I ran outside and stopped by the river. I could see them clearly now.

There were two people slowly walking towards me, one covered in silver and orange armour, and one in yellowish white. One was rather small, about two metres I'd say, but the other was much bigger, more than twice as large. They were now on the bank of the river, looking right at me.

The small one, in the pale armour, was carrying two short swords; both blades were uneven and wavy. They were very light silver. He also wore a mask. It was white and rusty, and looked rather like a dwarfish helmet, but a little smaller.

The big guy was the tallest, bulkiest, and strongest-looking person I'd ever seen in my life. He was covered in armour that had small streams of lava and ash all over it, and the armour itself was black and silver, so I guessed that the lava was what had made it look orange. He wore a mask as well. His had an open mouth, with small spikes all over it. He looked pretty human from what I could see, except for his feet and hands. Or claws I should say. There were three of them on both his arms and feet. They were jet black, turning silver at the tips. Just looking at him frightened me. I wanted to have him as my leader. Wherever there was skin showing, it was scraped and bloody, making him look non-human.

The tall one was staring at me through the eyeholes in his mask, and it gave me the feeling that he was searching for my weaknesses. Anyone would have been scared, but for some reason I didn't run.

They both crossed over the fallen branch to get to my side of the narrow creek. I was surprised that the branch could hold the big guy's weight. It turned out it couldn't. Just as they stepped onto the other side, the branch snapped and fell into the cold water below it, taking the big person's foot with it, which he only just saved by stepping out of the water before it sank.

He looked over at it, and then looked back to me. When he spoke, he sounded similar to Ravenwood, loud, so I could hear his voice through the crash of the waterfall. It was like a deep growl. Perhaps he was part animal, for with the claws, I would not be surprised.

'Who are you, and where am I?' he asked.

'I'm Wolf. You're in Wouldlock, one of the five Eromies, sir.'

'Nice to meet you Wolf,' said the sandy guy, in a friendly, polite way. 'I'm Peldor, and this is my friend Ardor. We're Orians from the Seven Gates.'

I knew about Orians. First, they are Arigor. An Arigor is the same size as a human, but at the age of ten starts to grow at a rate of two centimetres a week until they are full height. Talk about a growth spurt. Once this process is complete they are considered an Orian. I've heard that their traditional sport is called railing. Railing is kind of like fencing, but they wear full armour and helmets, and use any type of weapon.

Normally, Arigor and Orians lived at the Seven Gates. The Seven Gates are seven doorways to the seven elemental kingdoms. It is the place that the Orians and Arigor keep their element safe. Now that we humans are destroying so much of the Earth, they need to keep the natural parts safe. The elements there are ice, fire, nature, rock, water, and sand. The last door is to our world. Technology – that is, in my opinion, the worst of all the gates. Apparently there are all sorts of cool animals in the Seven Gates. I'd really like to go someday. I had never been there before. It's somewhere in Elrolia, so it's kind of hard to get there without being spotted by an Elrolian. As Ravenwood said, they don't trust us.

Peldor looked like an Arigor, though.

Peldor was looking at me curiously. He seemed to know what I was thinking. 'I am an Orian, you know. I'm twenty years old. I just never grew when I reached ten years old. I was exiled by the clan leaders for being different.'

'That's not fair!' I said.

'Well, that's my sister. Unfair.'

I stared at him. 'Your *sister* exiled you?'

He nodded sadly. 'She was the leader, and she was embarrassed to have a brother that was … different. Then, after that my other sister, Senabell, had a raile – a fight – with her to see who would be leader, and the one who exiled me, Harenelle, lost, but I was already exiled, so I couldn't come back unless *all* of the leaders agreed, and Streltzia, the Rock Leader, saw me just as Harenelle had. She didn't want me back. The same happened with Ardor.'

'I'm sorry. That's horrible. Is that why you two aren't at the Seven Gates?'

'Yeah,' growled Ardor.

Then I froze. I had just heard a growl, and not from Ardor. I turned around. There was the bear. It was back. Maybe it had lost interest in the crysillium. Whatever the case, it seemed to have a liking for me. Ardor had seen it too, and was staring right back at it, with his sad but angry eyes. It was about seven metres away. I would think that someone as large as Ardor would scare it away, but it didn't seem to care. It was really angry with me for entering its cave.

'Be careful,' I whispered.

I tried to think of what could scare it away. It was coming closer, slowly, but surely. I then remembered the lava on Ardor's armour. Slowly, I bent down and picked up a small branch. It had probably come from the trees by the Tigers River. I pulled myself up from the grass and turned to Ardor. I carefully put the branch against Ardor's armour, and as I had hoped, it caught fire and blazed with heat. I waved it in the bear's direction. The animal backed away, and then when I made a sudden great wave with the branch, the bear turned and galloped away.

'Thanks, Wolf! That thing could have killed us,' said Peldor.

Ardor made a growling sound in his throat. 'It could have killed me….'

I tossed the branch into the river. 'So, Ardor, were you exiled as well?'

'Yes,' said Peldor.

Ardor looked at him. 'I do not think it's wise to share too much of our past with him.'

'Ardor, he saved our lives. He deserves to know, if he wants to.' Peldor turned to me. 'Excuse my friend. After what has happened in his life, he does not trust anyone but me.'

'Why *were* you banished?' I asked.

'I don't like to talk about it….' Ardor grumbled.

'As you can see, my friend is also rather … unique. Unlike my abnormality, his prevents him from doing ordinary things. We do not know how this happened though. His parents were both normal Orians. Anyways, his mother, Incandesia, was the leader of the Fire Clan. She protected Ardor from being banished, even though most of the others wanted him exiled. But then his parents died when Hunter came to try and take over the Seven Gates.'

'*Hunter?*' I asked. 'The one who betrayed the Elrolians?'

Peldor nodded. 'Yes, him. He failed to take our home, but he managed to kill Ardor's parents. They were extraordinary fighters, but they sacrificed themselves to save us. Then, when the battle was over, they had a raile for a new leader, and someone called Flailyia won. She was just like Harenelle. She wanted everything perfect. She exiled Ardor without thinking twice.'

'She didn't have any brain to think about it with in the first place,' muttered Ardor.

'So then we met up, and we've tried to survive our best since. And we've been trying to find out why Ardor has … inhuman abilities.'

'You mean why I have claws, and why I erupt in fire every time I'm angry.'

Peldor nodded.

'You erupt in fire?' I asked, amazed.

'Yeah. Sometimes I can't control it. Got me in quite a bit of trouble when I was younger,' he said.

'Does it hurt you?'

'No. I'm from the fire element. I'm immune to fire.'

'Oh. Wait, I thought you could just choose your element, not actually get powers from it. Isn't that how it happens there?'

'Normally yes, Arigor choose an element, and then when they become Orians they get their elemental weapons, but I was born with fire. It happens every once in a while. But in my case, it's no privilege. Fire is my curse. I went to nine people to find out what was wrong with me. Each and every one of them said I would one day have extraordinary abilities.' He sniffed. 'Like that's true. They just don't want to give me bad news. People are scared of me. No one except Peldor here actually respects me.'

'People respect you, Ardor. Whenever you ask Inflamia or one of the other Fire Arigor to do something for you, they do it.'

'Still, that's not respect, that's fear. They're afraid that I'll get mad at them and burst into fire, or kill them.'

'Wolf, do you happen to know if there's a shelter around here? I don't want any more animals coming for me.'

'Yeah, there's a camp over there. You guys want to come inside? Maybe get a drink, or some food?'

It looked like Ardor would say no, but Peldor spoke instead. 'That would be lovely. Thank you so much.'

I led them into the camp, explaining to them about how we had made it. After a while, I figured I was getting boring to listen to.

'So are you guys going to stay here for a while?'

'Well, if that's okay with you and your team,' said Peldor.

'Peldor, we don't need to.'

'We need rest. Wolf has offered for us to stay, I say we accept. Look, I know you don't trust them, but if you keep doing everything yourself, you will fail. They might know something about your … condition. Wolf, you said that an Elemental Lord lives here, right?'

'Yeah.' I had told them about Ravenwood earlier. 'We can go talk to him if you like.'

'I think that would be a good idea. What is his name?'

'Ravenwood.'

'No!' growled Ardor. 'It can't be. Ravenwood what?'

'Ravenwood Sphalerite Spears. Do you know him?'

Peldor looked at me. 'Ravenwood Sphalerite Spears saved Ardor's life once.'

'Many more than once! I want to see him,' demanded Ardor.

'Right this way,' I said, leading them to where Ravenwood usually worked in the camp – his room. We had offered him the forgery, but he like his place better.

Sure enough, Ravenwood was in his room, studying an old map, comparing it to another, newer one. I had never been in here before. At least, not since Ravenwood had moved in. There were all types of weapons and other strange items I'd never seen, displayed around the room. I saw the Ice Axe lying on an empty chair, the eyes on the skeleton glowing icy blue. When Ravenwood saw Ardor, he jumped to his feet.

'Ardor?' he asked, looking at him in disbelief.

'Ravenwood! Well you haven't aged a day, my friend!'

'You're here! The last time I saw you, we were fighting off that Lorothian Lynx!'

Ardor laughed. 'The good old days! Remember the time we climbed up Mount Careus in Elrolia?'

Ravenwood smiled too, like I'd never seen before. 'And then it exploded? How could I forget? And Peldor! It's been such a long time!'

Peldor smiled as well, and then they were all talking like old friends.

'Um, you guys know each other?' I said awkwardly.

'Yeah,' grunted Ardor. He was much happier than he had been just a minute ago. 'We were great friends. And still are!'

'Oh, Wolf, the adventures we had. And all the times we saved each other's lives!'

'Yeah. And Ravenwood, I still owe you for that time in Raverand, with the liaser at the river.'

'I told you to forget it! We've had plenty of close calls together.'

'Yeah, but that liaser almost took out your eye! And if I hadn't wanted to go into that cave, you wouldn't have it scarred now.'

'Ah, it just improved my sight. Now I have the sight of a falcon, not a very old man,' Ravenwood said, chuckling to himself.

I quietly slipped out of the room, leaving them to talk and laugh. It looked like those two Orians would be staying with us for a while.

BLACK AMBER

I got a good long nap, and I lazily went back out into the meeting area, wiping my eyes, and saw Stream bent low over some metal parts, sweating like crazy. He didn't seem to notice me coming in. He never took notice of anyone while he was working.

'And … finished!' he said to himself proudly, holding up a rectangular object to get the full effect. 'Ah, Wolf! I've just finished making the phones,' he said with a big smile, as he tossed me one. It was a small, rectangular, handmade phone, that Stream of course had been making himself for a while now. It had a dark night-blue screen, with a silver howling wolf on its back, slightly embossed.

I smiled in wonderment. 'Thanks, Stream! This is great.'

Stream beamed, delighted. 'You see, I've added a feature so you can project your screen onto a wall, and then using a touch sensor, you can control the screen displayed on the wall by touching the projection.'

He showed me how to work all of the functions. It was probably one of the most sophisticated things I'd ever held in my life.

'Stream, this is cool. Have you shown the others?'

'No, you're the first one. As you can see, I've added a picture of the person's favourite animal on the back. By the way, I saw two strangers coming in earlier…'

'Oh yeah, they're Orians, from the Seven Gates. They're staying here for a bit, I think. They're friends of Ravenwood's.'

'I see. When are they leaving?'

'I don't know actually. They didn't say.'

'Well, if you see any of the others, tell them to come to me. I need to hand out the rest of these phones. Maybe at the morning meeting…'

'Sure. Thanks again for it.'

'No problem.'

'I really can't believe you made these so fast, and well.'

'Ah, I was really devoted to it, like all of my projects.'

'Well, I'll tell the others if I see them.'

I went out into the cool, fresh air. It was hard to believe that just a moment ago it had been storming tremendously. I felt the air disk Viper had given me in my pocket. I was wondering what it would do. Viper had said it would create an actual tornado, but he'd also said that depending on what the thrower was thinking, it could change. He said that Stringer had invented the music disks for parties but then used other elements for other uses. He made loads of cool stuff. And so did Viper and his brothers.

There was Spirix, running madly out in the grass. The snow wolf's long legs helped her run extremely fast. She was faster than a cheetah, and could hold that speed for as long as a cheetah could hold his. An Elrolian Snow Wolf could go like that for a maximum of forty seconds, if it was healthy and fully grown. Spirix would be an excellent hunter – not that she wasn't right now, but she would become even better. I had read about snow wolves' methods of tracking down prey. They would first hide behind a bush, or maybe a rock, and then when the prey was close enough they would chase it. The cheetah uses the same hunting technique, but if the prey can avoid the cheetah for more than about twelve seconds, when it starts to get tired after going full speed, then the cheetah will give up. The Elrolian Snow Wolf, however, tracks its prey until it's dead or just can't go any further.

Then I noticed something was wrong. There were no animals in sight. I couldn't see a single bird. I couldn't even hear one chirping. All I could hear were the unclear voices from inside, and the gentle rustle of the leaves, along with the rushing waterfall by the river. I ran to the bank of the water, and gasped.

On a flat rock in the middle of the water was a dead tiger. It was soaked in blood, and there were puddles of the scarlet liquid all over the rock, gently dripping into the river. The tiger's body had been ripped open, revealing its bloody rib cage. There were claw marks all over it. What could have done this? No hunter. No, this was a predator, but what, exactly? I wasn't aware of any animal that killed like this. There were not many animals that killed tigers. But what about the mysterious killer that we'd been hearing of?

But there was an answer, and it was right in front of me. A single claw lay in the blood, like a ship in water. It was too hard to see it clearly, but if I got a hold of it, I could probably identify the creature responsible.

The rock was not that far away. I would be able to jump to it. I walked back a bit, and shook off my coat. I then ran forward and jumped. I slipped on the tiger's blood, but I kept my balance, and didn't go tumbling into the cold water. But I couldn't see the claw. I looked around carefully. I hoped I hadn't stepped on it and crushed it. But no, there it was, in the water. It was going farther and farther away from me. I had no choice. I dived after it.

I felt like my head had hit a rock. Maybe it had. The water was freezing, though not as cold as the Alrian Sea. I flailed my arms, trying to stay above the surface without my clothes pulling me down. I grabbed the claw and swam to the shore, and pulled myself out as quickly as I could.

I gasped, and lay there in the soft grass, trying to catch my breath. Then I got up and examined the claw. I had never seen one like it before. It was long, curved, and sharp, like most claws are, but what made it unique was the fact that it was a blinding shade of silver. It glinted like coins in the light. I was surprised that it had been able to float. I lightly traced my finger over the edge. I winced in pain as it cut through my skin, a small drop of blood forming on my finger.

This must have been from the same animal that had killed Earthum. But that tiger must have put up quite a fight to slice this off.

I hoped the other tigers had been lucky enough to escape. They would find shelter somewhere else, maybe near the rainforest. If this creature really was the animal that had killed Earthum and liasers, and if it kept killing like this, then the animals of Wouldlock would be in a lot of danger. Even if it did continue, what would we be able to do about it? We would not kill the animal, and I didn't like the idea of sending it to a zoo or something: I don't like the idea of captivity.

But that didn't matter now. I had to find out what this animal was. And here was my lead: the claw. Maybe I could give it to a biologist to examine. Maybe they could define what it belonged to. But who would know animals better than us, who lived with them? But maybe a biologist could give me an idea of where this animal could be living in Wouldlock. Then I could go and find it. I didn't know what I would do then. I would decide when the time came.

I stuffed the claw into my pocket, which was a mistake. It cut right through, and slid out. I caught my new phone that Stream had made me just in time. I picked up the claw again and decided to just keep it in my hand. Sadly, that got cut as well, but I didn't really care. I was trying to imagine what this claw was from. I shivered. The water was making me extremely cold.

I headed to the Black Rocks. Even though it would take longer, I would warm up. At the camp, that was how we would dry our clothes. I would not regret going there.

I walked slowly, listening to the trees and the wind. I still couldn't hear any animals, though, which bothered me. I'd have bet anything that the creature that this claw belonged to was what had scared them all away.

I stepped up onto one of the rocks. It was much warmer here. I lay down, letting the heat sink into me.

Then I heard a loud cracking sound, like a bullet being fired. I shot up onto my feet, searching for the cause of the noise. It was a branch that had broken off of one of the trees by Tigers River. The leaves on the same tree moved, and I saw a black shape through the leaves. It was not my imagination. Something seemed to be in the trees, jumping from branch to branch.

And then the thing leaped out of the tree onto the ground, landing very quietly. I could see it clearly, for it was only about twenty metres from me. It was about the size of a car, all jet black, except for its eyes. They were a bright orange, like fire. The animal had a snout shaped between a cat's and a wolf's. Not too long, but not too short either. It had four long, strong -looking legs, and a long bushy tail. And that wasn't all. It had wings. They too were black, and like the body, were furry. Right now they were spread out to what seemed their full length, which was about three metres long, clearly to try and warn me away. Then I noticed its claws.

They were identical to the one I'd found in the river: silver and deadly. And two of them were missing. All of the legs except one had four claws. On the claws was also something dark red: blood. This was the creature that had killed the tiger. And maybe even Earthum.

It stared at me, and I stared right back. If it wanted to kill me, it probably could. Not only would it be able to run fast, but also, this thing could *fly*. It started to walk very slowly towards me.

I turned and as slowly as I could, walked the other way. But then I saw another approaching me, identical to the first. And suddenly they were all around me, climbing out of trees, from behind rocks and bushes, about a dozen of them. I was trapped. They were all now slowly advancing towards me, growling menacingly. I hadn't even heard them coming – what was wrong with my ears recently? They all looked the same except for one that had sea-green eyes. This one was on the left of the first one I'd seen.

And then the first one tensed, took a few steps backward, and pounced. I jumped to the side, but it was too quick. It scratched my back, and I screamed in pain. It felt like knives stabbing my backbone. I felt warm blood soak into my clothes, devouring me. The creature crept towards me again and its claw scratched my shoulder, which also bled tremendously.

'Help me!' I screamed in agony.

Its claws scratched me twice more, bathing me in fresh blood. It would rip me to pieces. I would die like Earthum, alone, and in pain that only ended with death. All the creatures gathered around me, and I got scratched five more times.

Then I heard one of them make a sound. Very faintly – as if it were talking. It sounded something like "*alterus,*" or some such nonsense. I was probably hallucinating.

I was still screaming. What had I done? I had not threatened them. And then, they all stopped. I opened my watery eyes. My vision was blurry, but I saw a huge ball of fire. It was moving towards me, and the creatures had scattered. When all of them had gone, the ball flickered into a red speck, coming closer and closer still. But before it reached me, my eyes closed, and I knew no more.

When I next opened my eyes, I was lying in a place that definitely wasn't Wouldlock. First, I was not lying on the hot, sharp rocks, and I wasn't covered in blood. I was in a bed. I felt the places I had been scratched and discovered that I was instead covered in bandages. I was in a small room, with a desk, and a few chairs, and of course the bed I was lying on. There was a small table beside me with a mirror on it.

I sat up against my pillows and picked up the mirror. I looked like a mummy. I ripped off the bandages, which was a mistake. The places I had taken them off hurt almost as badly as when I had gotten the injuries, but after a minute they settled back down. At least they didn't start to bleed again. I looked at myself again. There were many long scabs, evidence of the claws that had injured me. I grabbed my shirt, which had been lying on a chair, and hurriedly put it on.

I was feeling a lot better than I had when I was getting torn to shreds, although my hands and toes were tingling, and I was feeling drowsy. I put the mirror at an angle so I could see my back. It was bad. The blood had stopped spreading, but I could still tell that the wounds were deep.

I felt in my pockets for the claw I had found. It was not there. My phone was in one pocket, but the other was ripped and empty. Then I remembered taking the claw out. I saw it on the table. Whoever had brought me here must have found it along with me.

I remembered the fiery ball that had scared the creatures away. I wondered what it was.

Then the door opened, and in stepped Lance and Ardor,

both extremely relieved to see me up. I looked at Ardor, who was, as always, in his mask. I desperately wanted to know what his full face looked like. I could hardly see any of it.

'Wolf! You're up. How are you feeling?' Lance asked anxiously.

'Hey. I'm okay. Just a few scrapes.'

'Just a few scrapes? Man, if I hadn't scared those beasts off, you would be dead,' said Ardor.

'*You* saved me?' I asked. Then everything fit into place. 'You were the ball of fire!'

He nodded grimly. 'Remember about me erupting into fire when I'm mad? Well, when I saw what those things were doing to you, I'll tell you, I was very angry.'

I flashed a quick smile. 'Well, thanks.'

'Wolf, there are a few others here to see you.' Lance opened the door.

Stream, Ravenwood, Rovia, Slare, Peldor, Sora, Raider, Blade, Viper, Mac, and Icon all came in, all looking very relieved like Ardor and Lance did.

'Whoa. You guys are all here for me?'

Viper smiled. 'Yeah, man. Stringer told us what happened, so we thought we'd drop by. He wanted to come, but he was too busy. You know. That's what happens when you're an Elemental Lord. You're okay?'

'I nodded.'

Mac and Icon jumped onto the bed, both with no smiles on their faces at all. I realised they were scared for me.

Mac waved at me, and high-fived me with his foot, his eyes opened to the limit. Icon stared at me seriously. 'You are definitely okay?'

I smiled. 'I'm fine.'

His face spread into a smile. 'Good!' He pulled something out of his small black backpack. 'Mini Widget! You can have,' Icon said.

He pushed a blue, robotic misticon the size of my fist into my hand.

'Hey, Icon, thanks!'

He high-fived me and then jumped off the bed along with Mac. Viper picked them up.

'Wolf, I'm sorry, but we need to go,' Viper said with an apologetic smile. 'Urgent business with that file I told you about earlier.'

'That's okay. Thanks for coming. Good luck.'

He nodded and left.

'Wolf, Ardor, what did the creatures look like?' Sora asked with curiosity.

We described them to her, but she showed no sign of recognition.

'I don't think I've seen one before.'

'Yes, you have,' I said, remembering. 'You saw it flying in the Silent Mountains.'

'Oh, yeah … that must have been it!'

'Those things really hurt you,' said Ravenwood, looking me over. 'You sure you're alright?'

I nodded, the image of the monstrous creature floating back to my mind. 'It traps you. Makes sure you can't escape. Leaves no possible way out. It's like amber engulfing an insect. Keeping it trapped forever. It's like shadowy, black amber.' I paused, and then added, 'It's no wonder Earthum couldn't escape.'

The others nodded, realising that this must have been the animal that had killed Earthum. It fit perfectly.

'Well, I'm glad you're alright. What can we call these creatures?' asked Raider.

'I think Wolf's idea was good,' said Lance.

I frowned. I didn't remember giving any idea. I definitely wasn't that tired.

'What idea?' I asked.

'Black Amber.' That can be their name.

'I like that,' said Ravenwood. 'Black Amber. It's like a force. You know? Not lots of Black Ambers, but more like, "I was attacked by Black Amber."'

The others nodded in agreement. I was reminded of the file I'd seen at Stringer's. Black Aqua. These names both were strong and good.

'Where will we be able to find them?' asked Slare.

'I don't know. Just look out. Those things are dangerous,' said Peldor, looking at my arms, which bore many visible scars.

'We should carry fire with us,' said Ardor. 'I scared them off with fire. I doubt this will be the last time we hear of Black Amber.'

Lance nodded. 'Good idea ... a very good idea indeed.'

'We could use fire disks,' I suggested. 'The ones Stringer made.'

'Another good idea!' Lance said happily. 'I'll ask Viper to acquire some for us. In the meantime, you should get ready to go. I think you've rested enough. After all, four days is a long time.'

'I was out for *four days?*' I asked in disbelief.

'Yes. There must have been some type of poison or some such thing on the creatures' claws. Anyone would have gone out after an attack like that. Well, I'll give you half an hour, and then come and meet me at the entrance. Okay? Just call for Nurse Helia – she's been the one taking care of you. She'll show you out.'

I nodded silently.

'By the way, Mac, Icon, and Viper are going to stay with us while Stringer is off working on a special project.'

'We're going to be packed. Our whole team except for Shade, and then also Ravenwood, Ardor, and Peldor, and Viper and his brothers.'

Lance smiled rather wearily. 'We'll manage.'

They all wished me luck in recovering, and then left, leaving me alone in the quiet room. I rubbed my scars. I would have them forever, no doubt. We were all in danger from this ... Black Amber. I thought the fire disks would be a good idea. We would need them soon though. I could only imagine if Black Amber tried to attack one of us while we were on watch duty, or even if they attacked the camp. Maybe we could set up fire around it as well. Just a few torches or something like that.

I didn't really have much to collect. I don't normally need that many things when I go out. Just myself. I put on my coat from a hanger and studied the map of the building that was on the door. It seemed that I was in a hospital in Spheria, and a very small one for that matter. I didn't want anyone guiding me out, so I went out of the room and turned at a few corners, and spotted Lance at the door talking to someone very seriously at the entrance. He spotted me walking towards him.

'Wolf! This is nurse Helia. She was taking care of you and your wounds.'

'Hello, Wolf! Are you feeling alright?'

'Yeah. Thanks, um, for everything you've done.'

She smiled warmly.

'Well, we'll be off,' said Lance, with a polite nod to the nurse.

We thanked Helia again and strode out into the street. We got a taxi and went to the border of Spheria and then walked back to the camp from there.

I kept looking around anxiously.

'Hey, Lance, I should know this, but did Ravenwood mean that we say Black Ambers if there are many? Or is Black Amber plural?'

'I think we'll call them "Black Amber." It's like Ravenwood said. It's a force. "Black Ambers" just doesn't sound right. More like "ten Black Amber," or "Black Amber has attacked."'

I nodded. I felt like a fool for asking a simple question like that, but it cleared things up for me at least. English … so insanely complicated, even when it's you who invents the words.

On the way I told him about the tiger at the river, and showed him the claw I'd found there.

'This is interesting. This claw is made of Elrolian Onyxus. The material Elrolian weapons are made of. I don't understand how that could be naturally included on an animal. Someone would have to genetically modify it. It would have to be an Elrolian. No one else would have the material.'

'Wait, does that mean that it could kill an Elrolian?'

'Well, if I'm right about it being made of Onyxus, then yes. And if the creatures' claws are made of it, maybe their bodies could be coated in it too. Creating an animal with the power to kill the creator is a dangerous idea. If they have made this, they have created their own weakness.'

'You mean that if the body has an Onyxus covering, even if someone wanted to kill it, they couldn't?'

'Yes. It would be hurt, but it would only die of age, or perhaps sickness, like an Elrolian. This is very interesting.'

'Wait, so you mean that this could be a genetically modified animal? Not natural?' I asked.

'It's possible … in fact, it's very probable.'

'Why would anyone do that?' I frowned.

'I'm not sure…' he said, though it seemed like he was giving this a fair bit of thought. 'It could be used as a weapon.'

'What?'

'Never mind. We're here now. Let's go in.'

We entered together, and Lance went into his room, supposedly to work on his very important lock. I went into mine. I took off my things and stepped back into the arena. I was extremely bored. A few days ago, a pack of Black Amber was ripping me to pieces. Now I was standing in an empty arena, with nothing better to do than stare at the archery targets hanging off the wall.

I wanted to know what Lance had been about to say about Black Amber being used as a weapon.

I went into his room. He sat at his desk by the large crack in the boulder – his window.

'Lance?'

He turned. 'Yes?'

'I was wondering what you were really going to say about Black Amber being a weapon.'

'Oh, really, Wolf, it's nothing. Could you do me a favour?'

'Sure.'

'Viper is going to be here in a minute with the fire disks and with Mac and Icon. Could you greet him and get the disks for me? I'm going to call the Crystal Miners. We still haven't got that order from them yet.'

'Alright.'

I went out and closed the boulder. I heard a muffled grunt, and cocked my head to the side. Nothing. I turned around and was face to face with Lance.

'Lance?' I said in surprise.

'Oh! Wolf! I needed to ask Ravenwood something.'

'How did you get out here?'

'Oh, I came out with you. I didn't mean to scare you.'

'Okay. I'll go … get the disks,' I said frowning slightly.

'What disk? Oh, right! Sorry, my head is somewhere else.'

He smiled apologetically and left.

I continued going and saw Viper at the door. He looked just has he had at the hospital, his hair still up, dressed in black and silver, with his amazing gloves on. I couldn't see the knives though.

'Wolf! You're here! I thought you were still at the hospital.'

'No, Lance said I was looking good enough to go. So, you have the disks?'

'Yeah. Here you go.' He handed me a box. 'There are fifty in there. Stringer wanted to be generous.'

'Thanks, Viper.'

'Also, I've brought Mac and Icon – hey guys! Come on!'

Mac and Icon came running to him.

'Spirix nice!' said Icon happily.

Mac nodded energetically in agreement. 'He good!' He tugged at my sleeve as if I hadn't heard. 'He good! He good!' he shouted.

I smiled. 'So you guys are staying?' I asked Viper.

'Yeah,' said Viper. 'I just need to go and get my stuff off the turtle.' He waved vaguely at a giant turtle that I recognised as the one that had brought me to Stringer's place.

'See you. *Knives!*' he muttered, and he shot towards the turtle.

'That's so cool.' I murmured.

'You have the Mini Widget?' asked Icon.

'Yeah, right here.' I pulled out of my pocket the small misticon he'd made me.

He smiled as if this was the best thing in the world.

'So, you want to go inside?'

'Yeah! Yeah! Go inside,' said Mac, who was just getting up from rolling around in the grass.

'Okay, let's go.'

I showed them around, and at every room they gasped and applauded at everything, until they met Ardor. Then they screamed and cowered behind me.

'Monster!'

'No, this is Ardor. He's a friend.'

Mac peeked out his small head. 'Big.' He looked at me. 'He big. He a skinny metal elephant.'

'Hello there,' said Ardor. 'Remember me from the hospital?'

Both of them shook their head.

'You big. I would remember you,' Mac said, although it was rather hard to understand, and doesn't always pronounce the Ds in words – he's three.

'Well, it's nice to see you again.' He winked at me and went back into his room.

'We want Spirix.' Mac said.

'Okay, she's outside.'

They rushed out into the cool air to go find her, leaving me alone again. I still couldn't get Black Amber out of my head. Where could I find it? If I didn't stop it, we could all get killed. And if it wasn't natural, then who had had made it, and why? Something much bigger than just Black Amber was going on here. I wanted to find out what.

Everyone had seen them around either the Silent Mountains or the Beach Tree. They probably wouldn't go to the Beach Tree because there were no longer any animals there, after they killed the liasers.

I didn't know what I would do then, but I had to go. They had killed the liasers. They had killed Earthum. They had killed a helpless tiger. They had tried, though failed, to kill me. I was going to go to the Silent Mountains. To search for Black Amber.

THE SEVEN GATES

I stepped back into my untidy room. I grabbed my phone, the claw, and my knife. I also put on my winter coat, for it was cold out. I sighed. My scars from Black Amber ached. My whole body ached.

I went out of my room and found Ardor and Slare, Slare's head on the table, both of them looking bored.

'Hey, Slare, Ardor. I'm going to the Silent Mountains for a bit,' I announced.

Ardor raised an eyebrow through his rusty mask.

'I want to find the Black Amber pack again.'

'The ones that almost killed you? I see. Well, I've got nothing to do, so how about we go together? I could protect you like last time.'

'Thanks. But,' I added, 'I thought you didn't trust me.' I looked at him sharply.

'Yeah, I don't, but I still don't want you to die. You saved my life from that bear, more or less.'

'You could have handled it yourself, but okay, let's go.'

'Can I come too?' asked Slare.

'Sure.'

'Cool! This will be fun.'

I stared at her. 'We're going to track down a predator that killed Earthum, the liasers, and a tiger, and almost killed me.'

'It'll be an adventure!'

'Okay,' I said rather awkwardly.

I saw Mac and Icon with Spirix outside. They were throwing fallen sticks and branches for her to catch, which she did one hundred percent of the time. She would leap up and grab them in mid-air. It looked like they were all enjoying themselves immensely.

'Hey, guys. We're going to the Silent Mountains for a while, okay? Could you tell Lance for us?'

Icon nodded, while Mac hid from Ardor's sight behind Spirix, who also looked rather scared.

'Small big one!' yelped Mac, looking at Ardor, and he ducked back behind Spirix.

'Bye, guys!' said Slare, smiling brightly.

We started walking. It was rather awkward, because I had nothing to talk about – at least not with Ardor. Slare was as talkative as ever. She asked about what the Black Amber encounter had been like, and all about their appearance, how they communicated, and everything else.

I tried to look out for Black Amber. If it came, I didn't want to be caught unawares. But we met nothing. It might have been that Ardor had scared all the animals, and none dared to come out. If I was Black Amber, or any creature in fact, and I saw Ardor, I would run and hide. I had been surprised that the bear we had encountered hadn't done so.

We went cautiously around the side of the mountain, with Ardor taking extra care not to fall into the water. We looked around for a sign of the animals. We saw nothing.

'Maybe we should climb to the top,' said Slare. 'Then we might see them more easily. That's where everyone else saw them.'

Ardor seemed to have been thinking along the same lines. He nodded. 'Good idea. You two ever rock-climbed before?'

'Yeah, we do some in training,' I said.

'Good. It shouldn't be all that difficult.'

'I hope not. It'll be a long fall if we lose our grip at the top,' I said, looking at the highest point of the mountain.

'Well, we might as well start now,' Slare said brightly.

We found foot- and handholds, and sturdily made our way up the side. In training, we do two different rock climbs; one with equipment on a hard rock to climb, and one with nothing, but up an easier rock. This one was a mixture of both. No equipment, and a *very* hard (I mean difficult, not solid) rock, or mountain, in this case.

I only stumbled a few times, and didn't die, which was good with me. I wasn't great at rock-climbing. Slare was okay. She also slipped sometimes, but managed to stay on.

Ardor, however, was an expert. Perhaps it was his claws. They dug into the mountain, giving him a great grip. If ever his feet lost their grip, his huge claws would be there to save him. He had probably had practice with Peldor, having to survive in nature. Nature is a beautiful thing, but sometimes deadly. It seemed to have given Ardor a taste for adventure. Though we live in nature, it doesn't threaten us as much as it did them. But with Black Amber prowling around in Wouldlock, our safety might start to become more compromised.

I looked up at Ardor, who was far ahead of me. I lifted my foot, and slipped. I fell past Slare and tumbled to the ground, and fell on my back. I must have broken an arm or something, but I wasn't sure. My whole body was in pain, like I was on fire. The rocks below had almost penetrated my back. From a fall like that I was surprised I could still move, as pain throbbed through my body. Though not worse than Black Amber attacking me, it hurt all the same.

Ardor looked down, and even from a distance, I could see that through his helmet, his eyes were full of concern.

'Wolf?' Slare called.

'Wolf!' Ardor roared, 'are you okay? Wolf!'

'I don't know,' I groaned and rolled to the side. I saw a grey thing to my right, which definitely wasn't a rock. It was a human body. I couldn't see it well enough to check if it was someone I knew.

'Here!' Ardor threw down a heavy silver rope, which hit me square in the face. That's how I discovered it was heavy. I coughed and managed to grab it with my good arm, though I still had some trouble with it. I wrapped it around my arm like a bandage and gripped it as if I were hanging from the top of a skyscraper.

Ardor gave a great tug, and I was hanging, not from a building, but from a huge mountain. It wasn't much better than a building though. There was still a chance I could die. I looked down at the body. It was even harder to see it now. My arm felt like it was near to detaching from the rest of my body.

Ardor heaved the rope again, and I crashed onto the top, gasping.

'You alright?' he asked.

'Yeah, but I might have broken a bone or something.'

He gave my right arm a nudge, and I yelped in pain and surprise.

'Yeah, it's broken. It'll be okay though.' He poked around a bit more, and told me that besides that, I was fine, and I should have been glad I wasn't dead.

'There was a body down there.'

'What?' exclaimed Slare.

'Someone was dead,' I said with certainty.

'Who?' Ardor asked. 'Not someone we know was it?'

'I'm not sure. I hope not. I couldn't see the face.'

'Well, we should forget about that now,' said Ardor. 'We need to do what we came here to do. Look for Black Amber.'

'Yeah. I hope that if we find one, I'll be good enough to escape if it comes for us.'

'I'll make sure you do. You saved my life, and I saved yours, but I'll do it again. You're a good man, my friend.'

I smiled weakly. 'Thanks.'

'So, where would they be? I'm starting to doubt that they live here. It's too open. No good habitat for a creature like that. Even less likely that a pack of them live here.'

'But everyone has seen them over here. And no animals live here for them to feed on, so why would they come here?' I wondered aloud.

'There must be something they want here,' said Slare. 'Something that they like that is here, but nowhere else.'

'But what?' said Ardor.

'I don't know. We never come here in our training. Or really ever, because no animals live here. There's no reason to come to look here. It's empty.'

'Well maybe that's the reason they like it. And how do you know that for sure if you never come here?'

''Cause …' I tried to think. How *did* I know nothing was here? I just had a feeling that this place never held life. I remembered the body. Maybe it only held death. 'I … I don't know. Maybe, but I really doubt it.'

'Well, we should scout it out,' said Slare.

'You mean split up?' asked Ardor sceptically.

'No, we can't do that. Lance said it's best to stay with someone else, *because* of Black Amber. It won't do any good to split up while searching for them.'

'We don't have to split up. We should go back down and look. Maybe that body that you said you saw could help us,' Slare said.

'Yeah,' I said. 'It could have been killed by Black Amber! That would be our lead.'

'How would it being dead help us?' Ardor asked, frowning.

'We would know for sure that it was here, and that it might even live here. I think we would all be able to tell if Black Amber did it or if another animal did. They have their signature way of killing, that's very easily recognisable – ripping their victims apart.' Slare said, wincing in pain from my arm.

'Good idea,' I agreed. 'Let's go. See what we find.'

'Ah, don't worry, I'll get him.' Ardor used his claws to sling me onto his shoulder, and I almost burnt my face, for the lava on his armour was a centimeter from my nose, and I was sure my arm would never mend again. He went to the edge and slid down, and I saw Slare following. It was like skiing, just without skis, not in the snow, and not going down for fun or a competition, but to investigate a dead body.

Ardor came to a stop at the bottom of the mountain, about eighty metres away from the body, and got me back onto my feet. Slare slid down too.

'Thanks, Ardor.' I said, wincing.

He nodded.

'Let's check out the body,' said Slare.

We walked slowly over to the grey thing. I hoped it really was a body, and I hadn't just mistaken it for something else, for that would be truly embarrassing.

'That's a body alright,' said Ardor. Then he stopped, and held his claw out in front of us for us to stop too.

'What? Is it alive?' I whispered. We were still fifty metres away, and I don't know how he could have known, but I saw that through the eyeholes of his mask that he had seen something else.

Slowly, he raised his arm and pointed to a high point on the tallest mountain on the other side of the valley, a bit behind us. I followed his arm and saw a black shape. It was coming closer, and was not on the mountain anymore – it was flying towards us, growing larger and larger.

'Black Amber,' whispered Slare. 'How did it find us?'

I looked at Ardor. He was not exactly leader of this expedition, but I felt he would have a solution.

'I don't know. But we can't hide from it now,' he said.

I shook my head. 'You're right. We need to run.'

Slare nodded and we all ran away from the sea and Black Amber, to the waterfall. I was getting tired, but I kept pushing myself. This was a matter of life and death. I looked around. It was about a hundred metres away from us, and was still coming.

'We won't make it to safety!' I panted.

'Yeah,' said Slare, 'We can't go back to base, we'll endanger the camp!'

Ardor nodded. He picked both of us up and slung us over his back. Then he bent down onto all fours and went faster than a cheetah, his huge claws speeding him up. He was going at the same speed as Black Amber, but still it was almost upon us.

'I can't keep this up,' snarled Ardor. He swung us both off, and rose to his full height, facing Black Amber. He looked terrifying. They both did, although I must admit I was still more intimidated by Ardor at the moment, despite what Black Amber had done to me.

Ardor stared at Black Amber with his fiery eyes, like he wanted to rip it up.

'Go away now, or I'll make you,' he snarled.

Black Amber stared at him, not moving a muscle. It clawed the ground menacingly. I glimpsed its eyes. They were green. This was the same one I'd seen when the pack attacked me.

'Okay. I'll make you.'

He roared so loudly that the trees rustled as birds flew out of them.

That seemed to have no effect on Black Amber though. But Ardor was not out of options. He roared even louder, like a lion into a megaphone, and then his whole body caught fire.

It seemed to come from nowhere. A small spark, then he was just engulfed in flame. I jumped back, and I could see a bit of his outline in the fire, but the light nearly blinded me. Sadly, this Black Amber seemed tougher than the others. It stayed where it was. I noticed it had a scratch on its back. I wondered in alarm if Ardor had scratched it to scare it away that time they had all tried to kill me.

'Okay,' said Ardor, when his flame had died out. 'Now we can run.'

We darted away towards the waterfall, avoiding rocks and boulders that had found their way here. I saw the dead body in a flash of colour, but again, I couldn't make out who it was. I could hear the water rushing. We were close. We climbed up the side of the mountain until we were at the waterfall.

Ardor picked me up and swung me over the water, and for a few moments I felt like I was flying, until I crashed hard on a stone on the other side. Ardor didn't have time to be gentle. He did the same to Slare, who landed a few feet beside me, and then leaped over himself, landing between us without crushing us.

I didn't turn around to see if Black Amber was still following us. I didn't have time. I slid down the other side of the mountain, on the other side of the water, and landed close to one of the lakes that came from the waterfall. I think I saw a grey wolf at the Wolf Lair – a huge rock inhabited by the wolves – but kept going. We went past the Lion's Tree as well, though I saw no lions, and that's when I stopped.

'Ardor!' I called. He stopped too. 'We're going out of Wouldlock!'

He shrugged, and he and Slare kept going. 'This whole place is Wouldlock!'

I followed. They didn't understand what this meant. We were going out of Wouldlock … and into Elrolia.

I turned around to see Black Amber almost upon us. Man, it really wanted revenge for something. I started to believe even more that Ardor might have actually scratched it.

'It's coming!'

They both turned which was a big mistake. They tumbled through a doorway about my size, which must have been some entrance to the chamber they had fallen into. I don't know how Ardor went in, seeing how he is so big, but he did, and I followed.

I felt myself roll down some hard marble steps, and when I opened my eyes, I was in a place I had never seen before.

The Black Amber that had been following us tried to get in, but the hole was much too small for it. It snarled and tried to scratch us, shoving its head through the doorway, but then, when it realised it would do no good, it roared angrily and left.

'Oh no,' said Ardor, looking around. 'Not here.'

'We're in Elrolia,' Slare said.

'Yes, and no. We are in Elrolia. But more specifically, we're in the Seven Gates.'

'Isn't this where you were born?' I said carefully, looking at Ardor.

He nodded. 'My home,' he said bitterly.

I looked around. It was very quiet. We were in a big, circular room, with seven large metallic black gates all around it. One was the one we had just come through. I could see no sign of Black Amber. Over each gate was a circular symbol. Over the one back to Elrolia, which we had just come through, were a bunch of lines going out from the centre, with dots at the end, kind of like a clock. On its right, the symbol was an ice flake, then a wave, then a flame, then a tree, and after that one a few rocks, and then finally a mountain of sand.

'The Seven Gates,' I said, looking at all of them in amazement. The crafting was beautiful. A thousand times better than that of Spheria.

'This is amazing,' said Slare in awe.

'We should go,' said Ardor, stepping back towards the gate we'd came through.

'No,' said Slare. 'That thing will still be out there. It might expect us to come out soon.'

'She's right. We should wait a while. Explore.'

'Alright then. But the people here will recognise me, of course. And remember, they exiled me? That sort of means you're not to come back.'

'Well, we can insist you stay,' said Slare desperately. 'I'm sure you'll be able to stand up to them. We should go meet some people, so they don't think we're intruders.'

'Okay, then. Which one should we go through?' I asked uncertainly.

'I don't know,' said Slare. 'Ardor, which element has the kindest leader?'

'Probably Sand. Peldor's sister Senabell is the leader, and she's fantastic.'

'Okay, we should go through there then,' I said simply.

Slare pushed open the clean, silent gates to the Sand Element and we stepped into soft white sand. Suddenly I heard lots of voices. There must have been some enchantment on the gates, because from inside I hadn't heard a thing. There were loads of people, all in the same colour armour as Peldor's (silver and sand-coloured), with different masks on. There were lots of little caves where I could see people inside, and the whole place was sand, with little tornado-sandstorms that twirled around minding their own business. The storms seemed to be normal here. In the centre of all of this was a huge boulder, and standing on top of it was a tall, elegant woman, with long brown hair streaked with white, though it must have been dye, for she was very young. She was holding a white and bronze staff, looking at the people, smiling. I noticed she had no mask on.

Ardor saw her, and even he smiled. He walked over to her, and Slare and I followed.

'Senabell!' exclaimed Ardor.

She saw Ardor and her smile widened. 'Ardor! You're here!' She jumped down from the rock and walked towards us.

People were staring at Ardor, and, I noticed, so was I.

'What are you doing here?' the woman called Senabell asked.

'We were chased by some creature. It was about to kill us, and we fell in here. These two –' he gestured to us – 'they convinced me to hide here.' He glanced around at everyone staring at us. 'You haven't changed the rule about different Orians crossing gates, have you?'

'No,' she laughed, 'they're just surprised to see you after … you know.' She stopped smiling. 'I'm once again so sorry I couldn't stop them from exiling you. Wait … what happened to Peldor? My brother … he is okay, right?'

'Yeah, he's fine. I've been taking care of him.'

'Oh, thank you. So, have you seen Flailyia yet?' she asked, her relief quickly turning into concern.

'Not yet. I figure I'll come across her sooner or later. By the way, this is Slare, and this is Wolf. They're … friends of mine.'

'It's great to meet you,' Senabell said warmly, shaking our hands. 'We should go and see Flailyia before someone reports you to her. I think it's better to let her know you're here by showing up yourself.'

She led us back to the entrance to the gates and this time we went through the Fire Gate. This place was a lot hotter, and the ground was a black hot rock, like in Wouldlock. There was lava running in streams all over the ground, and there were fountains of it too. There were cabins of dark wood and stone around the place as well. The people there were pointing at us, and whispering – well, at least at Ardor. Of course, they would know he had been exiled. Probably the only reason they weren't going straight to their leader was because Senabell was with us.

Ardor silenced most of the whispering by staring at the Arigor and Orians who were doing it, and they looked away, frightened.

Then I saw the woman who must have been the Fire Leader. She looked very strong, but also looked like the type of person who wants everything perfect. She was barking at a little Arigor to do something for her.

'You useless little people! I will say it once more, Inflamia, get me a sharper sword, *now!* Look at the blade, girl! You should know quality when you see it, and be able to clearly identify poor crafting.'

The Arigor nodded, terrified, and scrambled off to find something for her.

'Flailyia! I've brought someone to see you,' said Senabell, bitter disgust on her face.

Flailyia stared at her, and then saw Ardor.

'*You!*' she screamed. 'How dare you show yourself here! I exiled you! You are not welcome here!'

'I came here to hide from a creature that would have killed me and my friends if I hadn't come here.'

'Oh, really, you have friends? Now, who in their right mind would want to be friends with a monster like you? You should have let that animal kill you.'

Slare looked at me. 'These people are…'

I nodded. 'I know. They're strict,' I said, trying to be as kind as I could, though I didn't like the feel of this place – or at least not the Fire Leader.

'Strict doesn't come close to it…' Muttered Slare.

Senabell stared at Flailyia. 'Flailyia! What has happened to you? You are saying this to someone in your element, in front of all these Arigor!'

'So what?' Flailyia spat. 'It's like I said last time, it's a disgrace to have this monster related to me in any way, even if he's just in fire. It makes the whole Fire Clan look bad because of this creature. His parents were too arrogant to admit that they had this monster for a child.'

Slare gasped. 'How could she say that?' she whispered to me.

Ardor's eyes narrowed. Everyone was staring at him. 'You have called me a monster and a "creature." You have insulted my parents. They loved me. They respected me. *I want to rip you apart!*' Ardor roared, and he burst into a massive eruption of fire.

I pulled Slare back, and everyone else scrambled away as well.

'Senabell! Look at this idiot! He can't control himself! Get him out, or he'll kill everyone!' said Flailyia, some fear audible in her voice.

Senabell started to speak, but Ardor, still in the fire, interrupted her. '*The only one I want to kill is you!*'

Then the fire went out, and he dropped to his knees heavily, breathing deeply through his mask. 'I've never gone that long before,' he muttered.

Everyone was looking at him. He pushed himself back up with his claw.

'See! You uncontrollable monster! You don't deserve to live!' Flailyia screamed.

'If you say one more thing about me, or my family, I will kill you.'

I gasped. So did many others. Ardor had said it with so much certainty, I could tell if he was actually serious or not.

'He's out of control,' Slare whispered to me again. 'He would never say that.'

Then I heard people coming in from the gate. I turned to look. They were undoubtedly the other four other Orian leaders.

'Senabell, Flailyia,' said the one in black, in a loud, commanding voice, 'I heard some serious yelling. Even through the enchantments ... what is going on?' She had on a mask as well, with spikes like Ardor's, but even more exaggerated.

'It's him, Streltzia,' Flailyia said, pointing at Ardor. 'You see, I exiled him, yet he has returned, and now he has again lost control of his emotions and burst into fire.'

'Oh, really?' said the Orian in white and blue – obviously the Ice Leader. He held a silver knife whose blade was transparent – diamond, I thought. 'Well, I've known Ardor since I was five, and he never gets mad unless he's provoked, and I've known you for a while too, Flailyia, and I know that you can be quite ... provocative.'

'Thank you, Clustus,' Ardor said to the Ice Leader. 'She was insulting me and my family.'

'Yes,' said Senabell, 'Ardor and his friends Wolf and Slare were hiding from an animal that was chasing them, and they came here, and then Flailyia started to be *very* provocative.'

'What? Me? He almost destroyed this place with his fire! Surely at least you, Veltrimus, Nature Lord, can understand that fire would kill us? It could have spread, and then burned your forest.'

'I do agree, it could have,' said the one Flailyia called Veltrimus, 'but, as you can see, it did not, and I believe the enchantments on the gates would have prevented the worst of it. I believe also that if it had, it would be your fault.' Veltrimus was covered in green armour and vines and leaves.

'I agree with Veltrimus. You provoked him. You of all of us should know what anger could do to him,' said the one in blue – Water Leader, of course. 'I am Nympha,' she added, looking at Slare and me.

'Really Flailyia, you're like a child,' said Clustus. 'You irritate people for the fun of it. You are an Orian. You should know better. This really is what children do. If you continue like this, we will be in need of a new leader.'

'Are you threatening to take away my power as a leader?'

Clustus smiled. 'Oh, yes.'

Flailyia was speechless. 'How dare you?'

He shrugged. 'I'm a daring person. Surely you know that? Remember all of the things I've done in training?'

'What, like when you used a thin piece of wood to surf on lava? Or are you referring to one of the other thousands of stupid things?'

'One of the other thousands of stupid things,' he said.

'How can you tell me that you will take away my leadership, when you do so many stupid things yourself?'

'Because what I do does not affect others in any way. You, however, threaten, and provoke people. The choice to take away your leadership will be in the hands of the Arigor. If we think it should be taken away, we will announce it, and then your Fire Arigor will vote on whether you should stay or not. And sadly, with the way you lead, I'm guessing most of them will vote against you.'

'You are overlooking something important! I banished him! He should not be able to walk back here freely, as if he is welcome!'

'It seems that only you don't welcome him,' said Veltrimus, shrugging. 'It was a matter of life and death, we don't let Orians die unless we can't do anything about it. Would you like it if we threw him back out there to be killed?'

She ignored this last question. 'He threatened to kill me!' Flailyia screamed triumphantly. 'He did, you can't let him get out of this one! He should be punished!'

Veltrimus looked at Ardor. 'Is this true?'

'Yes,' said Ardor coldly. 'And I don't regret it.'

'Well, I have to agree with Flailyia. That is a big deal,' said Streltzia.

Senabell stared at her. 'He couldn't stop himself! You would say the same thing! And he is already exiled, what else can you do? If you hurt him in any way, I'll defend him.'

'What is this? You think it's okay what he's done? What he *is?*'

I couldn't stand her saying all of this about Ardor anymore. '*Shut up!*' I bellowed.

Every single Orian and Arigor stared at me as if I'd declared war on them.

'You treat him like he's a beast!' I continued. 'How would you like it if you were like him? If you had claws, and erupted in fire? He didn't ask for this! Show him some respect! He isn't disadvantaged, he is unique, and this is a great ability.'

'You are not one of us! Be silent!' said Streltzia, and she grabbed my arm tightly and flung me towards a stream of lava with amazing force. Clustus saw where I was about to fall, and he raised his knife and pointed at the lava, and it froze over. I crashed onto it hard, but luckily it didn't break, and I slid safely onto the other side just as the ice melted into the lava.

I gasped. These people were violent. Or at least, Streltzia was.

'Thanks, Clustus.'

He nodded 'You're alright?'

'Yeah.'

He turned back to Streltzia. 'You people talk about killing....'

Ardor bellowed in rage and swiped at Streltzia with his claw. She flew ten metres in the air and landed with a thud on the rock, falling unconscious, her body ragged, blood spreading all over her, staining her black armour with red.

Then everyone was fighting. It seemed that on one side was Flailyia and the other fire Orians (not including Ardor), and on the other, everyone else. The Arigor had sensibly decided to stay out of this. There were clashes of weapons, and blasts of staffs.

They weren't trying to kill, just fighting until the opponent surrendered.

'*Stop!*' yelled Clustus.

Surprisingly, everyone stopped. I didn't get it. Flailyia didn't seem like the type of person to take orders from others. Nor did any of the other Fire Orians. Then, looking more carefully, I saw why. All of the Fire Orians except for Ardor was frozen in ice, so just their heads were free. The ice was starting to melt around those who had elemental fire weapons, or who had lava on their armour. He put his knife back in his belt.

'I hate weapons,' he said to Slare and me. 'I only use the small ones like knives, because the others make it hard for your hands to move around freely.'

He turned back to the Orians, and spoke in a loud, clear voice. 'Fighting will make no difference. It will not help us, it will destroy us. And all over a simple case of someone insulting another! I say, all of us should all shut up. Especially Flailyia. You should shut up forever. Ardor is different, and that can be an advantage. It's nothing to be ashamed of, Ardor. You should be proud of who you are.'

Clustus looked around at all of us, staring into our eyes with his icy blue ones. 'My old friend Emrex used to say: Unique skills should not disconnect you from the world, but *bring you closer.*'

Ardor nodded. 'I apologise for getting so… angry,' he muttered.

'Angry?' asked Flailyia. 'You were more than angry, you little –'

'Clustus is right,' said Senabell, staring at Flailyia, silently warning her to be quiet. 'Let's forget this, and go back to normal. It might be a good idea to separate Ardor and Flailyia,' she added.

Streltzia, who had gotten herself up, finally walked away to her gate, furious. So did all the others except Senabell and Clustus.

Flailyia went past us, looking very angry. 'I'm not stopping just because you told me to, but I need to prepare to give an important speech to the Arigor.'

Senabell rolled her eyes.

'Wolf, you're sure you're okay?' Clustus asked.

'Yeah, I'm fine. Thanks for the save.'

'My pleasure. She could have killed you. Sometimes she's a bit too fierce. Ardor, it's still good to see you again. No luck with controlling the fire though I see.'

'Yeah. We're still looking.'

'Peldor's okay, then?'

'Yeah. He's doing great.'

'Good. I think I'm going to have to be going back to my gate now. See you later. Wolf, Slare, it was a pleasure meeting you.'

He walked back out of the hot rocky place to his ice gate.

I looked up, and saw rock for the celling. 'How big is this place?'

'Pretty big,' said Senabell. 'When we first came here, to Elrolia, there was a magic orb. One of the Orians learnt how to use it, and expanded the chambers, making them huge on the inside, but smaller on the outside. It made all of this possible.'

'Oh. That's cool.'

'Yeah. You want to go back to the sand gate? Out of this heat?'

'Yeah,' said Slare. 'This place is killing me.'

We went back into the grand Hall of Gates, and enjoyed the brief quiet and calmness before going back into the crowded, loud Sand Gate once more. I again saw that all around the place were small tornados of sand swirling about, even more strongly than before, which calmed as Senabell entered again. It was a nice place. I could only imagine how Peldor must have felt leaving. Exiled by his very own sister. It was terrible.

The people here didn't all seem that kind. Like Streltzia and Flailyia. But I guess I hadn't met that many of them, and some were friendly, like Senabell and Clustus.

I guessed that Black Amber would have left by now, but I didn't want to leave just yet. I wanted to stay and explore. This place was incredible, and there was so much more to see.

'Hey, if you want I could show you the Armour Circle. It has all of the different weapons we use in the Seven Gates. You could take one as a souvenir,' said Spyra.

'Why do you need weapons?' I asked.

'Well, our sport is railing, like fencing, but with any type of elemental weapon, and more advanced armour, and *much* more dangerous arenas with elements you can use to your advantage, like lava streams, or trees, or boulders. It's like jousting, but without the horses. I hate it, but the others think it's a great form of entertainment and sport. Fighting. It's horrible. And it's even worse when it's encouraged like this.'

'Well, I guess it'd be cool to see the tools you use,' I said, trying to be polite.

Senabell directed us to a huge circular wall, with different tools, armour, and weapons around it. They had been categorized in colours, or elements perhaps. They looked very sophisticated – and dangerous.

'You can take one if you like,' she said. 'As a souvenir.'

'No, it's okay,' said Slare.

'I'll pass,' I said. 'But thanks for offering.'

Ardor shook his head. 'I wouldn't be able to hold it properly if I did.'

'Okay. Well anyways, they get their equipment from here.'

'Let me get this straight, you live in places that represent each element, but you aren't physically elemental. Right?'

'Correct. Only a few of us, like Ardor, are born into an element. It is clear when you are, but it is very rare.'

'Wait,' said Slare, 'Do you have elemental armour?'

'Only the Orians and Arigor born with elements, and the leaders of the elements, like me. But all the others have silver armour. It is surprising how many people are born into sand though … it seems the most common.'

'But why does Ardor have mostly silver?'

'I prefer silver to red and orange. Natural fire and lava is fine, but I hate the colour that symbolised our element. I always wanted to be in the ice element, but I couldn't choose.'

'Okay. That's interesting. So how do you tell if the Arigor are in your element then?'

'We have the symbols on our armour and clothing. You know, the ones over the gates. It's not that important for us to know who belongs where. They're allowed freedom. It's just when it comes to competitive sports or team games when we need to know.'

'I remember those. Flailyia took my symbol away from me when I was exiled,' said Ardor.

'We should go now,' said Slare. I agreed with her. I didn't want another huge argument about Flailyia.

'Yeah, we probably should,' said Ardor. 'Black Amber will have gone by now. We need to get back to camp soon I'd imagine. Sorry for … intruding.'

'It's fine,' said Senabell. 'Sometime you should try and meet me somewhere. Not here, because of Flailyia, but maybe closer to Wouldlock, so I could see Peldor again.'

'Sure,' I said. 'We'll try to arrange something later.'

'Well, I hope you have a safe journey. Don't let that animal eat you. Tell Peldor I miss him, and I send my love.'

'Umm, alright,' said Ardor. 'Thanks for standing up for me back there, Senabell. And you too Wolf, that meant a lot to me. I hope Streltzia didn't get you too bad.'

'Oh no, I would have gotten much worse if it hadn't been for Clustus.'

'Yeah, he's a great guy. He was probably my best friend, besides Peldor. Well, anyway, thanks for everything, Senabell. I hope I see you again sometime soon.'

'Bye! Have a safe journey!'

I looked once more at the seven marvelous Gates, with those seven elemental symbols, and realised just how much it had meant to Ardor, leaving his home. I turned around and stepped back up those same marble steps and turned to get a better sight of the place. It looked like a small silver dome, but I knew that there was much more going on in there than it seemed. We turned away again from the Gates to see another amazing sight. One I would never forget as long as I lived. The very place Ravenwood had told me about, the place I had dreamed of. It was the Castle of Elrolia.

THE TRAITOR RETURNS

The Castle of Elrolia was the most beautiful place I'd laid eyes on in my entire life. I had been running *for* my life, so I had not seen it when I had entered the Seven Gates, which was probably a good thing, because I might have stopped and stared. But maybe that green-eyed Black Amber would have too. You really have to see it to appreciate the beauty of it.

It was like a huge Roman gladiator arena – a colosseum – circular and light grey, with a space inside, for meetings, training, or anything else I guess. It was built on the side of a humungous black rocky mountain, with streams of crystal clear blue water running down the stone, between tall, green pine trees that were growing on the mountain side. Some of the trees were covered in snow, although I didn't know how because it was not all that cold out here. I did say that weather changes quickly here. Elrolia counts as *here* too.

The castle itself was, as I said, circular, but it had four long bridges that came out on every side – North, East, South, and West – that led to four smaller circular buildings that went down to the ground as well. On all five of the buildings, vines were growing down, but it didn't make it look bad. If anything, it made it better. I saw that winding through the towers was a small stream, not exactly a moat, but it added more beauty to the grand place. I could see even more pine trees around the castle, covered in snow like on the mountain. I could see no sign of electronic technology. Elrolia seemed to be an old-style castle. I liked that. New isn't always better.

Around the main circular building were lots of arches used as windows. I noticed that there was only a little glass on it. Only in a few places – most were just open windows, without glass, letting air flow freely through. It was amazing. The carving and detail around it was brilliant. It must have taken years to build this place. Even from a distance, I could see the tilted square above the arches – the Elrolian symbol of the mines.

I wondered if the Elrolians were inside. But as hard as I looked, I couldn't see any sign of life. I desperately wanted to see one. On the other hand, they might think us intruders, and after what Ravenwood had told me about them, I didn't want to get on their bad side. No one in their right mind would.

The grass that surrounded the castle was either brilliant green, or it was covered in fresh white snow. The water on the side of the mountain was flowing too quickly to freeze, though.

Slare and Ardor, I saw, were also staring at the castle in amazement, and looking at it as if it were a pile of gold and jewels, given to them along with their own personal dream home. I couldn't blame them. I figured I must have been looking at it the same way.

'It's…' Slare started to say, but stopped, finding it better to enjoy the view of it than to speak of it.

'It's Elrolia,' I said. 'It's better crafted than the Seven Gates, by far.'

Ardor nodded in agreement. 'I saw this place before, when I lived here, but it amazes me every time.'

'I wonder who built this place,' Slare said. 'I'd give anything to meet them.'

I hardly heard her, for I was still looking up at the castle in awe.

'We should ... we should, um, go or something,' said Ardor, staring with us.

I blinked and nodded. 'Yeah. Right. The team will be wondering where we are.'

'Okay,' said Slare, tearing her eyes away as well. 'Alright.'

We walked away in silence, stealing glances at the castle, not really talking all that much, just listening to the birds, and the loud rush of the waterfall that was coming closer and closer to us as we walked.

'How will we get across?' Slare asked as we approached the bank of the river.

I had just remembered that the log that we usually crossed had broken when Ardor and Peldor had crossed before, so it left us no clear passage.

'I could throw you again...?' Ardor suggested.

I rubbed my broken arm. 'No, I don't think we should do that. There must be another way.'

'Couldn't we swim across?'

I shook my head. 'Not with my arm like this. Besides, the current is too strong. Normally when we go to check on the animals we go across that branch, and I'd been meaning to tell the others that we needed a new one when it broke, but I was so distracted by everything else that was going on that I forgot.'

'We can try jumping.... Oh my!' Slare had noticed the dead tiger on the rock on the middle of the river.

'Oh, yeah. Black Amber killed it. I forgot to tell you. We can still try to jump though. I did it the last time. Ardor, you should go first so you can catch us if we fall. I did last time.'

'Okay.' He knelt down then sprang out on to the rock, his claws gripping the rock to steady himself.

'Alright, careful now. Slare, you go first,' he said cautiously.

She went back a bit, then ran up and jumped. She landed neatly on the rock beside Ardor. Then she jumped to the other side with no trouble, leaving space for me. I did it fine, and got across with only a bit of steadying from Ardor. I got onto the grass on the other side and Ardor followed, jumping high above our heads, and landing with us safely as well.

'Well that was easy,' I said. 'At least, easier than I thought it'd be.'

I tried to look for the Elrolian castle, but it was hidden behind the rainforest, up North. How I wanted to see it again. I couldn't even imagine living there.

'You can't see it from here,' said Ardor, as if reading my thoughts. 'You probably would have noticed it before this.'

'Yeah. We never go that far out. The animals there get taken care of by the Elrolians.'

We started to walk through the grass again, back to the camp. I rubbed my arm again. I hoped I wouldn't have to go back to the hospital. That would suck. I hated it there. It was so boring. Maybe someone could knock me out so it's like I'm asleep. Maybe we could just put my arm in a cast ourselves and leave it, but if one of my other injuries from the fall was more serious, then there might be no choice.

We arrived at the large boulder doors, and Ardor and Slare helped me push them aside to get in. At the wooden meeting table were Lance, Ravenwood, Sora, Rovia, Stream, and Peldor sitting around on the tree-stump chairs. I couldn't see any sign of Mac, Icon, or Viper though.

'Wolf!' Lance said. 'Are you okay? What happened to your arm?' he said, peering at the one I'd injured.

'I fell from one of the mountains.'

'When?' asked Lance in surprise.

'We went looking for Black Amber,' said Ardor.

'*What?* Looking for that violent creature?'

This was not like Lance at all, to say something like that about an animal. We stared at him. Was he feeling okay? I couldn't believe those words had just come out of his mouth.

'Lance, are you okay?' asked Sora uncertainly, thinking the same thing as me.

'Yes, I'm fine,' he said, trying to calm down. 'You went to look for it where?'

'At the Silent Mountains,' Slare said.

Lance flinched. 'What did you see?'

'A body,' I said. 'Dead.'

His eyes widened. 'Did you see who it was?'

'No. We were stopped by –'

'Black Amber,' Lance finished. 'So you have no idea who the body belonged to?'

'No,' said Slare. 'Wolf wasn't sure. We didn't come close enough to see it properly.'

Lance looked almost relieved. 'Well, we're all here, so it wasn't one of us. I do not suggest you go looking for the creature again, though.'

'Alright,' I said, frowning. 'Sorry.'

There were four loud knocks on the boulder door that echoed through the camp.

'Who could that be?' Ravenwood wondered aloud.

Slare shrugged and went to the front to get the door. She came back a few seconds later with someone I hadn't expected to see ever again. That no one had expected to see. Shade.

I stared at him, and Sora and Rovia actually stood up. At that moment, Raider and Blade came in talking, and stopped dead in their tracks, looking at Shade.

'Why are you here?' asked Raider, completely forgetting about his 'big words' thing.

'I came to talk to Lance. *Alone,* please,' Shade said emotionlessly.

'Right this way,' said Lance, directing Shade to his office, as if he had been expecting him. They went in, and firmly shut the boulders behind them.

Ravenwood put a finger to his lips and went to the room, putting his ear at the wall. He listened for a few very intense seconds, while we waited intently for news. Then his eyes widened in surprise. He came back to the table, stunned.

'He asked Lance to join him with his new job. Hunting animals in Wouldlock under the lead of the Spherian president, Dormanant Scale.'

Everyone gasped.

'No way!' said Blade, astonished, his voice alarmingly loud.

Ravenwood nodded grimly. 'Lance agreed,' he whispered.

There was complete silence. I could tell he was not joking. Not about something this serious.

'Lance would never do such a thing!' I said with utter certainty.

Ravenwood looked at me. 'I've been watching him carefully. That is not Lance. He has been very different lately. He has ignored our ideas, not trusted us with important jobs, and this is what made me sure. When you were gone, an eagle was found, with its wings cut off, definitely by a hunter, bleeding madly. He told us to leave it, because we had other things to do. Encouraging us to let animals die if hurt, saying we have more important things to do than saving animals. This is not Lance,' he repeated.

'What happened to the eagle?' I said, my eyes wide with concern.

'It's fine,' said Rovia. 'I helped it in secret under Ravenwood's orders. I would have anyway, of course,' she added.

'I believe Lance has been kidnapped, and this fool has replaced him. As of now, I suggest we pretend we do not know anything.'

'Can you be our leader then?' asked Sora desperately.

Ravenwood smiled. 'If … if that's what you all want.'

We nodded vigorously.

'Okay. But we must all act as if I am not, and Lance is.'

We agreed at once.

'Why though? What'll happen if they know we know?' said Raider, and some of the others nodded in agreement, looking at Ravenwood for an explanation.

'Well, imagine why someone would kidnap our leader, and then make the fake one give us instructions to stop protecting animals, and let them die. Those people probably aren't the good guys,' growled Ravenwood. 'Now listen. I will volunteer to join. It'll be a good idea to have someone on the inside of this … thing. No one else volunteer, no matter what they offer,' he said fiercely. 'When I am gone, I want Ardor to lead you.'

'What?' Ardor asked, alert all of a sudden.

'Please? For me?' asked Ravenwood, and in his eyes I saw the alliance he had with his old friend.

'Yeah!' Stream said. 'That's a great idea!'

After lots of encouragement, Ardor agreed. How could he not? Ravenwood was possibly his best friend.

Just then the boulder to Lance's office slid open again, and Shade and Lance strode out. Now looking at Lance, knowing he was a fake, I saw how he had been so convincing. It was very hard to see, but if you looked carefully, you could see that there was a screw on the side of his neck. It was very hard to see, and would only be spotted if you were looking for it. He was a robot – a very, very convincing robot. I bet a Spherian scientist had created it. First they'd made the bomb, then the snake, and now this. The technology they had was extremely advanced.

'Okay. I've come here because of Earthum's death,' Shade said. 'I don't think it's okay that something killed him, and we completely ignore the animals that did it, and even more, help them to survive. They killed one of us. I come here to offer you a new career. Alongside the Spherian president, we will hunt *them*.'

We pretended to be surprised.

'Now, before you say no, let me tell you that Lance has already decided to join.'

'What?' Raider said in surprise, very convincingly.

'Yes. I have. I see Shade's point, and agree with him on all accounts.'

His voice sounded exactly the same as the real Lance. I wondered how they had achieved that feat.

'The president will be awarding anyone who joins a large amount of money,' Shade prompted us.

'Shade, I see your point, and I understand how you must feel,' said Ravenwood.

'Are you about to tell me not to do this, Ravenwood? Because I will ignore you, nothing will change that.'

'No. I want to join.'

'No!' said Blade. 'We need you Ravenwood!'

He shook his head sadly. 'I'm sorry.' He joined Shade at the front of the room.

'See?' said Shade. 'The two wisest members of your team accept. I suggest you should too.'

'I'll join,' said Rovia, going to Ravenwood.

Sora stood up. 'No, Rovia! How could you?'

This was not in fake surprise – what had just happened?

'I'm sorry, sister,' she said, not sounding all that sorry.

I looked at Ardor. His eyes warned me not to do anything. We had been told not to join, yet Rovia had. Was she doing this to help us spy, or because she actually wanted to hunt animals as well?

'What's she doing?' Raider whispered to me out of the corner of his mouth.

'Don't know,' I whispered back.

'Slare?' Shade asked. 'Will you join me?'

She shook her head. 'Never. You idiotic, stupid little –'

'That's enough now, I get the point,' Shade said. 'Wolf, I know you'll never join. Raider? Blade?'

They shook their heads as well, and Raider threw a spoon at Shade, which hit him on the side of the head, then fell down his formal suit, which he pretended to take no notice of.

'I reject your imprudent request,' he spat, making Shade take a few deep breaths to calm himself.

'Stream? We could use someone like you, a technology expert. Your skills would be valued.'

'No. Never,' he said, shaking his head. He obviously couldn't believe what was happening. If he *had* joined, there would be something very wrong with him.

'Alright. And you two – Orians, Lance tells me. Would you like to help me?' Shade asked, taking a step back when he saw Ardor staring at him.

'No, thank you,' said Peldor, who, despite the situation, was trying to be polite, as always.

'And then you, sir?' he asked Ardor.

'Not in your dreams, or reality,' Ardor growled, making Shade step back some more.

'You want to hunt animals? How about I hunt you?' Ardor said, lunging towards Shade, although not hitting him, just scaring him some more, which was tremendously entertaining for the team.

'Shade, you can't do this,' I said, about ready to fight him. 'For your whole life, you've protected animals, and because of this, you want to kill all of them, under control of the stupid little president? *I* won't let you do this.'

'I am doing this for someone much more powerful than the

President, Wolf. I will not obey your commands. I am doing this for someone who, when you meet, will make you beg for mercy. And he will have no mercy,' he snarled.

I heard the boulders at the front slide open, and saw Viper come in with his gloves on.

'What's going on here?' Viper asked, looking around at Ravenwood, the fake Lance, and Shade and Rovia.

They explained to him what they were offering.

'You want me to kill animals? Let me ask you, is your head hollow?'

Shade stared at him, speechless. This didn't normally happen to him – well I guess he got this from Raider and Blade, but not from a stranger.

'If your brain, which you may or may not have, is telling you that the right decision to make is to kill animals for revenge, than in my professional opinion, your brain is the size of a jellyfish's.'

'Jellyfish don't have brains, you idiot.'

'Exactly.'

I stifled a laugh, and so did the rest of the team.

'Who are you, anyway?' Shade asked him.

'What?'

'Who are you?'

'Sorry, a bit louder, please.'

'What is your name?'

'I really can't hear you, can any of you hear him?' Viper asked us.

Many of us were too busy laughing to reply.

'*What's your name?*'

'Whoa, man, the neighbours are going to call the police if you talk that loud.'

'We don't have neighbours,' he said, not as loudly, trying to keep calm.

'Sorry, I can't hear you.'

Shade sighed and seemed to give up on him. Viper winked at me and I smiled.

'You really are just infuriating,' Shade said.

'What?'

Shade closed his eyes and ran his fingers through his hair, like he does when he can't stand something that Raider and Blade are doing to him.

'Did this guy teach you two how to be so exasperating?' Shade asked the twins.

'No,' said Blade excitedly.

'But I'll pay for lessons every hour,' said Raider.

Viper smiled. 'I'm going to check on the little guys.' He pushed open the boulders and went into their messy room. The fake Lance nudged Shade and nodded his head in the direction of the exit.

'Alright, last chance, does anyone else want to join me?'

No one said anything, and Blade, Raider, Ardor, and Peldor shook their heads and went to their rooms. Shade looked around once more and then gestured for Lance, Ravenwood, and Rovia to go out.

Then Viper stepped back out of the room, looking furious, his gloved hands shaking. Shade and the others stopped in their tracks. Viper held up two pieces of cloth.

His voice was full of anger. 'Someone gagged and tied up Mac and Icon, so they couldn't move or speak. *Who did this?'*

Lance walked towards him and punched Viper square in the face, sending him sprawling to the floor.

I stood up and stared at him. Shade rubbed his forehead. 'Oh no,' he muttered.

Viper blinked and got himself up. He narrowed his eyes and looked at Lance's neck. *A screw.* He mouthed to himself.

'Knives,' Viper said, and they shot up out of the sheaths on his belt and into his gloved hands. He spun them around in his hands so the point faced down, then stabbed the robotic

Lance in its metallic little heart. He grabbed the knives from the body and pulled them out, turning to Shade, a furious expression on his face.

The people who had left came back out of their rooms and saw what was going on. There were wires sticking out of Lance's body, and it was easy to tell what was happening.

Shade smiled, grabbed Rovia and Ravenwood, and all three of them dissolved into black dust.

'What – how – what's that body doing there, and how did he do that?' asked Raider.

'The body is a robot, and I have no idea how he did that,' said Viper, putting his knives away again.

'And why did Rovia join them just now?' Blade asked. 'She wasn't supposed to, right?'

'No, she wasn't. I don't know why. She may have actually believed in what Shade was saying, and joined him because she wanted revenge too,' said Sora.

'Okay, never mind that, how did they disappear like that?' asked Stream, who never believed in the supernatural.

'Let's all sit down and talk it over,' said Ardor.

There was silence. We sat, and all were deep in thought.

'He used the Element of Darkness,' said Peldor after a while.

'What?' asked Sora.

'If you can master the Element of Darkness, one of your abilities could be that you could crumple into ash in one place, and then reform in another. It's just a thought.'

Slare nodded. 'I think you're right. There isn't any other way he could have done it. There's no other possible way.'

'How can we know for sure?' I said. 'We need to know where he is, who he's working for, and what else he's got planned. He gagged Mac and Icon, he might have been planning to leave us with Lance and then … a bomb.'

'Give me a knife,' I said to Viper. He tossed me one, and I

tore open the robot's body. There was another bomb, resting in place where the heart should have been.

'Stream!' I said.

He nodded. 'I'm on it.' In thirty seconds it was disabled. They should have learnt this didn't work by now.

'We need to find someone who can help us with everything. Black Amber, Shade, Lance, this whole Spherian thing,' said Stream.

'Androma Faithly,' said Ardor absently.

'What?' I asked.

'She's an Air Rider. She's known for her elemental power. She's mastered the Element of Time. She can see the past, everything happening in the present, and sometimes tells flashes of the events that could possibly occur in the future.'

'Where can we find her?' I asked.

He raised his eyebrows. 'You want to look for her?'

I nodded. 'She could help us.'

I remembered what Ravenwood had told me about Air Riders. There were three. One of them was evil, one hard to get to help you, and the last one, an Elrolian. I hoped it wasn't the last one.

No such luck.

'She's an Elrolian.'

ANDROMA FAITHLY

'Elrolian? We've got no chance,' said Blade flatly.

'We may,' said Ardor. 'Androma doesn't live in the castle. If we go carefully, without anyone seeing us, we could manage it. She lives in the Tree Cave, alone. If we maybe bring a little gift or something, she might be willing to help us.'

'What kind of gift?' asked Slare.

'Something small, and rare.'

'The feather of a pigeon dipped in syrup?' suggested Raider.

We all thought about the possibilities. *The claw.* It was unique, and even though it was made of Elrolian Onyxus, which they would already have, it would be interesting to show it to them, and get the Air Rider's thoughts on it. She would never have seen the claw before. I decided to see what the others thought.

'We could give her the Black Amber claw,' I said. 'You know, the one I found that day the pack of them attacked me?'

Ardor smiled through his spiked mask. 'That's a great idea!'

'Should we go now?'

'Why wait?' said Slare, getting up.

'Wait,' said Ardor. 'The whole team can't go. Someone should stay here and guard the camp. Shade is out enemy now, and so is almost all of Spheria.'

The others nodded, realising what we were up against.

'This isn't about money, like the President said,' Stream told them.

'Yeah,' I agreed, 'not at all.'

Ardor nodded, glad we were starting to catch up. 'Yeah. It's a whole lot bigger than money. This is about the lives of a million animals. Any organisation in its right mind would flee.'

Viper shrugged. 'We aren't in our right minds. I don't know about you people, but I'll defend Wouldlock at any cost.'

I smiled. Viper had the right attitude. I was extremely glad he was on our side.

'So will I,' I said, which would have been very obvious to anyone who knew me.

Everyone else nodded in agreement.

'By the way everyone, I'm Viper, son of Industria, Lord of Energy,' he added.

They greeted him warmly and introduced themselves, since not all of them had met him at the hospital. He is so cool.

Peldor smiled. 'Ardor, my good friend, this is what I'm talking about. You've got more than friendship from these good people. You've got respect, *and* loyalty.'

'Alright. There are now...' he did a quick count ... 'nine of us, including Mac and Icon. I suggest three of us go. Is that alright with everyone?'

They nodded.

'Now, this is going to be dangerous, going this deep into Elrolia. Wolf and Slare, you know how to get there because you've been there before, or at least into Elrolia. You don't know where the Tree Cave is, do you?'

We shook our heads.

'Peldor! Could you? We stopped at the Seven Gates and Senabell said she wanted to see you. You could stop there on your way,' Ardor suggested.

'She did? Senabell?'

Ardor nodded.

'Of course I'll come! I know where the cave is.'

'Good. You can head there right away.'

'Did you tell Senabell I was going to meet her?'

'I said we would drop by,' Ardor growled. 'I didn't say when, but she'll be expecting you. I advise that you don't go inside if you can avoid it. We did, and we had some trouble with Flailyia.'

'Oh. I see. Well, I'll be careful to avoid her.'

'Okay. Good luck. Come back straight away after you talk to Androma, alright?'

'Sure,' Slare said. 'We'll try to hurry.'

We had almost everything we needed. I just needed the claw. Peldor had his two wavy swords in sheaths on his belt, with his sandy armour on. I didn't know why we would need any weapons, but I brought my knife just in case. You never know. It was good for climbing. I should have used it when climbing the mountain. It may have stopped my fall. There were so many things I should have done differently.

I went to my warm room and saw, on my desk, Ravenwood's axe. It had a note on it. I picked it up. When had he written this? He had obviously been in a rush, as the paper was torn in places, and the writing was an untidy scribble. The name at the bottom was unclear, but it seemed to hint that it was from Ravenwood.

Wolf,

I hope you are doing okay without me. I am writing this as you are in Elrolia. I figured sooner or later I would have to leave you for some reason, and I may not have the chance to give you this axe before we are separated. I'm sure you'll figure out some way to use this. Good luck.

I stared at the note. He wanted me to use the axe, maybe even to own it. I was amazed. I didn't understand why I would need it any time soon, but I strapped it onto my belt and took it with me. I grabbed the claw too, and kept it in my hand.

I looked around my room for anything else I would need, saw nothing, and joined the others outside.

'Hey guys, Ravenwood … he left me his axe. I think I'll take it with me. He said I might find a way to use it.'

They nodded, but didn't seem to think it was that much of a big deal.

'You have the claw?' Slare asked.

'Yeah, of course. Oh, by the way, we'll need something to use to cross the river. The log broke, and jumping isn't that safe,' I said.

'Okay, I can help you bring something,' said Ardor.

Together we went out of the camp and stepped into the long grass of the field, which was swaying gently in the wind, like waves on a beach, searching until we found a good long, strong log to replace the fallen one. Ardor hauled it onto his shoulder and brought it to the river, where we laid it down across the water. Slare, Peldor, and I walked cautiously across it. Luckily, it was sturdy enough to hold our weight.

We made it safely across and continued through the grass, walking along the bank the same way we had gone the first time, earlier today. I saw more animals around, and the general feeling was more calm, which suggested that Black Amber hadn't been seen for a while, at least not around here.

That was very good for us. I wasn't interested in having another chase. I just wanted to get to the Tree Cave, or whatever it was, and have a quick talk with this Androma Faithly. Hopefully she would be able to give us some answers. When had Lance been switched with the fake? That was one of my questions, but after thinking a bit about it, I realised it must have been when I was going out of the office, to meet Viper. The fake Lance had appeared outside while the real one was being taken, which explained the muffled shrieks.

But I had other questions. Who was Shade working for, and what was that body doing at the Silent Mountains? Who did it belong to? I should have asked them to take a look. And then there was my biggest question of all: what exactly *was* Black Amber?

These questions kept popping up in my head, as well as possible answers, but none of them fitted. I hoped that the Air Rider would have some. After all, that was the reason we were going. I felt the claw in my pocket. I hoped it would be enough to convince her to help us. I wondered why Ravenwood had not taken the axe. I felt it, too, on my belt. What use would I find for it? Would there be something I would have to freeze sometime? He knew I would not use it to attack any living thing, so why leave it, and especially, why leave it to me?

Again, we passed the Lions' Tree, and found ourselves at the imaginary border between Wouldlock and Elrolia.

'Ready?' asked Peldor.

'As ready as we'll ever be,' Slare said confidently.

We stepped over and looked around while we walked for any Elrolians that might see us. What would happen if they did? We could tell them the truth, of course, that we were going to find the Air Rider, but after all that Hunter business, they might not believe it.

'What exactly is the Tree Cave, Peldor?'

'It's like it's called, a cave made of trees that naturally formed into a shelter. It's just a bit past the Seven Gates, but if you don't mind, I'd like to stop there and pay a visit to my sister, Senabell. You met her, right?'

'Yeah, she was really friendly.' Slare smiled at the thought.

'So we can stop by and talk to her for a few minutes, then go to Androma, and come back. It should be simple.'

'Should be?' I asked.

'Well, you know, he has a point. Last time you went here you fell from a mountain, broke your arm – which you still haven't had properly treated – got chased by Black Amber, and got thrown towards a lava stream by an Orian, stuff like that. Your luck sucks,' Slare said.

'Yeah, I know,' I said, thinking about the other events that had happened.

We walked on until we saw the Elrolian Castle again, and Peldor stared at it.

'Look at that crafting! The way the arches curve around with the whole building, and the streams, and trees! It's stunning.'

'We know! Oh how I wish I could go inside there!' sighed Slare.

'Yeah, me too. It must be great, being an Elrolian,' I said.

We finally reached the Gates again, went down the cold, hard marble steps, and found ourselves once again in the Seven Gates. I looked around again at all of the symbols. They were amazing; each of them crafted out of a gemstone in a relevant colour. Water was sapphire, nature was emerald, ice was aquamarine, fire was ruby, and so on. The decoration on the gate we had come through showed all the colours together, and there wasn't any particular symbol, just the colours, and in my opinion looked the worst.

'So should I get Senabell, and you two stay here? She'll remember me, and so will the other Orians. I'm not exiled,' I said.

'Alright,' Peldor said glumly.

I opened the heavy metal gate to the Sand Element, and the chatter of voices and crackles of small campfires filled my ears. I looked around and spotted Senabell in the same place she had been last time. Not many of the Arigor bothered to look this time as I walked to her, perhaps because Ardor wasn't here.

Senabell saw me just before I reached her. She jumped down and came to greet me.

'Wolf! How are you? Is Ardor here?'

'I'm fine. Ardor isn't here, but I brought Peldor.'

She smiled. 'Oh, thank you so much! Is he outside?'

I nodded.

'Let's go see him,' said Senabell, a large smile on her kind face.

We went back to the gate and closed it behind us once we were inside, drowning the room in silence.

'Peldor!' Senabell said, hugging her small brother in a tight grip.

'Senabell! It's so good to see you! How have you been?'

'Oh, I've been great! You, um, haven't grown since I saw you last,' she said, smiling. This was obviously an inside joke they had shared many times before. They both laughed.

'And Slare! So good to see you again!' They hugged each other too, and smiled. It had only been a couple hours, yet they were extremely excited to see each other again, as if it had been years.

'So, are you here just to see me, or are you on your way somewhere else?' she asked, a mischievous smile on her face, echoing our mischievous plans.

'We're going to visit Androma Faithly,' said Peldor.

'Oh, you want to be careful, there's an Elrolian over there right now.'

'Really?'

'Yeah, a young man went there about five minutes ago, I think. I saw him when I was coming back from a meeting. Be careful he doesn't see you. I don't think he, or any Elrolian will trust a human or even an Orian like one of you. I can only imagine what would happen to you if they discovered you were sneaking around Elrolia.'

'Well, thanks for all of this, Senabell, but I think we're going to go now. I think Ardor wanted us back as soon as possible.'

'Okay, you all take care of yourselves, okay? Good luck with Androma.'

'Bye!' Peldor said.

'See you soon, I hope!' Senabell said to us.

We went out of the gates back into Elrolia, and Peldor led us to the cave we were going to, which was very close, no more than a five-minute walk, until we caught sight of it.

'What about the Elrolian?' I asked.

'Well, I think we should take our chances. If we tell them were friends of Ravenwood, who's a friend of Elrolia, they might let us talk,' said Peldor.

'Are you sure we shouldn't wait?' Slare asked.

'Yes. What's the worst that could happen? The Elrolians won't kill us unless they are one hundred percent sure we are a threat to them. You said Ravenwood left you the axe?'

'Yeah,' I said.

'Did he leave a note?'

'Yeah, he did, I brought it with me.'

'Good, we can show it to the Elrolian if he doesn't believe us.'

We continued walking, meeting no one, until we got to the place Ardor had told us about.

'Here we are,' said Peldor, 'the Tree Cave.'

Now I could see why it was called that. It was about a dozen thick trees that were all bent over, so it looked like a cave. It was pretty big too. There were vines and plants growing all over it, and there was a stream of water that ran down beside it too. It was very long, so I couldn't see anyone from where we were, but I noticed there was more space between the trees at the end, providing lots of natural light.

We went deeper into the cave and I saw two people at a desk, in deep conversation, taking no notice of us.

The first person was a woman. She must have been Androma Faithly, the Air Rider. She had very long jet-black hair that fell almost to her waist, and had lots of strange necklaces and bracelets. She had a crown on – an Elrolian crown, I realised. It was silver and had lots of spikes, with one big one in the middle. In the crown, on the three biggest spikes were three gemstones, all amethyst. Her clothes were all a very pale blue, making it look like her dress was glowing.

The other one was a man, and he must have been the one Senabell had told us about. He had charcoal-black rough hair, similar to the woman's, but much shorter, and spiked up and messy like Viper's. He had no crown on. He was covered in black armour, and under that a thin silver shirt and black jeans. He had a small, untidy beard, and dark brown eyes. Also, around his neck was a necklace with a small silver key on it. He radiated power, and without even knowing him, I feared him more than Ravenwood, even more than Ardor. But he did not give off any sense of evil.

He was looking at something that Androma was showing him on the table, and both of them looked very focused on what they were studying.

We went up a bit closer and they both looked up at us.

Androma spoke in a whispery tone. 'Are you here to see me?'

'Um, yes,' said Peldor.

'Just one moment, please,' she said. 'Let me finish with this young man first.'

'No, no, Androma,' said the man, looking at us carefully, 'We can finish after, it looks like these people have more urgent matters to discuss with you.'

'Alright, then, if you say so.'

'Thank you,' I said to him. 'Are you sure?'

He nodded. 'It's fine. Go ahead. This isn't too important.'

'Thanks,' Slare said.

'So, who are you three?' Androma asked.

'I'm Peldor, originally from the Seven Gates, and these are Slare and Wolf from Wouldlock.'

'Humans?' she asked, a hint of distrust in her voice.

'Yes.' I said. 'I know you don't trust us, but we are not here to attack you or anything, we just want some questions answered.'

'I notice you have an Elrolian Ice Axe,' said the man, who was now leaning in one of the corners, watching carefully.

'Yes, I don't want you to think we stole it, or will use it against you. It was a gift from an Elemental Lord, Ravenwood. I have a note to prove it.' I showed it to the two Elrolians.

'Okay,' the man said. 'Sorry to interrupt. I believed you, by the way. I have no problem with humans.'

We turned back to Androma.

'Well…' started Slare.

'That Ice Axe,' Androma said, looking at it with wide eyes. 'It will save a life, if in the right hands.'

'What? Whose hands?' I asked, expecting her to say that mine were the right hands.

'His,' she said, looking at the man in the corner.

'What?' said the man.

'You must have the axe. It will save your life, in quite a few situations possibly.'

We looked at each other, and at the axe, which was now in my hands.

'Are you – are you sure?' I asked. I didn't feel all that comfortable just handing it over to a stranger. But Ravenwood had said I would find a use for it. Maybe this was the use.

'Yes, the note from Lord Ravenwood says you will find a use for it. I believe the use will be saving his life.'

'Wait, that was from Ravenwood?' he asked. 'I couldn't make out the name.'

It seemed that everyone I met knew about him: Ardor, Peldor, and now this guy.

'Ravenwood who?'

'Ravenwood Sphalerite Spears.'

'I knew him! Or at least, my parents did.'

'Well, if you're sure it'll save his life…' I said.

'It will,' she said firmly. 'He must have it or else he will die.'

'Give it to him, Wolf,' said Peldor. 'I think it's a good choice. Ravenwood would have respected it.'

I handed it over to the man, and he thanked me greatly.

'Do you know *when* it'll save his life?' Slare asked Androma.

'Not exactly. It will happen sometime when you are fighting together.'

'What? Together? Fighting whom?' I asked.

'I don't know, but it will happen when you two are together.'

'Thank you,' said the man. 'Here – in return for the axe.' He took off a necklace, and on it was a claw. A *Black Amber* claw.

I stared at it, and took the claw I'd brought from my pocket. Identical.

We all looked at both of them.

'Where did you find this?' I asked.

'On the ground outside the Seven Gates. I don't know what it's from.'

'I do. We have had experiences with the creature it belongs to. It's from what we call Black Amber.'

'Black Amber? The animal's name?'

'Well, we named it that.'

'It sounds good.'

'Here,' I said, giving my claw to Androma. 'I brought this to give to you. It's made of –'

'Elrolian Onyxus,' she finished. 'No, you keep it.'

'Okay. You keep yours too,' I said to the man.

'Well, I think we should have a little chat together after you're done,' he said to us.

'Good idea,' said Slare.

'Well, anyway,' said Peldor, 'this Black Amber creature – what exactly is it?'

'It is an animal that was illegally created using cross-breeding,' Androma said, her eyes wide again, staring out into nothing, as if seeing the answers in front of her. 'Created by an enemy of us Elrolians.' She looked straight at us. 'Created to destroy animals, and Elrolians. Created by Hunter.'

STORM

Silence. I couldn't believe this, and didn't know what to think. This creature was indeed not natural. And worse, it was created by an archenemy of the Elrolians, and was right now living in our forest. Why would Hunter do that?

'Hunter? Why?'

'I cannot see any more of this *Black Amber*,' Androma said. 'That topic is too far to see now. What else do you want to know?'

'Wait, today someone called Shade came to us, and said he was working for someone who was hunting animals…'

'He is working for Hunter,' she said simply.

'Oh no,' said Slare. 'Then that means that –'

'They're going to use Black Amber to destroy Wouldlock and its animals,' said Peldor. 'Then Hunter and his army will attack Elrolia.'

'Thank you,' I said to Androma, standing up. 'I need to talk with …' I looked at the man. 'What's your name?'

'Storm,' he said, extending his hand. 'Storm Orthoclase.'

I shook his hand. 'I think Ravenwood might have mentioned you to me. I'm Wolf. Just Wolf,' I said, rather tired of introducing myself to so many people by now.

'Nice to meet you, Wolf.'

'Same here. This is Slare, and this is Peldor.'

'Hello,' Slare said.

'Pleasure,' Peldor said, bowing.

'Let's go out and talk,' Storm said, extending a hand towards the exit of the cave.

'Sure.'

We thanked Androma again and went out into the soft Elrolian grass that was swaying in the gentle breeze. We went over to a few boulders by one of the streams and sat down, listening to the water rush down and weave between the trees and stones.

'So, Hunter's back then,' Peldor said.

'Who exactly is Hunter?' Slare asked.

'He's a … well, a hunter. He kills animals, and humans, mostly for revenge on people that have done something to him,' Storm said. 'He was really mad at my father once for something, so when he betrayed us, he killed my father. Normally he would have tortured him, but he decided my father was much too powerful of an obstacle. You haven't done anything to anger him have you?'

'No, no. I've never even seen him,' I said.

'Good. If he wants to hunt you, he'll make sure that when he's done with you, you're worse than dead. And if he wants to hunt you, there's no chance of escape. Not even for an Elrolian.'

'So no one has *ever* escaped?' Slare said.

'Nope. Like I said, if he wants to get you for something, he won't just kill you. It just isn't his style. He finds out what you care for most, what you love most, and he destroys it. If he's sending things into your home, you better hope he's not angry with you. If Hunter is trying to kill someone we're friends with, then we're in danger too.'

'Why haven't the police killed him, or at least captured him?'

'Well, he's very hard to find. If he has the skill to kill an army of Elrolians, then he can easily hide from the police. They're scared of him. Scared that if they try to find him, then he'll hunt them. They allow him some space because of that. He has to be the smartest human ever to live. He would have made a great ally to us. He has so much skill, I sometimes wonder if he's Elrolian.'

'Do you have any proof that he isn't?' I asked.

Storm thought for a while. 'No. I guess not. When he came to us, he said he was exiled from his home when he was a little kid. Something about his leader sending his sister on a mission that got her killed. They say that he still wants revenge on the person who did it. After we let him join, we soon realized he was already partly evil. He was searching for the person who had sent his sister to her death. Then he killed twenty of us, along with my father, Elrace, and left forever. I have no idea why. Neither does anyone else.'

'So why would he do it here? Do you think he's mad at someone in Elrolia?'

'Maybe. I certainly hope not. Like I said before, if he's mad at someone we're close to, then we're in danger.'

'Why would he make Black Amber though?' asked Slare

'I … I have no idea. Maybe as a distraction, or a weapon.'

'That's what Lance said. What do you mean, a weapon?'

'Something to attack for him. If he wanted to kill all the animals in Wouldlock and Elrolia, he wouldn't just get a bunch of hunters and come in and kill them. Hunter's the type of person who only risks being out in the open if it's absolutely necessary. Black Amber is his way of attacking his target without doing it himself. He's concealing himself.'

'So what or who exactly is he after?' asked Peldor.

'I don't know. I know how Hunter works, not whom he tries to attack. Now, we've been talking a fair amount about Black Amber, and as I said, I think he might use it as a weapon. I think we'll need to pay Black Amber a little visit.'

'Do you want to kill them?' I asked, astonished.

'No, no, they didn't choose to do this, I would never kill an animal. Never, no matter what it may have done.'

I was starting to really like Storm. The regret I had had from giving him the Ice Axe was starting to drain away.

'What I'm suggesting is we possibly get them onto our side.'

Slare frowned. 'How could we do that?'

He looked away from us. 'People say that there are creatures in the Black Trees that can translate human and animal speech. We could talk to them, get them to translate for us.'

Storm didn't exactly understand these creatures.

'These things have tried to kill me, twice. They don't listen to reason.'

Storm shrugged. 'They listened to Hunter. Sure, we may have to use a little force to make them stay in one place long enough for us to talk to them, but I think that's when this Ice Axe could come in.'

We looked at each other and smiled, a plan starting to form in our minds.

'What are we waiting for?' Slare said. 'Let's go!'

'No, we can't just yet,' said Peldor. 'We need to tell the team. We might be able to convince Ardor or Viper to come.'

'Good idea. We shouldn't have too many people, though,' I said. 'Hey, Storm, are you going to come with us?'

He nodded. 'You bet. This is very important. We should go now. The quicker we get there, the sooner Hunter can be stopped. We should search the Black Trees. It's perfect for Black Amber.'

Then a terrifying thought crossed my mind. 'We'll have to fight him anyway, won't we? Any way this goes, he'll come eventually.'

Storm nodded gravely. 'You're smart, Wolf. Yes, any way this ends, we will have to face him in the end. And no matter how hard you try, I don't think that you're going to be safe from danger, if you do decide to go after Black Amber.'

'Black Amber is too dangerous to be under his control. I'm with you,' I said.

'Well, we should start going now,' said Slare. 'We all know we can't back out of something like this.'

We got up from the boulders and started to walk through the grass. I talked to Storm on the way there.

'Don't you have a crown?' I asked suddenly.

'Yeah, but I don't like it. It's kind of distracting. It's pretty valuable too, so imagine if there were a war or something, and it fell off. Do I just walk over there in the middle of the fighting and grab it? I would be dead, or at least hurt, if they didn't have Elrolian Onyxus. Also, I don't like everyone bowing to me. They do it out of fear, not respect. I hate it.'

He reminded me of Ardor. Being feared because of their abilities, and not respected by anyone. He had it better though. At least his own people respected him, while Ardor was treated like a dangerous beast by almost everyone.

'Ravenwood said you have a sister.'

'Yeah. I did. She disappeared after the battle with Hunter. Never saw her again. I don't like to talk about it.'

'Oh. Sorry.' I tried to change the subject. 'Whom were you fighting against in that battle?'

'Lanxians, they're called. They're creatures with no shadows, and they're scaly, human-like, with scales that blend in with swamps and forests – green, and brown. They're bigger than normal humans, and very strong. I haven't seen one for a long time.'

'Why did they attack you?'

'Well, they wanted food, for one reason. Also, I think Hunter teamed up with them before the battle, so they were doing it for him. He'd probably offered something in return. That's what he does. Now, if he's back, he'll have some big friends at his service from favours he's done a long time ago.'

I shifted uncomfortably. 'In the battle, did you um … like, *kill* them?

'No! No, we would never do that unless there was no other choice. We use the elemental weapons that can be used to trap them, which is to say, all of them. Ice freezes them, fire circles around them leaving no escape, nature wraps vines around them, and sand makes them fall into quicksand, and stuff like that. I think we killed ten of them though, only for self-protection and by accident. I personally never killed them. I was very small when the battle happened. We set them free after an agreement with the queen.'

'So you think there's going to be another battle?'

Storm thought carefully. 'If Hunter thinks he could achieve something through it, then yes.'

'When?'

'I really don't know,' he said. 'There's so much I don't understand right now.'

We walked past the border of Elrolia and Wouldlock, and continued in silence until we had reached the waterfall. The log was still there.

I still could see no sign of the tigers. I hoped they were doing okay. After all, there were lots of places in Wouldlock where they could hide from Black Amber. We walked across the log and Stream looked at our camp.

'Is that where you live?' he asked.

'Yeah,' said Slare. 'It's really nice.'

'Looks like….' He didn't seem to be able to name it. 'Kind of … unfurnished.'

'Yeah,' I said, laughing. 'We try not to use poles and stuff to keep it up. When our leader, Lance Ocrinus, found this place, he knew it was perfect. We use as few human-made things as we can. Also, it helps keep away the animals we don't want near us. You know, the vicious ones. It would attract too much attention if it looked like a modern building.'

'How do you sleep? You have beds, right?'

'The team sleeps in sleeping bags, but we do have normal beds for guests.'

'So what do you do all day?' he asked. He seemed pretty interested in how we lived.

'We do our job. We protect the animals and the forest.'

'From what?' Storm asked.

'Hunters that come here to get animal skins and stuff,' said Slare.

'That's so cool. It must be pretty awesome being so close to nature, having more animals as company than humans.'

'Well, it's kind of normal for me,' I said. 'I've been here practically my whole life. I don't know any other way of living.'

'So you've all been here since you were children?'

'No, not me,' said Slare. 'Peldor and I just came. I'm a member, and Peldor's a visitor. He's friends with Ravenwood.'

'So Ravenwood's here now?' Storm asked.

'No. Not anymore.'

I told him about how he had gone to spy on Shade for us. And, if Androma Faithly had been correct, he would be spying on Hunter too. I wished he were here. What would he have thought of Hunter creating Black Amber? And what would Lance have thought?

Lance. How I wondered where he was. Who had taken him? Shade as well? He had something to do with it, definitely. They had placed a fake Lance there to give us orders that Hunter wanted given. Not protecting animals, but actually joining a force created to kill them. If Hunter, or any of his associates, killed any animal at all, I would make sure that he would never forget how wrong he was to do that.

And I wondered about Storm's idea. Would talking to Black Amber work? Hunter would have made sure they would not switch sides easily. He would have offered them fresh food, and priceless things. He had created them, and he would know their needs and weaknesses. I had no doubt that he may have threatened to kill them too.

I had only heard about this criminal, Hunter, from a few people, and hadn't really heard much, yet I felt like I knew him. What he would do in certain situations. The thought of him reminded me how much death and destruction he had caused.

We finally arrived at the camp and I pushed away the boulders, stepping aside to let Storm, Slare, and Peldor in. I followed them. Storm was looking all around at the various things we had displayed. Things like awards from animal charities, the maps of Wouldlock, and the blood samples that we had collected from all of the animals to make sure they weren't sick, and were fresh and healthy.

He didn't ask many questions, he just followed me to the back, where I found Ardor and Viper entertaining Mac and Icon. Viper was throwing his elemental fire disks, and Ardor would hit them high into the air with his claws, where they would explode like fireworks. Every time, Mac and Icon would go crazy, leaping up and trying to catch the little sparks that fell down, laughing in delight.

'Hey guys, this is Storm. He's an Elrolian from, well, Elrolia. He wants to come with us to the Black Trees, and search for Black Amber.'

Before they could ask questions, I told them all about what Androma Faithly had told us. They had heard of Hunter, and didn't like the fact that he was against us, even sending his animals into our home. Ardor was probably the most uncomfortable with this.

'We need to get Ravenwood,' Ardor said immediately.

'Why?' I asked.

'He'll be with Hunter! He will kill him!'

'Yeah, but if he thinks he's on the same side, he'll be fine.'

'No, you don't understand. Ravenwood told you about Hunter, right?' Ardor asked.

'Yeah, he did.'

'Did he tell you they are life-long enemies? Did he perhaps tell you that Hunter is his *brother?*'

We all froze. What? How could that be? He would have told me … wouldn't he? Well, maybe not. Would I share something that personal? I guess not. Who would?

'I'm not sure if he would like me telling you this, but you need to understand what is at stake now. When Hunter and Ravenwood were children, they went off into the woods one night. They were chasing a wild fox, like any curious children would. They got lost, deep in the woods. Ravenwood was much older, and Hunter looked up to him as a leader. He expected Ravenwood to get them back home. When morning came, Ravenwood told Hunter to stay where they had decided to camp, and went to scout for the way out, leaving a trail of orange stones for a way back. A Lanxian came and chased him away, when he got to near to Elrolia, and he didn't leave any more stones. When Ravenwood finally got rid of the Lanxian, he could not find his way back to his brother, no matter how many times he tried. Ravenwood grew up by himself, every day looking for his brother. Hunter, in the meantime, believed that Ravenwood had abandoned him. He grew up by himself as well. He made up a new name for himself, and one day found that the stones his brother had left led to Elrolia. He didn't dare enter there, because Elrolian Stone Wolves guarded the castle. When he was older, he finally gathered the courage to enter the castle. He wanted revenge on his brother. He went in there, and betrayed the Elrolians, as I'm sure you have heard. He was angry with Ravenwood, and as I said he wanted revenge. And is still looking for it.'

'Ravenwood had been in Elrolia already?' I asked.

'Yes, indeed he had.'

'Okay, but wait, Ravenwood said he's part Elrolian.'

'Yes, he is.'

'But only one of his parents was Elrolian, so he didn't have Elrolian Onyxus on his heart. What if it was the opposite for Hunter? What if the reason he is so skilled, so smart, so hard to kill, is because he is Elrolian, and having only one Elrolian parent made him even more powerful?'

'I don't know,' said Ardor, looking thoughtfully at me. 'It's possible.'

Mac and Icon were bored now, and had started jumping on each other's backs, and doing summersaults in midair.

'Let's go discuss it with the rest of the team,' Viper said. 'Mac and Icon, you want to stay out here with Sirpix?'

'Yeah!' said Mac, nodding his head and body like he was bowing. 'Yeah!'

We went back into the camp and got everyone into the meeting room. We all took seats on the hard wooden stumps. I introduced everyone to Storm, and repeated to them what I had told Ardor about the meeting with Androma, and Storm's idea of talking to Black Amber. They were all very taken aback.

'*Hunter?*' asked Raider, astonished. Even he could not joke about something as serious as this.

'He's leading the animal hunt?' asked Blade. 'His brain is the size of a jellyfish's as well. Which is to say, nonexistent.'

'So some of us should go to the Black Trees, and try to communicate with Black Amber.'

'Won't they just try and kill us if we get close?' Blade asked.

'No,' said Storm. 'We'll freeze them with the Ice Axe.'

Nobody asked why Storm now had the Ice Axe. They probably didn't care.

'So what we need to decide now is who will go and talk to them,' Slare said. 'We know that Storm's going, and I'd like to go too. And maybe three other people?'

'I'll go,' I said immediately.

'Okay, so that's three of five.'

'I'll go along too,' said Viper. 'If that's okay with everyone.'

They nodded.

'Anyone else?' Slare asked.

'The rest of us will need to stay at base,' said Ardor. 'We still need to protect the animals, and we'll need a group of at least this size to do so. If you four are going, then that'll mean that nine – eleven, including Mac and Icon – will be staying here. That's good. You won't need that many people going. Some of us will need to go and try to get Ravenwood out of there.'

'Okay, well we don't want to delay,' said Slare briskly. 'Let's move.'

We went back out into the open and told Mac and Icon that we were going.

'I come?' said Mac.

'Um, it's okay,' I said. 'We're going very far, you should stay.'

'Okay. Bye,' said Mac, waving his hand up and down.

'Bye!' Icon said.

So, the Black Trees, eh?' said Viper. 'This'll be fun. Hopefully we'll have some exiting stories to tell when we come back. So, Storm, how are we going to communicate with the animals? You know Black Amber-ish?'

'No, there's a creature in the forest that can apparently talk any language. If we can get it to help us, Black Amber might listen.'

'This reminds me of a guy I saw in Alria once,' Viper said.

I listened intently. Viper's stories were interesting. He had been all over the Eromies.

'So this guy is selling pizza, right, so he's outside the restaurant, you know, like advertising their place and stuff, and then he sees this dog, like a golden retriever or something. So he – the pizza dude – starts first acting like a chicken that's had too much sugar, and then starts barking at the dog like they're communicating to each other. Then the dog comes up to him, the guy leans down so they're nose to nose, and then the dog spits in his face and slaps him with its paw, and he gets really mad, so he tries to kick the dog, but it dodges, and he breaks the walking stick of the old lady who was holding the dog's leash, so then I get mad, because he's just smiling at her, not apologising or anything, so I go up to him, say that he looks like the backside of a ugly donkey, then I slap him, and apologise for it.'

I stared at him. 'What does that have to do with us talking to Black Amber?'

'The guy was an ugly donkey!' he said, as if this explained everything.

I slipped my hands into my pockets and felt a few hard things rattling around.

'Oh, yeah, I forgot to tell you. I need to go feed the goats,' I said. The things in my pocket were small polished rocks. The goats eat rock. Yeah, I know, you must be thinking that they have hard teeth. They do.

'Where are they?' Storm asked.

'Oh, not far. They're on the way.'

'Oh, I love them!' Slare said. 'They're so friendly, and energetic.'

'Yeah, sorry, I meant to go before, but we were too busy. As I said, they're on the way. You don't mind, do you?'

'Oh no, not at all. It'll be fun,' said Storm. 'I work with animal at Elrolia, but not even close to as many as you work with.'

We walked on, and I thought about what we were doing.

We were trying to save our lives, and the lives of the animals around us. And we were being pretty much threatened by Hunter, for some unclear reason. That's what Black Amber is. A warning. Telling us what we're against. Black Amber. It all rotated around them. Hunter, the Elrolians, Ravenwood, Wouldlock, everything. It was Black Amber that connected it all.

We continued walking until we caught sight of the goats. They were by a large rock, just across the river. We all crossed the nice new log, and it held all of our weight easily. Viper nearly slipped off though, when a huge bald eagle swooped past his head.

'Whoa!' he said in alarm, steadying himself.

He jumped off the log and onto the other side of Wouldlock, and Slare, Storm, and I followed.

There were about fifty of the goats that I could see, and most of them were very young. Their fur is black, brown, grey, white, or a mixture of some of them. They're pygmy goats, and are adorable. *Not* cute. No, maybe adorable, but not cute. I can't stand that word. I don't know why, I just can't. Now, pygmy goats *are* different from domestic goats, mainly because of their size. Pygmy goats are much smaller, and usually more energetic.

Females are called does, and males are bucks. Males, or bucks, are usually heavier than females, weighing up to thirty-nine kilograms, while females normally go to thirty-four.

The little ones were racing around wildly, much faster than the average human could run, jumping up to incredible heights. It was crazy, because you hardly saw them bending their legs to spring up. It just seemed like there were a bunch of flying goats around you. The older ones, with the horns, were fighting, as usual.

You may not know how a goat fight works. Usually only the big ones do it. They get up on their hind legs, turn their head to the side, so they can see better (Their eyes are on the side of their heads) and then smash their heads against each other, then they hold it in that position for a few seconds, then do it again. It goes on for anywhere from four to ten rounds. Usually only two goats fight each other at a time, but I've seen three before.

When they saw me, they all rushed up towards me, the big ones getting up on their hind legs, putting their front legs on my waist. The small ones were charging into my knees, and then looking up at me expectantly. Some of them, I knew, wanted their hard little heads rubbed, while most of them were looking for food. Sadly, we can't let them eat whenever they want, because they'll eat too much, and that can cause problems, so we have to control their eating habits or they'll get overweight and sick. That's why wild pygmy goats usually die relatively young. The ones here live longer, mainly because of us.

I nearly lost balance, with so many goats on me. I threw some of the rocks, which took care of the hungry ones, then started to rub their heads, two at a time. They absolutely love that. Even if you just leave your hand hanging there, they'll satisfy themselves sooner or later. Slowly they decided they'd had enough, and one by one went off to eat as well.

'Wolf, you're really good with animals,' said Storm.

'Yeah, you would get to be too if you worked with them for so long,' I said modestly.

'Do they all have names?' Viper asked.

'Yeah,' Slare and I said together.

We started pointing them out, naming them as we walked through the crowd.

'Stone, Brick. Crash, Lash, and Nash. Boulder and Thunder and Silk....' I named a few more, and turned to Viper. 'Good names, you think?'

'Yeah,' he said. 'One of them should be called Viper.'

I smiled. 'Maybe.' I threw some more rocks over to them, and rubbed a few more heads. I turned, and after I took a few steps, Slare warned, 'watch out!' and I got run over by one of the little ones. I groaned and turned over. The little goat started treating me as if I was a trampoline, which wasn't the most comfortable thing in the world. It was Crash of course. He was a very, very small goat, the third-youngest in Wouldlock. His fur was a nice coffee-brown with some black running down the back of his head and spine. Like all goats his age, he didn't have his horns yet, but some small furry pointed ears. I got myself off the ground, on to my knees, and he climbed up onto me, and started to eat my hair.

'No, no, Crash, there's food over there,' I said, desperately trying to tug my hair away from him. It was like a tug of war competition. I was losing against this tiny little goat. He stopped and stared at me, then licked my chin and went for my coat zipper, then my shoe, which he somehow managed to get off.

'Can we take him with us?' Slare asked. 'He's so –'

I closed my eyes.

'Cute!' she said loudly, giving me a playful nudge.

I sighed. 'I don't think so. It could be dangerous. We're going into the Black Trees. That's no place for goats. Especially one as young as Crash.'

'Please?'

I sighed. 'If he follows us,' I said.

He followed us.

'Okay,' I muttered. 'If you're sure.'

Crash ran ahead of us, then did a quick U-turn and came galloping towards us. I smiled. He was extremely playful. Just before he hit my foot, I jumped up, and he raced right under my legs.

The little goat turned back again, trotted up to us, and kept at our pace.

'Do you know exactly how to get there?' Viper asked.

'Yeah, I know Wouldlock very well. I have a map just in case, but not of the Black Trees. Once we're in there, we're lost.'

'Okay, cool,' said Viper, laid back, relaxed, and confident as always.

Storm was looking at everything, his eyes never fixing on one place for too long. He seemed to be analysing the surroundings, looking for any kind of threat, and any ways we could make a quick escape. He was so powerful. As I said before, I could tell this without even knowing him that long. I was very glad he was with us on this journey. He was the type of person who made me feel that I would go anywhere, as long as he was there too.

'So, Storm, what's it like being an Elrolian?' Slare asked him.

'Not easy,' he said.

And that was all he said.

Slare laughed. '"Not easy"? That's all? Tell me more.'

'We have to train in combat, survival, and defence for three hours every day. You know, like fighting using weapons, surviving with only a few things in wild, uninhabited places. You feel like a weak child if you aren't fantastic at everything. You have a lot of things to live up to if you're an Elrolian. A lot of high expectations. And then we also practice defending ourselves from attacks, which we don't get all that often. But every once in a while, someone crazy enough decides to challenge us.'

'That must be why you're so good at fighting,' I said. 'All that training.'

'Yeah, partly. We use absolutely horrible weapons, to get used to bad quality, so we can perform miracles with good quality things. But also, it's how we're born. You know about Elrolian Onyxus, right?'

'Yeah.'

'Well, when we're born, it can cover other parts of our body, not just the heart. It can sometimes give extra skills to people with that type of thing. Like if it encased your legs, you might be able to jump especially high, or run faster. Or if it covered your arms, you could become stronger, or throw objects farther. Stuff like that. It might make your hands faster. Most Elrolians have at least a bit in their arms, making them faster when they fight, and more skillful.'

Wait,' I said, remembering our conversation about Hunter's amazing skills. 'What could happen if it surrounded the brain?'

'I don't know,' he said. 'A person might become really intelligent. The mind can be more powerful than the body. Especially if used in the right way. The mind is very interesting to me. I want to learn how to master it completely. Imagine how powerful you'd be then.'

We all thought about that for a while, until Viper spoke again.

'We should get some sleep.'

'Yeah, he's right,' Slare agreed.

'How about we rest over there?' Storm said, nodding at a large collection of jagged boulders.

'Sure.' I said.

We went down towards the boulders. I'd only just realised how dark it was getting. The sun was nearly down, and we were covered in the beautiful fiery colour of the sunset, shadows dancing like ghosts around us.

We dropped our belongings, set out our sleeping bags that we'd brought from camp, and one by one we fell to sleep, with no one left to be on watch for Black Amber, or any other animal that might sneak up on us.

That was our big mistake.

WHATS SO FUNNY?

I woke up to laughs, all around me. Not the type a sane human being would make, but a soft, rather hysterical type of sound. Some of them though, were louder, and rougher. I opened my eyes, and almost tore my sleeping bag, for I shot right up very quickly.

The others were just waking up as well. It was light out. We'd had a great sleep. This completely ruined it.

I saw Crash by my foot. He was chewing uneasily on my jeans.

Viper opened his eyes dreamily. 'What's so funny?' he asked, rubbing his eyes.

Storm shot up onto his feet and scooped up the Ice Axe, twirling it around in his hand.

'What's going on?' asked Slare, getting out of her sleeping bag.

I looked up at the rocks around us. Hyenas. Everywhere.

Maybe a dozen or so, all staring down at us, making those loud laughs that they're so well known for. They were large, brown, and furry, with spotted coats: spotted hyenas. I'd seen them around here before, but I didn't know they lived here. Or at least that's what I assumed. This was probably their territory, and we were in it. I should have known.

Some of them were big, some of them about a tenth smaller. The smaller ones, I knew, were male. They had downward-sloping backs, with long forelegs, but shorter hind legs.

This situation reminded me eerily of the time when I'd been surrounded by Black Amber. Nowhere to escape, pain and death merely a step away.

One of the bigger hyenas barked loudly, and the others laughed. It seemed like they were laughing at a joke she'd just told, but I knew what it really was. The one that had barked was probably the leader. The others were laughing because it was their way of showing submission to the leader.

Viper and Slare realised what was happening.

We were trapped. There was no way we could get out alive. When you invade a hyena's territory, they don't forgive you easily.

'My good friend Emrax used to say, that if you strike hard enough in unknown waters, something will come up and strike back.'

'Very good, but what do we do here?' Slare asked, turning to look at all of them.

'Strike again,' I heard Storm mutter. It was a good meaningful saying, but we needed to focus.

'We all need to get to safety,' I said, 'in whatever way we can. Viper, you have your knives?'

His mouth twitched, and his shiny knives shot into his gloved hands.

'Throw them as far as you can, and fly to them.'

'What? No! I can't leave you!'

'Do it.' Slare and Storm agreed.

Viper stared at us. 'Guys –'

'Go!' we said in unison.

'Okay, okay. Here, I'll get their attention, you run. Don't worry I'll be fine. Okay?'

He jumped toward the big hyena without waiting for an answer. They had been very slowly advancing while we'd talked, but it was Storm who set them off. He ran toward the Black Trees, and half of the pack went for him. Viper moved in the other direction. Howling, they closed in on him. We ran towards the Black Trees, following Storm, but we hadn't outsmarted them. Viper flung his knives in the direction of the camp, but just before he could go to them, a huge, furry hyena bit his right leg. He screamed, and I saw fresh blood spill out at an alarmingly fast rate. He fought and tugged to get his leg out, but this hyena put up a fight.

'Knives!' he yelled, and he and the hyena, which was still on his leg, flew away to the camp. I didn't see the hyena stop attacking him, even while he was in the air, which meant Viper would be in even more agony, and also that the hyena would be able to easily invade the camp. All the other hyenas were mad too, mostly at Viper, but it seemed that they would settle for trying to kill us instead, perhaps because of Stream's sudden move for the Black Trees.

So we ran. And ran. It was like one of those action movies where the heroes are running for their lives from the evil people. The good thing: In *most* movies like that, the good people get away. The bad thing: We weren't in a movie.

'Where are we going?' Slare panted.

'I don't know,' I said. 'Somewhere towards the Black Trees. Away from the hyenas.'

I looked back to see if Crash was still there, and was worried when I didn't see him, but then I caught sight of him way ahead of us, running like crazy, jumping high over rocks and fallen branches.

The hyenas were gaining on us. We wouldn't make it to safety, for there wasn't any. I knew that sooner or later, they'd catch up, or we would trip. Sure enough, a moment later, one of us tripped. Sadly, it was I. The others only noticed when it was too late.

The hyenas were on my body in seconds, snapping at anything they could get their mouths on, laughing like this was a fun game.

Right then was the second time I'd been attacked by a wild animal in, what, a week? More pain flooded through my body, and I was almost killed. But yes, fortunately I said *almost* killed. I survived. And it was because of an Elrolian.

There was a blinding flash of white light that lasted for only a few seconds, and the hyenas yelped and scattered, galloping back to their territory. Crash came up and started to chew my ear, hitting me with his foot to try and keep me still.

I looked up. A tall woman was standing over me. She had long, straight, black hair, and armour just like Storm. She also had a crown, which I knew was an Elrolian crown. It was beautiful, and very elegant. It was silver with a purple gemstone in it, kind of like Androma Faithly's.

'Are you okay?' she asked me softly.

I blinked. 'Um … well …' I gestured to my body. No, I wasn't okay.

Storm pulled me to my feet and I winced. At least it wasn't as bad as when Black Amber had attacked me.

'Thanks! But, if you don't mind me asking, who are you?' asked Slare, staring at the woman who had just saved our lives – or at least mine.

'I'm Spyra Crysabell. An Elrolian Explorer. My job is to go

explore the land in search of threats or anything else I may come upon. There have been sightings and attacks from a certain animal we haven't encountered before, and I'm searching for information on the matter.'

Crash was jumping up and down wildly, trying to bite Spyra's light grey T-shirt. It looked like a nice, crunchy rock.

'And who's this little one?' she asked.

'That's Crash,' I said, a little defensively. 'I'm Wolf, this is Slare, and this is–'

'Storm?' she said.

Storm nodded and smiled. 'Spyra. I've seen you before, training in Elrolia.'

'Yes, I've seen you as well. You were the one who jumped off the Elrolian castle for fun, was it?'

'Yeah, when I listen to music that I like, I get a big urge to … jump off a cliff or something,' Storm said. 'Normally I do.'

'You work with animals?'

'Yeah,' he said. 'I train the animals. Also, I lead the Onyxus River Team.'

'What?' she said, astonished. 'You go *in* there?'

They continued comparing notes. I turned to Slare.

'You think Viper's okay?'

She smiled reassuringly. 'I'm sure he's fine. He wouldn't be … defeated by a hyena.'

I knew we were both thinking the same thing. The camp was endangered. Hyenas are dangerous, even just one of them. But they would be okay. They had Ardor, Viper, Peldor, Sora, Raider … yeah. They had almost the whole team to help them. They would be fine, just as Slare said.

Then something that Spyra had said before hit me. 'Wait, you're looking for an animal?' I interrupted, getting Spyra's attention.

'Yeah, I am.'

'We know it,' I said, suddenly very sure. How? Let's put it

this way: How could it *not* be? 'We call it Black Amber.'

Slare and Storm nodded as they realised. It was so obvious. Everything in Wouldlock had something to do with Black Amber, and almost everyone here was aware of it by now.

'What is it?' Spyra said, frowning.

'It's a huge, black animal,' said Slare. 'It was created by Hunter. You know him, don't you?'

'Of course. He betrayed us. Killed many of the Elrolians.'

'Including my father,' said Storm bitterly.

Slare nodded sadly. 'He created this animal to attack us or something. I'm not exactly sure.'

Storm nodded. 'He wanted revenge on someone. He's going to use Black Amber to get it.'

'So is that why you are here as well?' Spyra asked. 'To search for Black Amber?'

'Yeah,' I said. 'We're going to try and get it to stop trying to destroy Wouldlock and Elrolia.'

'Do you know what he wants?'

'No,' said Slare.

'So where are you going to look?' Spyra asked.

'The Black Trees,' I said, nodding towards them.

She raised her eyebrows. 'You're sure that they are there?'

'Yeah...' I said. But was I sure? I didn't know for *sure*. We had just thought of this place from a few encounters with the creature. What if they weren't here after all? What if we had come here for nothing? Sure, it wasn't that hard to get back to camp, but a lot had been sacrificed. A hyena had attacked Viper, I had been attacked by about ten of them, the camp could be in trouble, and I had a feeling that this wasn't the worst of our journey. We were going to the Black Trees. It could get much worse.

'Well, if an Elrolian is sure enough about something to work with a human, then I guess things should work out okay,' Spyra said. 'Is it just you three that are going?'

'Now it is. One of our other people got … carried away. Literally,' I said.

'Oh. Well, can I come with you instead?'

Storm looked at us. We shrugged. 'Of course,' Storm said.

So just like that, we set off together, sharing stories about our encounters with Black Amber. Apparently, Spyra had singlehandedly tied one of them up long enough to get to safety.

'So why call them Black Amber?' she asked.

I repeated the story of how we'd chosen the name in the hospital after they'd attacked me. She listened attentively.

'Wow,' she said. 'That's quite the story.'

Then Storm froze and his eyes narrowed. Within a second he started walking again.

'What's wrong?' Slare asked.

'Keep walking,' he ordered. 'We're being followed.'

My heartbeat quickened. He seemed mighty serious. I started to walk in long, fast strides. I went up next to him.

'By what?' I whispered, and Slare and Spyra listened intently for the answer. Even I couldn't tell what was happening.

'A human,' he said, uncertainly. 'I think.'

The Eagles Trees were up ahead. I pointed this out quietly to Storm. They were three large trees like points of a triangle, their branches and leaves interweaving like a blanket.

'We could hide there.'

He shook his head. 'We can go there, but we cannot hide.'

'Why?' asked Slare.

'It is like when a cheetah marks its prey. Once spotted, there is no hiding.' He looked at me. 'We are being hunted.'

'We have no choice,' said Spyra. 'We must face the threat.'

We were almost at the trees. They were three unnaturally large trees that were home to many types of eagles. The trees were very thick, and strong, very good for climbing.

I heard a loud, rough screech. It reminded me of the hyenas

laugh. But this one I had never heard before in my life. This one didn't think we were funny.

'Does it know we've noticed it?' I asked.

Storm nodded grimly. 'It knows.' He looked at each of us in turn, and we all got the message. *Run.*

And so we ran. Forcing our legs to carry us to the trees, jumping over stones and small streams.

I didn't hear it move. Maybe it could fly. It was clearly no normal human that was pursuing us.

We stopped in the centre of the trees, the shadows protecting us from the hot sun. We were all back-to-back, each of us scanning the area for the creature. I hoped it wasn't Black Amber. But from the way Storm talked about it, it didn't seem like it was. It seemed to be something completely new.

Then I heard Spyra gasp. She had seen it. And following her gaze, I saw it too.

It was perched high up in one of the trees, and it was very easy to see, for its skin was a blinding white. But no, it didn't have skin. It was just bone. No flesh, just the skeleton. It had a humanoid skeleton, but with two noticeable differences. One, it was crouched down on all fours, and had unnaturally long arms and legs; two, it had a pair of enormous skeletal wings. Wings like a bat's, but without the actual wing, just the skeleton, with sharp claws at the ends. It seemed like it worked with some kind of invisible flesh. It could fly. I saw proof of that as it swooped down towards a lower branch. It didn't glide – it actually flew. More little skeletal bits expanded as it spread its wings.

Now, the whole thing wasn't just plain skeleton. It had gleaming black-spiked armour on its lower arms, legs, and chest. It also had a black helmet, which made it look even creepier. In its mouth were two rows of razor-sharp teeth, like small jagged rocks.

It stared at me. As much as someone can stare at you without eyes. It was like the evil eye-socket.

'What do we do if it tries to kill us?' Spyra said, asking nobody in particular.

'We try not to get killed,' I muttered.

It lunged.

It glided to the ground, and sharp claws extended out of its skeletal fingers like talons on an eagle. We stumbled backwards, hitting our backs against one of the trees.

'We need a plan,' Spyra said.

Storm frowned. 'A plan? Who cares about a plan?' He jumped very high up, reminding me of Crash, and did a summersault in midair, landing on the ground two metres from the creature with his axe in hand, kneeling down on one knee with his empty hand supporting him.

The skeleton shrieked and tried to scratch Storm, and he almost got out of the way, but the skeleton creature was much too fast. It clawed Storm's chest, leaving three bloody lines just visible through his ripped T-shirt. He must have taken off his chest armour when going to sleep. His arms and legs were still covered.

He didn't show any sign of pain, and started spinning around his axe.

I couldn't stand to just sit and watch. And neither, it appeared, could the others. We all charged.

The skeleton used his arm to swipe Storm away, and focused on us. I saw its hands start to smoke. I only realised what it was preparing to do a second before it happened. Its hand erupted in a mass of blazing red flame and it shot three balls of fire at us, hitting each of us right in the centre of the chest. It hurt immensely, but at least the fire didn't burn us to death. The fire extinguished almost immediately after it hit me, but that wasn't all the creature had.

It pulled a chain out from what seemed like thin air, and swung it at us. I don't know how it did it, but it trapped all of us, leaving us incapable of movement.

Storm had recovered, and was again charging at the beast. He hurled his Ice Axe and the weapon twisted in midair, narrowly missing the skeleton's head, landing in the bark of the tree behind it.

Storm's eyes narrowed and he ran, at the last moment sliding down between the creature's legs. He grabbed the axe, and wrenched it out of the tree, twisting around and smashing it down, cracking the skeleton's spine.

It snarled, and seemed to be hurt a bit. It swiped at Storm again, and missed by a centimetre. Storm swung his axe in a circular motion back over his shoulder and he hit the skeleton point-blank in the middle of its chest, sending it flying – involuntarily – far away.

Storm took several deep breaths and turned to us.

'You okay?' he asked, smashing the chain, setting us free.

We nodded.

'That was brilliant,' I said, ashamed that I hadn't done much to help.

Storm seemed to read my thoughts. 'It's fine. It's gone now isn't it?'

'Are you okay?' asked Spyra, looking at the scratch.

'Yeah, it's fine.'

Slare raised her eyebrows. 'Doesn't look fine.'

'Ah, it's okay. Look at Wolf. Those hyenas gave him worse.'

'What was that thing?' I said, trying to draw attention away from myself.

'Don't know,' said Storm shrugging. 'That thing is like from a fantasy world. Seriously. A living skeleton with wings?'

'It might have been Hunter!' said Slare. He might have created it to attack us like he did with Black Amber.'

'How can that thing even be living?' I said. 'How could it fly, or anything? That's incredible.'

'Well I hope it doesn't come back for more,' said Storm.

I grinned. 'It's probably going to go to Hunter and hand in its retirement form.'

'Well,' said Slare. 'Do we just head into the forest?'

There was silence. We would have to go in there sooner or later – probably sooner – but none of us were keen. Believe me, you wouldn't be either going into a spooky, dark forest, trying to negotiate with the very creature that had tried to kill you so many times before.

'How about we get some food?' suggested Storm. 'I'm starving.'

We nodded excitedly. 'Good idea,' we agreed.

We all sat down and brought out our sleeping bags to rest on. Storm took off his armour and jacket, revealing his blood-stained, torn white T-shirt. He took that off too, and started to patch up the mark that he'd gotten.

I saw that on the back of his body were many other scars. Apparently he'd faced many other battles.

'You sure you're alright?' Spyra asked anxiously.

Storm looked over his shoulder. 'Spyra. I'm fine.'

'Okay, okay,' said Spyra.

'So, what've we got to eat?' asked Slare, digging through our supply bag.

'Some baguettes, some lettuce, cheese, enough for a nice good sandwich. Help yourself,' I said, gesturing toward the food.

We all fixed ourselves sandwiches and ate greedily. We'd had a tough day. Hyenas and skeleton people that didn't like us, like a lot of other animals. For example, Black Amber.

Crash was running around wildly, until he smelt the food, and he too started to eat up. I'd hardly seen him at the encounter with the skeleton, which was a good thing. At least he hadn't gotten hurt.

Hopefully the skeleton would be the last wild, human-killing creature we met until the Black Trees, or at least for today. But of course, a half hour after our meal, our next wild animal approached us.

I knew this one very well. After all, who wouldn't, when you're named after it?

FORESTS GOLD

As we all finished eating, we decided that we deserved a break. Just a small one, after all that we had gone through. I closed my eyes, laid my head against my rolled -up sleeping bag, and let my legs relax in the soft grass, under the cover of the shadows of the trees. Crash jumped on to me, almost knocking the wind out of me, and then settled down on my lap, closing his eyes and resting his small head in my hand.

I did not fall asleep, but I regained my energy and was ready after twenty minutes. I could hear the birds chirping, singing their amazing songs, filling me with happiness. I hadn't seen any eagles for a while, but I caught sight of one perched in a tree after a little bit. I think about fifteen bald eagles live in this area. It's fantastic for their needs.

'So, if you guys want to go rest up, I think I'll go explore. You know, just make sure that our way to the trees will be clear. Don't worry, I won't go inside.'

'Okay,' said Slare. 'Make sure you don't get killed.'

I smiled weakly. 'I'll try.'

I gently lifted Crash off of me, got to my feet and started to wander out of the cool shade into the hot sunlight. I hadn't really been keeping track of time, and didn't have my watch on me, but I guessed it must have been about twelve-thirty.

I didn't know exactly what I was looking for. Black Amber? No, not yet. I wanted to be aware of any obstacles that we could face, such as if Hunter had sent another creature here. If so, I didn't know what I'd do. I'd probably think up a detailed plan, whereas Storm, in my place, would charge without a second's thought. Slare would use misdirection and camouflage to attack. I didn't know about Spyra. We'd only just met her.

I steadily approached the Black Trees, wondering if something would jump out at me and tackle me to the ground. A small river separated the trees from the rest of Wouldlock. I realised we would probably have to swim across to get to our destination. This could prove a challenge, for the water was very deep, home to a few dangerous animals, and the current was very strong indeed. The good thing was that there were some rocks to cling on to that were strewn in the water. If we found the right place, we might even have a slight chance of being able to cross over by using the rocks as a pathway.

I had to keep on reminding myself that sooner or later we would have to face Hunter, and solve the mystery of Black Amber and why he was trying to rip apart Wouldlock. Everyone said it was revenge. Such a terrible thing it was.

It seemed more normal here, which worried me. What if Black Amber really didn't live here? And if it did, would we all survive another encounter? Being truthful, I worried not all of us would. Maybe Black Amber we could manage, but soon we would be dealing with a much bigger problem. Hunter. I didn't want to get on his bad side, but to protect myself, and all the animals of Wouldlock, it would be necessary.

It was then that I heard a loud bellow. I recognised it straight away. This was an animal I knew well. It was a red deer, one of the largest of the deer species – the fourth largest, to be precise. Storm had told me earlier that they called red deer the Forest's Gold, meaning they are the most valuable of all the animals in the woods. Looking at the sheer beauty of them, you immediately understand why.

I saw the deer come out from behind the tree where we'd been camping. I knew this animal was no threat. They eat mostly leaves and grass. But this one was not alone. It was male, and accompanied by what must have been its fawn. The small one's coat was light brown with lots of white spots all over its back. It had long, skinny, but powerful legs, and of course, didn't have antlers, as this small one was a female.

It was unusual for the father to accompany the child – normally the mother takes care of the young. I don't know why, it just works like that.

The big one, however, *was* a stag. It had large, strong antlers that were growing white at the tips, and a shaggy, dark-brown mane. Its body was a little lighter, but not as light as the small one's. The points on deer's antlers increase with age, and this one's were almost fully grown. Nevertheless, that did not exactly mean it was very old. It was healthy, and at a good age to be taking care of a fawn.

I'll tell you a little bit about this particular species of deer. The red deer is actually quite common, and not endangered at all. They were at one time rare in some parts, but as I said, never close to extinction. Various wildlife societies made hug reintroduction and conservation efforts, and this resulted in an increase of red deer in certain areas. It was unusual to see red deer in this area, though, because I was told that they prefer Elrolia, but this red deer I had seen before, and it seemed to particularly enjoy this area of Wouldlock.

I smiled, and without fear approached it, stroking its rough, newly developed mane. It appeared that this one had stopped feeding, and was losing a lot of weight. This was nothing to be concerned about, however. This is a natural stage in the red deer's life.

I saw that this stag had a scar over its shoulder blade. I knew this deer – he was called Cervus, named after its species name, *Cervus elaphus*. The little one was named Imber, meaning 'rain' in Latin.

'Hey there, Cervus,' I said, stroking his mane. You can call me stupid, but I like talking to animals. I do not, however, talk to them stupidly, like some people do with dogs and cats. You know, like saying ... stuff. You get the idea – like 'Oh, who's a good kitty?' or 'Aww, you're tired, aren't you, you poor little dumpling?' It's usually incredibly stupid.

'How's it going?'

He snorted fondly. He understood.

'And what about you, huh?' I asked Imber, getting down on my knees.

She stared at me, and then licked my face.

I shook my head smiling. 'I love you too, Imber.'

She stared up at me with her round, brown eyes.

'No, no, you're not getting me with that.' I looked at her again. 'Okay, what do you want?'

She tugged off my jacket.

I sighed. 'Okay, there you go.'

She chewed it for a few seconds, then got bored and dropped it.

'Thanks,' I muttered.

I didn't especially want to get into that jacket now. But that was okay. It wasn't that cold out. I would live – for now, at least.

I heard another sound, from another animal. It was a spine-tingling howl. You know what it was from just from an explanation like that. A wolf. The very animal that *I* was named after

– and it was close. The deer had heard it too. Yet they did not run. They stayed. Those deer were called 'forest's gold' because of their incredibly bravery. Why is it that I so often hear animals before I see them? Sometimes. Sometimes it's the other way around.

My heart started to beat faster than normal, and my eyes darted around, searching for the wolf. It occurred to me that I might have been intruding in the wolves' territory, like the hyenas. I mean, first the hyenas attacked me, and now this. Why me?

Also, I knew what the howl meant. Sometimes they would howl just if another wolf had started them off, but normally the purpose is for a wolf to attract attention from its pack, or to announce its presence to other animals, or another pack. These howls can be heard from fifteen kilometres away.

This meant that a pack could be close behind. It knew I was here. Packs are normally made up of six to ten wolves that live and hunt together. I regard them as the deadliest of all predators. Not just because I share their name.

Grey wolves are the largest members of the dog family, and perhaps the strongest. Despite all of the movies that show it, they rarely attack humans, thought it has happened before. Unfortunately for me, this was a grey wolf, not an Elrolian snow or stone wolf. If it had been an Elrolian wolf, it would have been no threat, as they are trained, and only attack if commanded to.

Wolves are very famous, both in the wild, to those who are hunted by them, and to us. We humans have written more books about wolves than about any other wildlife species.

Then I saw a movement behind one of the trees, and I froze, just as it came out into the open.

The animal was terrifying, but stunning at the same time. It had a white body, but its back was grey. It had long, powerful legs, and its whole body was covered in thick fur to trap its body heat in the winter. It had large feet, with sharp claws, and its powerful jaw was also filled with very strong and sharp teeth, used to rip apart the flesh of its prey.

Do you have a dog? If so, is it smart? Well, a wolf's brain is a third larger than an average domestic dog. They're very smart. The wolves, I mean. No offence to your dog.

This particular wolf seemed to be quite young. Maybe nine years or so, yet it was still a threat. A healthy pup is strong enough to travel with the pack by the time it's three to five months old. Grey wolves are considered "young" from one to eleven. Their diet consists of mostly meat – and unfortunately deer. I didn't know what was making the two red deer with me stay. I realised that this particular wolf didn't want me – it wanted Imber and Cervus.

I had only seconds before it attempted to kill the deer.

'Run!' I shouted, pushing them away with some force.

It growled and raced towards the deer, its long legs letting it run much faster than the deer, which was frantically trying to get away.

Before I could do anything, five more wolves, all the same size or a bit smaller than the first one, came speeding out from behind the tree, running furiously, intent on killing those deer. Their heads nodded up and down as they ran, their paws tearing away at the grass. They were breathing hard. They had obviously been chasing this scent for a while.

The one that had been in front was now second, for a brown, yellow-eyed, much stronger-looking wolf was racing ahead with unbelievable speed.

I knew their hunting tactics. Wolves know that large prey can be dangerous to them if the prey decides to fight back. But a pack of wolves hunt as a team, almost always getting what they want done. What they want is to get their prey running. That way, they can chase it out until it's too tired, or too slow, or even just until it makes a wrong move – its fatal move. The alpha leads the hunt, so the new one – the brown one that had replaced the first one – must have been the alpha.

Once they've got their prey, they surround it, preparing to make the kill. They bite and tear the animal apart, feasting on its flesh, leaving the rest for other animals, mostly carrion-feeders, to have their turn, creatures such as vultures or hyenas. The hyena in particular will locate the carcass by the smell, or the sound of others feeding, or by watching birds of prey like the vulture descend to the dead body to eat.

Sometimes, if another animal is interrupting a wolf hunt, the wolves will make sure to get the interfering animal out of the way before moving on. I have seen wolves fight bears and coyotes that have been interfering.

I knew very well our rules about interfering with animals hunting, but I couldn't stand it, even knowing what usually happened to others that tried to take away prey from wolves. But I knew these deer, and they were like family to me. If I could just lead the deer to safety, and get the wolves to go away…

I could still see them being chased. I took a breath and ran, just as I had on the day the bear had chased me, as if my life depended on it.

The deer were circling, coming back this way. They shot past me, and the wolves slowed down, noticing me blocking their way. If I went out of the way, they would continue pursuing the deer. I had to draw their attention even more.

So I picked up a rough boomerang-shaped stick, and threw it at the alpha's head.

It roared and they all reared up in anger and started to pursue me. We were at the area of grass by the hyena's lair. I needed to get up onto a tree. I continued running, heading for the Eagles Trees. No, I couldn't go there. Storm, Slare, and Spyra would be in danger. So I went for the Lions Tree.

I passed the trees where my friends were, having no idea what was happening, but the wolves were advancing quickly. I needed to get there. And, after plenty of running, I finally did.

I whipped out my knife, and jumped as high as I could, stabbing it into one of the low branches. I climbed up, but not in time. One of the wolves, a black one, jumped up and bit my right foot, its huge jaw snapping closed as hard as it could. I screamed, and the wolf dropped back down, taking my bloody shoe with it.

Whimpering in pain, I climbed up a few more branches until I was at a height that they couldn't get me at. They continued jumping though.

I looked down at my foot, and almost screamed again. My foot was covered in sticky blood, but that wasn't the worst of it. Two of my toes had been bitten right off, severed from my very foot. It was pain like I'd never felt before. I'd gotten scratches, but even the ones that Black Amber had given me didn't hurt as much as this. Blood rushed out like water from a broken dam. I could only imagine how Earthum must have felt when his hand had been bitten off, although he may have been dead long before that.

I looked down, and saw that the wolves were being chased away by a huge, muscular lion. It was gigantic, with a messy mane of hair, and a long tail. It roared loudly, and the wolves scattered. It yawned like this was a normal, everyday thing, and went back to the base of the tree, lying down lazily by a female.

I looked back at my horrible foot, just a few stumps, covered in blood. And it was everywhere, dripping down the branch into a large puddle on the ground. Think of your worst injury, the one that gave you the most pain, and multiply that by a thousand. Got it? You're not even close.

This was a big problem. I was losing way too much blood much too fast, and my vision was blurring. And there was no one around to help me. So I grabbed a large leaf that was hanging near me from a tree branch and ripped it of its stem, wrapping it around my foot.

And how it hurt.

It was like putting lemon, or salt, on a wound. No, not even close to that, much worse. This would be there to remind me for the rest of my life.

I made sure it was secure, and tried to lower myself down, but failed, and crashed down to the floor. Luckily, the lion didn't notice somehow, and continued to rest. Or maybe it did but was just too lazy to do anything about it.

I limped off to the Eagles Trees, and after five minutes slumped on the ground, moaning, right outside the trees.

I heard voices die down, and then all three of the people who were in there came rushing out.

'Oh my god…' gasped Slare.

Storm stared wide-eyed, and asked if I was okay.

Spyra wasted no time. She rushed back into the trees and came out with the first-aid kit, instantly wrapping my foot up, wincing as she put it on. She was no fan of blood, I could tell. Well, neither was I.

I told them what had happened. The whole story, starting from the deer, then answered their many questions.

'Can you walk?' Storm asked.

'Barely…'

'Wolves did that to you?' said Slare, recovering from her brief shock.

I nodded. *I* was in shock. No animal had ever done something this bad to me before. But the good side was that Cervus and Imber were safe now. Two toes for two lives were definitely worth it. But this was so much. This injury was something that would change my life. I just couldn't believe it had actually happened. If I'd been just a second faster, I might have gotten to safety in time. If I had known this would happen, I would have them with me right now … right?

But the pain was horrible. It was impossible. I couldn't believe that a human could stand it without dying, for that was what I had wanted when I had received the injury. Death. You've probably had an experience when you've wanted only death as well.

I was still trying to imagine when I had seen so much blood. More than I'd ever seen in one place before. I wondered how much I'd lost. I felt very weak. Not at all in good condition for when we entered the Black Trees.

Slare seemed to be thinking the same thing.

'We can't go with you in this state,' she said, looking at my bandaged foot.

I knew what she meant. *I* couldn't go in this state. The others would have no problem. But I wanted to go. I really did. I knew animals, and could protect the group from them. Black Amber was my problem too, and I wanted to see it resolved.

'You guys go ahead,' I said, averting my eyes from their faces.

'No,' said Storm, shaking his head. 'We can't. You need to come with us. No matter what pain you feel, Wolf, we need you.'

'Yeah,' agreed Spyra. 'You're the expert.'

'Since when have Elrolians started to trust human so much they need their help?'

'I don't believe that all humans are as evil as Hunter. And a human killed my father. But I don't see why that means that every other human is evil too. I trust you,' Storm said, his face expressionless, yet his eyes full of emotion.

He trusted me. I felt privileged to know that.

'But still, this might be too much for Wolf to handle,' said Slare.

I thought about this. I knew she meant well, but I didn't want her thinking me useless because of this injury. But we couldn't wait too long. 'A day,' I said. 'We can stay and rest up for a day, then move on.'

'That seems fair,' said Slare, nodding in agreement.

'Deal,' said Spyra.

So we set down our stuff, and lay against the bark of the massive trees. I realised how tired I really was. Crash, who had been running in large circles seemed to be tired too, so he came to me, and curled up on my chest, licking my chin, and biting my long hair.

I smiled to myself and looked up at the trees, and how the light shined in rays through the branches. Then I heard the laughing, but not from an animal. I wasn't sure how exactly, but knew it was from a living creature with one intention – death.

LYPHERACE

Crash sprang to his feet and leaped off me, which hurt a lot, although obviously not as much as the other injuries I'd received today.

'Oh, not again,' sighed Storm wearily.

'Storm, if you want to go deal with this yourself, you're welcome to,' I said.

This was turning into an everyday thing. I heard the laughing again, and that was when I realised it was human. It was normal laughter, unlike that of the hyena. And I heard voices too.

'That's enough! It's not funny … those things are disgusting,' one voice muttered.

'Yeah, well what'd you expect would happen, when a vulture sees a dead animal, huh? You expect it to leave it alone?'

The voices were deep, and sounded evil.

'Yeah, but it was our kill!' the first one said in an almost whiny voice.

'I told you already, they don't care, Starlio! It's free food to those monsters.'

'Okay, okay. But you know he'll be mad. He wanted some deer skin, and we don't have any no more.'

We were silent, listening absorbedly.

Slare frowned. 'They killed a deer?' she mouthed to me.

I nodded gravely, and then continued listening.

'Listen, this is a forest. It's like a zoo. There'll be plenty more for us to take.'

The one called Starlio replied in a quiet tone. 'What if we see a shadow wolf?'

'Don't worry, he said that as long as we wear the armour on our arm, they wouldn't attack us. They know we mean no harm ... to them, at least.'

Storm frowned. 'Shadow wolf?' he mouthed.

I shrugged. I didn't have any idea what that was. But I did have an idea of who they were. They were hunters. They wanted to kill a deer for its skin. And from what I'd heard, they'd already killed one.

I had heard enough. I was about to jump out and attack, when the one of the people grunted, and I heard fighting. People breathing hard, flesh and bone clashing against another human's skin, and then I heard someone running, and then silence.

I mean real silence. I couldn't hear anyone breathe anymore. It was like I was alone, and the others had left. It was truly suspenseful.

I turned back around and jumped, as I saw a man I'd never seen before staring at us. He had a short black beard, a headset (I mean the thing that spies usually have coming down to their mouths), and a silver and black suit that covered him like stretchable rubber, which must have given him a lot of movement, for there wasn't armour that got in the way or anything, yet it was rather bulky. It was very cool, something worthy of

Viper's workshop. He had black sunglasses – you know, the type that other people can't see through, that made him look really spy-like and intimidating. Everywhere I looked on him he seemed to have some type of fancy equipment, yet it didn't make him look too … weird.

Storm jumped to his feet, and there was a lot of blurry commotion and then we were all in chains on the floor, even Storm, with the stranger hardly breaking a sweat.

I was amazed that anyone could have chained Storm or Spyra, and certainly not together, but he had the element of surprise, kind of.

'I'm agent Lypherace, from the Wildlife Intelligence and Life Defence- WILD, for short. I know, it hardly makes any sense, but it sound good,' he said apologetically. 'I place you under my custody for killing animals.'

In an instant we were angrily protesting, and Storm and Spyra somehow freed themselves, stepping up in front of the man.

'We would never!' we shouted.

Storm dropped his axe, which he'd used to break the chain, and smashed agent Lypherace against the tree, holding him in place by his neck. Not hard, but so he couldn't escape.

'I'm Storm Orthoclase, an Elrolian, and I have never in my life attacked an animal.'

Storm let go, but the agent stood there, staring.

'Hear us out,' I said. And I told him about the Animal Defence Organisation, which he seemed to recognise. He immediately apologised to all of us.

'I'm sorry. I thought you were hunters, like him,' he said to us, nodding in disgust at the man he'd tied up, and who was laid against the tree, and who had obviously been knocked out. One of them had gotten away. 'Wait, these aren't yours, are they?'

'No,' I said. 'They're hunters alright.'

'I'm once again very sorry. I'm an agent, and my job is to capture hunters that try to interfere with animals or nature. I work for a secret organisation known as Delta. The whole WILD thing was kind of a lie.... So, yeah, we've received word that some terrorist is forming a team of about a hundred hunters in Spheria, and for over two months now has been sending them to places to destroy nature and kill animals. We're trying to stop that. We're the people who deal with the really significant problems ... like this one.'

'With skills like that, you should be in the Elrolian castle right now,' said Spyra, impressed.

'Why thank you,' he said, nodding his head gratefully.

'Spyra,' she said, introducing herself. We followed her lead, shaking his hand and giving him our names. Like me, he seemed to have only one name. Or at least he only gave one. If it was his last or first name, I wasn't sure.

'So what are you people doing out here?' he asked us.

We explained to him how we'd encountered Black Amber, and why we were here now. It seemed that he was familiar with the concept of a great black flying creature.

I could tell he was interested. 'Could I come along?' he asked.

Of course, we agreed, and he went off to get his bag.

'You're all sure about this?' Spyra asked.

'Yeah,' I said. 'He seems okay. I've never heard of Delta before, though.'

'I don't think we're supposed to have. It sounds like a kind of top secret organization,' said Storm.

He came back a few minutes later with a massive camping bag.

'You moving houses?' I muttered.

'Not quite yet,' he said, smiling.

'I've packed my essential equipment with me.' He caught sight of Crash. 'Who's this?'

'That's Crash,' Slare explained. 'He decided to come along with us here.'

'Well, he's one brave goat.'

'Yes he is,' I said, watching him jump up on Lypherace, looking for food.

I threw a few rocks to him, and he caught them in his mouth in midair, crunching madly.

'Whoa, what happened to your foot, man?' he asked, staring in horror.

'A wolf,' I said dismissively. I hated drawing attention to myself.

'What?'

'It bit two off my toes off.'

'Oh man. That's horrible. I'm sorry to hear it.'

'Well, it could have been worse,' I said, sighing.

'We should go before more hunters come and try to attack us,' said Slare.

'No, we can't. There's still at least one hunter out there right now who's going to try and kill a deer, remember?' Spyra said.

'Right,' I said. 'We need to track him down.'

'How?' Storm asked.

'He could be anywhere.'

'I can try and locate him,' said Lypherace. 'I have some equipment that could help. I put a tracker on him in case I lost him.'

He unpacked his huge bag and took out loads of radars, and wires, and computer screens, doing a lot of complex things to the equipment, occasionally digging through his bag.

Storm and Spyra had lived in Elrolia for most of their lives, and had never seen anything like it. They would ask Lypherace questions, and he would answer, full of enthusiasm.

In less than five minutes he had discovered where the hunter that had escaped was.

'He's by … this place,' he said, showing me a map, pointing to an area very close to where we were.

'Do you want him for questioning?' I asked.

'Yeah,' he said nodding.

'Then we'd better get him soon, because he's approaching the hyena territory. They'll rip him apart.'

'Wolf, he isn't like us,' said Slare gently. 'He will kill the hyenas.'

She was right. Just because I would never kill an animal, didn't mean that others wouldn't either. He was a *hunter.* He did this for a job. My job was to protect the animals, and his was to kill them.

'We need to go get him,' I said.

'You can't,' said Slare. 'Not like this. You'll be very disadvantaged.'

'Don't worry,' said Lypherace cheerfully. 'I've got the perfect solution.'

He started to dig through his camping bag, and pulled out two silver and black objects, that looked rather like ice skates, just without the blade. Instead it had a rubbery black thing that jutted out like an animal's leg.

I frowned. I had never seen anything like this before. 'What are they?'

'My own personal invention,' he said proudly. 'I call them … well I don't really know what to call them. Anyway, they'll help. See, they help secure your foot, so it makes sure trees will bash it, not your feet, and it won't irritate them. Plus, I built them for special terrain uses, so it can keep you steady on land, rocks, grass, even ice. You can keep them.'

'Thanks.' I examined them more carefully. The bottom (the rubbery bit) was padded with small rubber spikes. I pressed a button on the side, and out of the blunt rubber spikes came sharp steel ones. On the sides were symbols. Silver, leafless trees.

'Is that the WILD team's logo?'

'Yeah. I voted for a mountain, but the others thought this was better.'

'How many of you are there?' I asked.

'Oh, not that many. Including me, nine.'

'Nine?' said Spyra. 'Is that enough to defend and explore nature?'

Lypherace smiled. 'Yeah. Trust me, we're very skilled. The best of the best, you know. Maybe not me, but the others,' he said modestly.

'No, man,' said Storm, 'you're amazing.'

He smiled again. 'Thanks.'

'How long have you been doing this?' Slare asked.

'Fifteen years actually.'

'Wow,' Slare said in surprise.

'Well we should start to go now,' Storm said. 'We've waited much too long. I think Wolf's as ready as he'll ever be with your shoe things. Where is the hunter now?'

Lypherace checked the map. 'Still there. The same place.'

'Let's go,' I said, finishing fastening my leg brace. It really was helpful. I couldn't feel a thing. It was as if nothing had happened to my toes. And it made me fifty times faster. It was like springs, throwing your body forward, but also like running at the same time.

'Wait, what about him?' Spyra asked, pointing in disgust with her foot at the hunter Lypherace had captured.

'He'll be fine, trust me. The net he's in is top of the line. He won't be getting out of that anytime soon.'

'Okay, then, let's go,' said Slare.

I scooped up Crash, and held him in a secure grip in my arms, then raced foreward at an alarming speed. An awesome, incredible speed. I could just imagine being a cheetah, this speed being normal for them.

On the short way there, I had a thought that rather puzzled

me. When we had gone with Peldor to Elrolia, we had had no obstacles or anything that stopped us. We just easily went to Elrolia, just like that. But now, going to the Black Trees, we had encountered hyenas, wolves, skeleton monsters that wanted lunch very badly, and hunters, and I was sure there was more to come. It was like someone was trying to stop us.

For a minute I thought that there was a possibility that Hunter was doing all this, but then I convinced myself that it couldn't be true. How could he know what we were doing? We'd discussed it all in camp.

In seconds I was standing at the edge of the hyena territory, at a safe distance, waiting for the others to catch up. I saw no sign of the hunter.

Crash stared up at me with his round yellowish eyes. Unlike humans, instead of a *round* black thing in the centre, they had a straight vertical line. I looked back at him.

'What?'

I got down to my knees and he rubbed his head against my bearded chin.

'Okay. But just until they get here.'

I adjusted my grip on Crash, and used my free hand to rub his head. He pawed my arm. That meant he wanted it harder. I did it harder, but he didn't seem to think so. He pawed of my arm again, telling me to keep still, and he did it how he liked it, his own way.

'Okay, but I'm sorry, they're here now.'

'Any sign of him?' Storm asked, looking around carefully.

I shook my head, getting to my feet. 'No. Not at all.'

'Well I think we've learned from our other adventures *not* to split up.'

'I agree.'

We all searched the rocks with our eyes and saw nothing for a while. Until …

'There!' Slare whispered, and we all sped out, Lypherace in

the lead. And he was fast. He was extremely fast. As fast as me even with the feet things on. Of course, he'd been training for fifteen years. He climbed up the rocks like a hyena (they're good at climbing) and threw himself off the tall rock.

It looked like slow motion. He fell, his arms spread out like wings, and the hunter turned, just in time to see Lypherace before he smashed him down on the ground with his feet.

But that wasn't all. The hunter whipped out a knife, and stabbed Lypherace's leg.

I saw blood spill out like crazy, running down his leg like rain down a window, completely soaking his suit.

The hunter tried to dig it in more, but Lypherace roared in rage, and grabbed him by the face. And with impossible strength, he flung the hunter straight into the rock, where he collided with the mass of stone.

Lypherace sank to his knees. I ran up to him.

'Are you okay?' I averted my eyes slightly. I just couldn't help myself. I mean the knife was still in his leg, the handle just visible.

I motioned for the others to stay back. He needed some space.

I looked back, just as he grabbed the knife and yanked it out, holding back a scream. Blood rushed out, as bad as when I'd lost my toes.

Spyra rushed over as well and handed over a bandage.

'No,' he groaned. 'The bottle.'

'You need to stop the bleeding!'

He didn't listen. He grabbed the small bottle from the first aid kit, and poured it on his injury, inside the large tear in his outfit. He winced, but I saw his suit close up and repair itself, like two bits of water joining together.

'That'll stop it,' he said, as if nothing had happened. Man, this guy was tough.

He picked up the knife by the blade, and dropped it into a

zip-lock bag from the first-aid kit. He zipped it up and stuffed it into his pocket.

He went to the hunter and crouched down. 'Who are you?'

The man groaned, and muttered something, barely loud enough to hear it. 'Garmax.'

'Did you kill any animals?' I said furiously.

He smiled tauntingly. 'Yes. A deer.'

I narrowed my eyes.

He coughed and continued smiling, looking at me this time. 'Are you going to kill me in return?'

I badly wanted to say yes, but of course, I wouldn't. Never. I would be as bad as he was. So I didn't answer.

'Whom do you work for?' Lypherace asked, cautiously rubbing his leg.

'It was under the President's orders.'

'And how many more hunters are here, besides you and your friend?'

'None. But you will find answers in Alria.'

Lypherace nodded, and turned back to us. Garmax shot to his feet and pulled out a second knife, but just as soon as he had, somehow Lypherace was holding the knife across his throat, and had the hunter's arms in pair of black handcuffs, his free hand gripping them tightly.

'Those handcuffs will tighten when you struggle, so don't be an idiot and cut off your circulation,' Lypherace warned cheerfully.

He's amazing.

'How did you do that?' Storm asked.

'Fifteen years, man.'

'Wait, where is he?' Slare asked, looking over Lypherace's shoulder.

'He's …' I turned.

The handcuffs were on the ground, unbroken. The hunter

was nowhere to be seen. It had been but a second! But there was a trace, a pile of black ash. Just like when Shade had vanished.

'Darkness,' I murmured.

Slare nodded. 'Like with Shade.'

'Wait, you've seen this before?'

Slare nodded, and explained.

'Wait,' said Storm. 'If he can do it ...'

He looked at Lypherace. 'The other hunter.'

Lypherace turned to me. 'Wolf, can you go check? We'll catch up to you.'

'Sure.'

I scooped Crash up again into my arms, and started to run.

I had a bad feeling about this, but I checked anyway. We had had a lot of, well, horrible luck lately, and I didn't think it was about to change. If that hunter could escape like that while being metres away from two Elrolians, and three humans, than another one could probably do it while being alone.

I approached the trees, and heard nothing, nothing except the animals, and the trees. So I guess another way to say that is that I didn't hear our prisoner.

Sure enough, when I turned the corner, he wasn't anywhere to be seen. And he wasn't the only thing missing. He'd taken Lypherace's tracking computer. We wouldn't be able to find them anymore.

I let Crash back down, and he looked around, sniffing random things like they might be suspicious. Yeah, I know, we've got a little detective with us here. And he seemed to have found something.

He nudged my shoe, and nodded towards a clump of sticks. But not just any clump of sticks; it was a nest. The twigs were cleverly woven together, preventing it from falling apart. The inside was covered with soft moss that would comfort the birds inside.

There was only one bird inside it at the moment. It was a small golden eagle. Now you may not have heard of the golden eagle (yeah, I know, here I go again). The most famous of all eagles in the bald eagle, of course, and most people only really know about *them*, but I personally like the golden eagle more. I like animals that most people don't care about or know of. Although I still adore the bald eagle species.

Golden eagles prefer the cold, and these trees are perfect for it. This eagle was young, so its feathers were chocolate brown, with a few white patches on its neck and wings, and on its tail base.

Also in the nest was another eagle, dead. I knew why. You see, normally, two eggs are laid at the same time, and the first bird to hatch kills the other, giving the survivor access to all the food brought to the nest. Yeah, you think you've got family problems?

Golden eagles are birds of prey. They don't eat worms and stuff; they eat rabbits and other mountain birds. They are typically very fierce.

It looked up at me and seemed to be thinking, 'What do you think you're doing here, buddy?' Or something like that.

I wondered how it had gotten here. Probably some other bird had knocked the nest off.

Crash started eating some grass. I couldn't help feeling sorry for him, so I tossed him a large black rock that he crunched up with his hard little teeth, grinding it into dust before swallowing the powder.

I heard breathing, though not from Crash or the bird. I spun around, finding myself looking at a small cat. An ocelot, the national symbol of Spheria.

It resembled a jaguar with black spots, or at least outlines of spots. Unlike the jaguar, it was very small. It was about the size of a house cat. But don't let that fool you. I've seen them take down grown deer. They are not as innocent as they look.

Though it eats many things, like turtles, anteaters, monkeys, and other animals, they eat birds the most. This cat wanted the eagle. The bird was completely helpless. Free food, lying in an almost unguarded nest, nothing to stop the ocelot, except me.

I wouldn't just watch an ocelot killing an helpless little bird. I know, we have our rule, but what would you do? These are some of the challenges of being a wildlife ranger. These animals had to eat. But I still loved them all. I'd broken the rule with the wolves. Why not do it again? Maybe part of this was because of what Black Amber had done. Showing me that they could kill at will, and our own rules protected them from us. Once more. One final time I would save it.

When not hunting, the ocelot is quite beautiful. Normally it is a nocturnal hunter, but since when do animals pay any attention to little facts like that? The ocelot is very adaptable. It inhabits almost any place where food and water can be easily found, but they like places with lots of dense vegetation.

The cat looked at me dangerously. It wanted that eagle. I could see what it was thinking. Bird, *dead.*

THE BLACK TREES

'Don't even try it,' I muttered, watching the ocelot carefully.

In snarled, and reared back, ready to pounce. My eyes narrowed and we stared at each other. It leaped. In a high arch, in went right for my head. I ducked, but only just in time.

I whipped around and grabbed the nest, pulling it away just as the ocelot tried to seize the baby eagle with its sharp claws. It bared its teeth, growling quietly in its small throat.

'Go get food somewhere else,' I said.

It didn't listen. It jumped up, just about to scratch me, and I attempted to get out of its way, but ended up with its claws digging into my arm, stained with my blood.

Crash saw what was happening and came to my aid. He leaped up and smashed his little head against the ocelot's body.

It fell down and turned to the little goat, eyes filled with fury. I took this opportunity to get the nest to safety. I held it in one hand, and climbed up one of the tall trees using the other. Some of the branches were much too weak, and snapped when I placed too much weight on them. I got to a safe height and placed the nest there, then tried to climb safely down.

But just as I was starting to get down, I saw that the ocelot had injured Crash. His leg was bleeding badly.

The ocelot was going to kill him.

I looked down. I was very high up, maybe twelve metres or so. But I needed to save Crash. I jumped down, snatched the cat and lightly flung it away.

I felt pain in my back again, but it didn't hurt as much as other things have that I've felt.

I saw the cat get back up and snarl again, or do whatever cats do when they're angry. I hadn't wanted to hurt it, but I had no other choice.

It seemed to lose interest in us, or so I thought, until I realised it had been scared away by the others who'd just arrived.

'Wolf!' said Storm, running up to me, and looking at Crash. 'What happened?'

I told them the story while I fixed Crash's leg. In two minutes it was not perfect, but better. I had bandaged it, and put on a small brace to stabilise it, so he could run without it getting any worse.

'An ocelot did that?' Spyra asked. 'Wow.'

'Aren't they the symbol of Spheria?' Slare asked me.

'Yeah,' I said bitterly. 'Spheria doesn't deserve it.'

'Guys, if those people are working for Hunter, which I'm pretty sure they are, then he's already here for all we know, planning his attack. We can't give him time.'

'So you're saying we should go now?' Spyra asked.

'Yes. Like, right now.'

Lypherace nodded and packed all of his things quickly into his bag, until it looked as if we'd never been here. 'I'm going to leave my stuff in one of these trees. I don't really want to have to haul it through those ones,' he said, nodding at the dead-looking black trees. 'They took my computer,' he added severely.

'Yeah,' agreed Slare. 'We should put our stuff there too.'

I offered to take it up, but Slare insisted she did, so she and Lypherace quickly climbed up one of the trees, and placed our bags carefully on one of the sturdy, thick branches. I have to admit, with hunters roaming around here, I wasn't too happy that we were leaving our things out in the open, but it was the best thing to do.

We approached the river around the Black Trees, the water lashing against the banks like a bear in a cage, trying to give itself more space to flow. But it was flowing all right. The rapids were threating to sweep away the stones in the water, and most of it was white foam. I saw occasional fishes through the water, but not many. The bears would love this place. But I guess it's just too close to the Black Trees for them. Much too close.

'How do we cross?' Slare asked.

'The stones?' suggested Storm.

'No...' I said, thinking carefully. What supplies did we have with us that could help us? We needed to make some sort of bridge or raft to get across the water. I thought back to how we'd gotten across the waterfall. Ardor. But that Orian wasn't here with us.

Wait ... an *Orian*. In the Seven Gates, Clustus, leader of the Element of Ice had made an ice bridge over the lava with his elemental ice knives. We had an elemental ice weapon. And we needed a bridge. If Clustus could create an ice bridge over lava and have it stand up to the heat, surely we could create one over water.

'Storm, your axe.'

He frowned for a second, then understood. 'I don't know,

Wolf. I've never tried using elemental power with this before.'

'We're losing time! Every second! We need Black Amber, and we need them quickly. Try it!' I urged.

He went up closer to the river, until he was at the very edge of the land. He took his axe out of the straps on his back, and held it firmly in his hand.

We all watched intently as he raised the axe, and, concentrating as hard as he could, he thrust it forward. Nothing happened. Then, the axe started to glow icy blue and growing brighter at an alarmingly fast rate. Out from the blade of the axe shot a stream of water that froze into pure, crystal-clear ice.

Storm took a few steps back, but was only surprised for a few seconds. Then he smiled, and ran across the bridge, keeping his axe in hand just in case.

He stopped at the other side of the river, and invited us across.

'Awesome,' he said. 'That is, like, way too impossible to be possible.'

One by one, we crossed over his makeshift bridge.

'Should I destroy it for now?' he asked uncertainly.

'Yeah,' said Lypherace. 'We don't want to be followed.'

He made sure we were all across, then held his axe high above his head and swung it down. The moment the axe made contact, the bridge shattered into a million pieces, littering the water with tiny shards of ice.

The skeleton eyes on the axe momentarily glowed icy blue again, then, like lights in a game show, they slowly dimmed, until there was no light left.

Now we were at the Black Trees. We were actually here. Searching for Black Amber in the dark, almost dead forest.

Why are the trees black? There are many stories I have been told over the years. I don't exactly know which one I believe. I can tell you some of the tales I have heard.

One of the simple stories that Stream had told me before was that they had once been marvelous trees, and then were poisoned by a hunter, killing them. Why did the hunter do it? Stream said no one knows. I didn't quite believe that story.

Lance told me they were Elkwood trees, burnt down by an uncontrolled forest fire. That made sense. Elkwood, as I said before, is extremely strong. Fire would harm it, but not kill it. The Black Trees were not dead. This seemed the more logical explanation. Yet, like the other story, there was a flaw. As I said before, Elkwood trees usually grow separately, far from one another. The Black Trees grew close together, providing a fantastic protection from sunlight. There were, however, some places where there were no, or at least few, trees in an area.

Each of the trees looked like a monster, growing slowly out of the brown grass and dirt. Many of them had no leaves, and those that did were blackened with many holes in them. On the leaves was what looked like torn black fabric, or maybe it was ripped leaves too.

It was strange. Looking back across the river it looked like a paradise. Fresh running water, healthy green leaves, and elegant trees. Looking the opposite direction gave you the sense that you were stepping into a nightmare. It was like in one of those movies, someone goes into the dark, old, dilapidated house, and you know right from the start that something bad is about to happen. Or at least it felt like that. You always want to tell them, no, don't go in the creepy house you idiot!

Now, where would we find Black Amber? The Black Trees covered a huge area of Wouldlock. It was mostly very dark in there, but like I said, there were some places that were unoccupied by trees.

Slare was thinking along the same lines. 'Where do we begin?' she asked.

'We might as well just go in, for a start,' said Lypherace.

We slowly and carefully entered the darkness, looking

down to make sure we didn't trip on anything. None of us wanted the dirty ground to have anything to do with our fragile faces, faces that had seen more than enough dirt and blood for one day.

I saw loads of the animals and bugs and other creatures that you really don't want described to you. Especially not if you've just eaten. I did see some amazing creatures, though. I saw a massive anaconda, and also, up in the trees, a beautiful Lorothian Shadow Eagle. Even in the dark it's easy to identify these unique animals.

So we went in, searching for Black Amber. We weren't exactly looking under leaves (although considering the size, they might have been there), but I didn't know what I was expecting to find. Would I find a pack of the creatures sleeping in a tree, maybe? Having a kind of meeting? Either way, it would be hard to spot them in the darkness. I know I said the others were easier to see, but not a creature of that colour and speed. It would blend in wonderfully with the trees and darkness.

'Is that it?' Spyra asked in a whisper, nodding towards a large black animal.

We froze.

I looked carefully. It too stopped moving. Then it stepped forward one step, landing its face in a ray of bright sunlight. No, it was not Black Amber. But close. It was a wolf. An especially large wolf. Its rough fur was an extremely dark shade of brown, like an Elkwood tree, or maybe a little darker. It was stunning. It was everything that a good, healthy wolf should be. Immensely strong, long legged, making it very fast, and from its look, it seemed that it got plenty of food easily enough. It had intimidating yellow eyes that bored into me like an x-ray machine. The point of its snout was lighter, though – almost white. So were its paws.

It growled deep down in its throat.

'Slowly walk away,' I said to them, my toes tingling. I just didn't want *another* wild chase. It might cost me more than toes this time.

Luckily, it dismissed us and prowled on through the darkness. Yeah, I know, just like that.

I wondered how a wolf had gotten across here. It may have crossed the rocks, though I don't know how or why. Hunting purposes? I highly doubted it.

I went ahead to catch up with the rest of the team.

'You okay then Wolf?' Storm asked. 'All eight toes?'

'Yeah, I'm fine. It was just passing.'

'Wait, where's Crash?' Slare asked, her voice showing no laughter.

We all searched around the area. It was dark, but there were a few beams of sunlight shining down on us.

'He did cross with us right?' Lypherace said.

'Yeah, he did,' I said, racking my brain to remember where I'd last seen him. I'd carried him across the bridge then let him down, and he'd walked ahead a bit, then…

'Tracks!' Spyra said nodding at a patch of light that was shining over a few small hoof prints.

I raced ahead again, totally forgetting to be quiet. My modified shoes made tons of noise against the ground and tree roots, and crackly dead leaves.

I only lost the track a few times, but always caught it again. He couldn't have gone far with his damaged leg, so at least I would find him in here soon.

I looked ahead and saw him. He was curled up on the ground, his little chest rising and falling. Luckily, no animal had found him before I had. Plenty of predators out there would love a snack like a goat. Lucky that that wolf hadn't got to him.

I picked him up gently. Why had he ever come? This was much too dangerous for him. He didn't even have horns to protect himself with!

Then I heard Slare's voice. 'Wolf! We found it!'

A few seconds later, all four of them came out of the darkness, panting. Wait, not four. Five.

With them was another creature. Its body structure was human-like, but it looked reptilian, with green-grey and brown scales, metallic-looking, like silver. This was something Storm had told me about before. A Lanxian.

I stared at it. Not exactly polite, huh? Why were these people presenting to me this creature like it was a golden medal? I mean, saying, *we found it?* Seriously? What, were they actually looking for a Lanxian?

I saw that Storm and Spyra weren't exactly thrilled. Seeing how they'd had a confrontation against the Lanxians at Elrolia, It was clear why.

'Did you find Crash?' Storm asked.

'Yeah,' I said, distracted, stepping into the light to show them the goat. 'And who'd you find?'

'Our translator,' said Slare.

'Our … oh.' This was the creature that could supposedly translate for us when we encountered Black Amber. I hadn't even thought about it.

'We found him in a cave,' said Lypherace smiling. Not a *funny* type of smile, but a genuine smile that seemed etched in his face permanently, that I hadn't seen him without since … never. People say smiling makes you live longer. Lypherace will live a long time.

I stepped up to the Lanxian, rather awkwardly.

I tugged nervously on my T-shirt. 'Hello. I'm Wolf. We need your help.'

The Lanxian stared at me.

'Can you help us?' I said, louder.

For a second I thought we had the wrong Lanxian, but then, ever so slightly, it nodded.

'I feel like an evil school principal,' I muttered to myself.

Suddenly Lypherace yelled out to me in warning, and just as I ducked, not having a clue what was going on, he shot over my head like a gymnast. As I rapidly turned around, I saw a quick glimpse of Black Amber, just like I'd seen before: the thick black fur, the wings, and the diving knife-claws.

Lypherace had single-handedly tackled it, protecting me from those teeth that had been so intent on ripping me up.

Storm also jumped in, pulled Lypherace off, and with a spin of his axe, the creature was frozen solid in a layer of two-inch thick ice. The only free part of its body was his head. The creature growled, desperately trying to free the rest of itself. It seemed to shine, or at least the bits of it in the light did.

The Lanxian frowned. He opened his mouth to talk, turning to Storm and Spyra, who I imagined had caught the creature.

He spoke extremely slowly, in a rasping voice. 'You want me to … talk to it?'

Lypherace walked back to us. 'Yes.'

Slare nodded as well. 'We need you to help us communicate with them.'

The Lanxian nodded slowly. 'Yes.'

I shifted around uncomfortably, until I couldn't stand it. We were treating it like a … a bad student. I didn't know its name, or even gender.

'Do you have a name?' I asked, trying to be kind.

'Yes. I am Altralz. I am from Lexanuth.'

'Okay. Thank you for helping us, Altralz.'

Altralz nodded.

'Let's go a bit further first,' said Spyra.

We continued walking past the frozen Black Amber. We were obviously quite close.

I walked to Storm and looked at him. He seemed to know what I was about to ask.

'Female,' he said. 'The males don't have the spiky spine. Females do.'

I squinted back at Altralz and saw that she did indeed have a thorny spine. Like that dinosaur, you know? I mean, not *that* big, but similar.

Then, I saw them – all of them. Not just the original dozen I'd seen at my first encounter, but about thirty, maybe more. Thirty fierce Black Amber, all together, right in front of us.

We all froze, each seeing the same thing at the same time. Sadly, the time we had seen them was when we were about thirty metres from them. And if I'd learned anything, it was that these creatures had mighty keen eyesight. I hated to say it, but Hunter had done an exceedingly good job with them.

The green-eyed one was in the middle of the circle they'd formed, and it had turned all of its attention on us.

I was surprised they weren't attacking immediately. What were they waiting for? Did they want us to come closer? I looked over my shoulder and saw that Altralz was walking towards them, seemingly of her own free will.

She came to a halt five metres away from the closest one, which gazed at her affectionately. Did they know each other? I wasn't sure.

Then, something strange occurred. They communicated. No, not English. That would be incredible, and stupid. This is not a fairytale. The Lanxian gave a range of barks and deep growls. The same way a Black Amber would. The green-eyed creature responded in another assortment of growls.

It really was absolutely incredible. Two animals of different species, one of which was human-created, were actually talking together. Just imagine what things we could learn from that!

'They're talking' I whispered in awe.

The others silently nodded.

Storm went up to Altralz and spoke something in her ear. He was telling her what to say to them. They continued talking, and I saw the Black Amber pack start to settle down. They might start to agree!

After a few more long minutes of watching, Altralz nodded to Storm.

'One minute,' Storm said.

He came over to us and smiled.

'I think we may have got them! She told them about our side, and Hunter's, and what they'll gain on ours, and lose on Hunter's. Anything to add?'

'Yeah,' said Slare. 'Thank them for not ripping us apart.'

Storm smiled. 'Sure.'

He went back and nodded to Altralz, then whispered something else. Why whisper though? We were standing next to Black Amber. Whispering wouldn't do anything. Although I guess I would whisper too if I were in that situation.

He walked back quickly.

'They say they'll help us, but on three conditions. We don't harm them, first of all. Also, they don't have to answer to our commands.'

I frowned.

'They mean they don't want to be useless. They want to help discuss what to do, not have us doing all the planning.'

'Okay, that works,' I said.

'And they want better protection.'

'What?' I exclaimed. 'They have Elrolian Onyxus!'

'They don't know that.'

'Tell them,' Spyra said simply.

He went back, and relayed our information, and after a suspenseful minute, he turned and smiled yet again.

'They're with us.'

I breathed out a sigh of relief. We had, on our own side, Black Amber.

PART II

THE ELROLIAN

THE HUNT OF WOULDLOCK

Allow me to clarify this. *I am not Wolf.* I am Storm Orthoclase, son of Aria and Elrace Orthoclase. Being an Elrolian, I see things differently from the perspective of a human. I am much more cautious, observant, and powerful, and much more modest. No, I'm kidding about all that. I am trained well, unlike most humans. I am born with a specialty in my blood. All of these things I mostly chose to be. Any human could be this way – except for missing the Onyxus in their blood. I suppose there may be a way of injecting it into you humans, but I've never heard of it. Elrolians tend to have higher expectations of themselves, and therefore are usually more powerful.

Anyway, first, I am constantly on the lookout for anything suspicious. Whenever entering a building, or a closed and unknown area, the first thing I do is search for all possible ways out. This is essential. You never want to be trapped in any situation. You should always know everything about where you are, and what things you can use to your advantage in your environment.

Second, I devote much of my time to learning important things. For example, I spent twenty years of my life training in combat, survival, and archery. The first step in life is learning how to defend yourself. So that is what I did. If you don't need to know something, don't learn it at all. I am sure that when you were in school you thought some of the things you learned were absolutely meaningless. When will you need to know how to draw a perfect circle? Or what the sums of the angles on a triangle are? Who cares about those types of things?

But let's move on. Survival is the next step. Sometimes, the biggest threat is not how to protect yourself from weapons or humans, but from nature. You need no know how to survive in any situation imaginable. It is not worthless to know. You may think that these skills will never be needed. But they can be. It is something you must know. It's like a car. You wear your seatbelt for safety (or at least you *should*, for I know people from other Eromies that drive and don't care about them – stupid, I know), and this is so that if you crash, you don't die, but you almost never actually come across a situation when you need the seatbelt, or one where it's injury or death. It's the same as survival. You can be prepared without knowing for certain you will need the skills. You get the idea.

Now the fourth thing is trust. When Hunter betrayed the Elrolians, that time so many years ago, we never gave trust to any human again. Well, I did. My mother, my dearest friend Emrax Treestone – a specialist in survival and the element of nature – and I, and a few others, all still had the belief that not all humans were bad. We believed in trust.

That is why I trusted Wolf and Slare and their team. Some people are bad, yes, but some people are wonderful. It is a privilege for me to share company with these fantastic people.

Just because one is bad, it does not mean it is the same for all. I don't know why the other Elrolians don't see it like this as well.

So, we'd just finished convincing the Black Amber creatures to support us instead of Hunter. It wasn't easy. You see, they don't really have a sense of justice. They don't know that what Hunter is doing is wrong. They do know that he created them. It really was difficult, but, as you can see, not impossible.

Now, we all knew that Hunter is going to come and attack. He wanted revenge for something that occurred a long time ago. So he would come, and destroy everything in his way. It was inevitable. But we also knew that when he came, we would be prepared to fight back. Millions of lives, even species, were in danger. When the time came, we would need to gather all the forces we could. And that time was coming very, very soon.

Hunter wanted revenge on Ravenwood. Wolf told me that earlier. But why come here, to Elrolia? Maybe Ravenwood wasn't the only one being hunted. Maybe there was someone else out there as well. I felt sorry for them. They would be hunted until they were worse than dead. How could you live knowing that? The answer: you couldn't.

And I honestly didn't know I if would be able to do anything about it. But if I could, I would. All – or I should say *most* – people simply want to survive. They don't want to be killed. But of course they wouldn't be. Not by Hunter. As I say, he would give them much worse.

So I started to talk with the team again, discussing what we needed to do next.

'Listen,' said Wolf, 'we need to get more allies. Just Black Amber isn't enough.'

Slare nodded. 'He's right. How about Wolf, Lypherace, and I go back to camp and round up the team and explain what's happening, and you and Spyra go to Spheria,' she said to me.

'Yeah, you can get the rest of your team, sure, but why should we go to Spheria?'

'Beause if the President is under Hunter's control, he may have information! You go to his office and get it out of him.'

Spyra nodded. 'Good plan. But who will stay with Black Amber?'

'They don't really need taking care of. But I guess Altralz could stay?' Wolf said.

I turned to Altralz and told her our plan. She nodded, and passed the message on to the Black Amber leader (I assumed the green-eyed one was in charge).

'They're okay with that,' I said. 'How 'bout we meet up at your camp in … four hours?'

'Sure,' Slare said.

So just like that, we went our separate ways, leaving Altralz and Black Amber there in the Black Trees. On our way out, we only saw some minor animals, like insects, maybe a few snakes. I guess not exactly minor, but not the big predators, you know?

Rarely was I alone with only other person, for in Elrolia, almost all of the activities are completely independent, or else a group activity, rarely just pairs. But for some reason it was no different being around Spyra than being with, say, Wolf, who though I hadn't known for long, was like an old friend, or like family even.

Yeah, Wolf is such a cool name. I imagine it has some significance to it though. My name … I guess you could say it also has significance. I am always very energetic, and I was from the day I was born. My mother told me the first thing I did when I learnt to walk was to try and run out of the building, which I actually did do later in my life. I don't know if that really qualifies as significant though….

'So, you think he'll have any information?' I asked Spyra.

'He'll have to. I mean, Hunter would have told him what he

needed to say to the Spherians, and all his plans and stuff.'

I nodded in understanding. 'Yeah, I guess so.'

We arrived at the border of Spheria quickly because after all, we had been in the Black Trees, extremely close by. Only about fifteen minutes away. So in no time (I mean like the fifteen minutes kind of no time), we were able to see and hear the quiet traffic, the rushing buses and cars. Yeah, quiet. I bet you'd love that. That's what you get in 2084. Awesome, eh?

It was pretty busy. Rush hour. So we approached the sidewalk, and the glass traffic light glowed white, and we crossed safely. It's a great place, Spheria, but it is *way* too fancy. It's like the whole city is a huge wedding or something.

The President's building is almost right on the border. Just about three blocks away. And this place was fancier than the whole of Spheria. It ... you've probably been there, or seen the place before at least, so there isn't any need to describe it, really. Someone's probably told you about it.

As soon as we entered, I started my procedure. I took note of all of the people currently visible, and the fire extinguishers, of which there were three, and the floor-to-ceiling windows. Ideal escape routes. In Elrolia, we were trained to use anything available to defend ourselves with. For example, I could use the metal rods on the curtains for spears or something. Probably would have no reason to use this in normal conditions, but, well, these weren't normal conditions. The President might try to kill us. Well actually, he was with Hunter, so he would probably send us to Hunter instead.

I went up to the main desk.

'Excuse me, where is the President's office?'

'Up the stairs to the right, but he isn't in yet, he'll be ten minutes,' said the woman behind the oak desk.

'Yes, he's a busy man,' I said, smiling. 'Thank you for your help.'

I went back to Spyra.

'Ten minutes.'

'Okay,' she said, nodding.

We took a seat at one of the comfortable couches in the lounge next to the staircase. The seats were velvety red, like that cake, and maybe the most comfortable I'd ever felt.

Someone came through the spinning glass doors – you know, the ones you push – the ones that are ideal playgrounds for children? Whatever. Now the reason that this person who had just entered caught my attention was that I'd seen him before. Garmax.

It was the hunter from Wouldlock. The one who'd stabbed Lypherace. He was carrying a black folder, and he was treating it like it was a breakable thousand-dollar object.

He headed straight for the stairs with no hesitation.

I nodded to Spyra in his direction, and we hastily got up and followed him up the spiral staircase. He seemed in a rush.

He went to a door marked 'President's Office,' and got out a golden key, which he inserted and twisted in the lock. He pushed open the door and stepped inside.

'Not yet,' I whispered, and we went against a wall.

'We need to! We can find why he's in there! If we wait, he'll lock the door.'

'Okay,' I agreed. 'But hide from him.'

It wouldn't be easy, but we wouldn't find what he was doing without going in now. I'd say we had ten minutes until the President came.

We slipped through, and looked around, again doing my check-the-exits procedure. The windows. Also there were two security cameras. That sucked for us. Garmax was at a desk, laying down the folder. Spyra and I quietly slipped into a closet. I opened the door, and being from Spheria, it didn't creak. I closed it slowly, but just as it was about to shut, I realised it was magnetic, so the magnets would close it, making a noticeable sound. It was too late. It slammed hard, and Garmax spun around like a cat.

Through the crack between the doors, I saw Garmax look all around the room, and then his dark eyes fixed on the very spot where we were hidden. I gripped my axe, and Spyra quietly drew two sharp knives from her black metal belt.

Garmax also drew a knife. It had a shiny black blade, and a silver handle.

He raised his hands, and both of the security cameras shut down – moving so they pointed downwards, a little green light on the side flickering into red. He obviously didn't want anyone seeing what followed.

He reached out to open the door, and I took the opportunity. I opened the door with full force, knocking Garmax to the floor, sending his knife sliding toward the main door, the blade going right through the small gap underneath it.

'You!' he snarled, his nostrils flaring as he recognised us from our encounter earlier.

He got to his feet, grabbed one of the chairs from the table, and with surprising strength, hurled it at me. It came towards me like it was in slow motion. It smashed my chest, and I smashed into the closet we'd just been hiding in.

Spyra flung her knives at him, and he ducked, missing the first one by a few centimetres. It landed between two books on a shelf, but the other knife scraped Garmax's arm, and he winced as blood spread from his limb.

'I'll kill you myself, right now,' he growled.

He launched himself at Spyra, knocking her to the ground, holding her in place, not letting her free despite her struggling. He raised his good arm, and his fist closed, ready to deliver a punch that would without a doubt break her face.

She then relaxed, and Garmax, surprised, was rather caught off guard. Spyra sprang to her feet, punching him hard in the back.

He howled and kicked her away.

I leaped up and, using the same technique as I had in the Eagles Trees with the skeleton creature, I raised my axe above my head and swung it, hitting Garmax in the chest with the flat side, sending him flying to the window. Just as he was about to make contact with it, he disintegrated into that same black substance he had become before.

The cameras very slowly raised themselves, thankfully not yet operative, for the light still hadn't turned green again yet.

I breathed deeply and gave Spyra a hand up.

'Thanks,' she said.

I nodded. 'Thank *you.*'

'Let's get this place back in order.' We cleaned up until it was as good as it had been before. The chairs back in place, and no knives sticking out of anything. Spyra took the folder, and we went back out, closing the door just as someone came up the stairs. The President.

He nodded to us and smiled, pushing open the door. I hoped he wouldn't realise it wasn't locked as it had been before. He didn't.

'Excuse me, may we have a few words with you, sir?' I asked.

'Of course. Come right in.'

Despite what Wolf had said, he seemed pretty friendly. I couldn't imagine him being evil. But I suppose that would be what Hunter wanted: someone who does seem like a good, reliable leader.

'I am Dormanant Scale, President of Spheria.'

'I am Spyra, and this is Storm,' Spyra said, a cheerful smile on her face. 'We're Elrolians.'

The president's face was blank. Then after only a few seconds, he was over the surprise.

'It's, um, a pleasure to meet you, Spyra, Storm. Very pleasurable indeed. So what can I help you with?'

I looked at Spyra, and we came to a silent understanding.

I shot up from my seat and in an instant had the President's hands behind his back, his head on the table, and Spyra had destroyed both of the security cameras with her knives.

'Do you work for Hunter?' I asked, loudly, almost growling.

'I don't know what you mean…' he groaned.

'Yes you do! Now tell me, do you work for that killer?' I roared.

'Yes, yes,' he confessed as I pushed his head harder, and his arms together more. 'I do!' he cried.

'You are setting up a plan to kill animals? To hunt in Wouldlock?'

'Yes!' he wailed.

'Where is Hunter?' Spyra asked softly.

He didn't respond.

'Answer her,' I demanded, with a little kick of his chair.

'He's at the Spherian University of Science.'

'Good. You will call off the hunt.'

'I can't. I really can't. Well, you see, it's just too late. The hunt of Wouldlock is moments from beginning. It is unstoppable,' he said, chuckling softly.

I slammed him once more against the table. That idiot. He was working for a murderer and he was actually supporting that murderer.

'Let's go,' I said. Spyra grabbed her knives from the table she'd been resting them on, and stuck them back in her belt.

I flung open the door, and we hurriedly rushed down the stairs, and out the door. We ran down the busy streets and back into Wouldlock. Who would the President tell what had happened? Who would care? Maybe Hunter, but I wasn't worrying about that right now.

'How did they not notice your axe? I mean, the security guards?'

I frowned. 'I don't know actually.'

'Well what now?' Spyra asked.

'We meet Slare and Wolf, and then gather reinforcements. Can you check out that folder?'

As we were walking, we took a look at the file.

'Okay, so they say that they're launching a hunt of … three hundred,' she whispered.

I stopped. 'Three hundred? How will we deal with that?' I asked myself.

'We'll need *lots* of reinforcements. Maybe we could get the Elrolians?'

I raised my eyebrows and smiled. 'That's an idea. We could try, sure. They would help us out a lot. But I don't know if they'd want to work with the humans.'

'Well, we could give it a shot,' she said.

'Sure,' I said. 'We definitely could. Does it say when?'

'Umm … yeah, they'll come tomorrow at one. They want to go early, when we have no idea of what's happening, probably,' she said.

'The good thing is they don't know that we know when they're coming, so we'll have the element of surprise. Garmax thinks the President has the files, he doesn't think we do. We should send them to him in fact. So the President knows when to attack.'

'What? Why should we send them? We don't want him to attack.'

'Yeah, but they're going to attack sometime. It's better if it's the time we want them to. Also, if Garmax finds out the President doesn't have the files, he'll know we have them, and they'll change their plan.'

'Yeah, I guess so. We can ask Stream or Lypherace to copy them then send them back to the President in Garmax's name,' Spyra said.

I nodded. 'Yeah. As soon as we get back to camp we'll ask them.'

'By the way, what about the President?'

'What about him? He just knows that he's attacking Elrolians. He thinks we don't know what time he'll come at. But we do. Maybe he's been scared off!'

As soon as I said it, I knew it couldn't be true. Hunter wouldn't care in the slightest. To him it would be another obstacle, nothing more.

Now, the big question that kept going through my mind was this: *should I kill him?* He murdered my father, and nineteen others in a war where we had given him our trust. So if I had the chance, *would* I kill him?

Now you're probably thinking I'm being too harsh. Put him in jail, you might say. But, no, no prison would hold him, much less be able to capture him in the first place. But was the solution to kill him? I had no idea.

We slowly passed through the forests and across the Tigers River. A few of the tigers were bathing, fighting with each other in a playful manner. The most notice they gave us were a few strange looks, but they quickly forgot, and went back to more important things, like sticking their heads in the water, then licking their faces.

I love tigers. They look so innocent at first, but then, with almost no notice, they strike. Lovely, eh? Yeah. Great creatures. Wow… I'm getting to be like Wolf. And that's not a bad thing. Cool.

We approached the camp. It really looks nothing like a camp though. It's incredible how so many people could live there for so long. It's pretty cool. I'm used to Elrolia, but I know that where I live isn't the standard. Anyone who believed that would be mightily disappointed in the rest of the world.

Wolf had told me they had everything they needed; beds, food, a few computers for research and stuff, and a library. Pretty neat.

The small guys, Mac and Icon, were out there with Slare.

'Wow,' said Spyra. 'This place is so cool.'

'Yeah,' I said. 'You could ask someone to give you a tour.'

'Yeah, that'd be great,' she said in awe.

'Hey Slare, Mac, Icon. How you all doing?' I asked.

'Great! So, what you got?' asked Slare, standing up.

Spyra gave me the files and ushered me in, and she started informing Slare.

Mac and Icon were playing catch with a small branch. And … wow! The three-year-old, Mac, he was throwing and catching with his tiny little feet! That, even I can't do. Remarkable.

I went inside, and found myself facing the members of the Animal Defence Organisation. They were sitting around the table with a neat pile of magazines on top. There was a loud conversation going on between the two brothers, Raider and Blade.

'It's a disagreement!' Blade said exhaustedly.

'No, an argument. Listen, a disagreement is a calm disputation between two people,' he said. 'This is not calm! You see, an argument is when two people discuss opposing views on *one* subject. A disagreement is when each person has a different view.'

'We can have different views on one subject!' said Blade.

Raider paused. 'Yeah … but who cares, this is an argument!'

'No, man, it's a damn disagreement!'

'Shut up,' Raider said.

'No.'

'*Please* shut up.'

'No,' said Blade again.

'Your face looks like a pink oink.'

'What the heck's a pink oink?'

'You tell me,' said Raider.

'I just asked you.'

'Hey, that's enough!' said Ardor. 'Storm's arrived.'

'Storm, great to see you again,' Ardor growled, nodding, his dark eyes staring almost right through me.

'Storm!' Wolf said. 'You got anything? Where's Spyra?'

'Outside. But listen up.'

I shared with the team what we had learnt, and also explained how Garmax had been there, and how we hadn't really gotten along.

'So, they'll come at one o'clock,' Lypherace clarified.

'Yeah,' I said. 'By the way, could you or Stream copy some files we got, then send the original to the President?' From what I'd already told him, he understood perfectly.

'Sure,' he said, nodding at Stream, his eyes invisible through his black sunglasses. 'We can definitely do that.'

I handed them the files, and they went straight to work, heading for Stream's room, which had all the cool fancy tech stuff that Wolf had told me no one but he and maybe Lypherace would understand. I wouldn't, at least. Elrolia doesn't have much technology, and the tech that we *do* have I still never really use. But I'm a quick learner. It kind of runs in the family.

Slare and Spyra came in and took a seat as well, so I started sharing our idea.

'As you can see, we are facing approximately three hundred trained hunters, all under the control of the legendary Hunter himself. He has the President of Spheria under his complete control, and they've no doubt found a way to authorise this attack, so any legal reinforcements are out of the question. I don't even think getting anyone from another Eromie would work. You all know how powerful the President is, he has lots of control over them.'

'So you mean, like no doughnut-eating police guys?' Blade said.

'Yeah, pretty much.'

'We need reinforcements of some kind,' Ardor said. 'We can't protect a whole country with … twelve people, not including Mac or Icon.'

'That's what we're getting to,' said Spyra. 'We need help, as

I believe everyone agrees, so.... We are going to turn to the Elrolians.'

Every single person in the room was making not a sound.

Raider and Blade stared laughing like crazy until they realised this was no joke.

'They'll never come,' Slare said. 'You might have, but they're different.'

'I know what the other Elrolians are like, but why not give it a try?' I said, a bit too fiercely. 'We need help. And it's up to us to get it.'

Stream and Lypherace came rushing in, grim looks on their faces – or at least on Stream's. With Lypherace it was hard to tell.

Lypherace spoke, his voice forbidding. 'Guys, we've got a big problem. A very big problem.'

BACK TO ELROLIA

'Alright everyone, we took a closer look, and according to these files,' Lypherace continued, 'they know we have Black Amber on our side. And now their priority is not to attack Hunter's targets, but to destroy Black Amber.'

'What?' Wolf exclaimed, 'but Hunter invented them!'

'Yeah, so he knows that having them against him is a really bad thing. So bad, that they need to eliminate them beforehand.'

'How'd they find out?' I asked.

I had not seen this on the file. But I guess I hadn't looked too carefully.

'Think about it. They would have records of Black Amber,' Lypherace said. 'Something Hunter has created as an ultimate weapon he would be keeping an eye on at all times.'

He was right. I couldn't believe I hadn't thought of that.

Now the whole Black Amber species was doomed. Sure, a human created it – a murderer, actually. Did that give it no right to live? They were living animals, just like all the others, and I would protect them.

Hunter didn't care though, like he didn't care about so many other things. So our first battle would be to protect Black Amber. Hunter could not get ahold of them.

'So we have to protect Black Amber,' I said. 'First, they'll come for them, and if they can, they'll take them away. They won't shoot them on sight; they'll probably bring them to a laboratory – the one he's staying in! They have Elrolian Onyxus in them, in their claws and probably their bodies, and probably many other precious things. They'll want to get it out. Hunter wouldn't waste something like that.'

'Wait, what laboratory?' Sora asked. 'You know where he is?'

'Yeah,' said Spyra, 'the President told us where he was staying. The Spherian University of Science.'

'So shouldn't we go there and attack?' Blade asked.

'No,' I said. 'We don't have much time. We still need to get the Elrolians.'

'Well, it's ... almost eight o'clock now, so you've got about five hours until they come.'

'Couldn't we change the time on the file we send the President?' Raider said.

It was a smart idea, but it wouldn't work. 'No, Garmax would have gotten orders from Hunter, and they'll come at one no matter what. Changing the time would get us in a worse situation if they know that we know when they are coming.'

'So who is going to Elrolia?' asked Viper, who was sitting in the corner. He had been awfully quiet for the last few minutes. His leg was in a metal brace he'd probably made himself for supporting his hyena-bitten leg. I wondered where the hyena was at the moment. It had probably run off back to its home. And Crash had gone back with them too, probably to his home as well.

'Well, I believe our two Elrolians will be essential, of course, and maybe one more, to show them who they will be working with,' said Ardor, looking around at us as he said it.

'They'll need someone who is a very good role model,' said Raider, rising from his seat proudly.

'Then it won't be you,' said Blade, tugging him back down.

'I'll go,' volunteered Lypherace.

I was a hundred percent for it. Lypherace was fantastic, almost as skilled as an Elrolian, probably the equivalent of some, and was a fantastic person overall. The others didn't know him as well, but I was sure he'd be the best for it.

'Yes, that would be brilliant,' I said smiling.

We actually might stand a chance! But then again, I didn't want to underestimate Hunter.

We set off right away, our precious five hours ticking away.

Lypherace, Spyra and I are quick people, and we sped through the grass and rocks to Elrolia.

I hoped Emrax would be there. He was, as I said before, a specialist in the element of nature. He can control the movements of plants, and air, and is starting to master the art of air riding. You've probably heard of the three legendary Air Riders. Well, people say he will become the fourth. He teaches elemental control in Elrolia. It's a very useful skill. And he has many skills – so many that he was offered the option of joining the Northern Elrolians.

You see, when you have learned everything there is to teach in Elrolia, and when they think you're good enough, then you have the opportunity to go to the north, to advance your skills to their best. The Northern Elrolians' castle is home only to the best. When offered, you have three options. To stay at your level, pretty much just grow to be an average Elrolian, maybe a bit better, or to become a teacher at Elrolia, or to go to the north. Then there are all the complicated rules about having your family go to the north as well, but it was Hunter himself who had wiped out Emrax's family in the battle of Elrolia, so it was just concerning Emrax in his case. But, Emrax had decided to become a teacher, and that's exactly what he was now.

As we approached Elrolia I realised that I had been away for two days. Now, people wouldn't be over worried – I was an Elrolian, I could very well take care of myself – but they would find it strange how long I was gone. Even for two days, Elrolians aren't really supposed to leave Elrolia without permission. The same would probably go for Spyra too, but it didn't matter. There was no punishment. But still, it was like being away from school for two days with no explanation.

Elrolia really is amazing. The circular building was created out of white plerauthus stone, a stone that we use instead of bricks and cement. It's like marble, just harder when frozen. It's said that the stone is the cause for the peculiar lights down on earth. Plerauthus reflects lights, and it's all around the base of the Eromies, leading to the event known as the northern lights down below. But for some strange reason, they still don't block the sky. I don't know too much else about it, though; this is more of Emrax's area.

The people who created Elrolia have long ago passed away, for they were what we call the Earthen, meaning people who were born on Earth, not on one of the Eromies, and had found their way up somehow. It was surprising how few were here. Although I guess it would be quite a perilous journey from down there all the way up to here.

I have never been down there, for I was never interested in leaving this place when I was younger, but now I feel it would be quite the adventure to go down there. But would I ever come back? I had no idea how the other people had got up here.

So, back to Elrolia. The front entrance isn't heavily guarded. But this was no problem. The guards are highly trained, and are able to easily distinguish normal humans from us. No one who isn't supposed to be there really has a chance of getting through the gates – they can alert the castle in seconds. I am very well-known in the community of Elrolia. Some people pity me for my father's death, others see me as a great warrior, as I have trained every day since my father's death.

The idea that always motivated me was the hope that one day, I might have the chance to confront the killer, Hunter. But again, the same question ran through my mind: Would I do it? Would I kill him? The time would come eventually … I could wait until then.

So as I gazed up at the elegant fortress, I was reminded of the terrible memory of the great Battle of Elrolia, as it was often referred to. I was only a small child then, but I can remember it as if it were yesterday. It is not easy to forget something that terrible.

I remember I was in the library, hidden in a secret compartment with my sister and my friend Emrax, as we watched the huge battle below. I was what, twenty then? Twenty-two, I believe. This is very young for an Elrolian. We tend to live much longer than humans. Our job was to ambush them when they entered the castle, and I could hear them coming, the huge army of Lanxians. But I had to see what was happening down there. My mother was down there, fighting away.

There were over a thousand Lanxians, all armed with dangerous weapons that served them one purpose – to kill.

Yes, they'd gotten hold of our weapons. You can thank Hunter for that. We'd foolishly given him the location of the Elrolian forge, where we created our great weapons and tools, and he'd done some serious stealing.

I could actually see Hunter, skillfully using an Elrolian Vortex, a weapon that can instantly change to anything of its exact volume by control of the user's mind. It was an incredible Elrolian invention, designed by the most famous Elrolian inventors, or engineers, the siblings Surplex and Velocito. My parents had met both of them, and I had recently met Velocito at a feast. She was amazing, so many incredible ideas and skills. Surplex was also cool. He was also a friend of my parents.

Hunter was dealing with ten Elrolians, that were one by one falling to his blade.

I was keeping my eyes locked on my mother, who was fighting fearlessly below, swinging her chain-mace. I saw her capture several Lanxians with it, and she flung them over to Emrax's father, Trelax, who instantly froze the captives in a block of solid ice.

Trelax was a skilled fighter, and like his son, he was an elemental specialist. Of course, Emrax wasn't at that time, but his father inspired him to be. Lots more happened after this, but the biggest event was when my father came back. He was with his nineteen accomplices, and had just come back from exploring one of Elrolia's biggest mountains, Mount Careus. The battle had started just as he was on his way back, and he'd arrived just an hour into it.

He got the gist of what was happening, seized his climbing knives, and joined the battle.

I called out to him, but it was much too loud for him to hear me. He went alongside my mother, and they worked together wonderfully, like they knew exactly what the other was going to do before they did it.

Very soon after, my father realised that his partners were in trouble, and he rushed to their aid. You see, Hunter wanted them dead – each and every one of them. I believe Hunter may have had some other personal experience with the mountain climbers.

After a bit of a struggle, Hunter achieved success. He killed the climbers, ending with my father.

Much more happened, but this is all I will say for now. After that little flashback, I realised I had stopped in the middle of the path, and quickly sprinted to catch up with the other two.

As we approached the gate, the crowned guards leapt down from their posts and came down to talk to us.

I recognised the guards, Glasus and Florez.

'Spyra, Storm! Where've you been? It's been two days since you left – and who's this?' Florez asked, nodding her head at Lypherace, who she'd classified as human.

'Lypherace,' he said, giving a small bow.

'Yeah, Florez, he's as good as Elrolian with the skills he has, let him in please,' said Spyra.

'Sure,' said Glasus, sending some signal to open the gates.

Both of them had been fighting alongside us at the Battle of Elrolia. They weren't even as good as Lypherace, to be honest. But then again, these young Elrolians probably didn't have the fifteen years of experience Lypherace did. Not saying that they're bad, but it's just that … well, Lypherace is better.

The gates were made, of course, with Elrolian Onyxus. It shone blindingly against the sun, especially when it was raised up giving us access to the dark wooden door that was embedded with the Elrolian symbol. Not the tilted square – no, that's for the Elrolian mines. The one here is the helmet of the queen – the doors to Elrolia. The symbol was shiny chrome silver, and it covered most of the wood on the doors.

With great strength, Glasus and Florez pushed it open and invited us inside. There was a massive atrium, the walls lined with weapons, precious uncut gemstones, and Elrolian armour of all different sizes and all of those awesome metallic colours. All of these were prizes and awards – special stuff.

There were fabulous chandeliers, and the crafting on everything was excellent. At the back there were two sets of marble spiral staircases going left and right, the steps of which were covered with a lovely lake-blue carpet.

There were also more doors on either side that led to the other armouries and rooms. The castle is seriously, really big, and every room looks fantastic, with high ceilings, and none of them were rushed in the making in the slightest. There are twenty huge levels, and I think about twelve or thirteen of them are just for residential purposes. There are many Elrolians here, so we do need quite a bit of space. Of course Elrolians do live in other places, but I would say that *most* of them live here.

As you can see, I did not do my standard procedure. I am in my home. Firstly, nothing would attack me here, and if it did, I would not flee, or have any need to escape, unless of course, this place is on fire or some such thing. The only reason I do these procedures is for a situation like that, if I needed to escape. Secondly, I know this place very well, having been raised here. Of course, I do not know all of the chambers here, but I would say I know maybe eighty percent of it.

We went up the stairs three floors, and arrived at the meeting room. As usual, it was empty. It was only full when there were important meetings taking place, so I hadn't expected anyone to be here, but decided to check just in case. There were rows of seats where the audience – or whatever you call the spectators – sat.

'Where should we go?' Spyra asked once I turned my back on the unoccupied chamber.

'The King and Queen's throne room,' I suggested.

We started up the stairs, Lypherace observing everything as we went. I could imagine how he felt. I had felt the same way, the day I was old enough to appreciate the magnificence of this place. I was used to it by now, and didn't really think much of it since I was here every day, but others were never disappointed. Although as I said before, I know this isn't standard.

The throne room was with no doubt the grandest room in the castle. It held beautiful wax candles that had had different colour wax, so it looked very colourful, illuminating the room in a dim glowing light. On the candles, on the bit where you light them, was a special coloured material that made the flame that colour. Amazing, isn't it?

There were two delicate silver thrones sitting next to each other, which I didn't really understand, for there was nothing to do there, and it would be extremely boring. One of the walls was covered with an enormous bookshelf. There were on the other wall more displays of sparkling gemstones, giving a nice colourful light to the room. The windows were from floor to ceiling, with nice big arches at the top. A cool little fact: the windows were actually made with hand-cut quartz from Lorothia. It gives a much clearer pane to look through, and does the opposite of what normal glass does. Normal grass magnifies the heat, or at least it lets all of it in, making the room uncomfortably hot. The quartz makes it nice and cool, like a light natural breeze. Now there wasn't much to see out at this time of night, but when the sun's out, it's amazing. In the game room, the quartz is different colours, making it look like you're in the midst of falling through a rainbow. But it's awesomer that a rainbow. I know that awesomer isn't actually a word, but it describes what I'm saying perfectly, so who really cares? Anyway, this is one of the only rooms with windows in the whole castle – most are open arches.

Both chairs were empty. The room, however, was not unoccupied. Alterthus, King of Elrolia was practicing his archery by the window. He is not all that old – do not think of him, or the queen, in fact, as old. They are both around fifty, I believe. I know, right? Pretty cool. Not really old. The king has rather short black hair, slightly growing grey, and a grey beard too. He is always wearing his armour, or at least whenever I see him he is, and he is *always* wearing his special Elrolian crown, which is considerably different from mine or Spyra's.

I could not see the queen at the moment, but the king took notice of us the moment we saw him.

'Storm! Spyra!' he said in a gruff but friendly voice, almost laughing with joy, laying down carefully his large, black, custom-made bow. He came over, shook our hands enthusiastically, and went over to Lypherace. 'And who is this young man?'

'Lypherace, sir. I'm an agent from Delta, a secret organisation known only to a few. I came across these two when tracking down a couple of hunters the other day.'

'You are not Elrolian?' the king said, his voice not changing in the slightest, which rather gave away his confusion – or was it anger? We had just brought a human in. I could understand.

'We need the help of you and the other Elrolians,' said Spyra hastily.

I would have waited to see Queen Eleria for this part, for she was much more friendly towards humans, and a lot more understanding that some of them were good-natured, but it was too late now.

'We are about to come under attack,' I said, nodding. 'Hunter,' I added, knowing the question he would ask. 'He's back, and he wants revenge for something.'

I saw fear in the king's eyes, fear I had never seen before on an Elrolian's face. 'You are the second one who has told me this,' he said. 'At first I didn't think it possible.'

The second one who'd said this? Who was the first? I thought to myself, frowning.

I informed him of everything that had happened over the last two days, starting from when I had gone to visit Androma, until now. He got the gist of the story.

'Well, your story is very similar to this other person's. Maybe you should meet him.'

Finally! I nodded eagerly. 'Sure. Lead the way.'

He led us down a set of stairs to the residential rooms.

'I have met this person before, and at first was only a little bit hesitant to believe him, but an Elrolian carrying the same message ... well that's a different story.'

Alterthus knocked loudly, and a growling voice answered, 'enter.'

The king knocked, and pushed open the polished oak door. I stepped inside. It was not so different from my room – at least not the format of the place. The furniture was different. It was nice – filled with old armour and old chairs and tables and stuff. The stuff was also old. And so, it appeared, was the man who lived here.

He was sitting comfortably on one of the couches, and had long grey hair, armour – like all the other people here – and his eyes followed me the moment he entered the room.

He stood up and greeted us. 'Hello,' he said, searching us up and down with his observant eyes. 'I'm Ravenwood Sphalerite Spears.'

'I'm Spyra, and this is Storm. This is Lypherace, human as well,' Spyra announced.

Ravenwood studied me carefully. 'Well, Storm, I trust you are familiar with the man named Wolf?'

How did he know?

'Yes, sir. I am.'

'Ah, no need for the sirs! I should be sir-ing you, young Storm. You do not remember me? For I remember you, quite well in fact. Son of Elrace and Aria Orthoclase. I visited you, do you not remember? Your parents and I are good friends. I work for the Animal Defence Organisation. Well, kind of. For the last few days I have. I work alongside Lance, who is gone now, and Slare, if you remember, and of course, Wolf.'

'Well it's, um, nice to see you, err ... again, I guess.'

'Same here,' he said, nodding. 'I see Wolf gave you the axe. Yes, I know. I gave it to him in the first place. Now, what would you like to talk to me about? I assume you came in here for a reason?'

'Yes,' said the king, who had stepped into the room. 'They bring the same message that you brought me yesterday. That Hunter is coming.'

Spyra, Lypherace, and I exchanged stories with Ravenwood. They matched perfectly.

'You see,' Ravenwood was saying after we told our tale, 'I had gone over to Shade's side in order to spy on them, and found that Hunter was there. He did not recognise me for who I was, for it's been quite a long time indeed, but I did not feel safe around him nevertheless. So, after gathering a little bit of information, I left, for I knew I had to inform the king.'

'Wait,' I said, puzzled. 'How would he have recognised you? Does he know you?'

Ravenwood took a deep breath. I seemed to have touched a nerve, or a personal subject.

'What I am about to tell you should not change your feelings for me,' he said, getting up and closing the door. 'Hunter…' He paused for a moment. 'He is my brother.'

I froze. *No way.* Here was the sibling of my father's killer.

'Listen. I was in a forest with him, we got lost, separated. I never found him again. I came to Elrolia, and stayed here when I wasn't looking for him. He thinks I abandoned him. I left stones to Elrolia, hoping he would one day find the path here and we would be reunited. But I never saw him again in person, until four days ago. He had changed. He is known as Hunter now. And he will not recognise his own brother. He wants to kill me now.' His voice was shaking. That was terrible. 'He wants me dead.' He trembled.

'That's why he's coming?' Spyra asked gently, patting his arm awkwardly. 'To… find you?'

Ravenwood brought himself together, and gave a firm nod. 'He is.'

'Then, for the good of Elrolia, you must leave,' Alterthus said strongly.

I turned to him. 'You want to send him away so Hunter won't come here?' I said, disbelievingly. 'Send him defenceless to his death? No! We must protect him.'

'Storm, we will all die! Hunter will not rest until he has what he wants, you know that!'

'He got what he wanted easily when he killed my father!' I yelled. 'He will not kill Ravenwood! He will not get what he wants, not while I am here!' I said, trembling with rage. 'I've had enough of this! Hunter getting whatever he wants by using fear! You give in too easily! You care only for yourself!'

'You will endanger my people!' the king said, his voice rising as well.

'So you want him to go die somewhere else? *He is being hunted!* We cannot just throw him out to die! We must stand up to Hunter!'

'If we *stand up* to him, we will all die!'

'What lack of faith!' I spat. 'You would have this great man sent away to his death! What kind of king are you?'

Spyra grabbed my arm as I almost lunged at him.

'I am one that will do everything in my power to protect my people! I will not place my kingdom in danger for the life of one man – one that isn't even Elrolian! That isn't how I'm playing this game!'

'This is not a game!' I roared. 'This is battle! Fight!'

Ravenwood spoke, quite quietly, but very seriously. 'I am afraid that however much you want to send me away, it will do no good, for there is something else that lies in Elrolia that is what Hunter wants. I do not know why he wants it, but I am quite certain that he does.'

'And what is that?' Alterthus snapped.

'Why, my king, it is you. Hunter, the great, yet wicked Hunter, wants you.'

WILL YOU JOIN US?

The king stared at Ravenwood as if he were a dead man, and had just been told that he too was lifeless.

'What?' Alterthus said sharply. 'What have I done?'

'I have told you, Alterthus, I have no knowledge of the cause. But, as it happens, I know this, and I do not think you would have any reason to doubt me, seeing how I have used my resources so far. I gathered this information from Hunter himself.'

'What have you done, Alterthus?' I demanded. I know this is no way to speak to a king, but I didn't really care at the moment. Anyway, you know now how protective he is of the Elrolians. He would not throw me out of Elrolia for using a slightly angry tone with him. He would not even try. And if he didn't, I wouldn't leave. I just wouldn't.

The king was not usually all that secretive, but he was not giving anything away now. I wasn't sure that we had much of a chance getting the aid of the Elrolians to protect Black Amber. If we could keep Black Amber, we may not even need the Elrolians. Black Amber was everything. But then, so were the Elrolians.

'King?' Spyra asked. I could see anxiety on her gentle face. She was worried about the king. I was too. If Hunter wanted him, we would not really have any chance of saving him. He would, like all of Hunter's other targets, be worse than dead once Hunter had finished his job.

I know this is kind of off-topic, but I was aching to know Hunter's real name. I was in the room with probably the only one to know. Ravenwood. Would it be something normal? Like Bob, or Joe, or something? Or would it be some type of name that sounds like it's been named after some sophisticated crystal or something more like that? Whatever. We needed to focus on the main issue here.

'Well Ravenwood, is it just you two he wants?' Lypherace asked. 'It would be easier to focus on defending just a small number of targets instead of a lot of them.'

'Yeah, I'm pretty sure. But don't take my word for it. I mean this is just what I've heard.'

'So then, king, maybe we should go with your idea,' I said, almost smirking. 'Should we send you out to your death as well? It's what's best for your people, right?'

I didn't mean this, for I still believed what I said about us standing up and defending, but I wanted to see what he would say.

'You both are right,' the king said, staring out the window, focusing on what? Space? 'We must leave for the sake of Elrolia.'

I almost laughed. He actually thought this was right, and in a way it was, but not for us. We couldn't just leave them to die, like I'd said before.

I shook my head, looking him directly in the eyes. 'We will not abandon you – neither of you. All of Elrolia is prepared to defend you, and they will. But you need to understand. We need your help. We need to stop Hunter from taking Black Amber. Or he will kill the entire species, and the only ones stopping him from reaching his goal will be us, and a few humans. He will wipe out the forest if necessary.'

'What is Black Amber?' he enquired.

I gave him a short summary of the creature.

'And you want how many of us?' enquired the king.

'As many as possible. There will be at least three hundred hunters at your doorstep if you do not help us. Black Amber can aid us in this battle! You must help us protect them!'

'Well, if you're so serious, I suggest we take this to the queen and the superior council and then make the decision.'

'We must decide now,' said Spyra. 'We have no time to debate this matter. It is simple, you send out some other Elrolians to help us, and then if we safely keep Black Amber, we can come and defend you from Hunter! It's perfect.'

The king didn't look so sure. 'I will fetch the council, meet me down in the meeting room in precisely five minutes.' He left the room.

'Ravenwood, want to come along?' I asked.

'Of course. This is a matter of high significance. I will be there to negotiate.'

We made for the meeting room, Lypherace still marveling at the work of the castle.

'Hey, do you mind if we make a slight detour? I just want to check something. Actually, you know what, you two go ahead, I'll catch up with you,' I said.

'What do you need to do?' Spyra asked.

'Nothing much, I'll just be a minute, go ahead.'

Ravenwood nodded grimly. This was an important situation. I could only imagine how he felt.

I went along the same floor over to Emrax's room. He was a teacher, so he had this big classroom joined to his personal room. Well, I guess it's not so much a classroom – more of a training room. It has six separate smaller rooms for practicing each of the individual elements, but we also have a large dome where we have a high-tech environment simulator where we can practice elements in virtual areas where we may actually one day find ourselves. That's I think one of the only things that uses technology here.

In Elrolia we only focus on the most important skills in life, that we are one-hundred percent certain to need. The other stuff, things that normal people do in school, well that comes second – if we ever do learn it, as I said before.

Now, because I said he's a teacher, don't think of him as an evil replica of your math teacher. Emrax is almost the same age as me, just four months older, and is the best teacher here. He's young, and he's cool. Nothing against old people, by the way. Old people are awesome – normally.

Anyway, when we were in school together earlier, he would always push himself, and he was serious. He loved the art of mastering the elements. He especially found an interest in nature, you know, stuff like changing air quality, making plants grow, having mental connections with other living things. He has been practicing flying for five years now. Don't think of him flying like Superman either. Real flying, like no-gravity-type flying, flying that doesn't exist. He masters the art of air control. He can will the air to lift him, push him, and hold him. He can even levitate – himself and even other people.

Now, you may be wondering why every Elrolian isn't practicing air control if it's that awesome. Well, that isn't all that you can do. There are plenty of other things to master that are just as cool. Now, these things take time to learn – a lot of time. Like I said, he's been doing this for five years. He does have a slight advantage, though. Elrolian Onyxus is clouded around his brain, giving him an extra push when using his mind to control air. This is complex stuff.

In fact, I have a special ability too. Elrolian Onyxus clouds my throat. At first this was a problem. The extra weight would cause my throat to have problems, and twice I nearly suffocated. But later, I learnt how to control it. I have perfected it over the years to the point that I can now breath without oxygen for a limited time. So yeah, I can pretty much breath underwater. Actually, I believe I can only do this underwater. Scientists that examined me said that this only works when I convert the water to something suitable for breathing. So basically, I couldn't breathe in outer space. Just a little cool fact about myself. My mother nearly had a heart attack when she saw me limp with my head stuck in an overflowing sink.

I knocked hard against the door to Emrax's personal room, waiting for a friendly response. Nothing came. So I went around to the classroom door, and was about to knock again when I saw a piece of paper on the door.

Hello dear reader! I am out at the moment, but I'll be back at twelve p.m. tomorrow. Come by and see me soon! Have a nice day!

Twelve o'clock! I would not see him. That was a shame. He was an excellent debater. With him, we would have had a ninety-nine percent chance of receiving help from the Elrolians. Of course we still had a chance, for this was a good cause, and I didn't really see what could go wrong, but we would be much better off with Emrax than without him.

I took out the keys to the office that Emrax had given me, and unlocked the door, stepping inside. I went over to his desk and scribbled a very long note telling him what was going on, and about the meeting we were about to have. I left it on his desk where he would see it, and left the room.

Twelve o'clock. That would be after the Black Amber battle. Why? Why couldn't he be here to help us! Our luck didn't seem to be going our way today. Well really it hadn't been going well for a while. Why did Hunter have to be doing this? This guy would make all those villains that the superheroes fight, and all those other criminal masterminds look like ants – really ugly ants. Ants that bite a lot, but you never really feel the sting. Hunter is a different story. When he strikes, he stings.

But who says I don't sting? I hate Hunter more than anyone else. And I will strike him hard. I will make him pay for what he has done. We had strong people on our side. Spyra, Slare, Wolf, Ardor – all of the campers. And with luck – which we didn't have a lot of – we would have the Elrolians to help us too.

So I went back out to join the others at the meeting room. The council was tough, but we had a great cause, and I really didn't see the need for this stupid council meeting. It was simple, they send some Elrolians to help us, we keep Black Amber and fend off the hunters, and then we come back and defend Elrolia. Simple. This council was really unnecessary. But at least the queen would be there. She was incredibly fair and kind, definitely much more so than the king.

So I entered the meeting room, and heard loud voices. Had they started? It seemed they had. It was so different than it had been when empty. I almost never attend these meetings, for I am almost never invited, and when I am, they are usually extremely boring, although sometimes it is interesting to sit in on.

I took a seat next to Spyra and she filled me in on what was going on. Nothing. They were just settling down. Ravenwood rose and the room fell quiet as he took a place at the front of the large meeting room that resembled a court room, with the circular rows of seats and everything.

'For those who do not know, I am Ravenwood Sphalerite Spears, from Lorothia. Yes, I am a human, but your king and queen have trusted me since Elrolia was created. I bear your ring,' he said, holding his hand up to show a silver ring with the tilted square on one side, and of course, the helmet of the queen on the other. This ring was given to those who performed a service or was deeply trusted. Ravenwood had probably gotten it for both. 'I bring news that I have gathered from Hunter himself.' He looked at each of the nine council members in turn.

I saw Queen Eleria, elegant in her seat, looking over the meeting with her observing eyes. Guess what she was wearing? Armour! That's right! She was looking at Ravenwood like he was a diamond. She always paid her full attention to anyone who was speaking, and it gave that person such a wonderful feeling of really being important.

'I was spying on Hunter – you all know who he is of course,' Ravenwood continued. 'And I discovered that he has a plan to hunt down two people, two people that happen to be in this building – in this very room, in fact.'

There was silence as everyone impatiently waited for the names, each of them I could see silently whispering *not me!* And they were lucky. For it was not them that was being hunted. They knew inside they had done nothing wrong, yet the Elrolians' hearts beat as they waited in suspense.

'The first one, my friends, is I.' There were surprised faces I saw through the crowd of people that had shown up. They did not expect someone who was aware that they were being hunted to speak so calmly about it. Especially when it was Hunter who was hunting them.

'And the second one, Ravenwood?' Queen Eleria asked patiently, a sympathetic look on her face. It seemed they knew each other well.

'It is, from what I have learnt, your king.'

There were loud gasps, and then a rush of voices as Elrolians broke into deep conversation. This was their king, and this meant it was important. I thought it was stupid. No one was this concerned when they heard Ravenwood was being hunted. From what I'd gathered, he was a great friend of the Elrolians. Just because the king held power, and had more control over the Elrolians, didn't make him any more special than Ravenwood. The queen stared blankly at her husband.

To be honest, I am not really a fan of the king. The queen is fantastic, and is admired by many, but the king just too harsh, and takes it out of his way to defend his kingdom. Now, that part isn't bad, it's just how he defends. I could understand how he may have angered Hunter. He was rather ... arrogant, at times.

This seemed to be our cue. I tapped Spyra's shoulder, and we too rose from our seats along with Lypherace, and went up to join Ravenwood.

'Hello, I'm Storm Orthoclase,' I said, looking each person in the eye as Ravenwood had.

'And I'm Spyra Crysabell.' She smiled warmly despite the seriousness of the situation.

'And I'm Lypherace, of Raverand. I work for Delta, and I have recently been working alongside these Elrolians.'

'We bring the same news as Ravenwood. We received this information from Androma Faithly, Elrolian of the Tree Cave.' I was not afraid of crowds of people, so I started pacing around the room so I could give everyone a clear view of me. 'Spyra and I recently accompanied the humans Wolf and Slare of Wouldlock, who are not present at the moment, but all the same, we went on an expedition with them and found ourselves face to face with one of Hunter's own creations. It has been named Black Amber. Black Amber is an animal – a pack of animals. We have recently joined forces with these creatures, and this is a great advantage for when Hunter arrives. For him, when he comes, we must be prepared. And this is too great of an advantage for us for Hunter to withstand, so he is going to attempt to eliminate – kill – the Black Amber species. We are going to stop that.'

'Yes, indeed, Hunter is coming to attack Black Amber three and a half hours from now,' Spyra said, checking her watch. 'We need your help to defend these creatures. We saw files that stated the time of attack,' she added.

'Hold on,' said one of the council members with a dark brown beard. 'You want us to send out Elrolians to protect one of Hunter's creations? Do you think us idiots? How do you know they will not betray you? This is *Hunter.* He has never been known for creating something so easy to change their minds!'

'These things are living, with real hearts, and real brains,' I said. 'They are not connected to Hunter. He has not control over them. They have given their word they will aid us. These things can kill Elrolians. Their claws are made of Elrolian Onyxus, so they can tear you apart. You must take action. If they turn against you, they could kill you. But now, *we* have them. Anyway, he wouldn't decide to kill them unless he was sure there was no chance of getting them back. They're with us.'

'Hunter will come and attack us, we cannot risk any Elrolians! We need every one of them!' the king said.

'I have to agree with Storm,' the queen said. 'If Black Amber is so important that Hunter needs them out of the picture, then these animals could be very useful to us. This is Hunter we are talking about! He has killed Elrolians before, and if these creatures have Elrolian Onyxus in their body, then it means he has more of this material, so he can kill us. He has both the equipment, and the skill.'

The brown-bearded councilor cleared his throat. 'Even if we do agree, how many Elrolians do you expect us to send?'

Why was this thing such a big deal? The Hunters would come *after* they came for Black Amber, leaving more than enough time for us to return.

'Well about twenty would be acceptable,' Spyra said.

'Twenty!' the councilor said, his eyes widening. 'My dear woman, have you no sense? Lots must be done if we are to prepare for this battle, and twenty is more than we can afford to spare! After this, Hunter will come directly for us! We cannot risk anyone!'

'We're asking for only twenty Elrolians, you idiot!' I shouted, losing my temper. 'To protect an entire species! A living species! Hunter will kill those animals in the most brutal way possible! Imagine if it were you!'

'I will discuss this with my fellow council members, Storm Orthoclase,' the bearded man said dangerously.

As they talked, I turned to Lypherace, Spyra, and Ravenwood.

'I can't believe this! What is wrong with them! Just send some Elrolians to help us and we're done!'

'They don't understand...' Spyra started.

'Why not! It is so simple!' I said in rage.

'Spyra's right, Storm, these people just don't understand the importance of Black Amber. We know what it can do, they have no idea.'

'Well how are we supposed to stand up to whatever Hunter sends to collect Black Amber? We have two Elrolians, two Orians, and a few humans. We are all highly trained, but I don't know if we can win this battle.' I lowered my voice. 'This might be the battle we die in.'

Lypherace looked at me. 'That's not going to happen, man. We're going to win this thing. We'll protect Black Amber, Ravenwood, your king, and Wouldlock.' He looked at me, and I saw hope. 'This is for all of us, and all of us will battle for Elrolia, for the animals, for freedom. This is the time that we rise, and for our freedom from Hunter, we fight. He wants to destroy Elrolia? Or Wouldlock?' Lypherace smiled grimly. 'Let him try.'

'We have made our decision,' the leader of the council said. She was a tall woman with blonde hair, and a permanent smirk on her rather sinful face – the evil, female Lypherace. 'The council, along with the king and queen of Elrolia, have made its decision.'

'This decision was *not* unanimous, I must add,' said the queen.

The king rose. 'You are on your own. We will stay to defend our kingdom. Thank you for your time.'

The room cleared out, people talking about their opinions on the topic. Many of them, it seemed, agreed with the final decision. I was speechless.

I made for the king, needing to talk to him, and possibly to threaten to beat him up, but Spyra pulled me back. 'Storm, you can't change their minds,' she said sadly, but unquestionably.

I knew she was right, but I couldn't stand this. I felt abandoned. I asked for help from my own people, and they turned me down, like an outcast.

'Listen, I'll stay and help them prepare for when Hunter comes *here,*' Ravenwood said, giving a final nod, and then moving along with the others.

I looked away from Lypherace and Spyra a bit. 'Before we go, I'm going to stop by my mother's room. I need to say goodbye … just in case we don't return.'

BLACK SHADOWS

I left the meeting room quietly along with the others, and went straight for my mother's room. I knocked on the door loudly, and I heard her soft voice invite me in.

I pushed open the door and saw her shoot a silver Elrolian arrow, hitting a bull's-eye on the dartboard. My mother is quite young, and is always doing exercise and keeping up with her training. Her long brown hair is always running down her shoulders, and she never likes to tie it up much. Never have I seen a day when she hasn't gone out to do a few laps around the castle. She was greatly distraught by my father's death, but the event didn't make her any less friendly or caring. Of course, she was practicing late at night, for there was so much to do in the day.

She saw me enter, and smiled with joy. 'Storm!' She laid down her bow and ran over and gave me a bone-crushing hug, which I hastily escaped from.

'It's been two days, you've had me terrified!'

I raised my eyebrows. 'You were terrified that your thirty-year-old son, Elrolian survival expert, who was gone two days, was in some kind of trouble.'

'Storm, I'm your mother, I worry about you. I don't want you to leave me like your sister and father.'

Oh, well this was great. After what she had just said, I was about to tell her I was going on a dangerous mission regarding my father's killer and I might never come back? My life sucks.

Well, I'm still me. I came right out with it. 'Um, I'm going out to Wouldlock,' I said carefully. 'I'm going to … to, well, help protect some animals along with the Animal Defence Organisation.'

'Well, that's great! I think it's fantastic that you're making an effort to help protect animals. You always loved them. Wait … what exactly are you protecting them from?'

'Some hunters,' I said casually. 'We were sent a tip that some hunters would be arriving.'

'That'll be dangerous,' she said.

'I'm up to it. Anyway, I have to go soon, because they're coming in about three hours.'

'Well, I wish you all the luck I can,' she said, giving me another hug. 'Go save those animals, dear.'

I smiled and went out the door. I would be back. I had to come back.

I met the others back at the main entrance.

'You okay, Storm?' Spyra asked me.

I nodded, and did my best to put on a smile. 'Fine. Let's go, then. We need to protect Black Amber.'

'Wait, Storm, we still have three hours, we might as well get some weapons from the mines!'

Lypherace nodded. 'Brilliant idea! We'll need a lot though.'

'Let's go ask the king,' said Spyra, heading towards the stairs.

'No!' I said, pulling her back. 'He would never authorise us to give humans freshly made Elrolian weapons! We'd be exiled for betrayal! Bringing a human in here at all set off a spark in his head. We must do this in secret.'

Spyra nodded. 'We can't go directly to the mines, they're way too hard to get to.'

'We can catch them as they bring the weapons in. I know where the storage rooms are.' I was already moving.

'What type should we get?' I asked, almost talking to myself.

'A bunch of Vortexes,' Spyra said. 'They'll suit everyone.'

'Yeah, but they'll need to be elemental, we want to try our best not to kill them,' I said firmly.

'What are Vortexes?' asked Lypherace, confused.

'They're weapons that change at the user's will. To any weapon of the original volume,' I said, smiling at his amazed expression.

'It took an hour for our history teacher to explain them fully to us,' Spyra added.

'We'll get ten. Not everyone will need them,' I said, mentally counting the people helping us. 'Turn here,' I instructed, turning sharply to the left, passing the staircase we had just come down.

We went through a few more corridors until we reached the forge. As always, it was heavily locked. I took out a key from a necklace I was wearing and opened the first of three doors. My father, who had worked here for a few months when he was a student, had given this key to me. I valued it above even my ice axe, for it was a gift from my father. But it was not unique in any way, for every Elrolian over thirty had this key. I had my own, but this was the one I always used: my father's key.

The second door required a handprint of an Elrolian, which I could easily give.

And the third door was, well, just a door, nothing special about it. But of course, its crafting was of Elrolian standard, and bore the symbol of the Elrolian mines, the tilted square.

It was a candlelit, wooden room that, unlike the rest of Elrolia, was messy. The people that worked here didn't care about tidiness. Now just because it was untidy didn't mean it wasn't organised. Those two words don't mean the same thing. The workers seemed to be able to locate everything they needed, effortlessly.

The place was littered with tools, bits of scrap metal, and blazing fires. I had no idea how anyone could work there, but they did. In fact, I knew one of the people very well. But at the moment, the place was empty besides us.

But it was not quiet. No, not at all. The machines were always working, though there are few. They machines that we do have are simple, and all solar-powered. Yeah, very eco-friendly!

There was a huge box marked "package no. 1," which I carefully approached and opened. Nope, in that one were about a million silver arrows. Not what we were looking for.

Now this was not thieving. These boxes are here for the purpose of people taking the weapons in them. As long as you're Elrolian, it's fine. If you aren't, you simply don't have access to these tools. The rules weren't like this, as you can probably guess, until Hunter attacked. So much had changed since then.

I checked the next box, and almost found what we were looking for. Yes, they were Vortexes. Now, before you use a Vortex, when you haven't willed them to change form, they assume the shape of a simple staff. They come in different colours, but the standard is silver. I don't know how it's physically possible for this change to happen, but there's some person who'd know out there. Probably the creators I'd told you about – Surplex and Velocito. But, as I said, this wasn't exactly what we needed. These were normal, with not an ounce of elemental power in them.

I then realised that looking in this 'normal' section would do no good, so I moved into the second of five large rooms, where the elemental tools were kept. I easily found the box, and took out ten surprisingly light black elemental Vortexes.

I passed three to Spyra and three to Lypherace, and kept four to carry myself. We swiftly moved out of the room, taking care not to tread on any of the fallen objects. Well, at least we had something to attack with. I honestly didn't know what we would have done without these. I mean, even if the campers of Wouldlock *did* have some type of weapon, a simple climbing knife wouldn't do well in this situation.

'We've got about two hours and forty minutes, we'll get there with about two hours left, if we hurry,' Spyra said.

Lypherace looked at us, his eyes hidden by his glasses, with the usual grin on his face. 'Then let's hurry.'

We rushed out of Elrolia, and at the gates by the atrium came face to face with Emrax. He was, as I said, extremely young, very playful, and I'd never seen him when he wasn't smiling. He was the most understanding Elrolian here. He loved green, which is good, as nature's symbolic colour *is* green.

'Emrax!' I said with joy, almost dropping the Vortexes.

'Hey, Storm! Spyra! Good to see you two! Where've you been? And who's this young man?'

'Lypherace,' he introduced himself, shaking Emrax's hand warmly.

'Pleasure to meet you. I'm Emrax Treestone.'

'Oh, we've been out in Wouldlock,' I said.

'So, I see you've got a few fancy weapons there, my friend,' he said, his eyebrows rising slightly.

'Yeah, we're in a hurry, but I left a note explaining everything in your office.'

'Sure, no problem. But anyway, if you're going to take a weapon, best go for elemental, right?' he said, grinning.

I smiled. 'You bet.'

'Well then, I wish you luck with whatever you're doing ... if you need any.'

'Trust me, Emrax,' Spyra said, 'we do.'

'Well, I ... wish you luck. Come back in one piece. And, by the way....' Emrax came closer, looking over my shoulder. 'No... is that...?'

I turned to see what he was looking at, and saw nothing unusual, but then realised he was talking about the Ice Axe, which was still strapped to my back.

'Yeah, you remember Ravenwood?'

'Of course.'

'He found this, passed it on to someone named Wolf, and then Wolf gave it to me.'

'Wow, I mean, the real Ice Axe! Do you know, that –'

'Emrax, Emrax, I know. Whatever you're going to say about this thing, I know. You told us about it last week, and the week before, and the week before that.... You know, I think we get reminded of this thing *every* week.'

'I'm sorry, my friend, but you know how I love this thing. And you know why.'

Emrax's father had owned this axe once before, until he passed it on to an Elemental lord, Lord of Sound, who died, and the axe was never seen again until it was rediscovered by Ravenwood. I believe Stringer, Lord of Metal, inherited the Sound Lord's powers along with his own.

I nodded. 'Yes, I do. By the way, I thought you were only coming back at twelve?'

'Oh, yeah, well, things moved along faster than I expected them to. Anyway, if you're in a rush, you'd better get going.'

'Yeah, we should,' Spyra said, again checking that watch of hers. 'Bye, Emrax!'

'Bye, Spyra, Storm, Lypherace. It was a pleasure meeting and seeing you all!'

I smiled, and Emrax leaped up the stairs. He would be outraged when he saw the note explaining what was going on, and how they had to have a whole meeting to decide whether to help us or not. And he would be even angrier when he discovered what the council's final decision was.

'Okay, let's head for the camp. We can hand out the weapons and set up our final plans,' I said, already moving again.

'Where do you think they'll attack?' Lypherace asked.

'Probably the Black Trees. They know that's where Black Amber will be.'

We continued right out of the Castle of Elrolia to the gates. I nodded to Glasus and Florez, and we walked into the dark, eerie night.

Despite the fact I had not slept for a long time now, I did not feel tired in the least. And it was a good thing, for a drowsy Elrolian isn't much of an advantage in a battle.

We walked through the forest past the treacherous Black Trees, where I knew Black Amber would be lying, waiting for an attack, for they too knew what was coming, thanks to Altralz.

By this time I had been to and easily recognised almost all of Wouldlock, for I had probably had some type of encounter with an animal in every part. The skeleton thing, the hyenas, the wolves – or at least, near-wolves. Well, you get the idea. It was a pretty cool but dangerous experience.

So we continued on walking. *Walking*. I mean, we were on such a time-sensitive … mission, I guess? We didn't have much time at all, yet we were just walking. I guess it's okay, but in most awesome adventure stories, they have better ways of getting around besides using your feet. I'm not saying there are no action stories where people walk, but … whatever. I'll shut up about walking, and just walk.

We crossed over the log to the other side of the place, and *walked* through the field, tightly gripping the Vortexes in our arms. I walked up the jagged rocky steps, and pushed away the boulders, entering the loud, crowded camp.

All of the campers were talking, anxiety and fear in their faces, exchanging the little supplies they had. They barely noticed me coming in, but when Ardor did see me, he gave a loud growl and everyone stopped at once, gathering around the central table. We placed the Vortexes on the wooden table.

'Those stupid people are *not* coming to our aid. We won't be seeing them for a while.'

Wolf looked very put out. 'The Elrolians … aren't coming?'

Spyra shook her head. 'We're on our own.'

'We can't defend ourselves like this,' said Slare, who was hardly ever so discouraged. 'We've got Black Amber, two Elrolians, and a bunch of campers. And a couple Orians,' she added, looking at Ardor and Peldor.

'Now, we didn't come back with nothing. We got these,' I said, indicating the Erolian Onyxus-made staffs. I started to give a brief explanation of how they worked. 'These may look simple, but they are very intricate tools. They can convert into anything of their approximate size and weight.'

'No way …' said Stream. 'How is that scientifically possible?'

'It isn't,' I muttered to Spyra. 'No, I'm not sure. But I think you'll be able to come up with some reasonable explanation.'

'That is so awesome,' said Raider, who mostly thought everything was awesome, but this seemed to exceed his expectations. 'You mean these things are, like, mobile toilets? Who invented this?'

We were all staring at him, and I can imagine he felt rather uncomfortable. He cleared his throat. 'Sorry. Continue, Storm.'

'So these will be enormously useful in this … confrontation.'

This battle would be hard on everyone, and I could imagine just how nervous they all were right now.

Blade then voiced what I guessed everyone was wondering. 'Will we….' He gulped. 'Die?'

They all were looking at Spyra and me, and Lypherace too.

'Well, I certainly hope not,' Spyra said.

'Also, we met someone in Elrolia. Ravenwood.'

'Yes!' Ardor shouted with relief. 'He's safe! I knew it!'

The team certainly was very happy, but it was necessary for me to tell them what he'd told us.

'He and the king of Elrolia are the people that are Hunter's current targets.'

They gasped.

'I know, I know, but we'll put up a fight if he tries getting them.'

'Do you think he'll be here, trying to get Black Amber in person?' asked Peldor.

I nodded gravely. 'With a matter of this importance? I would believe so.'

'Well then,' said Ardor. 'We have about two hours left. Let's get our final preparations in order.

We gathered close around the table, and started discussing our plans as Ardor laid out a huge map of central Wouldlock. Raider, Blade, Slare, Sora, Stream, and Wolf each took a Vortex, along with Spyra and me. Many of us also had other weapons, like my axe, or Spyra's knives, but we took the Vortexes as well just in case. The others had other things. Ardor's claws, Peldor's swords, and Mac and Icon had millions of fancy things, including an incredible Elkwood hammer that Mac had built himself.

'Wait…' I said. 'Where's Viper?'

Wolf came up to me. 'Don't worry, he's fine. He went up

to Stringer's place to help him out with a project that they're working on called Black Aqua. He says it is too important for him to miss. He had to go. He said he was hoping it was ready in time to help us, but I don't think it will be.'

'What's Black Aqua?' Lypherace asked.

'No idea.' Wolf said, shrugging. 'Although it's something big and *top secret* as it says on the file.'

'So it's just us,' I said. 'Okay then.'

'So listen,' Ardor said. 'Storm, I was thinking that you and Spyra could be the main attack force. I mean, Elrolians, you know, it's perfect for you.'

'Sounds good,' Spyra said happily.

I nodded. 'What about you, Ardor?'

He thought for a minute. 'How about Peldor and I guard the other direction, so then the open sides can be covered by Wolf and Slare on one side, and Lypherace and Sora on the other.' They all nodded in understanding.

'Then Raider and Blade, maybe you could take Mac and Icon up into the trees and guard there? Remain hidden. Keep the little guys safe, but cause a ton of damage to the hunters.'

'You got it, man,' Blade said. 'But what are we centred around?'

'I don't know...' said Ardor. 'But that's okay, right? We could go around a tree or something.'

'Yes, we will be more than contented to instigate various quantities of undercover mutilation to these delinquents,' Raider said politely.

I could see Ardor's eyes frown at these words. 'Um, good. Is that alright with everyone?' he asked loudly.

Mac and Icon came into the room.

'No!' said Mac, as if we were a bunch of idiots. 'You forget ... black ...um, black ... Black Shadows!'

Wolf smiled. 'What's that?'

'Black Shadows is name of place in the future! I create! One day, I will find island, and call it Black Shadows. It sound cool. I call our creations Black Shadows too!'

'What creations?' Slare asked kindly.

He and Icon waddled back into their room, and came out a minute later followed by a dozen black and silver robotic animals. They were extremely accurate. The size and detail were just incredible. I would have thought it downright impossible for someone of his age to make these. There were tigers, wolves, snakes, and animals that seemed to have come purely out of Mac's imagination. One – I am not kidding – was *flying*. They actually worked!

Raider swore under his breath.

'Can these things be controlled?' I asked, kneeling down to look into his face.

Icon nodded. 'Yeah! Voice, for Mac and me, and also they sense movement with these sensors, and they have sound and biocognetic sensors down here, so they can be controlled by programming in commands!'

'Biocognetic?' I asked.

'We invent,' Mac explained.

'You don't mind if they get … hurt?' Spyra asked.

Mac shook his head wildly. 'They can't get hurt. Look, they made of … um, Elrolians' Onyxus.'

I frowned. 'How did you get that?'

'When Viper was doing Black Aqua project, he found Elrolian Onyxus down in the sea!'

'Ardor?' I said, still staring at the robots in amazement. 'Get a place for these on your plan.'

'No problem,' he said. 'They can be defence, in case one of us is getting overrun by the hunters.'

I heard him scribbling a note on the map.

'I use programming on computer to make alive!' said Mac happily, stroking a snake that was making eerie and very realistic sounds.

‘These young men could give Stringer a run for his money,’ Spyra said.

‘Yeah, that’s all great, but we need to go out now. We don’t want to be late for these people,’ said Lypherace.

The team nodded.

Spyra took a deep breath. ‘Well, let’s go confront Hunter, and save Black Amber.’

HUNTER STRIKES

The team hiked out into the dark forest, leaving the old wooden camp with nothing living inside, although we had left one of Icon's lions on guard just in case anything happened. We would be able to see what it was seeing using our phones.

I could tell that Wolf wasn't thrilled, leaving his only home with hardly any protection, and neither were the other campers, but it was necessary for us to have as many people as we could get for this.

I still couldn't get over the fact that the Elrolians were doing nothing. It was an outrage. It was like having your family back out as you tried to do what was right. But maybe we were wrong. Maybe it's the Elrolians we can't trust, not helping us in any way like that. When Hunter comes for them, they'll be sorry. Or maybe they won't have time to be.

I started to wonder how this could actually work. We had

no choice. Hunter would not give up, and he would, sooner or later, get what he wanted. *That's* how this works. There really wasn't a way we could keep Black Amber from him.

But we would try.

'There,' I said. 'Let's take Black Amber there, to the border of Elrolia. That way no other animals will be in danger, it'll be far from your camp, and the Elrolians might see us and take pity on us,' I said, though rather doubtful about the Elrolians changing their minds. That was more of a wild dream then something that might actually happen. But I wanted to believe that we still had hope.

'Good idea,' said Slare, and we turned to face the border.

We walked over to the place I'd suggested, along with the dozen quiet animal robots that Mac and Icon had made to help us. Honestly, these two children might be more helpful than all of Elrolia.

I realised when looking at them that the two children each had a black arm brace on their right arms. They looked extremely complex, yet not a messy pile of scrap metal. They actually looked good, maybe even fashionable, in a way.

I slowed down until they two little guys had caught up with me.

'What are those?' I asked, nodding at the things on their arms.

As always, Mac was the first one to answer. As you've probably realised, he's very talkative.

'These are armour for our arms,' he explained. 'We made it! But that's not all! They have saw, laser, and touch sensor, and a place where a phone go in, a way to control my robots, a claw, a shooter, and even more.'

'What does it shoot?' I asked, peering at his arm.

'These,' he said, taking out a few solid black marble-shaped things. They have elemental sparks in them so they can explode with different things!'

'Wow. How long did it take to make?'

'Two months,' he said, a big smile on his face, as I could see in the darkness. 'I have got used to robots, so I make things easy.'

'Wow. Your robots will be great against Hunter.'

'Yeah! They will make him a– a– a pancake! He will be a ugly green, mashed-potato pancake,' he said with disgust.

I laughed. 'You got it.'

He gripped my hand tight, and he showed me how his animals worked as we walked. I didn't understand most of what he was saying, like stuff about gyro sensors, or infrared beacons, but it was cool to hear him tell me about them and even show me some cool stuff on them.

It didn't seem like any of the team was tired at all. I didn't see how they could be though, with something like this coming up. They were worried they might upset Hunter too much, and become his next target. Although honestly, I would like nothing better than to get him mad. Maybe I could find some way to break his arm or something. Something that would make me feel at least a bit better about my father's death. The event had haunted me ever since I saw it happen. Always I have wanted revenge.

I guess that was really all this was about. Revenge. Hunter taking revenge on Ravenwood and the king, me wanting revenge on him, along with so many others.

'Here!' Ardor barked. 'We can stay here.'

'Wolf, can you go round up Black Amber? Tell them it's about to start.'

Wolf nodded and we went over to the edge of the bank. I swung out my axe, and, using the same technique as I had before, created an ice bridge that sparkled visibly even in the night.

'Thanks,' he said, walking out fearlessly into the forest. 'Try not to start without me.'

'No problem. You got the Vortex?'

He raised it up for me to see, and continued on.

At the border of Elrolia was a large tree, which was perfect for an ambush. I wanted to have the element of surprise on our side, so we all climbed up into the tree, leaving the robots camouflaged against the tree. The tree was strong, with lots of thick branches and leaves, providing good space and cover for us.

The forest was quiet, as if the animals knew to be silent for what was coming next. It was maybe the most suspenseful moment of my life, besides the Battle of Elrolia, of course. At any moment, the hunters might come out ready to attack.

Raider and Blade climbed into the trees with Mac and Icon, pretending it was a race. When Raider laughed, and looked down, he was very disappointed when he didn't see the two kids there, for they were already far ahead. The rest of the team climbed up too.

But the hunters did not come. We waited and waited, and finally I heard quiet yet audible growls. It was, without a doubt, Black Amber, and sure enough, out came all of them, led by both Wolf and Altralz. He looked around for a moment, then realised where we were, and said something to Altralz, who gave a series of growls to Black Amber. They nodded, then, like a flock of birds, scattered, flying silently into the nearby trees.

I heard Spyra talking to me. 'Storm, come, we need to discuss final plans.'

'Spyra, I could barely deal with the planning we did in the camp, but when it comes to me, I never plan. Plans are too easy to manipulate. Look at their plan. Thanks to them *planning*, we now know exactly what they're doing. You see, you are the type of person who plans everything beforehand. Wolf, for example, plans when he sees a problem. I don't plan, I just do what I want.' She didn't look too sure. 'Trust me.'

I waited one more minute, and then just couldn't stand it. I didn't endanger the others, just myself.

I leaped down from the tree, and performed a clean summersault to get back to my feet. I love doing that.

'HUNTER!' I bellowed. 'I AM STORM ORTHOCLASE, SON OF ELRACE ORTHOCLASE, ONE OF YOUR PAST VICTIMS, AND I REST HERE WAITING!'

I looked up, and saw the team staring at me in horror. I heard nothing but my own voice echoing back to me.

I actually don't know how else to say this, so I'll say it like this. I was extremely bored. Then, my brain sparked into battle mode. I jumped up into the air, involuntarily executing a mid-air summersault, at the same time taking my axe from my back, just as the space I'd been standing in exploded with hot red flames, and then instantly died out as quickly as they'd begun. I have no idea how I saw that coming, but luckily I did.

Then, the whole world seemed to go into slow motion, as I saw a silver javelin coming straight for my head. In a second, it was a metre from my face, and my axe swung up, deflecting it back perfectly. I didn't know how it had happened. I didn't think I could have done anything like that. This seemed too much of a coincidence. I wondered if this was what Androma Faithly had meant about this axe saving my life. It seemed so. It was so such a simple, yet meaningful event that had saved my life. For I knew without touching it that the javelin was Elrolian -created. Or else the axe would have shattered it instantly.

Hunter had arrived.

'Come get me,' I muttered, twirling my axe in my hand, ready to strike.

Then he came out. Slowly, he came into view out of the dark, shadowy Black Trees. Hunter himself. He was wearing nothing but black. He had on black jeans, and a black armoured vest, along with a black hood that covered most of his short, messy brown hair. He had a black metal thing over his mouth. Not anything fancy, just a hard thing that covered his mouth and nose. Even from this distance I could see that no air at all could escape from that. How he was living with that thing, or why he had it on at all, I had no clue. It was new to me, for I had not seen it ten years ago, the last time I saw Hunter, at the battle. And though he was hard to see now, my eyes were very keen.

Just from looking at him you could tell he was evil – he just had that kind of glimmer in his eyes that showed nothing but cruelty and contempt. He had a blank expression, but I knew that later on it would turn into a cruel smile that had absolutely nothing to do with laughter or anything of its nature.

'Well, my friend, wait no more.' The strange mask did not change his voice. It sounded just as it always had. He said it as if we were friends, as if he were a good person at heart. But I knew better. He was evil, nothing more. Nothing would change that.

He walked out calmly to the edge of the land, and walked across the ice bridge that I had stupidly left alone.

'Now, excuse me for my poor memory, but who are you? I mean, I know you're Storm, son of whoever, but who *exactly?*'

I snarled. He didn't even remember. He could remember that I'd told him I was waiting, but not the name of the person waiting? His memory really was horrible. I was Storm Orthoclase! What else did he want to know? I should have taken this chance to attack, but I would not be gaining any advantage whatsoever. I would merely start this battle earlier. I would wait until the right opportunity arose.

'As I said, I am Storm Orthoclase, of Elrolia. You killed my father when you betrayed us.'

'Yes, yes, that's right, of course. And naturally you want me dead,' he said, his voice not changing in the slightest. 'Or, if you're like me, you would wish for me to spend the rest of my life in eternal pain.'

I didn't reply. I could feel the others looking at me from the treetops. Hunter seemed to as well.

He leaned closer and whispered to me. 'How about you call your friends down here, and we can get this started? I'll get my friends, you get yours, got it?'

He smiled and walked back to the trees. I turned and nodded. They leapt down as I had and we got up into our positions.

'I'm going to tear his ugly face off his worthless body,' Ardor growled. 'And then roast it on my burning claws.'

I watched as about a hundred or so people emerged from the dark trees. Each of them held knives, and strange-looking long tubes that I imagined were some sort of gun. I hate guns. They're stupid. Then two more groups came from the other sides.

'I really doubt this will change your mind at all, Storm,' called Hunter, 'but you have the option to walk away, untouched. You haven't upset me; I don't see any reason I would need to do this to you. I do not want to hunt you, but if you make the wrong moves in this … struggle, then that may change.'

None of us moved, of course. We were staying to fight.

'You probably know by now that I have a spy in Elrolia. If you didn't know, I'm telling you now. I know that that arrogant bunch of fools didn't want anything to do with you. And in that matter, I'm completely on your side. You asked for help from your family, they gave you none of it. You may have some idea why I did what I did now. If you join me, I can assure you that you will get your revenge.'

'Shut up, and prepare to die,' I said, and we charged.

The robots went ahead of us, and took on a quarter of the hunters, biting, snapping, and scratching them.

I went straight for Hunter, but I saw a familiar face in my way.

'Hello again,' said Garmax, sneering at me. 'What can I help you with?'

I swung my axe, and with a few quick moves had him trapped, the handle of my axe against his neck, his back against a hard tree. He coughed, then with another quick manoeuvre, escaped.

He swung out a knife identical to the ones he'd used before, and stabbed the palm of my hand. The knife went straight through. I could the point of the blade sticking out of the back of my hand, which had quickly turned red with fresh blood. The blood flowed as if it were leaking out of a hole in a water pipe.

I pulled my arm away, not letting any sound escape my lips. I felt warm blood trickle down my hand at an alarming rate. I saw that it had stained his silver knife with bright red liquid. I wiped it against my shirt, and again went in to attack, wrapping my hand in my shirt, the pain overwhelming me.

I kicked out, and he grabbed my foot, throwing me into a tree. I pushed off as my feet made contact with the trunk. I shot back towards him, and used my back to knock him off his legs, falling with a thud against the hard ground, right on a tree root. Garmax clawed at my injured hand with his, and I couldn't stop a yell escaping my lips. I fell to the ground alongside him, and kicked him further away.

A woman threw a knife at me, which I easily ducked, and I grabbed her by the collar and swung her into the cold river with my good hand.

I went back to Garmax, and picked him up the same way, swinging my axe in my signature style, sending him flying headfirst into the Black Trees.

I could hear screams, both triumphant ones and those of agony, and could see swords, knives, and axes clashing against each other. I also saw a number of bodies being flung into the river, none of which were ours, thankfully.

I saw Raider lying limply on the ground, and weaved my way through the crowd, whacking people away with my axe as I attempted to reach the twin. I got to his body, and handed it carefully to Ardor, who had just finished kicking away a number of hunters. He nodded, taking Raider up the tree, and depositing him by his brother. It seemed he'd been knocked out. At least he wasn't dead. I had seen his chest rising and falling.

Mac and Icon were yelling completely random things while throwing little basketball-shaped items at the hunters' heads. I didn't see the effect that they had on the hunters, but I didn't imagine it to be good – for them, I mean.

I wondered what we would do now. Why weren't they searching for Black Amber? Then I realised that they'd already found them. Behind me, Black Amber and about fifty hunters were fighting, one on one, while the rest tried to stop us.

I went right up to Hunter. He was fighting Ardor, which, I was glad to see, was proving a challenge for him. Ardor fought fearlessly, swiping his claws at Hunter, which Hunter was having a hard time dodging. Ardor, I could see, was mad – very mad. I knew that Hunter had attacked his home before, and Ardor had not liked it.

I heard that many died then, and I imagine that Ardor had a relative who'd been killed as well. I took this chance. I grabbed an abandoned Vortex from the ground and it instantly transformed into a sharp sword. I adjusted my grip, and threw it like a javelin at Hunter's leg. It hit, and then, as the knife had done to my hand, it tore the fabric of his jeans and sank right through his leg, protruding out the other side.

I swallowed hard. Why had I done that? I was dead. Actually I was much worse than that.

One of Hunter's other associates took up the battle with Ardor. Hunter's face was, for the first time, contorted with fury, the blade of the sword still sticking out of his leg, bloody and full of dirt from the ground.

I was taking deep breaths, shaking from the sight. For the first time in my life, I was almost scared, for angering Hunter was not a good idea.

'You … did this to me?' he said, his voice a hoarse whisper.

I said nothing, and did nothing.

'You, Storm Orthoclase, are in trouble.'

He gripped the sword, and tugged it out of his leg, and fell to the ground.

'When I next see you, I will be hunting you.' He touched something on his arm, and like the others had done before, disintegrated, the calm wind blowing the black dust away.

I was not one to take time thinking about what to do next, especially in the midst of a battle like this one. I gripped my axe hard, and turned back to the battle.

I saw a robotic tiger charging at a badly injured hunter. I saw Sora's body lying on the ground, being guarded by one of Mac and Icon's beat-up rusty black metal lions, but it wasn't too bad – the Elrolian Onyxus was holding well.

I rushed over, hacking around, deflecting bullets and knives with impossible accuracy with my axe. I knelt down next to Sora. She, unlike Raider, was dead. Her blank eyes stared beyond me into space, eyes that would never see again. I turned her over, and found a bronze knife sticking out of her still-bleeding back. I tugged it out, and examined it. There was an engraving on it – probably the name of the owner – but it was no longer legible.

I took it up to the lion, and it looked at the knife with its black lifeless eyes. Then its head turned sharply, following one person. He was bald, and very muscular. The lion went back to guarding Sora's body.

The bald man was the killer.

I nodded in thanks to the lion, and sprang to my feet, and strapped my axe to my back, running straight for the man. I tackled him, and we both landed hard on the dirty ground. He punched me hard in the stomach, knocking the wind out of me. I rolled away, and got up, clutching my bleeding fist, which had been slammed on the ground with full impact.

'You killed her!' I screamed. 'We haven't killed any of your people! You cruel murderer! How can you live with what you've done? Why do you do this? For Hunter?'

'You've been throwing my friends into ice-cold water, man. And I just don't play by the rules,' he said in a voice that seemed to anger anyone who heard it. I wanted to punch his hard little hairless head.

I took my axe off my back, into a sturdy two-handed grip.

He smiled. 'Playing like that are we then?' He leant down and grabbed a Vortex that was currently in the form of a sword – it was the same one I'd used to attack Hunter. It turned into a colourless replica of my weapon, which angered me even more.

I growled, and lined up the top of the axe – the skeleton head – with his heart. Suddenly the silver blade exploded, the shards of metal frozen in the air. Then, without warning, they all shot at a speed faster than a bullet from a gun towards the bald hunter, leaving him no time to escape. The moment they made contact with him, they froze him. Unlike the time with Black Amber, I could not see the ice around him. I guess that was because the shards came back to me, reforming the axe, yet he still stood there like a statue.

I didn't have time to marvel at what I'd done. I just moved on to the next hunter, then the next. Not including the ones dealing with Black Amber, there were about twenty left. They had completely destroyed half of the robots, and another quarter of them were just not working. Probably their life cord had been broken. They had Onyxus too.

Well, on the good side, I wasn't dead. Yet.

I saw Lypherace dealing with ten hunters, and was about to help him, when he caught my eye, sending the message *it's fine*

– *look after yourself instead.* That left about ten of them. Ardor and Peldor were handling them, so I went on to help out Black Amber. They were not doing so well. Many of them were injured, and one looked dead. I used what was now plainly *my move* – the awesome, very effective axe swing. The hunters had cleverly formed a line, slowly moving in on the animals. This was absolutely perfect. I wondered if it could possibly work – using them as dominos.

I went up to the first hunter, and knocked him into the other, then into the next one and so on. I actually got five of them into the river doing that. Then, it came from nowhere. A body went flying across the hunters' heads, right in front of my eyes, literally centimetres from my face.

It was Wolf. I ran over to him without hesitation. If he were dead, I would find and nearly kill the murderer. Wolf had grown to be one of my greatest friends. He was like me. If he believed in something, he wouldn't give up on it, no matter how hard others tried to convince him.

'Hey, you alright?'

'Yeah,' he groaned. 'Storm, your hand!'

'Yeah, it's okay. Let's finish this off.' I sighed.

We turned back to the hunters to see them play their final card. They each stepped forward, touching each creature, and in unison, vanished. It looked like film editing. It *sounded* like film editing. First I saw all of them, hunters and Black Amber, fighting loudly. Then, in the blink of an eye, they were gone. *Including Black Amber.* The forest was silent.

Wolf looked around. 'Now, why didn't they lead with that?' he wondered aloud.

I shrugged. 'Hunter wants to hunt me, they have Black Amber, we only have injured or dead people with us now, and we have to go soon to protect Elrolia. We're dead.'

We all assembled together by the tree where we'd started, gathering the abandoned weapons from the ground. This place looked like a trash can. There was blood everywhere, along with broken armour, and robot parts. The first morning light was beginning to be visible in the distance.

I kicked the frozen bald guy away from us, and we started to discuss … stuff.

'First of all, who is dead, or seriously injured?' Peldor asked.

'Sora has gone,' I said.

'Yes,' said Ardor sadly. 'It is a loss we all regret. But she went to battle knowingly, and died for a good cause.'

Died for a good cause? We hadn't gained anything. But I got Ardor's point.

'I can't believe they killed her,' said Stream in astonishment.

I looked down sadly, and tried to get off this depressing subject. 'What about injuries?' I asked, looking around. Yeah, that's a better subject!

'Well we're fine,' said Blade, nodding towards the little guys, Mac and Icon, and his brother, who had recovered from his fall with nothing more than a sore head (or so he said) and a few scrapes.

'Nothing wrong with me, besides a few little scratches,' said Lypherace.

He wasn't telling the entire truth. His suit was ripped and bloody, and his whole right leg was covered in blood. It was hard to see the blood against his dark clothes, but my eyes had adjusted to the dark through the night, and the sun was giving off light now, peeking out from the treetops.

No one else was wounded much, except me, and I didn't see any need for the team to know of my hand injury. I don't like it when others think me weak. Nothing against the people there, but anyone who knew of this would have treated me like I'd lost my arm.

I had wrapped up my hand carefully in a grey scarf I'd found abandoned on the floor, and it was keeping most of the remaining blood inside.

A moment later, Mac and Icon came down from the tree they'd been playing in.

'Look-it!' said Mac, presenting to me a robotic bird that he'd just made out of the parts on the ground. Looking at all the other bits of machinery, I could tell that we'd have some cleaning work to do. We didn't want this beautiful forest looking like this. Although cleaning up wasn't something to worry about right now. They had Black Amber. That was our main issue.

'Wow, Mac, that's great!' I said, distractedly.

'We need to get Black Amber back,' Slare said, and we all deeply agreed.

This was a species, and just because it was created by Hunter didn't mean it shouldn't live. It had caused us trouble, but it was an animal. Like we were. And we would ensure its survival.

I nodded. 'We need to get them back. And I think I know how….'

THE MAP

The team leant in, listening intently. Any ideas for how to get Black Amber back from Hunter would be a start, no matter how crazy they were. The parts of armour, robots, and bodies were scattered all over, but we all ignored them.

'The President said Hunter has been staying in the Spherian Science Centre or something like that. We could go in there. Break in, and get Black Amber out.'

The team nodded in approval.

'It's a good idea,' growled Ardor. 'We should send some of you out to get them back.'

Wolf frowned. 'It'll be pretty hard. I mean, we'll have to get a map of the place, break in to their secure vault, past security cameras and guards and stuff – I don't know if it's possible.'

'Well, let's see, we have two technology experts, two Elrolians, two Orians, and all of you, with your specific areas of expertise,' said Spyra confidently. 'We can have some of us at the camp working on the computers, and we'll send the rest out to get Black Amber.'

'Well, we should get right on it,' I said. 'How about Lypherace and Spyra and I go, and Stream and you guys can do the complicated technology stuff?'

'Sounds good,' Peldor said.

'There's really no sense in delaying anything, so how about you go now?' said Blade.

Ardor shook his head. 'Unlike you, Blade, the rest of the team is badly injured. We should go back to the camp, maybe give Sora a nice burial, and then they can set off.'

'Sure,' said Blade. 'Sorry. But will we really have time for a funeral? I mean, things are getting pretty urgent now.'

'Yeah, maybe not,' said Ardor. 'Not yet. But let's head back. Lots to do,' he said, looking around at the mess we'd made.

The others were tired, but I was full of energy, and I sprinted ahead along with Wolf and those incredible shoe things that Lypherace had given him.

'So, you alright?' he asked me as we went along, gradually coming closer and closer to the camp. 'Your hand, I mean.'

I nodded. 'It's okay.'

'Who did it to you?'

'Garmax. Remember the hunter from Wouldlock, before the battle? The big guy who stabbed Lypherace as well? Him. That idiot.'

'Yeah, I remember.'

'Also … Hunter wants to, um, kill me.'

We slowed down. He looked at me, probably thinking this was a joke, but the moment he saw my eyes, he knew it wasn't.

'Why?' he asked quietly.

'I stuck a sword through his leg. Almost cut it off.'

He nodded, swallowing hard. 'He'll try to kill you, my friend. But I'm not going to let that happen. It *won't* happen.'

I nodded in thanks. This was the kindest human I'd ever encountered. Better than Ravenwood, or anyone. He cared about me like I was family. He really was a loyal friend.

'Thanks, man.'

He nodded grimly, and we started to move again, but at a slower pace. We crossed the log and entered the camp, which was just as we'd left it, the lion pacing back and forth through the different unlocked rooms. When it saw us, it nodded its head slightly, and went into Mac and Icon's room, this time staying in there.

Wolf and I went into separate rooms, and I took my armour and shirt off to clean my numerous wounds. I almost couldn't bear to do my hand. I unwrapped the scarf and saw that I couldn't see through it, which was a relief, but the amount of blood was abundant. It was absolutely disgusting.

I wrapped it with a thick layer of black silk, which surprisingly kept the blood inside, although it instantly soaked the soft fabric.

I cleaned off my back, chest, and arms with the various medicines that the camp had stored for any injuries they received, which must have been many, considering that they lived out here in the wild, amongst all these animals and of course, nature itself.

My face wasn't so bad, so I just left it. It is surprising how quickly the gashes turn into scabs and scars, for they already had, besides my hand, of course.

Sadly, I had no extra clothes with me, so I had to put on the same ones I'd had on in the battle, which didn't look pretty, but were better than nothing.

I went back outside to find Wolf in a clean shirt along with the rest of the team who'd just arrived. Lypherace went to get his leg and the rest of him sorted, and I sat down with Wolf and Spyra, who said she didn't want to clean up just yet, while the others followed Lypherace.

'So, Spyra, how did you do?' I asked her.

'Not so bad. Got a few of them into the river, prevented Stream from dying, twice, and kept myself alive.

'Well you did that very well,' I said. 'And Wolf? How'd you do in the battle?'

'Okay. These foot braces helped out a lot. You know, like with jumping, and all those agility moves and stuff. Except for when that guy threw me ten feet into the air at the end.'

'Lypherace was incredible,' remarked Spyra. 'I mean, he has the skills of an Elrolian, if not more. Every hunter he set his eye on ended up unconscious, lying in the river. I'm just glad he's on our side.'

'I'm glad you think so highly of me,' said the man himself, coming out of the room where he'd been quickly cleaning himself. He was, like me, dressed in the same ripped-up clothes he had on during the battle. 'The team's just getting finished up, they'll be out in a sec.'

He came over and took a seat opposite me next to Spyra. 'So, we'll have to go into the security office at the centre, and um, *borrow* a map of the building. They won't have the kinds of maps we need in the tourist section.'

'Well, this place is pretty important in Spheria – really important. They'll have top-notch security, and it'll be near impossible to get in unnoticed,' said Spyra. I wondered how she knew this.

'What's wrong with getting in noticed? We walk in with their security badges and clothes, and get the map. Should be pretty simple,' said Lypherace.

'Yeah, unless, like, *Hunter* is there waiting and he catches us,' I said.

'We won't get caught. Guys, this is some of what I do for a living. I spy on people, and protect what I believe is important. I've got fifteen years of experience. Don't be so discouraged, we'll get Black Amber back.'

'Well, you seem confident,' said Wolf. 'I agree with Lypherace, we can definitely do this. What's the worst that can happen?'

I raised my eyebrows. 'Quite a lot of things. But who cares, let's do this! I like danger – most of the time,' I said confidently.

'Okay, we'll inform the rest of the team, then we can go off,' said Lypherace, and as if on cue, the members of the Animal Defence Organisation came in to the lounge and took a seat on the circular plank of wood they used as a bench.

'So, what've we got planned out?' asked Ardor, taking a seat, lessening the pain in his muscles that had been at full motion in the battle.

'Well I think that Lypherace, Storm, and I will go and find the map, then get back here where we can plan how to get in,' said Spyra.

Peldor nodded. 'Sounds good. How long do you estimate it'll take?'

'Three hours from leaving to coming back, I'd guess,' said Wolf after calculating the events in his mind.

'Okay, we'll send out a team to clean up the area, or if Mac and Icon have some cleaner machine…'

'We do! Yeah!' said Mac excitedly. 'It clean all of trash, and make into other parts to build for me!'

'Well that's sorted, then, we'll just … chill,' said Raider, relaxing considerably.

'You sure you can handle these two?' I asked Ardor.

'Yeah, you guys go have fun, man. Ardor is responsible, he'll take good care of us.'

'No, man, they don't pay me enough to get me to deal with you two.'

Raider smiled. 'Yeah, we're a handful,' he said proudly.

'Okay, Stream, get your tracking stuff, whatever you need ready for when we come back,' said Wolf.

'Right on it,' he said, rushing into his room.

I rubbed my hands together. 'Okay, then, we'll get out of your place now, leave you alone, we'll see you in three hours,' I said.

We didn't need much. Lypherace grabbed a bunched-up layer of bubble wrap for some unknown purpose and we set off to Spheria, moving at quite a quick pace as we did when we had a group like this.

'Um, Lypherace, what's that?' I asked after a while, pointing to the bubble-wrap, for I just couldn't stand not knowing any longer.

'Oh, it's a clothes-changer. I programed it to assume the form of a security uniform from the Spherian University of Science,' said Lypherace, smiling at my look of what must have been bewilderment.

'What about us?' Spyra asked, obviously wondering why we didn't plan this beforehand.

'No worries young lady, you all look the perfect age.' Lypherace said.

'For what?' Wolf asked, as confused as I was.

'Students, guys! This is a university! Students don't have uniforms or whatever – you go in, they honestly don't care. Anyway, you three are brilliant at hiding from curious eyes, aren't you? It'll be fine, relax a bit!'

We continued walking – or jogging more like – with Wolf occasionally racing ahead, jumping to incredible heights with his feet things.

I really liked this part of Wouldlock. The trees were beautiful, and so were the rivers and grass. I'm not saying that it isn't nice in Elrolia, but there it's always covered with snow, and only pine trees live there. I like the range of nature here. The animals are fantastic. So many! It's incredible that these animals are as common to the campers as Elrolians are to me. In Elrolia we do have animals, but not quite as many. We're mostly known for our wolves, both snow and stone. They have more scientific names, the real ones, but we all call them by these simple ones. I think snow is a Lexphorus wolf, and the stone one is a Regaltum wolf. We also have others like deer, and foxes, and owls and stuff, but most of the animals here I've never seen before.

This time, it was rather different from before. The university was very far from the border, and we would not be able to walk there easily, so we caught a cab to take us.

It was a comfortable, sleek metallic silver vehicle, like all of the Spherians cars. Here, it's like it's only up to standards if it's blinding white or metallic, or has some precious gem in it. I prefer my place. New isn't always better. Emrax and I always believed in the old things that were forgotten, never given a moment of thought. It was those things that were special. That held the most power. Or so I believed.

I am not an easily worried person, but this time I was rather uneasy. I mean, who wouldn't be, after getting a warning like I had gotten from Hunter? I doubted I would stay sane for another month, with him on my trail. This was a serious thing … what would I be in danger of losing? My home? My family? Everything I love. Love is a dangerous thing. When you think of it, you imagine a good, strong bond between two people or things. But it isn't always so strong, for it is easily manipulated. Used against you. This is how Hunter attacks you. And soon, the same fate that had come to so many others would catch me, and I would fall as well.

I did not want to think about this. Especially when we were going to the one place Hunter was sure to be.

So I thought about the good things in life. The family I still had, my friends both in Elrolia and in Wouldlock that cared for me as if I *were* family. These wonderful thoughts were washed out of focus as we stopped outside the entrance to the university.

We paid the driver, and as he drove off, we turned to the building.

It was big. *Very* big. It was almost as formal as the President's office, except it was a university, so there were a number of changes that I could spot even just standing outside.

Above the entrance were the letters S U S, which obviously stood for Spherian University of Science. What better place was there to conduct experiments such as cross-breeding than a licensed building built for that purpose? Whatever Hunter did wouldn't have to be a secret, for in here it would be legal. He would have nothing to worry about, unless Black Amber escaped the building, causing havoc in the city.

'Lypherace, your clothes!' Wolf whispered.

'Right!' He strapped the bubble-wrap thing tightly around the clothes he had on, and like magic, the wrap did what he'd told us it would do. It assumed the form of a security uniform, with the university logo on it, and even an SUS ID with all his information on it, which I assumed was fake.

'Wait, what about yours? You can't go in like that!' Lypherace said, looking at our ragged clothes.

Spyra shook her head. 'Lypherace, it's okay. We're going to a science lab! Everyone will be looking like this.'

'Okay, if you say so ... I should have thought of this.'

I looked more closely at his badge, and sniggered. 'Widget Bibblesqueak?' I said, biting my lip to stop me from laughing any more.

'Yeah, I found the guy on the Internet, he's a bus driver or something.'

Spyra kept a straight face. 'Well, the name suits you.'

Lypherace smiled. 'Yeah, yeah, you guys go on and laugh, but I'll be the one laughing when someone asks for *your* name.'

We opened the doors and stepped in, facing the front desk, at which a bored-looking spectacled man was sitting, reading a magazine. He saw us and peered over his glasses.

'Students?' he said, putting the magazine down and placing his fingers over his laptop keyboard. 'And you're security?' he asked Lypherace.

'Yeah,' Lypherace said, keeping a completely straight face.

'Go on right ahead, sir.'

Lypherace went down the hall and turned right so I couldn't see any more of him. I made to go after him, but the guy at the desk stopped me.

'Excuse me, I need your names for the record of the science programme, please.'

Lypherace was right about the names – and I'm terrible at making up names.

'Oh, I'm, um, Bliggle Flatface,' I said, caught unprepared.

The guy looked at me like I was insane.

'Bliggle Flatface?'

'What? I didn't choose this name!'

He frowned, but typed in the name anyway, and waved at me to go on. I left Wolf and Spyra to give their names. I went the same way Lypherace had gone and found him waiting just around the corner.

'Mr. Flatface!' he whispered in mock surprise. 'How wonderful to see you again!'

'Shut up,' I said, smiling.

Spyra and Wolf came around the corner moments after.

'Okay, let's head up to the security office. They'll be sure to have some maps on the building that we can take for examination,' said Lypherace.

'So where's the security office?' Spyra asked.

We turned to Lypherace.

'What?' he protested. 'I don't know!'

'Yeah, but you should,' I said. I slung my arm around his neck. 'Fifteen years' experience, man.'

He looked away. 'These glasses do not go with this outfit,' he muttered.

I couldn't help laughing. 'What? Come on, let's find the place, guys.'

We didn't like the idea of splitting up – especially not here. So we went as a group, and whenever a professor or student walked by we pretended we were lost.

After a few minutes of searching, we found the office in a corner off to the side of the main hall. We were about to walk in when my eyes widened, and I gestured madly to the others to get out of view of the officer at the window.

'That's the guy!' I said. 'He killed Sora!'

Wolf bent over to look, and came back with a deep look of hatred on his face.

'He might not recognise us…' Spyra said hopefully.

I shook my head. 'I froze him in an invisible layer of ice for an hour. He won't have forgotten me – or any of us.'

'Okay, we'll need to plan how to get in,' Wolf started.

I patted him on the back, looking carefully at the murderer. 'Yeah, yeah, you guys have fun, just don't screw up.'

I strode down into the office, and five guards came at me at once. I took the phones from two of them, throwing them up into the security cameras which smashed instantly, and took the other three and broke two, keeping one for myself for later – if there *was* a later.

I grabbed the fire extinguisher as well, swinging it around, knocking out two of the guards. I did a kind of handstand, kicking another guard – I recognized him as one of the hunters from the battle. Kicked him right in the face while wrapping my feet around the fourth one, bringing that one down to the floor, capturing him in his own pair of handcuffs.

I turned to the last one, the killer, and without hesitation, jumped up onto the desk, then onto his back, slamming him to the floor as well, putting him into another set of handcuffs, ripping his shirt and using the piece of fabric to tie his legs. I used another piece as a gag, to stop his loud echoing screams.

I did the same to the last two, who had been making some noise as well.

Then another guy – a strong muscular one, much more fit than the bald killer – entered the room, humming loudly. He had a tough face, with a black earring in his right ear. Grasping the situation quickly, he sprang into action.

I caught his first attempt at a kick, and turned him over, pushing him into the desk. He growled as I put on another set of handcuffs, but still managed to grab a metal water bottle, and almost knock me out with it. I quickly disarmed him, and hit him strongly on the head with the bottle.

He didn't, however, fall unconscious to the floor like I'd planned. He got even more mad. The handcuffs slid off his sweaty wrists, and I realised that the guy's wrists were just too big to fit in them.

He growled again, sending a punch at me that almost hit me, but I dodged at the right time, jumping onto his back, and digging my elbow into it. He screamed and grabbed my foot, sending me flying into Lypherace, who had been attempting to get out his own pair of handcuffs while Spyra and Wolf dealt with another four security officers who'd probably been sent because of the enormous racket we'd been causing. My head hit the corner of the wall, and started bleeding badly. You know how it is when you get a head injury. It bleeds all over the place. I groaned, and then, catching him off guard, I sprang off the wall, crashing into him with my shoulder.

We tumbled into the next room, where we fought, punching and kicking until he made the one move that let me win. He grabbed my hand, and I pushed down on the joint connecting his thumb to his palm. He howled in pain, letting go of my hand, clutching his own hand, and I gave a quick, sharp jab on the side of his head. He collapsed like a doll.

I got back up, breathing heavily, coming out of the room just as Spyra finished off the last of the guards.

Lypherace shook his head sadly. 'I was really hoping to avoid that this time.'

I nodded, tearing off another piece of grey fabric that I kept pressed against my head to stop the bleeding.

'Sorry about that.'

'It's okay. Now let's grab that map and get out of here.'

We went into the room where the second bald guy was, and found the map displayed on a wall. I seized it, and we headed out of the building with Spyra leading the way, for she was the one who'd found this office in the first place.

We went out of the cool, air-conditioned building, and out into the breezy streets of Spheria. We hailed another cab, and sped out to the border.

We didn't talk at all during the ride. We weren't mad or anything, it was just that ... we didn't talk. We paid the driver and quickly set off to the camp, arriving there just after four-thirty. I figured we'd been out about two and a half hours, so we were good with the time.

We walked all the way back to the camp again, where we found only Ardor, Peldor, and Slare outside.

Lypherace nodded in answer to an unasked question that was clearly going through their heads.

'We got it.'

Ardor smiled. 'None of you dead?' he growled.

I shook my head happily. 'None!'

'Well, that's something,' said Peldor.

I laid the map on the table, and we looked it over for signs of any place Hunter could be keeping Black Amber. It was a very clear map, a large white piece of paper with golden ink that was slightly raised, like on books, you know?

On the map, I saw no place Hunter could possibly be creating a species of animals, and was worried that we had maybe the wrong map, but it did say SUS on the top right-hand corner, along with the very address we'd gotten it from.

'I don't see it,' I said, studying carefully.

We looked at each of the floors, and saw nothing of where he could be, only science labs, cafeterias, and classrooms.

'Maybe the back?' suggested Spyra.

We carefully flipped it over, and found some small handwritten notes, written in inky black.

Peldor read one out loud.

'The biology lab and crossbreeding labs are located elsewhere, at the Spherian University of *Biology*. We've got the wrong building. The wrong map.'

'Wait, if Hunter isn't at SUS, then why were his hunters from the battle there?' I asked.

'Well I would deduce that he did *part* of his work there – maybe gathering animal blood and DNA – but did the actual cross breeding here,' Peldor said, pointing at the written location of the Spherian University of Biology.

'Honestly, why can't they just stop this?' said Slare. 'Why have two separate buildings?'

'Because they have space and money,' muttered Ardor bitterly.

'But biology *is* science.'

'Space and money,' said Ardor. 'Two powerful things that Spheria has lots of. They take over people.'

'So we went all the way over there, did all of that for … nothing?' I said, disbelievingly.

'No,' said Ardor, 'you went there to get us Hunter's *real* location. So now, someone else will have to go get the real map.' He took a deep breath. 'I will go.'

I stared at him. 'Are – are you sure? I mean if he sees you, he'll be kind of…'

'What? Because I'm like this, I can't go where I want? This will give me a chance to share with the community my thoughts on what "different" people should be able to do.'

'Okay, but I'm coming as well,' I said firmly.

'Yes, you can come when we actually get Black Amber, but Slare was saying that you may have some other important things to do while I'm gone.'

Spyra looked up from the map. 'Um, Ardor, I'm not sure you'll be able to get there easily.'

We looked intently at her, waiting for her to carry on.

'It's on The Edge.'

Well, that sucked. The Edge is, well, the edge – the end of the Eromies. Unlike Earth, this place isn't a never-ending surface. On Earth, you can walk for your whole life, and never fall off into space. Here, it's just a massive, floating piece of land that has edges where you will tumble down into Earth's water.

Now, this isn't the bad part. The bad part is that each of the Eromies is like a country. Huge. And we're in the centre, with the other four Eromies surrounding Wouldlock. So that meant it would be a very long way to go before we got there. We would have to fly, really. There wasn't exactly any other way, except for going on land, which would take us much more than a week, time which we didn't have. Very soon, Black Amber would be utterly destroyed, with no living trace of them left on the planet. This wasn't any job for a taxi.

The team was quiet, for they knew as well how hard it would be to get there.

Then Stream came rushing in, sweat trickling down his red face. He was breathing heavily, but smiling like it was Christmas.

'I've done it!' he said proudly.

He went up to our table and carefully laid on it a wooden box. In it were small things like earphones connected to a little round cork-sized thing.

'These, my friends, will help us *tremendously*.'

'What are they?' Peldor asked.

'Mobile video cameras,' he said. 'If we're dealing with Hunter, then we need to be prepared for anything, so with these, we will be able to see and hear what everyone else is seeing and hearing, from right here in the camp. You can take it off in the shower and everything though,' he added awkwardly.

'Cool,' I said. 'That will be useful.'

'Yes, yes, I've even taken the responsibility of making some for our guests,' he said, handing one out to all of us except Wolf.

'Thanks,' I said, taking one and hooking it up to my shirt.

'Hey, no need for me,' said Lypherace. 'These glasses have got a camera, phone, and internet access in them. I can find a way to connect it to your computers. I'll never be without them.'

I shuddered, picturing Lypherace in his pajamas, wearing those glasses, with that same smile on his face. I dismissed this image from my mind.

'Great job, Stream,' Spyra said, and Stream flushed even redder with pride.

'Thank you,' he said, beaming. 'Now, how about we hook up your glasses now?'

'Sure,' Lypherace said, getting up and following Stream into his little workshop.

'So, what's this other important thing that I need to do?'

'Well, remember how when we were going to the Black Trees we met Garmax, and he said go to Alria? Well, I think it's time we did.'

Spyra nodded. 'Good idea. But where? Just explore around there?'

'I guess so. Anyway, I know this is kind of out of the question, but I got these tickets to a lemon factory, so some of us could go. They grow lemons, then use chemicals to enhance them.'

My spirits lifted. Going somewhere fun at this time would be great! Just to loosen us up a bit. I was *so* stressed.

'I've got four, and so has Stream, but if I take Storm, Lypherace and Spyra, and Wolf helps out Ardor with the Black Amber map thing, it'll be good!' Slare said happily. 'We'll look around for anything suspicious.'

'Where is it?' I asked.

'Oh, it's on the border of Alria and Wouldlock. Most tourist attractions are. It'll be great. Alria has the best lemons *ever.* People come from all over to taste them, and are never disappointed.'

'All right. Well if it's okay with you guys, I'll get Lypherace, and we can go.'

Ardor, Wolf, and Peldor nodded encouragingly, and we went into our different rooms to get what we needed.

I went into the room Lypherace and Stream had gone into, and found them sitting on the chair and bed, talking.

Lypherace was looking at me from the moment I stepped in, like he knew what I would ask him. I was about to ask myself how, for the door was closed, and I hadn't been that loud, but then, I knew. *Fifteen years.* Wow.

'Time to go?' he asked, getting up.

'Time to go,' I echoed.

We got up, went out of the room, pushed the boulders together, and setting out to walk the whole journey, we left Wouldlock.

SILVER CLAW

The land of Alria is an astounding place. It's a very hot place too, which is a big change from Elrolia. About forty percent of the land is desert. There are incredible cacti of all sizes, shapes, and colours, and the country is home to some of the most beautiful birds in the Eromies – besides Wouldlock, of course. There are numerous huge rocky cliffs, made of sand and stone, that somehow are completely solid. Alria is well known for its magnificent emeralds, and of course, as Slare said, its lemons.

But they also have a few cities. There are a few small villages around Alria, placed in the three states, Dentiris, Dester Arlgo, and Estel. Let's see … there are three capital villages in the state of Dentiris – the most important – and then there are about twenty others in all of them together. The three cities in Dentiris are by far the largest of all. There's Orenalth, Algatere, and Thramastus. The Lemon Kingdom was located in the biggest of all – Orenalth.

I had never been here before, but know all this because of history class. What a depressing thought. But I still had ideas on what it might be like. I imagined it as a large place with many cowboy-like villages: wooden, and all sandy or brown-coloured, old and broken down.

And the place wasn't all that different from my mind's image. It was more developed than I'd imagined, with a couple of modern cafés and hotels. The paths were just plain white sand, but the buildings were built on large wooden platforms. It was a nice place. It was a very big change from Elrolia or Wouldlock. We walked towards the village we'd spotted, which I assumed was Orenalth. It was incredible how quick the land changed from the forests of Wouldlock to the sandy plains of Alria. I saw a pack of striped hyenas off in the distance, but they kept their distance.

I spotted another nice café, and realised just how hungry I was after being up so long without food to satisfy my growling stomach.

I looked at the other three – Spyra, Lypherace, and Slare.

'Guys, could we maybe take a break and get something to eat?' I asked.

'Sure,' Spyra said. 'I'm hungry too.'

We went over to the place, stepped up onto the wooden platform, and opened the timber doors to a jingle of soft bells. The place was crowded, with lots of loud chatter and the clatter of silverware and glasses.

We took a seat near the door, and of course, my procedure automatically started working itself out. This was a good place, for there were numerous things to defend ourselves with – besides my axe, which no one gave a second glance.

I liked the feel of this place. The people looked friendly enough. A good example of this was our waiter. He had a small beard, long, tied-up hair, a single gold earring, and a smile rather like Lypherace's.

'Well hello there!' he said. 'My name's Plest, and I'll be your waiter today. Now what can I do for you?'

'We'll just have a round of ice water to start with please,' Spyra said, after confirming with us.

He nodded, and, looking at Spyra and me, said, 'let me guess … Elrolians?'

'Yeah,' I said, frowning. 'How'd you know?'

'Oh, I used to be really interested in you guys, so I found out how to identify you from other people. Like the guards at the gate, sir.'

'Very good. Honestly, even I don't know the difference,' I said.

He smiled. 'Yes, sir.' He went off to get our drinks.

I heard a distinct sound – a voice, whispers. But no one was whispering. I frowned, but didn't make much of it.

On the walls were large paintings of landscapes of Alria, like the desert and the unique cacti. I had a look at the small menu, and when Plest returned, we placed our orders, which, despite all the people, came within ten minutes, and was very good, and left a wonderful taste in my mouth. And of course, I got a slice of one of Alria's signature lemons, which, as Slare had said, were absolutely magnificent – sour, yet sweet at the same time, the purest yellow I'd ever seen, shining like gold.

I swallowed, nodding. 'This stuff is good.'

We didn't spend much time at the café though, for we ate, and wanted to move on as quickly as possible. Before we left, I spotted an abandoned newspaper on the table next to us, and something about it caught my attention – the symbol on the front page, a gleaming silver claw.

I picked it up and read the headline. *Silver Claw Strikes Again.*

I continued reading the first part, and didn't like it.

The Alrian police received a tip yesterday from the Spherian President that the Silver Claw organisation may be coming for a visit. We are unsure when the terrorists may be arriving, if ever, but advise all Alrian residents and visitors to stay indoors and keep high guard over themselves until this is over.

The Silver Claw, for those who don't know, is a terrorist society known for threatening cities with large predators – animals – with a silver claw on them, and then they take what they want in the midst of the confusion and fright. We do not have any confirmed news, but scientist Clapper Stirrs believes the event will occur on November 21.

It seemed too much of a coincidence. *Today* was November 21. Also, there was something I didn't understand. Why would the President tip a country off that the Silver Claw was coming? I mean Hunter would love for Alria to be destroyed to get whatever the Claw wanted.

I showed this to Slare and the others, and they had the same thoughts as I.

'Well, we'd better get inside quick,' said Slare. 'Let's go to the lemon place. It's close to here.'

'Okay.' I put the newspaper in a recycling bin, and stuffed my hand into my pocket, taking out a few hundred-dollar bills that I'd had from Elrolia. I left three on the table for Plest. He was a good waiter, and deserved this. I waved to him, and smiled as we left the café, his gasps of surprise audible even from outside.

Spyra looked into the window, and so did I, and I saw him bow, putting his hand to his heart, and then pushing it towards us.

I nodded, a large grin on my face and let Slare lead the way to the Lemon Kingdom. It was not far, but in this killer heat, it felt very long.

As we walked, I spotted a young man with a dog. The animal looked depressed, if a dog can, and I immediately saw why. The man kicked it. And by the look of it, it was a very hard kick – a kick you would give when you were angry. But he wasn't angry –it seemed like he just felt like it. The dog whimpered and walked on. The man tugged hard at the collar, and I was surprised that the dog didn't bark.

I went over to him, and he gave another hard kick. This was something I couldn't stand.

'Excuse me, I don't know if you noticed, but that dog doesn't like to be tormented like that.'

'You got a problem, man?' he asked lazily, giving another kick. 'I'll do what I do when I want to do it. This is my dog. You don't need to interfere.' After another kick, the dog almost howled in pain. If it could, I bet it would have cried.

'If you hurt that dog once more, I'll break your neck,' I said.

He smiled, and gave a kick that should have broken the dog's rib cage – would even have broken a human's.

I said nothing, but jabbed two fingers into his throat.

He didn't even scream, but dropped like he'd been knocked out – and I realised that he had, as well with a swollen lump on his neck. He deserved it. I released the dog, and it raced away, happy to leave its former owner. I realized I had been pretty violent these last few days. I was thinking I really should settle down.

The man grunted, and rolled over.

'I'm Storm Orthoclase – of Elrolia,' I added, turning from him and his shocked expression. 'Remember my name.'

Spyra was staring at me. Lypherace was smiling faintly, his eyes following the dog as it sprinted away.

'Let's move on,' I said, and Spyra and the others hastily started to walk again.

'That idiot,' I muttered. 'He deserved way more than what I gave him. People these days. They're horrible. The way they treat animals – it disgusts me. One of these days, I hope everyone who's ever done that to an animal learns their lesson.'

We walked the rest of the way, through the hot sands of Alria, and though it was tiring, it was well worth it. The place was marvelous.

It was white and gold, and looked extremely elegant. The place was sleek, like a five-star hotel. It had huge golden letters printed across the two wooden doors: *The Lemon Kingdom.* I didn't think it would be like this at all, judging from the quality of the rest of the village. The quality of the village wasn't poor, but just … not as advanced as this particular building, or as Spheria's.

We went in, and in the middle of a circular room was the tallest lemon tree I'd ever seen in my life. Growing right out of the ground, where a hole had been cut in the floor to allow its growth. Lemons were all over it, like Christmas balls that you place on a tree. They were massive, some close to the size of dodge-balls. The leaves were healthy green, and the bark a nice chocolate brown.

The place was almost completely empty, with just a few tourists and guards wandering around. It was no surprise. These people were taking the Silver Claw very seriously. The four of us went up to the main desk and handed in our tickets.

'These are for the factory tour,' the guy at the counter said glumly. 'This young woman will be your guide today.'

'Hello!' said the woman. 'Nice to meet you all, I am Clora, I'll be your guide today.' She was more or less repeating what the first guy had said, just in a brighter tone.

She took us through the factory, pointing out the conveyer belts that carried the lemons, the robots that packed the lemons, and how they were shipped off. It would have been interesting, but I just wasn't in the mood for this type of thing. I had had higher hopes.

'So then this is where we scan the lemons for any infections, and if they are poisoned in any way, they go down to the cacti.'

'Why?' Lypherace asked.

'The juice helps them grow. Has a lot of nutrients in it,' Clora explained.

I didn't really know why anyone would bother going here, but it got a bit better at the testing point, where we each got a lovely yellow lemon. And these, fresh from the giant tree, were even better than the slice I'd had at the café.

'Very good!' Slare said, trying to lighten our moods.

I was only half listening when I heard muffled screams. My head jolted towards the source of the sound. It seemed to be coming from the entrance hall. Spyra, Slare, Lypherace, and I carefully edged forwards towards the screams of terror.

There were lots of them, if my hearing was correct. All of them were being scared out of their mind by something. I turned back, and saw Clora on the floor, her body rigid and soaked in blood.

I turned to full alert, grasping my axe, and the others, spotting the body, got their weapons as well.

'Shut up, split up, and don't die,' I instructed.

We each went in different directions, for the screams were coming from all over, echoing loudly, giving me a very eerie feeling. I jumped onto boxes and climbed up the jagged rock columns until I'd reached the top floor, where I could see all that was going on in the floors beneath.

There were about a dozen people in each room, all with some kind of staff in hand, and all of them bearing the same symbol on their black clothes: a sliver claw.

I closed my eyes. What was it about us that attracted all these killers to wherever we were?

I grabbed a fire-extinguisher and hauled it over the side, ducking out of view as it made contact with one of their heads.

I heard angry voices, but couldn't make out exact words. I turned to find myself face-to-face with a skinny man with an evil grin on his face.

He smiled like I was dead meat, and made to strike. I almost laughed, for without me moving, his hand crashed into the cardboard box next to me.

I pretended I was surprised. 'Ow,' I said, emotionlessly.

Then, I struck down hard on his arm, while swinging my foot out, hooking his thin leg, then pulling with all my force, bringing him down face first onto the marble floor. He bit my leg, and I felt blood seep out.

I kicked his face away, and with a sharp jab to the shoulder, he went completely still. I squinted.

'No...'

I looked closer, and saw that he had only one hand. The other was a shining silver claw. I'm not joking. And this wasn't a glove. His hand had been completely cut off, and replaced with a robotic metal claw.

I tore my eyes away from the claw, and saw that downstairs the rest of his people that were still in the entrance room were swarming in on a poor child, who was terrified, clutching a drawing of a lion or some type of yellow cat.

One of the guys went forward, snatched away the paper, and ripped it to shreds, laughing insanely with the others as the poor little kid cried.

Another of them grabbed a knife, and I knew what was coming next. He took the kid's hand, and started to pretend to comfort him, his hand with the knife slowly emerging from behind his back.

I had to get to him. He would kill the kid if he tried to cut his hand off, for in a place like this, blood would run out way too fast. But what was I to do? They were four floors down, and there was no way I could take the stairs to get down there in time.

I would have to jump. I gripped my axe for a second, wondering if I could try to freeze the guy, but there was no way, for even if I could send a bolt, it might hit the kid, and then he would be dead even sooner – and the Silver Claw would be aware of me.

I strapped my axe to my back and made to jump, but was

just too late. Someone was behind me, and punched my back, probably breaking my ribs just as I was about to jump. I grabbed my axe, and swung it, smashing the person into a wall, and leaped to my feet.

And then, once again, the screams started. So loud, they were deafening. Horror flooded my body, and my joints went numb. They were screams of a little boy having his hand sawed off.

I roared in rage, and swung myself off of the railing. I fell down four floors, and landed hard on the paper-ripper's head. I tackled the knife guy, and knocked him out easily, and then threw his limp body into the others.

'I'll make you feel pain like never before!' I roared. 'You hear me? I'll rip you apart, stab a knife through your head. I'LL KILL YOU!'

Spyra came racing down the nearest set of stairs, her mouth bloody, saw what was happening, and jumped down the rest of the way. She ran to me, and grabbed the child, bringing him out of harm's way while I finished off the rest of them, my ribs screaming in pain, like fire in my body.

I was absolutely furious. No one hurts a kid like that. No one hurts any innocent person like that. I kicked and smashed until there was no one else in the room moving besides us three.

I looked down at the man who'd done the dirty work. I started at him with pure fury. His eyes flickered open, and I stepped towards him.

The person who had cut the kid's hand off would have his nose broken for a while. That and five other parts of his body: his arms, legs, and his neck. I just couldn't stop myself.

We moved the bodies away and into the bathroom.

Spyra had torn the sleeve of her shirt off, and cleverly wrapped it around the kid's arm, softly whispering comforting words to him, trying to stop his echoing wails.

Lypherace and Slare came in, breathing heavily – even Lypherace – and with a grim expression.

'Oh my god…' said Lypherace, stopping in his tracks.

'Okay, do you know where your house is?' Spyra asked tenderly.

'No, but my big sister is at the café across the road,' he sobbed.

'Okay, I'll take you to her, and explain what happened and she can take you to a hospital immediately.'

She left with the kid, holding his good hand, trying not to look at the blood-soaked fabric over his other hand. Here there are ways of surgically reattaching limbs, so she gingerly picked up the other part of his arm. There was hope. He would be alright.

'What the hell were those people–' I started.

Lypherace put his finger to his lips, his face dead serious. 'They're still here,' he said, as if in a trance. He looked straight at me. 'And from what I've seen, they're here for us.'

My hand automatically went for my axe, but Lypherace shook his head sharply. 'We can't escape.'

What? Of course we could! We'd defeated them before.

Then they all came out of their hiding places, forming a perfect circle around us. The guy who'd torn the paper came forth, a large grin on his face.

'Hello, my friends!'

'Shut your mouth before I detach it from your face,' I advised.

'Right.' He looked at me very calmly, but with distaste. 'Cuff those three, bring this one to me for a minute,' he commanded, and the rest of the Silver Claw obeyed, dragging me unwillingly across, but I made no struggle.

'What's your name?' he spat.

I didn't answer.

'I thought so. You must be Storm,' he said, giving a little

wink. 'Hunter told me about you, my friend. I am Cloredolx.'

Then, again, I heard whispering, just like in the café, but even quieter, only audible to extremely keen ears.

'You know Hunter?' I asked, surprised, completely forgetting the voice.

'Of course! I wouldn't be here if not for him.'

'Why did you summon me five metres from where I was?' I asked.

'Oh, yes, about that.' He took a deep breath and started slowly circling me, his hands behind his back.

Spyra then came back in, being firmly held by another group of Silver Claw people.

Cloredolx ignored this, and continued talking.

'You see, in the olden days, on earth, in a place very much like this, if people with power ever had an old dog … one that wasn't any good for anything, do you know what they'd do with it?'

'Worship it?' I said humourlessly.

He smiled. 'Good guess, but not quite. They would kill it – but in an entertaining way. They would throw little white hot stones at it, until it … died.'

'So then why aren't you dead?' I asked.

He smiled like it was a stupid thing he couldn't believe I'd had the nerve to say, but it took a while for his team to catch on.

'Hysterical,' he said, his eyes narrowing.

'Now, I have orders from the Spherian president to bring you to him, but before that, let's give you a small taste of what it's like to be an old dog, shall we?'

I heard muffled screams from Spyra, who along with the other two was trapped in a zip-tie, her mouth gagged.

They all grabbed stones with their clawed hands, and as Cloredolx has said, the stones were white-hot, steaming even.

And then they fired. And all I knew was blackness, and ongoing agony, until I couldn't stand any more of the heat and force, and my eyesight blurred and blurred as my brain finally shut down.

Well, I wasn't dead. Not yet, at least. I was with Lypherace, Spyra, and Slare in a room, but the problem was, we were in cages. They were built along a hall, with hundreds of them along both walls. It seemed I was not trusted to be on the same side as my friends, for I was facing all of them, alone, for all I could see. The cage bars were spread out enough for me to stick my arm through, but nothing more.

The hall was not too long, for I could see the wooden doors at either end, but it felt much too small. Perhaps because I was in a cage built for a small lion. We were the only ones in the room, and there were ten cages on either side. We were in the middle.

My axe, knives, and armour had been removed, and I felt very cold. I could not be in Alria. No, I was probably in Spheria, where the President was. The hall was very fancy, and no place other than Spheria would spend this much care on a simple jail. Although Elrolia would, I suppose.

My hands were trapped in a plastic zip-tie in front of me, this time to taunt me, showing me that there really was no way out. My hands ached. These things would cut off my circulation if they were any tighter. But the Silver Claw was clever. They did not want me dead – or at least, Hunter didn't. Not yet.

I had been wondering for a while what he would do to destroy me. What would he destroy that I cared for? My family? Elrolia? Or would he go after the campers that had grown over a short time to be my friends? I would find out soon enough.

I saw in the corner of my cage a glass of water that could probably hold nothing more than fifty millilitres. There was also a small burnt piece of bread that crumbled in my mouth when I took a bite.

Spyra and the others were awake now, munching on whatever they had after taking in their surroundings. They had taken Lypherace's glasses, and he was squinting in the dim light, looking very angry. How weird that he looked like this. It's like if you have a teacher who wears her hair in a bun every day, but then one time she has it down. Or a he, I suppose it could be.

I coughed, getting Lypherace's attention.

'You got any helpful gadgets on you?' I asked.

He did a quick body search, but shook his head.

'Then how do we get out?'

A man came storming in. It was one of Cloredolx's rugged-looking servants.

'Hey, didn't you guys, like, hold some children once in here?' I asked, remembering a story I'd heard about elemental children being captured.

'Yeah,' he said bitterly. 'They escaped using, what, acid from a bird or something? They were after Hades.'

'Who's he?' Spyra said, frowning.

'A god. A god who tried to steal wands for something.' He looked at me sharply. 'Why you want to know?'

'Just wondering if I could use their techniques.'

He smiled. 'Oh no, see, we need you. Hunter has big plans for you. Last time I saw him, his leg wasn't doing so well.' He came up to the bars. 'And I think he knows who did it.'

He snickered and left, going off the other way, to do more important things.

I thrashed around with the zip ties, trying to break them apart. Pure plastic was holding an Elrolian captive? No. I could not stand for this.

'Isn't there a way for you to escape these? Like, without breaking them?' I tried using my teeth, tried just pulling my hands apart, but it left stinging red marks against my flesh.

'Well I've seen magicians do it, but...'

Another guard came in, keys in his hand. He was going to free us! I could tackle him easily. But then twenty more came in. *Twenty.* They were serious.

'Lord Hunter wants to see you,' said the first guard formally. 'Come. Don't be any trouble for us, and we'll do the same for you.'

They unlocked us, and I did nothing, for I truly did want to see Hunter – to find out what he had in store for me.

They brought us out into a place that made me one-hundred percent sure this was Spheria. It was like a lounge, but the size of a whole house. There were what looked like real rocks all around, as well as a huge pond with a rocky bridge over it. I guessed this was the home of the Silver Claw, for Hunter wasn't one to stay in such a natural place. He preferred technology much more – the things he had total control over. There were very high ceilings, and the doors were frosted glass. The floor was hard black slippery marble, sparkling in the light.

Hunter was right there, sitting comfortably on a grey couch, his leg in a metal brace. That sword had injured him quite a bit then. That didn't help me out.

'Storm Orthoclase,' he said, his voice perfectly normal, even with that creepy mask, and considering that I'd given him the worst injury of his life. He sounded even happy. But that was cause he was about to get his first part of revenge.

'I'm sorry to have had to bring you here like this, but it was necessary. I see that the Silver Claw has very neatly captured you. Another flawless job,' he said, bowing his head slightly to Cloredolx.

'And of course, it was also a good idea to bring your friends along,' Hunter said, spotting Lypherace, Spyra, and Slare.

'I am here today to start off with your punishment for your

actions.' He gestured down to his leg. 'This is not something I forgive. Nor is trying to obtain the help of my proudest creations ... or what used to be my proudest creations.' Hunter's eyes flickered towards a small stream running through the floor, a few rocks in it serving as a pathway to the opposite side. 'Now, your punishment will be simple, but long. I will make happen to you again all the terrible things that have happened to you over the course of time. First, will be desperation. Let me tell you a little story about this topic.'

The guards pushed us on to a couch and resumed positions by all the exits. For the first time, I saw the water moving. Something was in there, although I couldn't see exactly what it was. But it was big.

'Let me tell you about the way I got this mask. I was experimenting with some animal blood – you know how I like to experiment, right? I created what you call Black Amber.'

How did he know so much? How did he know what we'd been saying and doing?

'But, like all good inventions, I didn't get it right on the first try. I knew the basis of cross-breeding, for I'd done it many times before, and you, in fact, may get to meet another of my creations soon. But back to the point. I had created a few successful creatures in the Black Amber species, and they were one by one growing larger and better. But one of them went out of control, as all animals do. Of course, I don't like animals, for they can't be easily controlled, but if you teach them in the right way, they can be quite easy to manipulate. But this particular creature was not behaving well, and before I had time to kill it, it scratched me, so deep it ripped the wall of my lungs apart.'

My attention went to his chest, but I saw nothing unusual.

'But I have a good team of scientists, and they had a mixture of chemicals ready beforehand. What they did was allow me to breathe without air. So this mask constantly feeds me that solution. But for that minute, when blood was rushing out of my body, my ribs exposed, no air to breathe, I was truly desperate. It was a sincerely terrible feeling.'

He took a moment to pause, allowing me to soak it in.

'Now, I want to show you exactly how this feels.'

He walked over to the pond, and at that second, my mind sparked and I knew how to escape these horrible plastic zip-ties. I used my fingernail to pull down the little tab that stopped the tie from loosening. I pulled down, and the zip-tie loosened until it was off. I twisted it to reattach it the opposite way, under the cover of my shirt, and tightened it again. Set up this way, I could pull and I would be instantly free, for the jagged part was facing the top: nothing held the tie in place. It's complicated, but works perfectly. So now, I was no longer captive, except for the fact I was in the Silver Claw's base.

Hunter pointed into the water, and an animal's head came out, a head like a seal. The creature must have been one of Hunter's creations, for it was not an animal that I believed existed in nature. It was like a combination of a snake, shark, and crocodile. I don't really know how to explain it, but it didn't look friendly.

He stroked the creature's large scaly head, and it showed off its sharp teeth, and I realised it was in the middle of chewing up a dolphin, or some other sort of sea creature.

'This is Quantilos. I created her nine months ago. She's a very well-behaved animal, and does exactly what I want, when I want it. So, what would you do if you were stuck in a pond with her? Just the three of you, no one else. How about we find out?' Hunter said, his lips curling into a smile.

'In your zip-ties, you'll be completely secure, so we can start,' he said, taunting me.

The guards slowly filed out, and as Hunter briefly turned his back, I took the chance, quickly undoing Lypherace's and Slare's zip-ties.

'Well, good luck.' Hunter vanished, black dust falling to the floor in a pile.

We leapt into action. We fought like never before, disarming the Silver Claw members of our own weapons. Once I'd gotten my axe back, I focused. Elemental power could save me here. And just like that, a wave of water spread out, smashing the Silver Claw, freezing most of them instantly. I did the same to the creature in the pond, freezing the water around it so it couldn't move.

Two of the Silver Claw was still standing. I punched one in the face, and elbowed the other in the back, and both dropped to the floor, not dead, but not going anywhere for the moment.

I noticed I'd missed Cloredolx. He put up a long fight with Lypherace, until he made the wrong move, and skidded across the floor, where I threw him into a waterfall, and he fell down to the frozen pond, still.

'That was easier than I thought it'd be,' Spyra said, and I agreed with her.

'Now how do we get back?' I said, looking around the lounge, which was in a state of destruction, unconscious bodies everywhere, as well as broken tables and chairs.

'Well first let's get out of this building.' Lypherace said, and we scanned the place for any weak spots.

'The waterfall! It's real, it'll lead out!'

We climbed up the rocks on either side, but it wasn't easy. It was like wall-climbing, which I do in Elrolia often, but this was much harder, for this was not made with foot-holds and hand-holds. Still, we train for climbing in Elrolia, and Lypherace could do it fine. It was only Slare who needed a bit of help, for even though she had had some practice at Wouldlock, she was still struggling.

It was a very nice place, and reminded me of home. I knew that if there were this many natural things, we must be close to Wouldlock, for everything natural in Spheria is, except for a few bits, like parks and zoos and stuff.

We made it out, and found ourselves facing the forest of Wouldlock, with Spheria behind us. We were very close to the camp, by the field.

'I can't believe they actually thought they could keep us there,' said Slare. 'Look how easily we escaped!'

'I have a feeling that if we'd let all of the guards get out of the room before we tried to escape, we wouldn't be so lucky,' I said. Hunter wouldn't have let us out that easily, and I bet that we would have had no chance if they'd left.

We walked back to the camp, along the path we'd taken so many times, but was still no less interesting, for nature is always full of surprises.

We slid aside the boulders and entered the camp. What a difference between hot Alria and here, or even Spheria.

When we got into the camp, the team looked like they were expecting us, and I realised they'd been seeing everything through the images from the camera Stream had given us, and from Lypherace's glasses, which he'd managed to retrieve.

I saw Ardor and Wolf as well. Why were they still here?

'Are you all right?' Ardor asked.

'Yeah, fine. How did it go with getting the map?' Spyra asked.

'Oh, great,' said Wolf. 'We didn't have to go after all. Stream hacked their main computer, and he's receiving the copies now. And we know you guys got nothing,' he added.

'By the way, I was trying to talk to you. You know we can communicate, right?' asked Stream.

'Oh ... you must have been the one whispering!' I said. 'Sorry, I didn't know.'

He quickly showed me how to talk, and we got back to the discussion.

'So that guy, Garmax, must have said to go to Alria just to mess with you,' said Raider, nodding in understanding.

'Yeah, it was a trap. The Silver Claw was waiting. I just don't understand how they knew we were coming,' I said.

They looked at each other.

'Come with me outside,' Peldor said to us.

I frowned, but we didn't question him, and followed him out of the meeting room.

'What's up?' Lypherace asked.

'Well, we know how they found out,' said Peldor grimly. 'Mac and Icon were playing around this morning in the meeting room, and they spotted a video camera. It's been recording since Shade left. He put it there. They've known everything we've been doing since he left. That room is where we do all of our planning.'

'So did you take it down?' Spyra asked.

'No,' Peldor said. 'This is our advantage. We can feed them false information.'

I nodded understandingly.

'It was Wolf's idea. He's a smart fellow,' Peldor said, nodding his head.

'It's a good idea,' Slare said, impressed.

'What do we do now, though?'

I didn't look at them, for I was starting to think of what to do already. 'Now, we go get Black Amber. We really get Black Amber this time.'

AQUARIUS SEABELL

There was no way possible we would get to the Spherian University of Biology to find Black Amber with the resources we had, in the time we had. So we needed other resources – and Wolf knew the person we needed to contact. He was an Elemental Lord by the name of Stringer.

I knew him from the days when we'd been recovering from Hunter's attack. He'd given us the materials for more weapons, sadly not Elrolian. But he would have what we needed.

So, Wolf, Spyra, and I set out to visit Stringer. He was across the Alrian Sea, his mansion built from scratch with his metal. Wolf was sure that Stringer would have a flying vehicle

of some sort, and that was exactly what we needed. But how could we get there to ask him? Well, even if they couldn't build a flying thing to carry us, Mac and Icon could make us a nice raft with an engine that boosted us far ahead, and in less than ten minutes we'd almost reached Stringer's place, just as the engine was just fading. Although we had to swim a bit, we got there in one piece.

Stringer must have seen us coming and from wherever he was in the building given the command to open the doors to allow us to enter. A flight of stairs slid out into the water. We climbed up into the building, and immediately hot waves of air from the walls blew us dry.

I had never been there before. The place was very fancy and impressive. It looked like a high-tech starship, but much more awesome. I was not used to this, for there is hardly any technology in Elrolia, as I'm sure I've said before. And this was the most high-tech place ever. The wood contrasted nicely against the metallic white walls and silver handles. There were three massive crystal chandeliers hanging in the lounge. Stringer came down the spiral staircase, his armour retracting into one small breastplate as he walked.

'Hello there! Wolf, nice to see you again, and let's see...' he bit his lip trying to remember our names.

'Joe and Glag,' he guessed.

I shook my head.

'Tim and Serine?'

'Nope,' said Spyra.

'Mr. Leo, and Ms. Da Vinci?'

'Storm,' I said finally, helping him out a bit.

'And Spyra,' Spyra said, shaking Stringer's hand after me.

'I knew it! I was right! Elrolians, yes? Yeah, telling Elrolians from humans is becoming a more widespread skill – but not for me.'

'From that long ago?' I asked. 'You have a good memory.'

'Why, thank you,' he said, bowing deeply. 'Now, I doubt you came over here to relax in my wonderful home, and swim in shark-filled oceans, so let's sit down and get to business.'

'We need your assistance,' Wolf said to start off with.

'Yes, what exactly?'

'We need a flying vehicle,' I said.

'You mean like, one that flies?'

'Um, yeah,' said Spyra, confused.

'Well, I've got one.'

'Great!' I said. 'Can we borrow it for a day?'

'Well, it doesn't work. I need a crystal. It will act as fuel.'

'Wait, why? I mean, couldn't you just use a helicopter or something?'

'No. You can't get where you want to go by air,' Stringer said.

'What? Why?'

'I know where you want to go, actually. Ardor contacted me. But there's a barrier around Hunter's base. Made of pure darkness. I have no idea how it works, but it is indestructible, and will kill you, or possibly do worse if you go around it. This guy goes out of his way to defend his residence. So, you'll need protection from darkness, and the only thing in the Eromies that will shield you is the Flaming Crystal of Atlantis.'

I frowned, and he fetched a map from a closet.

'There are forty-seven different Flaming Crystals in Atlantis at the moment. You need to go down and get one for this vehicle, to prevent you dying. You keep the map, set your eye on one of these, then get it and bring it here. These things hold *tremendous* power. Only few people are capable of creating one – the last of the Atlantian species. And they're incredible ... anyway, the flaming stone.'

'How could this shield us?' Wolf asked.

'Well, the Atlantian people were very powerful. And those who are left still are. Atlantis itself is one of the most incredible places in the world, and the place itself is very powerful, even supernatural, people say.'

'So we get it, bring it to you, and you install it, then we can go?' Spyra asked.

'Yeah, that's about it. I can lend you a submarine or something to go down there.'

I nodded. 'That would be good.'

He looked at me. 'You know what ... I might be able to help you out a bit more....'

I smiled.

'Just a second.' He ran up the stairs to get something

'Well, I didn't think it would be this hard,' I said. 'Hunter is really scared of this thing – Black Amber. Putting this much security on it... I just hope we're not too late.'

'Well, I would imagine we'd be just in time. Extracting Elrolian Onyxus would be a tough thing to do,' Wolf said bitterly. 'It's just not right what they're doing. Killing an entire species because it's a threat? It's just wrong.'

'We'll get Black Amber back,' Spyra said confidently as Stringer made his way back down the stairs along with another person.

He had short light brown hair that was sticking up, but being so short it was hardly noticeable. He had a muscular body, and beads of water on his forehead. He was wearing a black swimsuit, with blue lines that seemed to be glowing, or were maybe even lights.

'This is Aquarius Seabell, professional deep-sea diver. He discovered the largest crysillium stone in the world, worth 2.5 million dollars. He has not sold it, yet he is still very rich.'

Aquarius Seabell smiled awkwardly, as anyone would have done when introduced as a rich person, especially in front of us in our shabby clothes.

'I did sell one ... but the other I kept. Anyway – hi there!' he said. 'I hear you're heading down to Atlantis? Well, kind of.'

'Yeah,' I said, nodding.

'Well, I would be honoured to come and help you out.'

We nodded.

'That would be great,' Spyra said.

'Yeah, thanks.'

'No problem. We'll get you in some suits and get a submarine started, and we'll head off.'

We got up and walked up the stairs behind Aquarius. Stringer smiled, and gave me a wink.

'Good luck,' he whispered. 'Don't get eaten alive.'

When Stringer said he'd lend us a submarine, I didn't expect him to lend us one like this. It was as elegant as his house, but unlike the other projects he'd made, this one's colours were black and blue, like Aquarius's suit. I wondered why, until I saw that printed on the side of the vehicle were the words *Black Aqua*. So this was something from Stringer's brand new series! Awesome.

I had noticed that he had been tearing apart his other creations to either get their parts or disassemble them, replacing the orange with that same bright blue. Probably this new colour scheme was improving it somehow. He'd told me before he left that different colours usually meant different levels of technology, blue being one of the most advanced. This blue technology was something he'd recently discovered – not bought, but *discovered*.

The vehicle was being controlled from up at Stringer's house by Stringer himself. He would lead us down through the water to the approximate location of the crystal, and then he'd let us dive out to actually pick it up. He'd given us some special diving equipment that would allow us not to be crushed by the pressure of the ocean.

The submarine was huge, and I started to explore it a bit before we reached our destination. There were a few wooden tables that had been pinned down to the ground in case of any underwater turbulence, I guessed.

But the coolest part was at the front of the sub. There was a large sphere, which you could walk into, and the thing was, it was glass. Through the two-centimetre-thick crystal-clear glass, you could see all of the incredible sea life. The multicoloured fish and coral – it made you just want to jump in and swim, no matter how cold the water could be. It was like being in a movie. I couldn't believe this truly existed.

You would think the fish would swim off at the sight of a vehicle like this, but it seemed instead to draw their attention. They came so close, they almost pressed against the glass. And it was not just fish that were so interested. I even saw a small hammerhead shark. It was like they'd seen something like this before, and knew it was no threat.

It was truly amazing. The life that was so overlooked because of how hard it was to get to.

Aquarius came inside, and we started to chat. I wanted to know a little more about him.

'Hey man,' I said. 'Thanks for taking the time to help us out here.'

'Oh, no problem. It's always worth coming down here,' he said, gesturing at the school of fish.

'So how exactly does this thing work?'

'Well, we're experimenting with Black Aqua technology. This is our forth project, not including the biggest of all, which I believe Stringer wants kept as a secret. He's up there using a sonar map to find our destination, and there's a camera out front to help him see. Actually, there are cameras on all the sides.'

'Wow. That's awesome.'

'Yeah. And it gets better the deeper we get. You can see some pretty awesome creatures. You know what, in a few minutes you might catch a glimpse of a Lorothian Scarback. It's a type of shark,' he added after seeing my confused expression.

He smiled once more, and left.

He was right. The further we travelled, the larger the animals got – and the thing is, the deeper we were, the darker it got. But soon enough, strong lights flickered on outside the vehicle. Stringer could see from his place, I guessed. It provided enough light to see the animals, but there were starting to be fewer.

I heard Aquarius's voice through the speaker at the top of the glass sphere.

'We are approaching the crystal. It's small, so you won't see it, and when we go out there and get it, it won't be easy. That thing is still heavy.'

I stared out into the dimly lit sea. I would be going out there. Emrax's old but meaningful saying came back to me again. If you strike hard enough in unknown waters, something will come up and strike back. We would be approaching unknown waters, taking something from it. The creatures down there, they could strike. Like Aquarius said, this would not be easy. We needed to find it actually take it back to the vehicle, then go up and get it installed.

Aquarius's voice rang through the sphere again.

'All divers to the diving port,' he commanded.

I got out of the sphere and made for the double doors. The others were already there, strapping on their equipment.

Aquarius helped me out with mine, and my heart started pumping. We were hundreds of metres down in the sea. What if these suits couldn't stand the pressure? Would being Elrolian save me from being crushed like a plastic bottle? I was not sure, and didn't care to test it out.

'Okay, can you hear me?' Aquarius's voice sounded as if he were talking right in my ear. I jumped, realising we could communicate through the microphones in our suits. I also knew Stream would be seeing me through the camera he'd given me, and before I completely locked my suit, I plugged in one of the earphones so if Stream was talking I would be able to hear him, but at the moment I heard nothing except the others in the submarine testing out the communication system.

'Alright everyone, we go through the airlock compartment one by one, then out into the sea. Now, make a final check to make sure everything's secure.'

Wolf winked at me, and I nodded as we stepped through the first door, and it slid shut, automatically locking airtight.

Aquarius nodded to everyone, and the second door slid open, revealing the cloud of darkness. We filed out of the submarine and the powerful flashlights on our suits lit up the darkness.

'Okay, it'll be somewhere within a five-hundred metre radius of the vehicle, so check everything, under every rock, in each piece of seaweed. It's glowing hot orange, so it shouldn't be too hard to miss from this close,' said Aquarius.

We swam out into the ocean, and I didn't like it. It was so dark. Things that were a metre away could only be spotted if we shone a light directly on them. It was too easy to be caught unawares here.

We spent five minutes scouting the seabed without a glimpse of the crystal. I occasionally would hear someone start a hopeful sentence, but it would trail off when they found that it was a false alarm.

I spotted a large boulder, and tipped it over, but again found nothing.

I went down further from the vehicle and saw a cave-like space. I swam into it, my light up ahead, searching for any sign of life or crystal. The only thing of interest was a large piece of crysillium, which wasn't that helpful to me at the moment.

As I went deeper, I saw a faint glow. I hopefully turned the corner, but again found nothing more than crysillium. I sighed heavily, and then heard a scream. It was Spyra's.

I shot out of the cave. 'What? What's wrong?'

'It bit me! The shark bit me!'

My eyes narrowed, and I rushed off, spotting her in the light.

'Are you okay?'

She nodded. 'Sort of. The thing was small, but still....' She showed me that blood was escaping. My heart beat faster.

'You're going to drown!' I said. If blood was coming out, it meant her suit had been punctured.

Her mouth fell open, but she quickly recovered and swam at top speed for the vehicle. I looked at her and saw that she was shivering. The water had gone into her suit. The vehicle was still a hundred metres away. The good thing was that she hadn't crumpled up. The Elrolian Onyxus was holding her together.

'Aquarius, the door code!' I yelled as we approached.

'Triple-seven, five, eight,' he said.

I got to the door and tried to enter the code, but I realised that though the suit was not so large, the gloves were so big that they made me unable to press a button without pressing the ones surrounding it. Only Aquarius didn't have the gloves. But that didn't matter. I snatched the gloves off my hand, and looked down in horror as it ripped off the entire arm of my suit. Freezing water climbed up my arm. I didn't let this distract me, but by the time I'd opened the door, my suit was filled with ice-cold water.

Spyra climbed in, but her suit was filled too. I did what I had to do to keep her alive. There was no time for me to get in. If I went in, it would be plainly too late. I'd have to climb in, lock the door – everything. It was meant to be individual – there was simply no space for two people at once. I closed the door, and knew she had the sense to open the second one. She was safe. But I was not. I took off the entire suit, for it was of no use to me except for the light. All it really did was to limit my flexibility. It was the breathing that was the problem. I was underwater, with no oxygen.

Was this really the way I'd die? In the cold, wet darkness, my last action saving an Elrolian, looking for an orange rock?

The darkness was terrible. So empty, yet so full, and though my Elrolian body prevented me from being completely crumpled, we might have been so deep that the pressure still threatened me. Threatened to destroy my bones, crush them into powder that would linger forever in the wet shadows of the sea.

But I was losing air. My lungs wanted me to breathe freely. Then, just as I was about to punch in the code to open the door once more, I felt a tentacle across my foot. Without light, I could only imagine what it was. An octopus maybe? I was not sure, and didn't want to open my eyes and see, but it was grabbing me and dragging me down, and when I finally escaped its slimy grip, my mouth burst open, and cold water rushed in as the few remaining bubbles escaped my lips.

As it happened, the thought hit me like a boulder. My lungs were built for this! Why had I not thought of it before? I felt the flesh on my neck tear slightly, gill-like, turning the water into something suitable to breathe, just as Hunter's mask did for him.

It was beautiful, breathing after those seconds when I had no air. Even if I'd remembered about my special skill, down here I would still feel rather scared. I opened my eyes, and incredibly found that I could see – see everything. It was better than light. It was as if the light in the suit had prevented me from seeing like this. I remembered what Emrax had told me once. That if there were light, my eyes would use that to see, but if there were none, my eyes would kind of … make their own, I guess, or something unimaginable like that.

I used my free fingers to type in the code, and after going through the doors, found myself facing Spyra, who looked deeply relieved, yet puzzled at the same time. I was about to explain everything when I heard Aquarius's voice through the speakers again. 'Okay, Wolf's found it. Is everyone okay?'

'Yes!' Spyra shouted in relief.

'Good. We're heading over.'

I explained to Spyra what had happened, and about the water-breathing thing I could do. I couldn't help but remember another of Emrax's sayings – his favourite of all. He said that unique skills should not disconnect you from the world, but bring you closer.

I smiled as I remembered.

I heard the doors slide open, and a moment later Aquarius and Wolf stepped in, water flooding through the lounge, then flowing out through unseen drains, leaving the floor fairly dry. Wolf laid down a large orange crystal and took off his suit. It was beautiful. The crystal, I mean, not the suit.

It was uncut, but there was an Atlantian engraving on it, filled in with gold. I did not speak nor read the language well, despite the classes I took for a year at Elrolia. I mean, I could sometimes remember short phrases, but when they tried to get me to speak it underwater, it came out as an eruption of bubbles. It was something about the way you used your tongue that allowed it to sound normal. In class they tried to teach us how to shape our mouths the right way and blow correctly so that the words sound normal under water. But I had a hard time.

'What does it say?' I asked.

Spyra, who had always exceled at reading Atlantian, squinted at the stone and then read aloud: '*From the depths of Atlantis, this stone was made in fire. Those who find it hold the greatest of all power.* There's some more, but I'm not sure exactly what that part says.'

'Well, that's pretty useless. Let's get this to Stringer.'

As if on cue, the engine started, and just like that, we were moving up towards the surface. The others studied the stone, but I took the opportunity to take another look at the marvelous sea life. I went into the glass sphere and just sat on the floor, watching the fish from all of the different angles I could.

It seemed to be faster going up than going down. The sea got lighter and lighter, like the rising sun in the morning. We kept going until we had reached Stringer's place. The submarine went in and Aquarius gave us a hand out.

Stringer came down the staircase.

'You got it! And you're all alive!'

'Yeah,' I said, rather surprised myself.

'Well, hand it over, and I'll have the vehicle ready in five minutes.'

Wolf passed him the stone, and he set to work, right in front of us, on another vehicle. Another Black Aqua project, I noticed. Stringer was not sparing any expense. He opened a chamber in the vehicle and inserted the stone in the centre. The vehicle glowed with power like a rocket entering the Earth's atmosphere.

'There we go! Ready to ride.'

We got in, and gave our final regards to Stringer and Aquarius. Then, with no more hesitation, we started the vehicle, and with Spyra at the wheel, we flew off to The Edge.

BREAKING IN

I wasn't sure what we would find when we got to the university. From what Stringer had told us, there would be a dark force-field type of thing, and I was aching to see it. Hopefully, with the firestone installed, we would not be blown up when we entered the area. I still wondered how they managed to harness the dark energy at all. It seemed like it would be impossible, but with Hunter, I guess not.

I still had my doubts about whether we would get there in time. If Hunter had already gained what he needed from the Black Amber species, then he would have no further need for them, and would immediately kill them, or worse. All of this would've been for nothing – travelling to Stringer's place, going under water to get the stone, almost dying, and even the map that we got from the other university in Spheria. All of it would've been for nothing.

As we flew off, drawing closer and closer to the university, I wondered two things. First, I where were we going to land,

and second, how did Spyra know how to steer this thing. In Elrolia we don't have many vehicles, and certainly not anything this high-tech. Stringer had volunteered to bring us himself, but he'd done so much already, and we didn't want to bring him into any danger, even if he was an Elemental Lord.

As we moved closer to the university, it dawned on me that Hunter himself might be there, waiting for us. The Silver Claw would've informed him by now that we had escaped, and this time we might not be so lucky. We had escaped the Spherian University of Science, and Silver Claw, but Hunter would have learned from his previous mistakes and would be much more careful, especially where it concerned us. He isn't the stupid kind of villain that gets tricked every time and gets angry, losing control and becoming reckless. He learned from his mistakes, and he always got his way in the end. If he had wanted me dead (which he thankfully did not), he would have me dead.

Flying on the Black Aqua vehicle was much faster than anything I've ever been on. It would've taken us much longer even in a standard jet, or helicopter. It didn't take long before I caught sight of the place, for it was massive, with the name of the university painted on the top floor so we could see it from above. It seemed that Spyra was now starting to think about landing as well. We had no clear space, and were hovering over the university. We made it in through the invisible field, but how were we going to actually land?

The shield hadn't harmed us in any way, and we were still here, and if I hadn't known we had been close to death, I never would've guessed that we had been in any danger at all. I hadn't actually seen anything, but perhaps felt a little tremor in the vehicle, like a bit of turbulence. It's a good thing we had gone to Stringer in the first place.

Spyra turned around. 'Where do we land?' she asked.

Wolf looked around trying to find a good spot. 'I'm not sure. How about on that rooftop?'

The building was very close to a mountain, I noticed. We could land on the mountain instead!

'No,' I said. 'We can land on that mountain top. It's not too far from the University, and they won't spot us as easily.'

Spyra nodded, and made way for the mountain, which was good enough to land on. After a gentle touchdown, she shut the engines down, and we opened the door, stepping out into the fresh breeze, with various scents from the plants filling the air.

'Well, that wasn't so hard,' I said, with a little smile.

'Well you weren't the one driving,' said Spyra, with a grin as well.

It felt incredible, running down through the soft grass. Just running down through the nature made me feel so relaxed. Of course, that all ended when we caught sight of the huge Spherian university that we would be soon going into, and would probably be meeting some of Hunter's friends. That would be the end of relaxation for me.

'So how do we get Black Amber back to Wouldlock again?' I asked, suddenly worried.

Wolf spoke. 'Well, Ardor said he would fetch Altralz to translate where we wanted them to go. I mean they should be able to fly, unless Hunter has already done something to them. We'll just use the video camera and audio things to pass on the message.'

I nodded. 'Right. Good idea. But when did he say that?'

'When you weren't there,' Spyra said helpfully.

We entered the building, and besides a few changes in the furniture, the format of the building seemed the same as the other university, but I had no doubt that the inside was different.

We had no need to present ID or anything; we really just walked ahead, which I thought was strange, but didn't question it. The security office, as I saw on the building map, was in roughly the same position that it had been in the other place, maybe a bit easier to find though.

Luckily, there was only one guard, and he appeared to be sleeping, so we went in without struggle. I didn't recognise him from the battle, anyway. Below his coffee mug was a stained map – the one we needed. The guard gave a snort, and my hand went for my axe, but he continued sleeping. I took the map and handed it to Wolf, then grabbed a sticky note and wrote this:

Hey man, just took the map over to the cleaners, be back in a minute.

Nothing suspicious about that, was there? It didn't really matter. It was better than nothing. On the back of the sticky note, I scribbled *Hunter sucks,* just for fun. If anyone wanted me hunted as much as he did, provoking him more wouldn't make much of a difference. Risks were sometimes what made life fun.

We found a lounge on the next floor, where we settled down on the red velvet couches and studied the map. The place was quiet, though not empty. It felt like a library.

The map we'd gotten hold of was similar to the other one. It was very clear, and easy to understand, but it was very big, and searching for a place Hunter could be was rather difficult. We had no real lead on what to look for. We thought it would be a large place, maybe a lab of some sort that would provide enough space for Hunter's experiments. Somewhere that would no doubt be marked 'dangerous chemicals,' or something like that.

I wondered how he'd managed to haul a pack of Black Amber into a university like this one. Being who he was, I had no doubt that he'd managed to find a way. I wouldn't have been surprised if every scientist in this building was supporting him.

We ordered a round of sparkling water, and studied the map further.

'This lab looks pretty big,' Spyra remarked, pointing to one on the map.

'It does...' said Wolf. 'How about we give it a shot?'

'Wait a second, what about this one?' I pointed out a large room marked 'The Lord.' I was pretty sure this was his. It was big, simply marked 'hazardous chemicals,' and I just had this *feeling*.

Wolf nodded. 'Fourth floor, lab 56A.'

We finished off our drinks and left a tip for our waitress. The room was easy to find. The building had good maps and markings, and the people were very helpful, but having this master map was the most helpful, and we got there in about seven minutes.

There it was, on the door, 'Lab 56A,' printed in blinding gold. The people had been clever enough not to mark this as 'The Lord' as well, but I had no doubt that we'd found the right place.

Something didn't seem right though. Last time, twenty guards had been launched when we tried to get a map – one that we didn't even end up needing. But this time, we'd got the map, left a note insulting Hunter, ordered drinks while studying a top secret map, found the room that Hunter was operating in, all without a single fight, or even a second glance. It felt too good to be true, you know what I mean? But I was prepared for disaster to break loose at any moment. I am, as you've heard me say before, not one to be caught unawares.

I don't know what I was expecting to see. Blood? A mass of bones? A bunch of scientists practicing surgery on Black Amber? Whatever I thought, I didn't expect to find it empty – but it was. We needed some type of card to get in, but instead I destroyed the lock with my incredible axe. Our footsteps echoed eerily in the large room, like pebbles falling on stone.

'Wait, where is everyone?' Spyra asked.

'I don't know...' Wolf said, looking around.

'Wait...' I went to the side of the room and saw a huge tower, covered in a large white sheet. I tried to tug off the sheet, but it seemed to be weighted. I tried again, with all my strength, Spyra and Wolf helping me. It fell off, and it seemed to pull a trigger, releasing all the sound in the room. Terrible howls, barks, and roars. It was Black Amber, each and every one in a separate cage.

Wolf stared, immediately realising that we would only have seconds until a dozen guards were upon us. I sprang over to the wall, where the electricity box was – you know, with the master light controls and stuff? I ripped off the video camera and audio thing that Stream had given me, and tore off the band over the cables, so the silver wires were sticking out like broken fingers. I also ripped off the audio button, connecting the wires, and then I flicked the switch, and there was a burst of noise, like static from a microphone.

Our people on the other side of the communication system seemed to hear the growls, and assume they were from Black Amber. In a second, Altralz was on the line, speaking Black Amber tongue, which silenced the creatures immediately. Then Altralz went quiet, and I disconnected the microphone, and reconnected it to my dirty shirt.

Now, how were we going to break the cages? I swung off my axe and stoked the blade lightly. Elrolian Onyxus would break the locks like butter, but we would not be able to do it by hand in time.

I raised up the axe and concentrated, every lesson I'd ever had with Emrax coming back to me. Then, like the other time, the axe shattered, the whole axe this time, into a million pieces. Each and every piece shot towards a lock, and though I couldn't see the shards, I saw the locks explode like glass, and at once the shards soared back to my hand, reforming into the ice axe. Wow. This axe held lots of power. I'd only been using a small bit of it. What I had seen was probably only the tip of the iceberg. And Androma had been right. This axe had saved my life. Multiple times.

As Black Amber broke free, I was afraid we'd take a while to get them out, but they knew better than to walk out the front door. They soared up into the air like a flock of birds leaving a tree. They broke through the roof and smashed their way out of the building, pieces of the ceiling raining down, but not harming us.

'That was easier than I thought,' I muttered to Spyra and Wolf.

They nodded in agreement, but at that very moment, the doors of the lab opened, and about a hundred people poured out. Scientists, security guards, hunters, and Silver Claw members, all stampeding through.

I saw that they'd left one door alone, and while they were taking in the situation, I grabbed Spyra, seeing Wolf spring towards the door. We raced along, and barely made it, running hard through the hall, and finally out into the open, just in time to see the last of the Black Amber fly away.

I then realised that they wouldn't be able to make it. The dark field! But they passed through without any harm. The Elrolian Onyxus in their blood must have saved them! Well, that was one problem taken care of, but what about us? We ran at full speed towards the mountain. We needed to get to the vehicle – Wolf needed protection.

The hunters ran out, chasing madly after us. Our surroundings were a blur of colours as we ran. A mass of green, grey, and brown trees like abstract art. But then Wolf made his mistake.

His leg brace caught a log on the way up the mountain, and he fell to the ground. The hunters were too close for us to do anything.

'No!' I screamed. 'Wolf!'

'Go!' he called back in agony. 'Leave! Save yourselves now!

If I'm killed, do one thing! Save the animals of Wouldlock! Save Lance – '

Before he could finish, he realised how close the hunters were, and though he knew he could not possibly escape, he threw himself off the cliff, his arms out like a bird. The hunters down below swarmed in, and he was gone. He was not dead, but in their hands, he wouldn't live for long.

I was about to make for the hunters, but knew it was no good. If I tried to save Wolf, I would fail. There just was no chance, so I reluctantly hiked further up the mountain, the rest of Hunter's team following us.

But we didn't make it. Just as we reached the top, a hunter – a very agile one – raced behind us, and then pulled out a staff, or some such thing, and shot a black orb of darkness at the vehicle. As it made contact, it exploded, just like the locks had, but with much more force. This held up the hunters, for fire was now between us, but it made no difference, for we now had no way out. But, we continued running. Running and running.

Then, I made the same mistake Wolf had, and tripped on a plant, falling on the hard rocky ground.

Spyra, who had turned, also tripped, and we lay on the ground helplessly. We would not escape if they caught us. But they didn't. As the first five came towards us, they all disintegrated into the black dust – but why? Would they appear behind us, and encircle us? And why hadn't they just teleported before? Perhaps they were not fully in control. Maybe they could only do it when they were relatively still. But I found it odd, for if that was the case, they had done just that, teleported, right in front of my eyes.

But it happened to every other hunter who came too close. And it happened at the same place, like there was a line... But there was! The field! We'd gone through it! And we hadn't died because we had Elrolian Onyxus in our blood, like Black

Amber. When those creatures had done it, I thought it was only they who could do it. But no! We'd made it out safely, for it seemed that the hunters couldn't teleport inside the field. We really were safe. Except for Wolf.

I wanted to go back. I had to! Wolf was my friend! I could not abandon him to Hunter! But it was the same as last time. I just couldn't. Even if I could go in there, we wouldn't make it out.

I got up, and we watched the other hunters breathlessly pace around the field, none of them daring to go too close. So we walked away, just like that.

A moment later, another of Stringer's inventions was hovering over us. Stringer had come to save us! I sank to my knees, and realised how exhausted I was. So exhausted, that when I got to the ground, I fell unconscious, darkness filling my eyes, seeping the last of the light out of my vision.

When I woke, the first thing I thought of was Wolf. I was in a comfy bed. My own bed. I was in my room, in Elrolia. I blinked. Wolf was gone. That was all that mattered. Hunter wanted me to feel pain, and now he had something very powerful to use against me, something that would be much worse than physical pain for me. He had Wolf.

Lance… I was sure he'd mentioned the word before, but I couldn't remember what it was about. Was it a name? A place? Some sort of special object in their camp? I had no clue.

My room was comfortable, but I couldn't relax. Not with what was going on in my brain. There was my axe, lying next to me, and I gripped it tightly. There were archery boards, paper, old scrunched-up and ripped homework, and a picture of me, my sister, and my parents at the top of a mountain – all this was lying on my desk.

I heard a breath by the door, and shot out of my bed. I found myself holding my axe blade up to my mother's throat in the rounded corner of my room, next to the bright sunlit window.

I blinked, and lowered my axe. 'Sorry.'

My mother smiled. 'It's quite okay. Your skills are up to speed.' Her voice went quiet, and I knew what was coming next. 'I heard that your friend was taken.'

I nodded gravely. 'You know it isn't over?' I asked. 'He's coming. He wants Ravenwood and the king.' I gulped. 'And he wants me.'

She sighed. 'I know, my dear. Ardor of the Seven Gates informed me a few hours ago. You will survive. I will not lose you.'

I didn't want to get too emotional. I hate when people are sad. But I was very much of that right now, and didn't want any more of it.

'Right, now listen,' I said. 'I'm going to go see Emrax, see you soon.'

She nodded, and I strapped my axe to my back and went out.

'Oh, Storm – he's in the meeting room with some of your other friends, and I forgot to tell you, Heraxus – Heraxus Starscrapper – wanted to see you. He's with Emrax also at the meeting room.'

'Okay, got it. Thanks.'

I ran down to the meeting room, where I found it packed with Elrolians. But not just Elrolians, others too. All of the campers were there, chatting with the Elrolians.

I spotted Emrax talking to Ardor, who was drawing quite a lot of attention to himself by his huge size.

'Ardor! Emrax!'

Emrax smiled. 'Hey, Storm! I convinced the king and queen to let your campers in. After you let out what they call Black Amber, we guessed Hunter would be coming soon, so I suggested we decide what we're going to do here.'

I smiled. Only Emrax was capable of doing that.

'Great. And how are you, Ardor?'

'Oh, fine my friend. We're about to start an official meeting – better find a seat.'

'Yeah, okay, you save me one, I'll be there in a second.'

I looked around for Heraxus, and saw him by Spyra, talking to Streakell Serpentine, one of Spyra's close friends.

Heraxus was dressed casually, with no armour. He hated armour, and loved being comfortable, which was why he was rarely seen away from the grand lounge or the comfortable arena seats. He had shiny brown hair that always seemed to look wet, and was pulled back so his wrinkled forehead was exposed. He saw me, and gestured for me to join him.

'How are you, my friend? I heard you've been on a little adventure for the last few days.'

'Yeah, it hasn't been fun.'

'Ah, it'll be fine. I just want to let you know, even if the other Elrolians decide to leave, I'll be at your side.'

I nodded. 'Thank you.' I turned away to talk to Streakell. 'And how are you?'

'Oh, doing well. And you?'

'Okay. Could be better.'

I forced a smile, and moved back off to find Emrax and Ardor, which of course was easy. I took a seat.

'Emrax, where is Black Amber now?'

'Oh, right outside the castle, waiting.' He smiled again. 'Don't worry my friend, we are ready for battle. Today, we fight for Ravenwood. For the king. For you. We fight for the freedom of Elrolia once more.'

ONE LAST TIME

The crowded meeting room of Elrolia fell eerily silent as the beautiful queen Eleria stood, taking a deep breath before speaking out clearly to her audience.

'My fellow Elrolians, and dear guests, we are here to discuss the dark matter of Hunter. He is coming. It is inevitable. Though the king would prefer for us to leave with all haste, we have decided to have an official council meeting to decide.'

'Again,' I muttered to myself. 'I'm not going to have an hour of this.'

Emrax tried to pull me down, but I got up and strode out to the front of the room.

'Elrolians and guests, I am Storm Orthoclase, and I am here to save us one hour. Now, the purpose of this meeting is, as the queen said, to make a decision. These are your options. You can flee, like the king would like, for your own safety, or you can stay. You didn't come to my aid that last time, but I expect each and every one of you to have the courage and responsibility to aid us. Fight for Elrolia, as you have done before!'

My audience looked at me like I was announcing a rabbit as king of Elrolia.

I shook my head. 'This is simple!' I said, rather exasperatedly. 'Three lives are at risk, and I would give mine for any of you, and you should be ashamed that you wouldn't do the same! Let us stand up for Elrolia one last time!'

They seemed to start to get the picture. I saw Emrax smooth his jeans and come up to join me. I couldn't help smiling. With him, how could they decide not to stay?

'I am Emrax Treestone, of Elrolia, Professor of the Elemental Arts. I'd like to support Storm with this case. You see, my brother, father, and mother all died in the Battle of Elrolia, by the hands of the wicked and devious Hunter. So did Storm's father, and many others that we have known and cared about. Perhaps this is the reason that you do not want to do this, to fight for Elrolia. Because you have not felt the loss of a loved one. Because you do not know how it feels to crave the chance to avenge them. My brother would always say that the death of one is equivalent to the loss of a million. Every life should be spared. And you should want to help. If you do not want to help because you don't want to avenge the lost, that is acceptable. But you should never be afraid to stand up for your life, or for that of others, for that is what life is all about. When you are that step, that very second away from death, that is when you understand life the most. We ask for your help tonight, to save the lives of more than just three, because each and every one of you is capable of so much more. The lives you can save, the changes you can make! Never doubt what you can do. *Question* what you can't.'

Well, that was quite something. I mean, what a speech! When I try to convince people of something, I usually enforce it rather hard. Emrax, on the other hand, tries to relate to the audience. See, he's awesome. And the effect it had on the Elrolians was priceless. Now I understand what video cameras are for.

Oerix Waterdue, another Elemental specialist, who was very close to migrating to the northern castle due to his incredible skills, rose from his seat to his full towering height.

'I will stand alongside you, Storm Orthoclase. We didn't come to your aid before, and I deeply regret it, as should everyone else in this room, but I stand with you, my friends, to any end.'

Then, one by one, every Elrolian, Orian, and human in the audience rose, and my fears washed away. This was what I wanted to see: the Elrolians fully uniting. And alongside humans too! Brilliant.

The king rose, and the audience were seated, watching him carefully.

'Emrax Treestone, and Storm Orthoclase, you present good motives to the Elrolians, and I do think it should be up to the people of Elrolia. And judging by your reactions to Professor Treestone's wonderful speech, I would say that we have decided to stay. And by life or death, let us remember this day, where we fight, as you say, for the lives of millions.'

Everyone clapped hard as the king descended back to his seat, a faint smile on his face.

'Before we all clear out,' I said, 'I'd like to say that not even the Elrolians together would be able to stop Hunter. They took Black Amber with only three hundred, and though we now have greater numbers, so will they. We need to gather as many reinforcements as possible.' They had to understand what we were facing.

'Storm is correct,' Emrax said. 'Is anyone here in touch with the Elrolians of the North?'

No one had anything to say.

'If I may, I will go and suggest they help us,' Emrax said to the queen and king.

'You may,' said the queen with a gentle smile. 'And that was a brilliant speech, Emrax,' she added.

Emrax was right. The Northern Elrolians would help tremendously. As I said before, only the best stayed there. I think only forty-seven Elrolians had actually achieved that rank and decided to go there – that's how hard it was. There were Elrolians that had been given the Northern rank here, but had decided to stay here, but we needed more. Maybe we could send someone to the Seven Gates to try and round up the Orians.

'Wait...' I suddenly thought back to our first encounter with Hunter on the Black Amber quest. He had said something about a spy....

'Wait!' I called out. 'There is a spy! Someone from Hunter's team is here!' They didn't hear me, and continued to go for the door, so I took off my axe and threw it at the door, a perfect strike, locking it, which drew their attention to me.

'There is a spy in this room!' I yelled, so everyone could hear me. 'And no one is to leave until I find out who it is!'

Every person was scanning each other's face, like they may be dangerous aliens.

'Listen, there's no time to explain how I know, but we need to find out who it is,' I said to the king and queen, who nodded, getting down from their seats to examine everyone.

'Where's Carest...' I murmured. Carest Florenel was an expert in facial expressions, and could detect lies with ease. I spotted her in the corner of the room, carefully studying the faces of the Elrolians.

'Carest!'

She was around the same age as me, with long braided caramel hair over one shoulder, dressed in white and grey, and like Heraxus, with no armour. She was studying sociology here at Elrolia, and getting very good at it. It was near impossible to keep a secret from her. She's a very friendly person – I'd worked with her when she was on the Onyxus River Team for a brief period.

'Oh, hey, Storm. So, a spy, eh?'

I nodded. 'If I could get you up on stage, would you be able to find the one?'

She shrugged. 'If I can ask them a few questions.'

We went up to the stage, and I attempted to yell and get their attention, but it was no good, for it was way too loud, and no one could hear my voice. I nudged Ardor, and, understanding, he let out a mighty roar, and that got their attention all right.

'I'd like you to give your full attention to Carest Florenel here,' I said.

'Hello, everybody, I'd just like to ask a question. *Who is the spy?*'

It was such a simple, straightforward question, but only a moment after she asked it, she nodded, and turned to me.

'He calls himself Warlon Quent,' she whispered to me. 'He has black hair, dark purple shirt.'

I scanned through the audience, identifying a man who fitted the description, and, without explanation, grabbed him by the collar and brought him to Carest. He didn't struggle or protest. He knew he was caught with no way out.

'Him?' I asked.

Carest nodded.

I brought the so-called Warlon to the queen.

'It's him. Do what you please, but just don't kill him.'

'I never would,' the queen said, calling a guard to haul him away. He made no objection, but stared at me with hatred.

I took back my axe from the door, and the Elrolians started to flood back out again through the hall. They would be going to the armoury, I assumed, to gear up for the upcoming battle. We would need everything we had – and more.

Emrax came up to me.

'Well, I'll be setting off to the north now,' he said. 'Let's hope I don't have to go over what we just did here. Elrolians these days are getting rather lazy.'

I nodded. 'Good luck. Come back soon- with the Elrolians.'

'I'll try.' He smiled once more, and went off to get ready to go.

'Hey, Peldor!' I said, as he came up to me. 'What's up?'

'I'm going to the Seven Gates. I'll try and get them to come help. Hopefully I'll be able to get some of them.'

'Thank you, my friend, and good luck.'

He smiled, and went off to follow in Emrax's tracks.

Reinforcements were being taken care of; now I needed to go help out with getting the warriors in position, and arming them with weapons. I had no idea what Hunter would bring upon us this time. This was the final round. But we had Black Amber, and I had a feeling that this time we would hold. This time we had an army of Elrolians, and would hopefully be getting more. I guess our objective was to really just hold our ground for as long as possible. Until Hunter backed out, I guess? I wasn't sure at all how long it would take for this to be over. But this was it – the climax, I suppose – of my brief but meaningful adventure. The moment that mattered most.

Just then, Slare came up to me.

'Hey, Storm. This place is beautiful! I saw it once with Ardor and … and Wolf.'

I nodded. 'We'll find him,' I said.

'Well, I just want to thank you for all that you've done for us. You might not have really thought about it, but you were a powerful leader to us. We needed you.'

I smiled. 'You people are the best I've ever met. It's people like you who get us to think twice about not trusting you.'

She smiled as well, and went off to join the other campers, who were starting to talk with the remaining Elrolians. Most of us don't have anything against the human race, but some of those whose families had been slaughtered by Hunter would not forgive. But there were some who remained because they were curious about what humans were like – Oerix Waterdue, Heraxus Starscrapper, and Icarell Ormea were only some of the Elrolians I saw. These were the ones I knew best.

I walked out of the room and down the carefully crafted stairs to the armoury, which was, as I suspected, packed with Elrolians. Those with personal experience with Hunter looked anxious – and so did the ones who'd never seen him before. Hunter was as dangerous to them as anyone. Being Elrolian would not protect them from him – nothing would. But to protect themselves from physical injuries, they strapped on armour anyway.

I went around helping them, comforting them while I did it. None of them were being forced to do this. They were doing it because they believed it right to do so – and so it was.

While I was doing this, I remembered the moment I'd lost Wolf. He'd told me to find "lance." What was that? A certain weapon? A person? A place? Whatever it was, I would find it, for this was Wolf's last request, and I would see it done. Well, no, not *last.* I would see him again. I had to. I knew Wolf had mentioned the word before. I clenched my fist in frustration.

A small Elrolian child came up to me. She was no older than five, and I couldn't believe she was doing this.

'Sir, can you help?' she asked, holding up a small breastplate.

I smiled. 'You are ready?' I asked, fastening it to her little chest.

She nodded. 'I liked Professor Emrax's speech. I want to help!'

'That's good of you, but it could be dangerous.'

'Well, my mother is died, but my daddy is still here!'

I smiled sympathetically. 'Who is that?'

'He is daddy!'

I laughed. 'What else is he called?'

'Daddy. And sometimes Heraxus, but only by the big people. He is upstairs, he is coming down here soon.'

Heraxus! I had known he was married, but I didn't know he had a child.

'What is your name?'

'Roll!' she said proudly. 'Roll Avertune, after my daddy's husky!' She peered at me. 'You are Storm Orthoclase! My daddy knows you! Does Hunter not like you?'

I nodded. 'You could say that.'

'Does he want you die?'

I nodded. 'Kind of. But I'll be fine.' I didn't want to get into this with such a little kid. I strapped on the rest of her armour, and, giving a warm smile, left to get some other people sorted.

'Hey, Rester,' I said, seeing one of my friends over in a corner. 'Need any help? I think you have to attach the Moranus Heel to the Overest Plate.' I gestured to the straps on his armour. "It's complicated.'

'It sure is … ' he muttered. 'Damn, why are there five holes in this thing? One for your head, two for your arms, and one for your waist. What's the other one for? Are we supposed to have tails?'

I laughed. There were always those few people who could make you laugh anywhere, any time.

Just then, Heraxus came in. 'Hello again, Storm.'

'Hey, Heraxus. I just met your daughter. She's wonderful.'

'I thought I'd already introduced her to you…. Anyhow, if you'd like to go back up, I'll take care of all these people.'

I nodded. 'Thanks.'

I left the room, closing the door behind me. It was so quiet suddenly that I was tempted to open it back up again to make sure I hadn't gone deaf. I didn't, of course, but I went up, with no idea exactly where I was going. I automatically headed for my room, but while I was walking, a voice called out for me.

'Storm! Come here!' It was Stream.

I walked over to him. He was in the guest room, and when I went in, I found all his equipment there. I closed the door behind me.

'Listen, Lypherace and I were working, and we have an idea.'

I saw Lypherace in a corner, nodding. 'Yes. We know how to communicate with Wolf. We gave him that video camera for a reason. If Hunter hasn't noticed it, which I doubt, we could be able to see what's going on, but I'm not sure. Hunter isn't deceived easily.'

'If we can do it, we will do it,' I said.

'He should still have it on. Even if Hunter has taken it, he might have put it somewhere where we could get a good look at them.'

Lypherace nodded. 'I'll start the computer.'

He took out of his bag a super-high-tech, billion-pixel HD laptop, that couldn't have weighed more than a basketball.

As the computer booted up, I wasn't sure if I thought what I was going to see would be any good. We might not even see anything. What if Hunter had destroyed the device? Or what if what we saw was Hunter torturing my friend? Well, we would see.

After a few complicated commands on the computer, our logo – a metallic orange deer's head in a sliver circle – appeared on the screen, showing us that the program had started.

'It's working,' I breathed, as a well-lit room came into focus.

'It's him,' Lypherace said, looking the screen with loathing. 'Hunter himself.'

TORN APART

On Lypherace's laptop screen, I could see the entire room Hunter and Wolf were in. The only thing giving out light was the window at the other side of the room, which should have made the scene strongly backlit, and it would have been hard to see with normal eyes, but the technology was advanced, and it was crystal-clear.

Hunter, with that strange mask on, was sitting on a comfy-looking black leather couch, opposite Wolf, who was on an identical couch. Wolf looked much less comfortable, for he was wearing handcuffs, and his foot was angled strangely, probably an injury from the fall when he had been taken. His face was cut, and there were still speckles of fresh blood on his grim face.

Hunter must have taken the camera and laid it down, and was unaware that they were being watched. I could see on the screen a small rectangle in the corner showing the view of nine other cameras – one each for the rest of the team. Lypherace's and mine showed too, both fixed from our point of view on the same larger image on the screen, the one showing Hunter and Wolf.

I noticed that my own camera had a little orange light on it, and hoped the light on Wolf's camera, sitting with them in the room, wouldn't give away to Hunter the fact that we were watching.

Lypherace hit the mute button, and I knew we were now free to talk. He hit another button, and I heard the conversation happening on the other end.

I hoped my eyes deceived me: for a brief second I thought I saw Hunter's eyes flash towards us, but he did nothing.

'You broke in,' he was saying to Wolf. It was as clear as if he were standing in the room with us. 'You took my creatures. What do you call them, again? Black Amber? A good name … very metaphorical. But I am amused by the fact that you even *considered* trying to take the creatures away. Even after that long boring battle at Wouldlock? You should have known better.'

'Boring?' Wolf asked. 'You almost got your leg cut off.'

'Yes, but the pain does not bother me when I picture the revenge I shall lay upon the one who did it. Storm Orthoclase. You are good friends, yes?'

Wolf nodded. 'You could say that.'

'Will you miss him?'

'I'm not going away.'

'Are you sure about that?'

'Not unless you're planning on killing me.'

Hunter laughed. 'No! I do not kill. At least, not humans. I used to, though. I'm sure you are aware that I managed to kill twenty Elrolians without getting a scratch? That's not quite my thing anymore. I like to bestow upon my enemies the things that have haunted me for my life. To make them feel desperate, feel alone, to lose everything you care about. Not death. But all of those things will eventually come upon dear Storm. Yes, in time.'

'I still hate that dreadful mask,' Wolf said, completely ignoring Hunter's previous statement.

'Ah, but I told you why I have it on. Some people say it is my weakness, but my weakness is not the mask. Death would not stop me from doing anything. Not that anyone *could* kill me.'

'Why do you want the king?' Wolf asked. 'I know why you want Ravenwood and Storm, but why the Elrolian king?'

Hunter took a breath.

'I guess it wouldn't hurt to tell you … it's nothing that you can use against me.' He nodded. 'It started a long time ago. When I went to Elrolia in search of Ravenwood. I met the king. I was with my sister.'

Wolf frowned.

'Yes, I have a sister. I'm not surprised you don't know. No one cared about her, or at least not enough to include her in my life's story. But I cared. She was beautiful, by far the nicest person on Earth. When Ravenwood left us, we went in search of him, and came across the fabulous Elrolia. We stayed there for five years, accepted and cared for. When my sister was nineteen, the king ordered a quest to seek out some sort of armour. He said that my sister would be the absolute best for the job. None of the Elrolians would do. It had to be her, he said. But I didn't want her to go. I knew it would be dangerous, going out there, even with other Elrolians, for we were not Elrolian. But the king insisted, and so she went out, alone.'

Hunter got up from his seat and started to pace around the room.

'She didn't come back for a week, and by then, a team of three was sent to search for her. I volunteered, of course. And so did the king himself, along with the great Elrace Orthoclase. And we found her, alive and well. But before we could even call out to her, she was killed. Torn apart by an Elrolian Snow Wolf – a Lexphorus wolf. The king did nothing, and neither did the other man. But I – I killed it. It had killed my sister, the last of my family. I did not consider Ravenwood part of my family anymore, for he had abandoned me. And now, my sister is gone forever. And because of what I did, because I killed a wolf, the king despised me. And he banished me. So I ventured out on my own for a year, and then came back, in the hopes that he had forgotten me. And so he had. I changed my look, my name, and tried to become a friendlier person, for I desperately needed a home. But I did not regret what I had done to that wolf. Forever did I want revenge on the king. For banishing me, throwing me away like a dirty rock, and most of all, for sending my sister to her death. Of course, Elrace got what he deserved for not helping a while ago, at the battle. But the king – I will make him suffer for what he did, more than I will do to Ravenwood or Storm.'

'He couldn't have known,' Wolf said. He would never have done it if he had. And if you couldn't do anything, how could Elrace?'

'It doesn't matter!' Hunter roared. 'The king is responsible. He might as well have killed her himself! So once I am done with the king, I will move onto Storm and Ravenwood. At least, that was my original plan. But it's changed, and now I am going to get all of them at once. But Storm Orthoclase, for causing me the most physical pain in my life, for being one of *them* – he will get pain too. For taking away Black Amber.'

'So what have I got to do with anything?' Wolf asked.

'You will aid me in destroying Storm. He cares about you like a brother, I understand. After only a few days! And soon enough, you will die. Perhaps he will too, but you will die in a special way. Storm himself will be responsible for your death. And forever will he curse himself.'

'So what happens to me now? Am I going to Elrolia?'

'That decision will be made soon. But now, will you come with me…'

They stepped out of the room, and I heard the door slam shut, and then silence. Lypherace shut the screen.

'How will you kill him?' Stream wondered aloud, which was probably what everyone was thinking.

I shook my head. 'I don't know.' I didn't like this. Hunter had said it like he knew a hundred percent what would happen – but how? I would never kill him! What was he thinking? But I wasn't sure. My heartbeat quickened. I knew right then that there was nothing else to do. Oerix was in charge of in charge of the animals. I needed to talk to him.

'Lypherace, can you print a clear image of Hunter for me?'

He nodded. 'Right away.'

'Thanks.'

He did some fancy stuff, and the live video we'd just watched replayed. He paused it and took a screen shot of Hunter's face, and in a minute, it was printed out.

'Thanks for everything guys,' I said, grabbing the photo and rushing out of the room.

I knew where to find Oerix. He would be at the gates, sorting out Black Amber and the Elrolian wolves. So I ran down the stairs and out the front doors.

'Oerix!' I called.

He turned. He was adjusting the head armour on a stone wolf.

'Yeah.'

'Can you get a message across to the animals?'

'Yeah, sure, what?'

'Tell them to tear apart this person on sight. At least make sure he doesn't get inside the castle.' I handed him the picture.

'Hunter….' He smiled, realising what I wanted to do. 'Very smart, but they won't be able to identify a specific person.'

'Okay … well, tell them to attack anyone who has this mask on.'

'No problem, man. But to communicate better, I'll need that creature – they call her Altralz.' He went off to find the creature to translate.

If Hunter laid a toe in the castle, he would be, as he himself had said, *torn apart.* Even if he wanted Wolf to get inside for some reason, Hunter wouldn't be going in with him.

I was still deeply worried. Hunter would have some plan that would not be as easily beaten as this. He would have prepared for me to do something that he could use to his advantage. If someone told you that you would make the choice that got you killed, you would take extra precautions … and sometimes it is those precautions that make it all happen. But I was not stupid. I was planning everything out. Hunter would not deceive me.

I then heard two loud thuds, and saw someone coming toward the castle at an alarmingly fast rate. Too fast to be humanly possible.

'Bows at the ready!' I called. But as the person came closer, I realised he was no threat, and recognised him, also noticing that he was not traveling on the ground.

'Down! False alarm!' I then shouted.

I ran down to meet the person.

I had met him before. I had met him a while back, when at the Battle of Elrolia, when he had come with Stringer. He was not one to be left out in a battle, for the skill he possessed was incredible.

This person had thrown a special set of knives, and flown to them. I would be surprised if you didn't know his name – especially if you know Wolf, for I believe they had met earlier.

'Viper, my friend,' I said.

'Storm! Oh dear, how nice it is to see you again. Emrax still here?'

'He went off to the North,' I said. 'But he'll be coming soon. Anyway, why are you here? Are Stringer and Cryslia coming?'

'Oh, you bet. I came here a little faster with the help of these, you know,' he said, spinning his knives. 'We're here to help. Aquarius was talking to Wolf, who told him about everything, who told Stringer who told me that Wolf had told Aquarius who'd told Stringer then told me, you know?'

I nodded. 'Right…'

'Well then, how about we go in? I should probably be stationed somewhere high. You also have always liked to fight from a far distance rather than close up, right?'

I nodded. 'You know me well. Just go up into the Atrium, there will be an Elrolian there, ask them.'

'Okay, thanks.' Viper nodded, and went off into the castle.

All these people were coming to risk their lives for three people … me being one of them. That was faith … this was even stronger proof that making our choice to stay away from humans was the wrong one.

Stringer and Cryslia came a moment later, and they followed the same path as Viper. I assumed these would be the last that needed to go inside.

I saw Peldor return, with no one else, it seemed.

Ardor was standing by the gate near me. 'Ardor!' I called. 'Can you tell them this is the last call for anyone who wants to go in or out?'

He nodded. 'LAST CALL!' he bellowed. 'IF YOU WANT TO GO IN OR OUT, DO IT NOW!'

They got the message, but all stayed where they were.

'So, no luck?'

He shook his head. 'Sorry, Storm. They don't think it's worth it … or at least some of them didn't. They aren't allowed to allow only some to come.'

I shrugged, and I took off my axe and swung it, prepared for anything. I had been in charge of the archers, or at least would be until I decided to give them free fire, which I always did quickly. I always did this job, and liked it.

'Be ready for anything my friends! Think of your favourite music, your favourite memories. Let them run by you as this battle occurs. But do not despair! Those happy memories shall not be your last!'

'Gate-keepers, do not open for anyone! There is no need! From this point on, consider this battle has commenced.'

I saw someone approaching in the distance. I knew it would not be help this time. One person – only one. Hunter? I doubted it very much. He would not come on his own. Maybe a messenger?

I heard someone call my name again. Lypherace. He sounded very serious.

'Wait!' I said. 'I'll be a second.'

Carest was one of the archers. 'Hey, Carest!' I called to her.

'Yeah!' she shouted back.

'Cover for me until I come back, okay?'

She nodded, and came up to take my position.

I ran over to Lypherace, who led me back to the guest room. He was staying in.

'Wolf's been attacked,' he said. 'Hunter let a rouge Black Amber loose on him. I know. I saw.'

'How?' I said, coming to the computer.

'I hacked the security camera. It wasn't easy. But and I took a video of it. Here.'

He started the video. Hunter had led Wolf into a room with no windows, but blinding lights all over. Black Amber was sleeping, and woke the moment they went in. Hunter pushed Wolf in, hurried out, and I heard the door bolt shut.

I didn't want to know what happened next, but watched anyway.

'Is he dead?'

'I don't think so. At least, not yet.'

The next three minutes were Wolf getting torn up by the monster. I wanted to scream. Then, he escaped one of the creature's lunges, and backed up against the wall. The creature tried to strike again, but missed, and smashed through the wall itself.

I saw Wolf desperately run out as Black Amber got caught by a falling piece of the wall.

I sighed in relief that he wasn't dead, but I couldn't be sure he would stay like that. That creature had really beaten him up.

'Storm, I don't want to have to say this, but I watched this carefully. The animal scratched his throat. I think he might have come close to tearing Wolf's throat. It may have blocked passage for air.'

'He might suffocate?'

Lypherace nodded grimly. 'I'm sorry, Storm.'

'I don't understand … why did Hunter do that … he wanted *me* to kill him. Why would he do that? He didn't have anything against Wolf.'

'Maybe he knew he was being watched. He is a smart person, Hunter.'

'But still…'

The door then flew open, and Heraxus was there.

'Storm! Oerix was looking out. He thinks he sees Hunter – with a mask, he says. He advises that you come.'

I nodded. 'Thanks for doing all this, Lypherace.'

'No problem. I'll be out in a second.'

I sprinted out, racing through the hall until I was back out in the open air. I ran to the archers. Carest was doing a good job of comforting them at the moment. These people were great warriors, but the one person who would undoubtedly strike terror into the heart of every one of them was Hunter. The man who had tortured and killed their families, the one who could destroy all of them almost with ease.

'Thanks, Carest!' I said, taking back the post, going to the edge of the building to look down one storey. Hunter was not too close, but still visible. A black hood covered most of his face, and I couldn't make him out clearly, but I knew it was that same mask.

The whole castle waited intently, their weapons at the ready, prepared for any kind of sudden attack that Hunter might bring upon us.

I didn't like this. He was walking willingly into the Elrolian castle like he was a friend. He would get torn apart, as I'd ordered, if he was stupid enough to come too close. But Hunter wasn't stupid.

And *why* was he here now? Alone? Where was his army of hunters? Why had they not brought Wolf? Something was very wrong.

'Bows at the ready!' I called out again. 'Keep your eyes locked on the target!'

The Elrolians raised their magnificently crafted bows, and fitted them with shining arrows, that went from jet black to chrome silver, with a sharp pointed tip at the end. All of them were pointing at Hunter. The Elrolians were magnificent shots, and would not miss anything.

'Wait...' I murmured.

The person below seemed dazed, like he was sleepwalking. What was going on? Hunter drew nearer and nearer, and then, all of a sudden, the Elrolian wolves sprang out, and were upon the figure, scratching him and biting at him very visibly as he fell to the ground.

'Stop!' I called. 'Stop them!'

Oerix relayed my order, and once again giving Carest my role, I ran down to the gate. They opened it thoughtlessly, barely able to refrain from going up to take a look.

The wolves drew back, snarling. I drew my axe, for I was not about to approach Hunter's body unarmed. Why had he given in so easily? I didn't think anyone would be able to live through an attack like that. Those wolves were, of course, Elrolian, and their claws would sink through any type of metal. Unless he was wearing Elrolian armour – which wouldn't really have saved him – he shouldn't have be able to live more than two minutes. How he would die, I really didn't want to know.

I steadily approached the body. The other Elrolians watching attentively, ready to jump to my aid in case anything went wrong.

The hood covered the face completely now. The fallen body was dressed in ragged clothes – black jeans and a grey coat. He had a ragged and ripped-up cloak on too, which held the hood, now stained with blood.

I gripped my axe tightly with both hands. It felt like a trap. Exactly what Hunter would do: pretend to die, then strike, but I bent down, raising my axe, and, my hand shaking, removed the hood, exposing the dirty, bloodied face.

It took me a moment to take in what I saw. The features were hard to make out. I quickly felt for a pulse. None. I pushed myself up, my body trembling, and, in pure rage, screamed.

BATTLE OF THE ELROLIANS

I couldn't stop myself. I screamed until I had nothing left in me. It was not Hunter who laid on the ground, dead, not a drop life within him. It should have been, but it was not.

It was Wolf.

The people around me who recognised the body almost screamed themselves, but none felt anger as much as me. Wolf was wearing Hunter's mask. That's why he had been attacked. He must have put on a duplicate when he was attacked by Black Amber. Hunter would have had plenty of backups of the mask that was keeping him alive.

I looked up to see another person coming towards us. It was, with no doubt, Hunter. I stood up, shaking with anger. I grabbed my axe, and walked out to meet him.

He took off his own hood, and smiled cruelly.

'Storm Orthoclase, my friend. Is something wrong?'

'You killed him,' I said.

'Oh no, I didn't by any means. I sent him back to you. You are the one responsible for killing him.'

He was right. I had been the one to give that order. Trying to avoid Hunter's threat brought it right up into reality. *I* had killed Wolf. *I* was responsible.

I wouldn't just talk to him like this.

'I WILL KILL YOU!' I screamed, and I raised my axe, ready to attack. 'I will torture you, I will stab you until you die. I will make you feel pain!'

'Let us begin,' Hunter said, and behind him, his army, more than two thousand people, came running in, all armed, riding all kinds of terrible monsters.

Arrows flew, and soon enough, swords, knives, axes, they were all clashing, sparks flying. I said no more, and took every possible strike I could at Hunter.

I summersaulted over him, and tried to attack him from the back, but he grabbed my axe, and twisted it. I kept a hold, and turned around with it, ending with a nice solid kick.

I would occasionally take a swing of my axe at a random hunter, but tried my best to focus on the man himself.

I saw Heraxus and Spyra fighting back to back, taking out hunters like bowling pins. I did not stop fighting Hunter until he smiled, turned to black dust, and appeared elsewhere, far out of my reach.

The hunters went for the castle, hacking at it until an Elrolian came to face them. The hunters wanted to get inside. They wanted the king, who was with Ravenwood, firing arrows from a concealed space in the southern tower.

I fought, every strike I made dedicated to Wolf's life, making sure I brought upon the hunters the pain I felt now. But I did not kill. Hunter was right. Death would solve nothing. I wanted revenge. An arrow flew towards me, and I ducked, but a second one came and scratched my shoulder, spilling fresh blood all over my armour.

I didn't use my element – ice for my axe – but was still successful. This axe wouldn't normally be my thing, for I preferred long-distance weapons, but something this powerful was much more effective, for it was elemental, and could also shoot at great distances.

I ran into a hunter, and nearly got stabbed in the back. I twisted around over the hunter's body, and gave a strong blow to the face, audibly breaking it.

A dinosaur-like horse monster came up to me, and tried to bite my face off. I dodged and, gripping its saddle, swung up onto its back, driving it out of control, crashing into several hunters along the way, finally swinging back off as the creature ran into a river, completely out of control.

An axe smashed the ground at my feet, and I jumped back. I grabbed the axe, and gave it a quick scan. Elrolian! Of course! The spy must have been transporting our weapons to Hunter. He was serious about this battle – he wouldn't hesitate to start killing Elrolians again – or at least, giving his army the privilege.

I wanted to rip Hunter apart. He had made me kill Wolf. His cunning ways had led to his death, and soon, he would meet his.

I turned my attention back to the battle, and saw that there was a big change in numbers. About half the hunters had vanished. I then realised that they'd done that annoying black dust thing. They were in the castle now. The gate was blocked, and I needed to lend some of my help to the Elrolians up there. I signaled to Carest, and she shot an arrow attached to a rope. I climbed up the rope to get to the archers. Soon, hunters were attempting to come up the same way, and just as they were about to climb over the wall, I cut the rope with a neat swing of my axe. The hunters they fell to the ground below.

A hunter came up to me and sent a punch right to my face. I grabbed his arm and twisted it, and as he winced, his arm bending at a strange angle, I pushed him off the tower and then gave a kick to another hunter, hauling her off the side.

'How you holding up?' I asked Carest, who was, like Heraxus and me, very close to joining the northern rank.

'Just fine. You?'

'Alright. Just a scratch or two so far,' I said, smashing the side of my axe against a hunter's chest, sending her flying away.

'We won't hold up!' Carest said, ducking along with me as the Elrolians sent a volley of arrows over our heads.

I nodded grimly. Nothing to do about that at the moment.

'Oerix!' I called. 'Release the wolves!'

I jumped back off the tower and, with a neat roll, landed just in time to see a stampede of Snow Wolves race out like cheetahs, ripping the hunters apart like bread.

I saw a buff woman throw a spear directly into the body of a wolf. The animal howled, and dropped to the ground, its soft white fur darkening with scarlet red. I roared in rage, and threw my axe at the hunter, hitting her chest at point-blank range sending her flying away into a river, my axe going along with her. I rolled my eyes. Well, that was one problem taken care of. And another one made. My axe would sink to the bottom of the river. But honestly, how would that stop me? I dived in, freezing though the water was, and saw my axe glinting in the water like a jewel. I swam down and grabbed it. Before I went back up, I just stayed there a moment. I was in peace. No noisy screams or clangs of swords. Peace. But it didn't last, for when I went up and pulled myself out of the water, I faced again the terrible battle.

And we were losing. I saw dead or injured Elrolians everywhere. I saw Heraxus on the ground, lying limply, and a hunter pleasurably hacking at his back with a club.

'Stop!' I screamed, and ran towards Heraxus, slamming his attacker with my shoulder, bringing him to the ground. I took Heraxus's hand and pulled him up.

'You alright?'

He nodded solemnly. 'Thank you. I think he broke my arm.'

I then saw a humungous robotic horse stampede into the battle, crushing Elrolians. Hunter had created this – a mechanical creature. It was bronze, and being steered by … no one. It was working by some sort of control elsewhere.

I ran to it, and jumped up, using the gears and bits of sticking-out metal to get myself up onto its back. I twirled my axe around and hammered it down, cracking the metal plate.

Where was its weak spot? Its battery? I smashed my axe all over it, and finally saw a load of wires. I tore them apart. Nothing happened. It was fake! To mislead me, or whoever else attempted to stop the creature!

A hunter got up onto the back of the robot as well, and tried to cut my hand off with a large sharp sword. He missed, but it was very close, and he then did a kind of handstand and gave a big kick, sending my sprawling back. My axe fell out of my hands and I tumbled of the side, and just managed to catch on a metal rod. I swung around, and let myself go, flying into the hunter, knocking him off with a powerful punch to his breastplate.

I grabbed my axe and went up to the head of the horse. I smashed both of its eyes out, where there seemed to be cameras, and it started to run around out of control, nearly sending me flying off its back. I saw a hatch. I opened it and swung down into a large compartment inside the horse. I saw a pillar of transparent orange energy, like glass. I smashed it apart with my axe, and felt the horse stop and start to fall sideways to the ground. I jumped out of the compartment into the river. I saw the robot explode as I fell, and pieces of its body descend through the water. I shot up to the surface and pushed myself out.

I saw Viper close by me. He was turning around, his arms held up, and all around him hunters were falling to the ground.

I saw his mouth twitch and realised he must have been using his knives. It was absolutely incredible.

I was just in time to see ten hunters appear on the field in their annoying darkness thing. In the exact same moment, they each drove a knife into a different Elrolian's body. 'NO!' I screamed.

They fell to the floor, dead, like so many others.

This repeated twice more – twenty more dead Elrolians. One tried me – but I was prepared. I gave a blow to his face and kicked his knee, bringing him to the ground, and twisted his hands until the knife dropped. I caught it by the blade, smacking the hilt against the hunter's head so he fell completely unconscious. Then, for good measure, I kicked his chest.

Suddenly I felt a scream of pain in my back, like fire against bare skin. I'd been stabbed. Blood flowed down my back, seeping through my armour, where the knife had cleverly found a weak spot. I turned around, the knife still in my back, and stared at the person who'd wielded it. Hunter.

'It's not Elrolian, my friend, but feel the pain,' he disintegrated once more, and I dropped to the floor in astonishment. It was pain like none before. I was almost surprised I was not dead, for if I was not Elrolian, I would have been. Your worst injury that you've ever had – it is nothing compared to this. Understand, I should have been dead – only the chemicals in my blood, surrounding my heart, saved me.

'Storm!' Heraxus said, pulling the knife out, his hand bloody.

I felt blood all over my body, like warm water on a cold day. I gasped. Taking it out did nothing to help. It made it worse.

'Put it back in!' I screamed.

'What?'

'Put it back in – to stop the bleeding!' I cried, kind of insanely, I guess.

'I'm not going to stab you!'

'There's a hole in my back with nothing to stop it now!'

Unwilling to stab me, he summoned an Elrolian to bring the first-aid kit, but I couldn't stand it. I picked up the knife and grabbed it tightly, my knuckles white. Just as I raised my arm to try and put it back in, which I thought at the time would help, an arm grabbed me. The first-aid people. They patched it up for me. Heraxus thanked them for getting there in time to stop me stabbing myself.

'You are crazy!' Heraxus cried. 'You actually thought that would help?'

I grunted.

All seemed lost. My home would be destroyed, Elrolians would and had been killed and injured, and there was nothing to stop the hunters from doing more.

But at that moment, something happened. Every living thing, both hunter and Elrolian, stopped in their tracks. They thought they'd imagined it. But it came again – a wolf's howl, loud and terrifying, piercing each and every person's heart. It seemed to shake the world.

And then, all hell broke loose as a hundred armed wolf-riders came riding in. They were on Elrolian Snow Wolves, which were armoured heavily with gleaming chrome that faded to black. They were huge – larger than horses – being ridden by the Elrolians of the North. Help had come. The riders were wearing magnificent silver crowns, armed with the most beautifully crafted weapons, and the finest armour. Emrax led them, a confident smile on his face.

They finished off the battle for us, destroying all in their path. Most of the hunters were stupid enough to stay. They had no idea that all their hope was lost, but the ones who knew who these people were fled immediately.

'Hunter!' I roared. 'Come back here! We're not finished!'

I knew he was gone, but wanted to see him. I wanted ever

so badly to kill him for what he'd done to me. But wait – he was not gone. Ravenwood and the king! Hunter believed I'd been taken care of with the knife, and had moved on – to the meeting room! He would be there!

I got up and ran with all speed to the gates, now standing freely open, for the gatekeepers had been killed long ago.

I went in and raced up the stairs, and pushed open the doors to the room to see Ravenwood, the king, and Hunter standing in the middle.

'Ah, Storm! Here you are, to complete the trio!' Hunter said.

I went in, drawing my axe, and closed the door.

'The knife wound treating you alright?'

'Shut up,' I snarled.

He smiled, and turned to the king.

'What do you want, Hunter?' the king asked. It seemed Hunter had only just gotten here too.

'Oh, well, you should be well aware by now that I am hunting you, for what you did to my sister all those years ago.'

'That was you…? But I – I did nothing! And I thought you dealt with that when you killed twenty Elrolians that time.'

'Shut up!' Hunter roared. 'I am not finished, and will not be until I drive you insane. And I'll have you know, that while you cower in this petty room, I have killed hundreds of your people. And there will be more to come! I slaughtered your family, your friends, everyone. I will just move on to destroying your home, and of course your dear wife, and then, I will be done. Or, you can kill yourself now … and you'll have nothing to worry about.'

The king stood, his eyes full of sadness and deep regret.

'If this is what it will come to … then I have no will to see it transpire.'

He grabbed the Elrolian knife from his belt, and with one second of hesitation, in which I saw fear in his eyes, he drove it into his body. He sunk to the ground, and stayed there, lifeless.

I stared. 'King?' I said in astonishment. I leant down and felt his pulse. 'Dead!'

How could he? He'd just killed himself....

Hunter smiled. 'I think we both knew it would eventually come to this ... but Ravenwood, my brother, what about you?'

'I? Brother, I always loved you. I never meant to abandon you, please understand. I always wanted the best for you and our sister.'

'You cared nothing for either of us!' Hunter spat. 'I see nothing for you but death. You have already lost everything. Except your life.'

At that moment, the second that Hunter took a step, the Northern Elrolians came stampeding through, on foot of course.

Hunter turned to look, then again disintegrated.

'Where is he?' one of the Northerners asked. 'Where did he go?'

'You won't find him anymore,' I said dismissively. 'Once he does that, he's gone.'

'You're Storm Orthoclase,' the person said. 'Son of Elrace and Aria? I was a good friend of theirs ... I'm Cydel Laximust. Are you okay?' he added, having seen the blood on my back.

I nodded. 'Thanks for coming.'

'Pleasure. The king...'

He stopped mid-sentence, looking at the king's dead body on the floor.

'Dead,' I said. 'Killed himself. He was driven insane by Hunter.'

Cydel nodded. 'I can understand that.... I also believe Hunter is hunting you. Will you do the same?'

'I certainly hope not,' I said. 'The king had nothing to live for. I have the rest of my family, and Elrolia … or what's left of it.'

'And what about you, Ravenwood? Do you remember me?'

'Oh, of course. I may be old, but my memory is as good as ever.'

Cydel smiled. 'Axial, could you take this body out of here? I'll help you, just start going.'

A woman came up and carefully dragged the body out, no emotion showing in her stunning green eyes.

'Well, Storm, Ravenwood. Good luck. I am sorry we arrived so late…. We could have saved many more lives.'

He gave a final nod, and he and the others left the room. Then one person came back in. Emrax.

'Hey, man,' I said.

'Storm! Your back!'

'Yeah, yeah, whatever … the bandage is stopping the bleeding.'

'Hunter?'

I nodded.

'Storm, you're going to the medical room, come on.'

'Um, no, I'm not. Not me. There are many others to be seen. It's not much – just pain, no chance of death. An Elrolian knife did not make this. Others have more serious injuries.'

'Have you ever gone to the medical room in your life? You probably have the biggest record of injuries in Elrolia – and usually very serious ones.'

'Well, I've read about the hospital. You send me brochures to try and make me go there.'

'And why don't you?' Emrax asked, a little smile on his face. He was always exasperated when I refused to see a doctor.

'It doesn't matter! They'll just stick some itchy cream on it or something and say to come back for a check in a month. I don't need that type of time-waster in my life.'

'I suppose you read that too?'

I smiled, and we nearly laughed. If Hunter took away

Emrax, I would, no matter what the cost, murder Hunter without a second thought. Emrax, my mother, my friends – they were what mattered. And he'd already taken Wolf.

'Do you know if any Black Amber or wolves were killed?' I asked.

Emrax nodded. 'Twenty-three in total. Pretty sad. Nineteen were injured, but it's nothing we can't handle. Hunter really aimed for Black Amber – they saved a lot of lives. I wasn't there for most of it, but every Elrolian I've talked to say they owe their lives to Black Amber. No wonder Hunter didn't want them included in the battle.'

'So now it's pretty much over. He just wants Ravenwood and me. If we don't go to him, he'll come back to us.'

'Well, we're prepared to fight for you,' Emrax said.

'Emrax, More than five hundred must have been killed. If we stay, even more will die.'

'Storm, if he wants you, he'll attack us anyway. It's how he works. It won't stop us from being killed.'

'You're right. But that's not going to happen ... because I'm going to kill him first.'

'That's the spirit. This thing turned from a simple injury to a death game – a game of chess. He's got all the pieces. But of course, that would never stop you.'

'Never,' I agreed.

He felt my shirt. 'Why are you soaking wet?'

'I took a swim,' I said simply. 'Well, two, actually.'

'Right...' Emrax said, looking at my uncertainly. 'In the middle of the battle?'

I nodded. 'Yeah.'

'So, um, who was that person who died, if it wasn't Hunter?'

'His name was Wolf. You – you never met him. He was a human. A very good human. And I gave the order that killed him. Me, his own friend.'

'Storm, you couldn't have known.'

'Everyone says that! But I should have. If I hadn't given the order, he wouldn't be dead! It was my fault, all my fault! If I had done nothing, or realised it sooner, he could be in this room, alive with us!'

'Nothing can change what has already happened, my friend.'

'Still! It's something I should have changed. For the rest of my life I'll feel like this! Like I personally murdered him!'

'Storm, settle down. There are ways of communicating with the dead, as you should know! The Elemental Lords! They're like gods! Some of them deal with the dead! The Ghost Lord, for instance. Or the Lord of Souls'

'The Ghost Lord?' I asked, especially interested in this.

'Dead people who still have a soul. The people that can still kind of live. They can bring messages from the dead to the living, but always for a heavy price. The whole story is really interesting, if you really care to hear it.'

'So like a million-dollar price tag?'

'Shut up,' Emrax smiled. 'Something like…'

'A stone!' I exclaimed.

'What?'

'A little pebble! No, I'm kidding. We found an Atlantian firestone that would cover the price. And Stringer's here! He might have brought the crystal with him.' I smiled. 'See you soon.'

I raced out of the room, and found myself face-to-face with Stringer himself.

'Stringer, have you got the…'

'I heard you talking,' he said. His chest armour opened up to expose a fragment of the crystal. He took it out and handed it to me.

'I've kept this broken part of it with me ever since you retrieved it. But use it well! I understand it almost cost you your life.'

I ran back into the room.

'Emrax, I got it!' I laid the stone carefully on the table. 'This will do, right?'

Emrax curiously examined it. 'Where on Ortus did you get this?'

'I didn't get this on Ortus. Got it *under* it. The bottom of the sea. Aquarius Seabell helped us out a bit.'

'Well, this holds a tremendous amount of power. I don't think anyone would turn down a gift like this one. Are you seriously considering giving this away?'

'Well, yeah, if I could talk to Wolf.'

'You're really serious about this,' Emrax said.

I remembered all the time I'd spent with Wolf, brief though it was.

'I really am.'

DO YOU BELIEVE IN GHOSTS?

Talking to ghosts, or even just encountering them, is the type of thing horror movies are based on, and visiting my dead friend could be just that. A horror story. Communicating with the dead! It was not a joyful thought … but what if I could take it a step further, and bring him back into the living world? I doubted it was possible, but would do anything to bring Wolf back.

And if I could talk to Wolf, could I talk to my father? Or see if my sister were dead? Sadly, I doubted there would be any option of bringing them back. I would not have been the first to get such an idea, and I hadn't heard of anyone succeeding, but it wouldn't stop me from trying. According to Emrax, this stone was very valuable. I had no idea what it could do, but didn't really care.

What was the best an Atlantian stone could do? Let you breathe underwater? I could do that already. Give you the full elemental power of water? Maybe.

I should have stopped it – Wolf's death. Elrolians were powerful people, and I was one of them … yet I had failed so badly. Because Hunter wanted me destroyed, wanted me to kill myself as the king had done. But what if I killed him first? We would see.

'Where exactly is the place?' I asked Emrax.

'Well luckily for us, it's not too far away. About twice the distance from here to the house of Androma Faithly.'

'Really! Let's go now! You can lead me, and we'll get there in half an hour.'

'I guess so,' hesitated Emrax. 'What do you want to tell Wolf?'

'I want to ask him what he did, and explain what happened to him. I want to try and bring him back.'

'Storm, I don't think that's possible. We live in a world unlike earth, with more advanced ways to manipulate science, and turn it into a form rather like magic. But death is the end. There is no way to bring him back my friend.'

'I'll still try,' I said, though Emrax was probably right.

'Okay,' Emrax said. 'Let's go.'

Spyra had met us at the gate, and, interested in what we were doing, trailed along with us. It was nice to have company. She had been affected by Wolf's death too. Maybe not as much as I had, but she still wanted to see him.

Hunter's damage had affected the whole of Wouldlock. First from the battle when the hunters took Black Amber, and also from the one we'd had just now. They had destroyed the trees, burned the grass. They'd done this seemingly for fun as they crossed over to battle us. Elrolia didn't look so great now. Rocks had been heaved against the walls, some small fires that had long ago been extinguished still left black marks against the marble walls.

But the more we drew away from Elrolia, the more untouched it became. Soon, we were at the Ghost Lord's castle, and it was in its own way magnificent as well.

It was dark, even in the evening light; it was as if all natural light had been sucked away. There were a few other lights here and there. They looked … well, like ghosts. Dim, and moving like snakes. The evil version of the northern lights.

The place was like a castle. Towers loomed over us, casting eerie shadows. Massive cobwebs, each strand as thick as your finger, Stretched al over the trees and stones. Cracked stone staircases led up to the main floor, to a large open space. I couldn't see the whole place from this distance, but we were getting closer.

I drew my axe, but Emrax continued walking normally. He had no weapon. He liked to rely on what he could do anytime, anywhere, which was his elemental power of wind and nature – both very strong, and usually underestimated. Wind could make huge natural disasters, create plants that could squeeze the life out of you. Emrax had mastered all of this, and had gone beyond what was in the books, creating new uses for these elements.

'So, someone lives here? With all of the ghosts?' Spyra asked, looking up at the castle.

'Kind of. The Lord of Ghosts is kind of the way of saying the Lord of the Dead. Ghosts are the physical forms of dead beings. There is no heaven or hell – there is death. And this is the death castle, the land of the dead. At the very border of Elrolia and the sea,' said Emrax.

Sure enough, I could see and hear waves crashing against the shore, very near to us.

'We are at the border. If you continue past this place, to the north, you would find the Northern Elrolians' castle. It's a beautiful place, you know.'

'Is it?' I said. I had never been there. You could only go if invited, which was only either for very important discussions, or if you had achieved the required rank, going past what Elrolia had to offer.

'It is … much different from this place…' Emrax said.

'I want to visit the north one day,' Spyra sighed. 'That would be awesome.'

We went up the stairs, our footsteps echoing through the castle. I heard the shrieks of bats, the flapping of wings. I wondered what creatures would dare to live here; it didn't seem suitable for anything.

'Do all of the ghosts live here?' I asked. 'It seems much too small.'

'Oh no, I don't think so. I'm not sure exactly how it all works.'

'Will we be safe? I mean, is the Lord of Ghosts going to be angry that we're invading his territory?'

'Perhaps … but that's what the stone is for, isn't it? He should accept it, and allow us to talk with them.'

'Stone?' Spyra asked.

'Yeah, we brought along something to give the Lord,' I said.

'Is that why people aren't always here, visiting dead family?' Spyra said. 'Because they wouldn't be allowed without something to give?'

Emrax nodded. 'Imagine what it would be like if people came in here every day. Millions of people die all the time, and have died, and millions more people would want to visit them. But not all of them have access to things that could be powerful enough to allow them entry. This is a special occasion.'

We came out at a large open area, and in the middle I saw a round rock pillar about a metre high. Floating a few centimetres above it was a round glowing orb, revolving slowly, mist like dry-ice slowly pouring out onto the floor, covering our feet.

I wanted to go to it, to touch it. What was it doing there? I stepped forward, but Emrax pulled me back. He shook his head.

'Wait,' he whispered.

I saw a figure coming out from an archway on the opposite side, cloaked in black, robe swirled slowly, floating like there was no gravity holding it down. The mist seemed to separate around the figure as it walked. Beneath the dark hood I could see only shadows, not even a face.

The figure was holding a staff in its large skeletal withered hand. At the top were three sharp revolving blades, making it look all the more terrifying.

'What do you want?' a voice whispered. It seemed to come from the castle itself, not the figure. It was not male, nor female. It was not human either. As it spoke, the crystal on the end of the staff grew brighter, then dimmed.

'I wish to speak to the dead,' I said. 'I have a gift to present in return for this honour,' taking out the stone from Emrax's leather bag.

'What do you have?'

I came cautiously forward, and showed the stone.

'This is an Atlantian Firestone. It holds great power that you may harness and use. You are the Ghost Lord, yes?' I asked uncertainly.

The figure took the stone, and examined it.

'Indeed. I am the Lord of the Dead, of ghost, souls, spirits – you may call me what you wish. My name is Hyloxophon. You are Storm Orthoclase, and you are Emrax Treestone, and Spyra Crysabell.'

Emrax and Spyra nodded, coming forward as well. 'Yes, Lord. We wish to communicate with someone who was very recently killed, someone by the name of Wolf. Just Wolf,' said Spyra.

I came forward even more. 'Also, if I may, could I talk to Elrace Orthoclase? My father?'

Hyloxophon nodded. 'You may.'

He led us over to the orb, and cast his skeletal hand over it. Then, he stepped back, and the orb spewed a cloud of dry ice, or something very much like it, and a glowing, ghostly form of Wolf appeared in the very air in front of me, his skin the colour of the moon. He looked as he always had, his bones safely in his body, not like the mangled mess I'd last seen him in.

'Wolf …' I said, as if in a trance. 'You're here.'

'Storm, Spyra,' he said. 'It's good to see you.… I'm … dead.'

I nodded. 'Wolf, I did it! When I heard what Hunter was going to try to do, I ordered that anyone wearing Hunter's mask be attacked. I didn't know that you would have it … and I was too late to help you. I'm sorry.'

He nodded understandingly. 'He set Black Amber loose on me. It ripped my throat. Only one of Hunter's masks could save me. I put it on. He knew I would, and he knew what you would do after seeing those videos. He knew you would watch them. He drugged me, made my reflexes weak. I couldn't do anything to protect myself.'

'How did they know I would order that? How did they know I would do any of that?'

Wolf smiled faintly. 'You're not so unpredictable you know? Also, you can bet that spy had some way to communicate with Hunter. Even if the spy was captured, which I imagine he was, he would have found out somehow, and got the message across. Anyway, he could have used darkness to escape at any time. There was nothing holding him back from freely searching the castle.'

I nodded. 'But I need to bring you back…'

He shook his head. 'No, Storm. I'm dead. I will stay that way. Death isn't the end for me, but I will never return to your world.'

'No!' I said, my voice rising. 'It must be possible! If you're here in front of me now!'

'This will become my home. Even assuming this form is tiring for both the Ghost Lord and me. I spent my life well. The animals of Wouldlock will hopefully live a better life because of what I did. I wish I could come back. I am not finished. I could save many more lives....'

'You said, when they took you that I needed to find "lance" ... what is lance?'

'A person,' Wolf said sadly. 'He was taken by hunter a while ago. He was my leader. Find him, and save him – if he still lives.'

'Tell me about him, what he was doing, everything.'

'He said he was working on a lock. He would disappear into his room to work on it. But when we searched his room, we found nothing. They might have taken it.'

'A lock?' said Spyra, confused.

'Yes, a lock. I have no idea what for, or really anything about it. Raider once saw it. He said it was massive, the size of a computer. But tell me ... I understand there was a battle after I died. Did anyone else fall?'

Emrax came forward so he was in full view. Wolf had not seen him yet. 'I'm Emrax Treestone. I was at the battle, and saw one of your friends die. His name was, I believe, Stream.'

I looked at him, surprised.

'He's dead?'

Emrax nodded.

Wolf looked down sadly. 'He was a good person. How did he die?'

'An arrow through his body. It was Elrolian, I think,' Emrax said. 'But not fired by an Elrolian. They had our weapons, which was why so many of us were able to be killed.'

'Yes.... So you're Emrax?' Wolf said. 'I've heard about you.'

Emrax looked at me, and I flickered a smile.

I turned back to Wolf. 'So, um, how does it feel?'

'Well, pretty normal, kind of. This is the first time I've seen this world since I was killed ... normally I stay in this castle, but when I look out, I see darkness. Normally this place is crowded with ghosts. Lots, all very quiet. But this time, you are the only ones here, and I see the world. Dying … was … strange. The pain, ongoing, and then it stopped. And I was here. I wasn't introduced to this place. I found out everything by myself. It's not too bad.'

I nodded. 'I'm sorry again.'

He smiled kindly. 'Well, Storm, Spyra, Emrax. Good luck. Don't die … at least not any time soon.'

'We'll try,' Spyra said.

Wolf nodded, and burst into a puff of smoke. Dry ice, I tell you.

The Ghost Lord came forward and once again repeated his gesture. The dry ice gathered together and Elrace appeared. My father. His colourless hair was wet like always, and pulled back over his head, giving him a sleek look. He had a small neat beard, and he had his usual smile on.

'Dad!' I said.

He smiled. 'Storm! My dear son! It's so good to see you. It's been so long. Paying me a visit.… That's good of you. Even in death there are things to look forward to. Do you remember me well? After all these years?'

I nodded. 'Of course. Mother is doing well,' I added, which softened him up considerably.

'Great! Tell her I say hi … and – Emrax! Spyra! Oh my, all of you have grown!'

'It's nice to see you again,' Spyra said with a smile.

Emrax, who had become very friendly with my parents, called them by their real names. 'Elrace! You haven't changed a day!'

My father grinned. 'Still has good looking as ever, eh?'

Emrax chuckled. 'Of course.'

'Oh, I've been so *bored!*' he said. 'It's great to see a familiar face. It's hard to find people you know around here.'

'Yeah, it must be,' I agreed.

He turned back to me. 'It's really too bad that your sister isn't here with you.'

'Do you know where she is?' I asked eagerly. 'I will find her if you can tell me! No one else knows!'

My father sighed. 'If I am correct, she is not still with Hunter. For all those years she had been with him, but not anymore.'

'So then where is she now?' I asked quickly.

'She only joined him because she thought it was for the best. You remember how she always had an interest in Orians and Arigor. Hunter promised her to save them, or so the dead tell me. But when he lied, and attacked their home, she tried to escape. Hunter didn't let her. He imprisoned her inside Elrolia itself, but no one ever knew where, or even that she was there.'

'She's in the *castle*?' I said, disbelievingly.

'Yes. Trapped. She may have died long ago.'

I shook my head vigorously. 'Not her. She would have survived. She trained in survival class with me. She's still alive,' I said confidently. 'And I'll search every corner of Elrolia to find her.'

'Well, my son, if that's what you say, I know there is no stopping you. Good luck. I love you!' He smiled warmly, and then, like Wolf, vanished. Seriously! I'm his son, and after three minutes he disappeared? He was *dead!* He shouldn't have been tired!

Well, whatever. I needed to find my sister, Swayvera. Trapped in the castle for more than a year. How could I not have known? And could she still be alive! Like I said, she was also a survival expert, but was she still alive? Was she able to find food and water? We would see. And I would only be satisfied when I found her, dead or alive. I wouldn't stop looking until then.

We went out, down the spiral staircase, and back into the evening. It was considerably lighter than the ghost kingdom.

'So your sister is trapped inside the castle?' Spyra said.

I nodded. 'Yeah ... somewhere.'

'Perhaps she was mistaken for a hunter and put in a cell without a second glance!' Spyra said.

I shook my head. 'We would have noticed. She's somewhere that no one knows ... that only Hunter knew about, and now Swayvera as well.'

'She could be anywhere – in a hollow tower, in a well – we have no lead. Only that she's in Elrolia.'

'I'll find her. Elrolia may be big, but I'll find her.'

'Storm...' Emrax said uncomfortably. 'She may not be alive.'

'We don't know that! I will only stop looking if I know she's dead!' I snapped.

'How long has she been down there?' Spyra asked.

'Well she would have betrayed them when they invaded the Seven Gates, so about two years I guess.'

'Two years...' Spyra breathed. 'How could she still live?'

'I don't know,' I said sadly.

Hunter had really got at me. My father, Wolf, Swayvera, the king. What would be next? My mother? Emrax? Elrolia, my home?

A long time ago, at the Battle of Elrolia, I was told something that really did change my life. Two people had time-traveled to our time from a few years in the future, and had warned us against letting in a stranger offering us power, but what really bothered me was that they said that in the future they had seen, I had committed suicide. Because seventy per-cent of the Elrolian population had been killed, and I had been in charge – I had led them into battle. So I'd killed myself. Not a pleasant thought.

My back still stung from Hunter's blade. Not a fatal injury, but still, no less painful.

I saw something move in the tree next to us, and whipped out my axe.

A snake crawled down and slithered towards us, its scaly body glinting. Glinting too much – it was not normal. It was, like the horse, robotic. It was like one of Mac's or Icon's creations, but more realistic.

It slithered down into a hole in the ground, and I realised what it was. A bomb.

'Run!' I yelled, and Spyra and Emrax obediently scrambled away as the snake blew up, exploding into a mass of flame. I felt the sleeve of my shirt catch fire, and hurriedly put it out.

I breathed hard. Fire had caught the trees around us. Luckily, we were not in a grassy area, and the flames did not spread.

'Wait…' I muttered.

I shot a bolt of ice at a tree, but it evaporated in front of my eyes. This was powerful, very hot fire.

'Emrax!' Spyra said. 'Blow it away!'

Emrax stared at the trees, and a powerful gust of wind caught them, blowing out the fire. The trees flattened, like in a tornado. We hadn't been affected by the wind; Emrax could control it well.

'It was meant for us,' Spyra said. 'Hunter did it.'

'It was meant for me. He wanted me to feel *pain,*' I said grimly.

Then, a thought came to me. The snake went underground. What if that was where Swayvera was? *Under* the ground!

'I think I know where Swayvera is,' I said.

'Somewhere in Elrolia?' Emrax asked.

I stared at the great castle in the distance. 'Under it.'

THE CAVERN

'Where ... where?' I muttered to myself. We were back in Elrolia, and I had told the queen about my sister, whom she had known very well. Although after the queen had heard about her husband's death she was in no happy mood, she'd sent a team of twenty Elrolian trackers to find Swayvera, with Ardor in the lead.

We had searched towers, prison cells, room cupboards, everything. The idea of her being *under* Elrolia sounded insane, and I only wanted to try it if all else was securely checked over.

Ardor was an excellent tracker. It seemed his unique form boosted his senses, which made him very observant.

We had found routes down below the castle, and were now searching them. It had not been easy to find them. All had been locked with solid Onyxus, or had been completely caved in. After a few hours of exhausting work, we'd managed to unblock twelve of them, and had started to explore.

'Water…' I said to myself, examining the walls. There was a stream running down the cavern. 'She had water … what about food?'

I ran down through the place towards a speck of light at the end of the tunnel. I saw that on the walls were drawings. I touched them carefully. Charcoal. She had done these. They were pictures of Arigor: the symbols, their unique masks.

I looked over and saw one of me and my mother and father. She was an excellent artist. She had written *My Loving Family* below it. I walked along the wall, looking at what she had drawn.

I backed up as tears welled up in my eyes. I missed her. And there had not been a day, it seemed, when she had not been thinking of me.

I collected myself before yelling, 'Swayvera! Where are you?'

I heard only the echo of my voice coming back to me. But she was here somewhere. She had to be.

Then, I heard Ardor. 'Storm? Where are you?'

I raced ahead, and saw another path to the left, where Ardor was standing.

'Ardor. Any luck?'

'None. I've been seeing pictures though…'

'Yeah, so have I. We're close.'

'The drawings aren't recent though,' Ardor said. 'She may have died already.'

'Why is everyone trying to convince me that she's dead? She isn't dead! We'll find her!'

'I certainly hope so. I just don't want to get your hopes up.'

I turned from him and rolled my eyes. Up ahead, there was light in the rocky cavern. I started to walk towards it, and soon burst into the light. Light. How could that be? We were far underground. My eyes adjusted, and I saw that a grid of lights were shining down on me. I looked around and saw plants, rocks, streams, bridges, everything. It was incredible.

'What is this?' I muttered.

It was like a zoo, but without all of the animals or stupid cages. I saw fish scrambling in the water, and colourful birds perched in the tall green trees.

It didn't seem right. I clutched my axe. I was naturally suspicious. There were other arches leading to more tunnels, where trackers were starting to come, examining the place like me.

The place was not so big. I went in farther, and saw a body lying on the ground next to a pond. I ran to it, and turned it over to see the face. Swayvera. I felt her pulse. It was going. She was alive.

I shook her harshly, and her eyes flew open. She took a moment to take me in, then gasped, and embraced me.

'Storm!' she cried.

'Swayvera,' I said, blinking.

'Two years! Now you've found me!' she said.

She was a mess. It seemed she had been wearing the same old ragged clothes for two years. Her face was scarred, and her arms scratched – out of rage of being trapped, I guessed.

'You wouldn't believe what it's been like. Trapped, alone. I've been waiting … I thought I would stay here until death … and I came close to bringing it upon myself a few times.'

'I … I can't believe it. We must get you out of this horrid place.'

It could have been a paradise, but to my sister it was a cold prison. And considering what it had done, I thought of it the same way.

The trackers came, and we took the shortest route out after calling to the others. I thanked them tremendously for spending their time and effort to do this. We returned to the castle, and first let Swayvera into my mother's room. There were endless tears of joy, which I watched over, a smile on my face.

'I missed you! I thought you were gone!' my mother said, tears running down her face. 'I was distraught.'

'I thought of you every day. If only dad was here.'

'He would have been delighted,' I said. 'He sent me here. I thought you had been killed.'

'I think this may have been worse,' Swayvera said. 'That's Hunter's style. I should never have joined him. I did because he said that he would do everything in his power to protect the Seven Gates. I wanted to help. I felt about the Arigor and Orians the same way you felt about animals. But soon, I realised he wasn't about protecting. He would try to get me to raid villages and everything. And finally, he attacked the Orians, and I just couldn't stand it anymore. But he didn't let me leave. He punished me. He sent me down and imprisoned me under my own home. I must have been mere metres apart from you sometimes. I found that place, and lived there. Just lived there, nothing else to do except trying to convince myself that there was still a point in living.'

It distressed me, hearing about this. About what it was like. Being punished for withdrawing from Hunter's service. Two years of her life, spent in misery, alone, and bored so much. There isn't even a way to describe it.

'When the other Elrolians find out about this, they'll have one hell of a celebration,' I muttered. 'I mean, about you being alive – not alone, of course.'

'Yes, Swayvera, I've kept you too long, go clean up. I shall inform the queen immediately of your arrival. She knew you well – she will be delighted.'

Swayvera got some nice clothes and went to take a shower, and my mother went out to the throne room, leaving me alone in her room. I remembered sleeping here when I was a kid. I would curl up on the bed, but I always would switch to the comfy round chair in the corner of the room. It overlooked everything. I liked that.

When Swayvera got out of the bathroom, her hair was nicely done, her clothes new and clean, and she looked like she thought it was Christmas, or better. She looked incredible.

'Hey,' she said, smiling brilliantly.

'Hey. You look beautiful! Shall we go get some air? Fresh air? I imagine you'd want to get out a bit after two years down there.'

'You bet.'

'Wait a second,' I said, and I put my head up against the door. I sighed. 'There are people out there. If we go out there now, you won't have a moment of peace.'

'Yeah. Let us join them, but just … later. I want to go outside just with you for now.'

I nodded. 'Stay here.'

I opened the door, and went out to face a pack of Elrolians, most of them female, I noticed, although one or two were guys. They were obviously here for Swayvera.

'Well, have you seen her yet? She's in the library! Come on, let's get a move on!' I said.

They blinked in surprise, and then excitedly started to walk off to the library.

'Well that was easy,' I muttered.

I opened the heavy polished wooden door and stepped back into the room with my sister.

'So where do you want to go?' I asked her.

'Just outside to get some fresh air,' she replied. 'Not far.'

We went out of the room to the archery stand, where a cool gust of wind met us.

'We had a battle just now,' I said, realising that Swayvera wouldn't have known. 'Many died, all at the hands of Hunter. I was even in the room when the king stabbed himself.'

She gasped. 'He is dead? Along with others?'

I nodded. 'Many others. Hunter and the others had Elrolian weapons.'

'So there were dark matters going on out here too.'

'Oh, many. You didn't miss much. At least not anything you'd have wanted to experience. Death and destruction.'

I shifted uncomfortably. Should I tell her about Hunter wanting to destroy *me?* She might be in danger because of that. All villains do that type of thing – threatening family. But Hunter excelled at it. I decided it was best not to worry her about this. Not yet.

'Hunter had created an animal to destroy Elrolia. We call it Black Amber. But it joined us, so he tried to destroy it. It was so powerful, he didn't dare fight it. He took it away from us, but we finally broke into his base and got it back. And then just now, we had the fight. No one really won. I guess. Considering the king is dead along with so many other Elrolians, you could say we lost. And he'll come again soon,' I said, trying not to look directly at Swayvera.

'Who else does he want? Why will he come back?'

'For Ravenwood,' I said. It was the truth, but just not all of it. 'He wants Ravenwood. They're brothers. Something bad happened between them.'

I wasn't in the mood for explaining, and Swayvera didn't ask me to.

'Should we go in now?' she asked.

'Sure. The others will be anxious to see you.'

We got off the bench and pushed open the doors into the castle. Our footsteps echoed across the atrium. It was very quiet. Where was everyone?

'Let's go to the throne room,' I said, which would be where our mother was.

We went across the hall, and when I pushed the doors wide open, voices flooded my ears.

'Welcome back, Swayvera!' they called.

She smiled dazzlingly and went off to thank the Elrolians and her friends. She was very happy. Who wouldn't be?

They had laid out drinks, food, and banners that the Elrolians had signed each with a warm welcoming message. They had prepared this with very short notice, but the things that they could do in a short time were unbelievable.

The people were quite interested in her story. It was incredible, how she'd survived down there, and the threats she'd faced. She repeated her story gladly to anyone who asked her to recount it.

I went around talking to people, seeing how they were recovering from the battle. They all bore marks that they would carry for the rest of their lives. They all had some type of injury, and I felt responsible. Hunter wanted me. That was why the Elrolians were in so much danger. The more I thought about it, the more I realised he had reason to be mad at me. I had almost cut his leg off, for starters. I had taken his most powerful weapon from right under his nose – Black Amber.

Almost all of them knew Hunter was hunting me, but they didn't talk to me about it. They seemed to think it would make me feel worse. I don't know which was better. There was no way anyone could encourage me. I was fated to kill myself. With Hunter on my trail, it wouldn't be so hard for him to achieve it.

Oerix came up to me. 'Storm. How are you?' he asked.

'Fine. You?'

'Good. I'm sorry about your friend. I should have realized. I should have stopped the wolves.'

I shook my head. 'You couldn't have done anything. But thanks for … understanding. I didn't mean to kill him.'

'Of course not. You must be happy that your sister is here. Two years down there … my god.' He gave a friendly nod and wandered off.

I went to the queen, who was sitting alone at her throne.

'Queen Eleria,' I said with a bow. 'You must be grieved because of your husband's death.'

'Quite, Storm. You were there?'

I nodded. 'Hunter was talking to the king and Ravenwood when I came in. He told the king how he would destroy everything – Elrolia, his people, you. He said he would be responsible for the extinction of the Elrolian species. The king was driven insane, like anyone would have been. He decided it was best for everyone if he were to depart from the world. And so he did.'

A tear fell down the queen's cheek and dropped to the floor. 'You will be next then?' She asked me carefully.

'Perhaps. Maybe Ravenwood. But he will come for me. There is no stopping him. Thank you again for all that you have done for us. And for all that you will continue to do.'

'You are welcome, young man. I congratulate you on finding your sister.'

'Thank you, my lady,' I said, I turned to see yet another face.

'Streakell!' I said. She was perhaps Swayvera's best friend. 'Looking for Swayvera, I presume?'

'Oh, I've already been talking with her,' she said, lacing her fingers through her long black hair. 'Two years underground and alone!'

'I know … it's quite something. It's great to have her back.'

'Yeah … so this whole Black Amber thing. Hunter created them?'

'Yeah. He likes to experiment with crossbreeding. I guess this was the result. It was a powerful weapon – strong, agile, and loyal. We just changed around their idea of which the good side was. Hunter wanted them badly. Just seeing them in action tells you why. They have Onyxus in their claws, making them lethal to us … and him.'

'Anyone you know die?'

'Stream – one of the humans – and a few others as well. I haven't seen the list of the dead yet. It's horrible. And he will be back.'

'Well, we'll just have to keep fighting,' Streakell said. 'Have a good day, Storm.'

'Yeah, you too.'

As soon as Streakell left, Swayvera came up to me again.

'Hey, Storm ... do you think we could go over to the Seven Gates? I ... have something to suggest to the Orians.'

I studied her carefully, but she gave nothing away. 'Sure. I'll ask Ardor if he wants to come.'

'Ardor?'

I smiled, imagining the look on her face when she saw him. 'Yeah, come with me. I'll get Peldor too.'

When I introduced the two Orians, the look on my sister's face definitely satisfied me.

'Take your time,' muttered Ardor. 'It always takes a while to get used to me. You're Storm's sister?'

She nodded. 'Swayvera,' she said, extending a hand, which Ardor decided to pass on, allowing Peldor to have the honour of shaking it.

'Peldor of the Sand,' he said, as formal as ever, with a deep bow.

'Swayvera,' she said awkwardly.

'We'd like to go to the Seven Gates,' I said. 'Want to come?'

'Sure! Why not?' said Peldor.

'Yeah,' Ardor agreed. 'Let's go.'

Within fifteen minutes we had reached the Gates, which always impressed me. Ardor spoke.

'Which one do you want to go in?'

'Sand?' Peldor said absently.

'Sure. Senabell was always nice,' said Swayvera.

'She's my sister,' Peldor told her as we entered, his face lighting up a bit.

'Really? Awesome!' Swayvera exclaimed. 'We were good friends!'

Senabell spotted us from her sand dome and came down to meet us. We got all those warm greetings – the old *'you've grown so much!'* And *'it's been such a long time!'* That kind of thing.

'Senabell,' Swayvera began, 'I would like … to live here.'

Senabell was taken aback. 'Really? That's brilliant!'

I blinked in surprise. 'Are there any rules about this?' I asked curiously, also rather sadly. For two years I hadn't seen my sister, but now, here she was, and she wanted to go live somewhere else?

She noticed my look of surprise. 'Is that okay?' she asked.

'Yeah, of course…'

'Well, I have never done this before,' Senabell said. 'I'll need to ask the council. Wait here. I will summon them.'

Five minutes later, the leaders of the elements were gathered around. Not all of them were thrilled to see Ardor, I noticed.

'What is this for? It's not about him again, is it?' The Fire Leader – Flailyia, I remembered – said bitterly, nodding in disgust at Ardor.

'Is it not possible for you to shut your mouth?' Ardor growled.

'Ardor, you are the one who should stop talking. You are an unwanted guest here,' she said.

'You're scared of me!' he said with a mischievous smile.

'You seem to think nothing of what *exiled* means. You should not be here.'

'Are you going to stop me?'

'This isn't about Ardor,' said Senabell. 'This is about Swayvera. You remember her. She defended us against Hunter two years ago!'

Even the Rock woman couldn't see anything wrong with her. 'So? Why are *we* here?'

'Because she would like to stay with us,' Senabell said clearly.

Clustus of the Ice Element smiled. 'It's a great idea! She's a wonderful person. I see no reason she should not stay, so unless you have an objection, Flailyia, then this is easily resolved.'

Flailyia shrugged. 'I guess so. But what if she's a spy?'

'Shut up,' Ardor said. 'You don't have to be so determined to hate everyone that isn't like you. Let her stay.'

'I agree,' said Streltzia, Lord of Stone. 'She is an honourable Elrolian. Her protection would be of great value to us.'

Swayvera smiled.

'Well, that was simple,' said the Nature Lord as they rose.

'Yeah, well I just wanted to check with you. No one has ever asked us something like this before,' Senabell said.

I pulled Swayvera to the side. 'Are you sure about this?'

'Yes Storm. I love you, and mother, but I need to protect these people. My help would protect them from much more. I could save lives! Being here would make that so much easier. I'm not far away.'

I nodded. 'Bye, then. I'll visit you. Does mother know?'

'Yes. She agreed with me that it was for the best.'

So I'd found my sister, yet now lost her all over again. True, she would be very close, but her choice made my heart fall.

I went out into the air, leaving my sister behind with her wish, another event that made my life just that much more sad. After this, what could happen to make my life any worse?

FINAL WARNING

Of course, after a bad event, there's always a worse one just around the corner! So what awaited my return to Elrolia? A bad event. But it didn't come immediately.

I entered the castle, where people were still celebrating Swayvera's return, despite the fact that the one being honoured didn't live here anymore. They probably didn't know. It was the perfect excuse to have a fabulous party.

I went into my room, and threw myself onto my springy bed. What happened now? It was hard to adjust back to normal. Would I be able to? Would I be able to live normally, knowing that out there, the most dangerous person in the world was after me?

I stood up on my bed and adjusted myself so I was hanging upside down from the horizontal pole that I have for that reason. Being upside down helps me think. But what was there to think about? Normally I think about homework, or upcoming sport competitions that I'm in, but my mind was just blank.

I slapped myself hard on the cheek.

Think, Storm. About something … anything, I said to myself.

I saw my axe resting on the table in the corner of my room. I tried to imagine myself without it. Would I have died, like Androma Faithly had predicted? What if Wolf had kept it? Would he still be here with me if he had?

Rock climbing. That was what I needed. Something dangerous. Maybe I would try without a harness. Yeah, that would do me good. Danger always got me spiked up and alert.

I swung down from the pole and walked out the door to the Arena. In the centre of the round Elrolian castle is an arena, and as you probably know there is a large rocky cliff cutting through the castle, which the architects had done well to work around, basically just leaving a space there for the mountain to run down. There was no need to add a wall, for the rocks pretty much acted like one for us. It made the structure look better than if it was fully constructed all the way around.

At a certain ledge on the cliff, there was a station where you could harness yourself for rock climbing. I try to climb twice a week at least. It requires strength, agility, balance, and concentration. Although I am still rather reckless at times, like now! Who needs a harness? Part of the fun of the sport is the risk you take while doing it.

So, I harnessed myself up, but only so I could easily descend to the bottom of the mountain, at which point I shrugged off the gear and started to climb.

Always try to make sure to have at least three points on the wall, the best being two feet and a hand, which gives you the most support. I know it was kind of stupid of me not to have the harness on, but I thought, what was the worst that could happen? A few broken bones? They would heal.

I was climbing 'on-sight.' I would be ascending the rocks without any aid or foreknowledge, for I would be attempting to climb a route I'd never tried before. I knew most of the wall very well – every ledge, every annoying area that I'm used to smacking, everything. But not this little sliver.

This was a different take on free-climbing, where you use your physical strength to climb, and don't rely on the rope or whatever for support. Here, I wouldn't even have the option of the rope for support. But enough of this, this is way too boring. Please accept my apology. Now, on to the climb.

I went fast, taking in every possible hold that I could use. I had to be careful. One hand slipped off, but I easily caught back on with my other one.

Only when I was half way up did I make my mistake. I reached out with my foot while trying to adjust my grip with my left hand. I went off balance, and tumbled off. I was falling, a drop of twenty metres. I saw an abandoned rope hanging on my left, and wildly tried to snatch it. I finally caught hold, but my hand got singed as I descended, the rope burning my hand.

A ledge was coming up, and I braced myself for impact. Three – two – one – crash. My bones ached badly. How stupid I had been. I had been so close to getting to a nice ledge where I could have taken a three-minute break.

I grunted as I felt my shoulder click back into place.

'I'm such an idiot,' I said, but I put on a smile and started to laugh. I hauled myself up. At least no one had seen me fall. But when I turned, Emrax was facing me.

'You *are* an idiot,' he said with a smile.

'Thank you. I was bored.'

'So you tried to get yourself killed.'

'I didn't try too hard.'

'Well, you ready?'

I frowned. 'For what?'

'Survival training? We both signed up a month ago! You know, when they drop us off somewhere in Lorothia and we have to survive for twenty-four hours without deciding to give up?'

'Oh, I forgot about that! When is it?' I asked worriedly.

'Two hours. You've got time.'

'Good. It's so quiet...'

'Yeah,' said Emrax, 'I think they're still at the party. The perfect excuse to have something fun to do for however long. How can you be bored?'

I shrugged. 'Just am.'

'Well, the chance of death is always something to relieve that,' Emrax said, looking up at the mountain. 'I suppose it's good preparation for survival training though.'

'Yeah. Let's go down,' I said, studying my hands. They were fine.

We locked ourselves onto the rope and slid down. I always loved doing that. It's like you are flying. Sometimes I would stop myself in the air, and would just stay there and read a book or something.

We touched down lightly on the rocky ground and unlocked the clip connecting us to the rope. We loosened and shrugged off the harnesses, hanging them next to the others on the rack beside us.

'Doesn't it seem so boring to you?' I asked suddenly. 'Life?'

'Not yours. Hunter is chasing you. It doesn't get much more exciting than that,' said Emrax, shrugging.

'But what's the point of life now? What do I do with my last few days alive? Black Amber – this whole thing – it's changed me. Lessons, training, jobs ... what's it all for? What are we supposed to do with the time we have?'

'Solve problems. Do what you can to make life better for others, because every life can make a change. Whether you are a child, an animal, or an adult. There is always something we can do to make our lives worth living. What you are going to do to make a change is your decision.'

I thought about this in silence. 'I'm going to make this a better place,' I said. 'I'm going to make the lives of the Elrolians special.'

'Storm...' said Emrax. His voice hinted at fear. His eyes stared over my shoulder, as if he could see the dead walking. '*He's here,*' he whispered.

I slowly looked around to see a lone person standing in the middle of the arena. Hunter. His hood was down, and his black mask made him look robotic in the light.

'Storm Orthoclase,' he sneered. 'I hear you've found your sister. Did she like it down there under her home?'

I shook with anger. 'I'll kill you!' I screamed, and I grabbed Emrax's knife from his belt and flung it at Hunter, who easily dodged, the knife piercing the wall behind him, trembling like a child shivering in the snow.

'Come and get me,' he whispered, just loud enough for me to hear him.

I raced towards him, and he too started to run, but he drew to a stop at the gates, where I crashed into him, and saw black dust fall to the ground.

'No!' I shouted, but it was too late. The next thing I knew, after a blur of colours, Hunter and I were in a different part of Wouldlock – the Silent Mountains. We were at the top of the highest cliff, a three-thousand metre drop before us.

He loosened his grip on me, and I stumbled to the rocky ground.

'Storm. My friend ... it's nice to see you again.'

'I'm afraid I can't say the same,' I breathed dangerously.

Hunter chuckled. 'Yes, yes ... you see, I need to talk to you. To give you a final warning, alone. I will not kill you. No, I will not. I will not harm you in any physical way. I will destroy you *forever.* I will crush everything you care for, murder and torture everyone you love, and make you kill yourself. I have given you small taste of what awaits you. You friend's death, with you responsible, and your brief capture by the Silver Claw was just part one.' He leaned forward and whispered in my ear. 'This is the second part.'

'When will you stop?' I asked. 'You're insane. How is this going to end?'

He moved back. 'Once you are dead. But I won't rush it. You performed your move, this is the beginning of mine. We are playing a game. You are going to lose.'

'What if I make another move? What if I kill you first?'

'Oh, that may be a more difficult task then you imagine. But I suppose you are still rather angry with me, so let me make this clear. I do not need to live for you to suffer.'

'What do you mean?' I asked cautiously.

'The world is dangerous – full of murder, lies, and agony. Yet every day, we fool ourselves into thinking we are safe. It's only when danger finds you that you see the darkness that threatens to devour you.' Hunter's eyes bore into mine, and his mouth curved into a wicked smile. 'I, Storm, am the darkness. And darkness needs no life.'

Very slowly, he approached the edge of the mountain, every step sounding like a hammer against metal, ringing through my ears. My heartbeat quickened as I stood there, wondering what would happen next. Would he suddenly turn and throw me off the cliff for a taste of more pain? I watched him, bracing myself for whatever came next.

'Goodbye, Storm Orthoclase. And good luck against the other obstacles I have set for you. I'll see you very soon.'

He turned away from me to face the beautiful sky of Wouldlock. He took one more step, and with only a moment's hesitation, he spread his arms like an eagle's wings and leaped off the edge, descending down to the valley below.

I stared, and ran to the cliff. I got to my knees, and below I could see very faintly a grey speck. Unmistakably Hunter's still, lifeless body.

'He's dead….' I said. I couldn't quite believe what had just happened.

'Hunter?' I called out, not sure what to expect.

No voice came back to me. Not even the echo of my own. Well, they were called the Silent Mountains for a reason. I blinked, and pushed myself back up. It was a trap. Or was it? He seemed to have left … left this world.

I turned around to face my home, and saw that it was glowing, in flames. I almost stopped breathing. Menacing red flames were sending out black smoke, poisoning the cold air, licking away at helpless trees. My home was being destroyed. Hunter's second move. Darkness was flooding through the legendary castle. Monstrous flames with lives of their own had been set free.

I couldn't help admiring the incredible force. Light … how it worked … it was fascinating. But this did not stop the dread I felt inside me.

Fire was upon Elrolia.

HUNTER MAKES
HIS NEXT MOVE

BLACK AQUA

COMING SOON